Crystal Balls

Amanda BROBYN

POOLBEG

© Amanda Brobyn 2011

The moral right of the author has been asserted.

Copyright for typesetting, layout, design
© Poolbeg Press Ltd.

1

A catalogue record for this book is available from the British Library.

ISBN 978-1-84223-468-6

Typeset by Patricia Hope in Sabon 11/14.5

Printed by
CPI Cox & Wyman, UK

www.poolbeg.com

ABOUT THE AUTHOR

Amanda Brobyn, originally from Liverpool, moved to Northern Ireland in 1999 where she lives with her husband and two children. Amanda's media career kicked off as a scriptwriter before moving onto novels, and she recently graduated with an MA in Film and Television Production, Management and Policy from the University of Ulster. She is already working on a feature film adaptation of *Crystal Balls*.

ACKNOWLEDGEMENTS

In an attempt to be inclusive, let me thank all those people who have played a part – no matter how small – in the making and publication of *Crystal Balls*, my debut novel.

I cannot even begin without firstly thanking Paula Campbell of Poolbeg Press for making my dreams come true – you had faith in me all along, Paula, and without you I might still be in the awful world of financial services, so from the bottom of my heart – thank you. Thanks to Sarah Ormston, also at Poolbeg, for allowing me to pester her regarding my hare-brained PR ideas and for encouraging me to bring more – you might regret that! A massive thank you to Gaye Shortland, my editor, who worked me like a slave over the Christmas holidays! Joking aside, your skilful eye for detail has left me glowing in the knowledge that *Crystal Balls* is the best it can be . . . and that is all down to you. Thanks to Paula Clamp who recommended Poolbeg to me and for carving out the pathway to my new career.

Moving on to family and friends, firstly thanks to Michael and Claire Noble who read the first draft of the book and returned the manuscript to me with a gold star! To my dear friend Richard Crawford without whom this book would not have been possible – you believed in me as a writer even when I doubted by own ability and it is you who has opened up this whole new world for me and I adore you. To John Brooks, one of the best friends I have ever had – you predicted that all which has happened, would happen, didn't you? Your strange insightfulness once again turned out to be as true as you are a friend to me – and I to you. For Karla Robinson of David M Robinson Jewellers, thank you for being a proud friend and for taking the time to help me with the book's promotion and for using your contacts to get it out there. The next favour is from me to you!

Thanks to Cyril and Doris for their creche facilities(!) and for buying me the time I needed to write in peace.

Thanks, Mum, for your constant encouragement, hilarious (and very true) anecdotes and for telling the whole world just how proud you are of me, and thanks to my dad for conceding when I got the publishing deal! I'm not sure you believed I would, but I can see in your eyes just how much my achievements mean to you. You are both extremely special parents and I hope I make you want to burst with pride.

An enormous thanks to my sister, Jo, who read and re-read every single draft of the book, bouncing back with copious notes – some good, some bad, and for making me see that I could write like all the other authors. I always believe you, Jo, because you tell me the truth and this book is for you as much as it is for me.

Thanks to my husband Stephen – who has never read the book but probably knows more about it than me – thank you for not buying ear-plugs and for listening to me over the years – I love you. To my beautiful children,

Josh and Harriet – for Josh, thanks for telling your teacher the book was actually called *Big Balls* and for making me explain to her that it was not indeed a top-shelf publication! For Harriet, thanks for never grumbling when I spent our entire maternity leave glued to the laptop – you were so good and now Mummy gets more time with both of you.

Finally, for those inexplicable situations which make your spine tingle and the hairs on your arms stand on end. For the times you spin around to see who is there to be greeted with an empty space. For the strange smells and cold spells you feel, but no-one else does. For the times the lights flicker or a cold breath hits the back of your neck. For the strangest feeling that someone is watching over you . . . they probably are. Thank you, too!

www.amandabrobyn.com

For Stephen, Josh and Harriet
with all my love.

Prologue

Slumped over the battered suitcase, she flings up her hood, protecting herself from the violent grey rain as it hurls down from the murky London skies. Each drop whispers words of failure, basking in its power to pelt her harder and harder. Gloating like a playground bully. Her torso is already numb but no amount of physical affliction can come between her and the gruesome mental punishment which holds her trapped in anguish and despair.

Unable to hold back, a tear escapes from her tightly closed eyes, followed by another and another, and she begins to sob uncontrollably, not caring about the weird looks from passers-by. None of whom are bothering to ask if she's okay. But hey, this is London.

"*This isn't how my life is supposed to be!*" she screeches hysterically, her voice breaking under the exertion. "I'm talented," she whispers, sobbing, "and I don't – know – what – else I can do – if I can't do – *this*."

She breaks down once more and her shoulders convulse with each sporadic heave of breath as she cries wildly. Red eyes squint from beneath the oversized hood and her face glimmers with an iridescent wetness as she continues to weep in desolation. She is now oblivious to the awkward glances from the foot traffic around her. Her best monologue yet, wasted on their closed ears and selective eyes. Wiping her runny nose on the arm of her sleeve, she hangs her head in remorse, immersed in a fog of blankness.

How can she tell her mother she's failed? Failed her.

Her mother had spent her own early years wanting to make it as an actress, under the constant repression of an unambitious family telling her to wise up and live in the real world. So from the moment her own daughter could walk and talk, she was pushed incessantly by a woman who was clearly living her dream through her offspring. Every ounce of energy her body possessed was injected into allowing her child to have the opportunity to become that very thing she never was.

"And I have failed her," the girl repeats again and again. "I have failed her."

The dream is no longer.

She stands, slowly and painfully, cold from being static for so long and stiff from putting her body through excessive auditions day and night, year upon year.

Dragging the heavy case behind her, she trudges heavily through the sopping streets of Soho, looking for a home and silently praying for someone to take her away.

1

Chantelle clambers up the stairs, thumping loudly on each one, with all the grace of a baby elephant. How is it that weighing in at only eight stone such a little thing is capable of creating a mini-tremor?

Breathlessly she knocks at the office door.

"Tina, are you in there?"

"No, I'm not here!" I answer with playful sarcasm. "I'm the boss and I've given myself the afternoon off!"

Chantelle enters, panting heavily, and plonks herself at the opposite side of the desk. An immediate emission of stale cigarettes fills the air.

"Chantelle! You told me you'd given up!" I exclaim with the disgust only an ex-smoker is capable of.

"Well, I've kind of given up so I wasn't lying," she explains, straight-faced and earnest. "I've actually cut back which in reality means I've given up what I *used* to smoke." She stares at me, looking smug and clever at her response.

I can't even contradict her – there's logic in there somewhere.

I trained Chantelle as a saleswoman, a better one

than even myself, but the downside is that she has an answer for everything and at breakneck speed.

I'm feeling mellow today after a joyous meeting with my accountant and it's a day for celebrations. Let her kill herself with lung disease if she wants to, providing she abides by the rules of no smoking on the premises or in front of the building or during any type of hospitality event. I guess I can't ask for much more, apart from asking her not to *really* kill herself of course. She's my right-hand woman and I'm not sure I could survive without her, but as much as I tell her, I'm not quite sure she believes it.

"Chantelle, don't you know how unattractive it makes you look?" I preach. "You're drop-dead gorgeous but you ruin it all by having a fag hanging out of the side of your mouth." I laugh off the frustration. "Very ladylike! And why do you keep knocking, you daft sod? If the door isn't shut tight, just come on in. Open-door policy, remember?"

Chantelle nods approvingly. "You know what, Tina, I got so used to being treated like a skivvy and a nothing in my old job, it still seems, well, kind of weird that you're the boss but you're so nice at the same time."

Her honesty and respect are admirable qualities although I can't help but feel that, at twenty-seven, she ought to be showing signs of greater maturity and aiming to work as more of an equal rather than being happy as a subservient. And this is why I made her the office manager twelve months ago, a recognition well deserved and well overdue in terms of her entire career span.

Needless to say, I headhunted her from Goldsmith

Kings which was easy given she hated it – well, hated the owner really, and for all the same reasons I had done. Her reputation promised her to be worthy of recruitment and, once the word on the street was out – that the chauvinistic pig's success was practically off the back of Chantelle – I made her an offer I knew she couldn't refuse and, after her obligatory notice was served, she was all mine. And I certainly didn't intend to lose her. I love her, the punters love her, the wives and girlfriends are taken in by her natural charm and flattery, and Chantelle graces her way through each day with the ease and simplicity of a woman who works purely for the passion of it, never asking for anything but always giving. She has been and still is indispensable.

"Earth calling Tina!" she teases.

"Sorry, Chantelle, I'm in a world of my own." I roll my eyes at her. I don't want to keep telling her how valued she is, knowing how uncomfortable it makes her.

"Penny for them?" She smiles at me affectionately. "Oh my goodness, talk about food for thought!" Bright-eyed, Chantelle suddenly jumps up, digging her hand deep into her jacket pocket and pulling out a newspaper cutting. Leaning over the desk, she quickly unfolds it, holds it in front of me, positioning it far too close to read. She dances around impatiently, hopping from one leg to the next.

"Please say you'll come, Tina, please!" she blurts out, looking down at me with big dark-brown eyes set firmly in you-cannot-say-no mode. Although, to see those eyes, you have to look past her ample chest first.

"Will you give me a chance to read it, for heaven's sake? I don't even know what it is!"

I scan my eyes quickly over the article while Chantelle childishly bounces around, twitching like she has heavily overdosed on speed.

She is clearly desperate to speak again and, seeing my eyes lower towards the remaining lines, she bursts out uncontrollably: "Will you come with me, please, Tina? I've always wanted to see one of those guys but I'd be too afraid to go on my own. Honestly, Tina, this means so much to me I can't tell you. Please come with me!" She takes in my reluctant face. "Pretty, please?"

"Chantelle, breathe," I tell her. "Just take deep breaths." I stare at her like she is a woman possessed. "I've never seen you like this before – you're usually so collected."

I flick through the article once more. My gut reaction is a no, but her excitement and near-desperation have stirred something in me. She opens her mouth to speak again but I silence her with my finger to my lips like a kindergarten teacher. It works beautifully. Why have I never tried it before?

"Hang on a minute. Just let me read it again. And will you keep still? You're making me feel sea-sick."

I digest the article for the third time, reading it slowly and mulling it over in my head, but I begin to feel quite uncomfortable at the prospect of it. It's fine for Chantelle but not for me. I'm not the lost little girl who needs to find herself. That was in the past where it will firmly remain and this is the here and now and, from where I'm sitting, it's looking pretty damn good. I know exactly who I am and where I'm heading and I simply don't see the point of paying thirty quid for some deranged spoof to impart a pack of lies. I can understand Chantelle's interest, however, and in her shoes I might well share her sentiment.

The article, a full-page spread, is promoting Liverpool's first Psychic Fayre where it aims to demonstrate communication and contact with the spirit world, through mediumship and clairvoyance. Fine if you're into that sort of thing, I guess, but the idea of it all fills me with ambivalence. I really don't like it. What if they ask you questions? Personal questions? What if the next thing you know is that some crook has stolen your identity, cleared out your bank account and eradicated you from your own existence? You are not really you any more. Someone else is you.

Shaking my head, I quickly attempt to figure a get-out clause.

"You know what, Chantelle, I really don't feel comfortable going if I'm honest. It's a complete waste of money and probably run by a group of phoneys." I hate doing this to her but in a way I'm also trying to protect her. "I mean, think about it logically, it can't be authentic, honest gov."

Chantelle leans across the desk, practically lying on it face down. "Please, Tina, oh please!" she begs. "I really need someone with me and you're just the person to keep me grounded. I can't go with Colin because he doesn't believe in that stuff and my nan would kill me if she knew what I was up to." She laughs. "My nan says it's the devil's work, not that I believe that but . . ." her black-olive eyes widen with innocence, "but I can be a little naïve sometimes." The corners of her mouth turn upwards and her thick lashes flutter prettily. "I get so taken in by it all. I really do need to have someone there with me."

What a performance, Chantelle! Move over, Hollywood.

"Look, I'm not really the right person to go with you," I point out adamantly. "I'm a cynic who is in control of her life because she made it happen. I am where I am because of sheer hard work and this time around I ain't gonna fail!" My voice breaks a little as I recall that very phone call to Mother asking to be rescued. "It's up to you, Chantelle. You have to create your own destiny and make your own luck in this life." I feel a sudden stab of pain. The fight to turn my life around came at a price but, still, I live to tell the tale and what doesn't kill you makes you stronger. Or so they say.

I watch her despondent face and mellow slightly. I step down from my invisible soapbox. "It's about action and about doing, Chantelle." I look around me. "Blood, sweat and tears has been injected into this business. At one point I only had the clothes on my back." I shake my head at her, conscious that I may have been a bit heavy. "A crystal ball can't map your life out, Chantelle. All it will do is make your pocket lighter." I take in her obvious disappointment. She's as transparent as they come, and wears her heart on her sleeve. I find her simplistic approach rather endearing. I endeavour to make light of the situation by grabbing her hand. With my index finger I trace the contour of her palm, holding the hand firmly as she tries to wriggle it away. My manicured nail trails slowly along her jagged lifeline, deliberately tickling it to torment her.

"You have a long life in front of you, my dear," I begin in jest, my voice quaking for dramatic effect. "You will live way into your nineties but your faculties will have left you long before." I stifle a giggle. "Your chest will go south and your pelvic floor will join it after having nine children . . ."

"Ouch!" Chantelle's eyes begin to water at the prospect.

"You will come into money, a lot of it, but you will always remain faithful to your employer!"

She snorts at me wickedly.

"Oh, and all nine of your children will have different fathers!" I put her hand down. "That will be fifty pounds, please!"

We both laugh as Chantelle examines her chest, thankful of its northerly position. Her face screws up and she pants heavily. "I'm about to drop another one!" She stoops down, holding the small of her back. "Get the towels, quick!"

I grab the cutting, crushing it into a ball, and hurl it towards her. "You're sick, Chantelle! And close your legs, will you? I can nearly see your kidneys!"

"Hang on a minute?" She regains her perfect posture. "*I'm* sick? Pot and kettle come to mind." She chortles. "I'm not the one who slept with a fifty-year-old!"

Bitch! "He said he was forty!" I retort. "My God, don't remind me of that, you big horror! I was only twenty-three at the time!"

"Which makes it even worse!" She tuts. "Slapper!"

My shoulders shudder with nausea. We were in the throes of foreplay when he asked me if I was ready? I replied yes but what was the question? After he noisily climaxed, alone, the cheeky bugger turned and said, "I thought you were ready? You've got a lot to learn, sweetheart." He got out of bed, still semi-erect, leaving me there naked and humiliated and not knowing whether to slap him or try again. I told Chantelle that story after a few too many!

Chantelle retrieves the crumpled cutting from the floor and throws it in the bin across the other side of the room. It lands perfectly. She smirks, turning back to face me. An impish devilry decorates her exquisite face – she truly has no idea how beautiful she is.

Every piece of displayed flesh shines with a dark-gold hue. Her thick black eyelashes protect eyes so dark a shade of brown they can be mistaken for black from a distance. Her dainty nose, a Hungerford inheritance, portrays an air of aristocratic exquisiteness and dark red lips in a permanent yet unaffected pout add the penultimate finish to perfection. The finale, however, is a heart so pure and full of virtue that humility would serve her well if it bowed down. As is expected, Chantelle is unaware of the degree of influence and control she possesses and, what she uses, she uses in jest. With her charm, ravishing appearance and a bit of Machiavellian practice, she could actually be quite dangerous.

"It ain't worked, Ms Harding!" She shakes her finger at me. "Stick to what you know about, girl, cos palm-reading and comedy just ain't your thing." She struts about the room in gangster fashion. Terrible American accent – piercing to the ears in fact. At least my gypsy voice was believable even if the content wasn't! "Seriously though, Tina, how about I just get a reading done and you can wait outside? At least then you're not wasting money and I get someone to go with?"

When you put it like that! I suppose I could consider it. Conceding, I mean. What harm can it do really? It can't be that bad if they're using the Royal Fort. People use that hotel for weddings and conferences. In fact, it's a pretty good endorsement for their business, using such a prestigious location. Perhaps that's part of the master plan? I'm not interested in having a reading but I guess there are no reasons why I can't support my own staff in doing so and it's very rare for Chantelle to ask for anything.

"Okay, okay, I'll go with you," I give in reluctantly. "But only book yourself in, Chantelle, seriously, and don't try to convince me otherwise. Anything to get you out of my office. Some of us have got work to do."

A jubilant Chantelle runs around the desk, bending forward to hug me. She's practically sitting on my knee!

"Thanks, Tina!" she grins. "You're the best. I can't wait!"

Skipping heavily to the door, she turns serious for a moment. "Oh yeah, Tina, Brian Steen's PA rang earlier to remind you about the meeting." Her eyes twinkle. "Don't worry – I told her you've been looking forward to it all week." With a cheeky smirk, she closes the door behind her and seconds later the floor vibrates with the thud of her descent.

What is it with that girl and how, once again, have I managed to succumb to her charm?

I thought I was the boss around here?

2

The prospect of the meeting with Brian Steen fills me with nervous energy. He is a familiar name to those in the trade. A ruthless property developer, with the Council heads and bank managers in his back pockets. Never refused planning permission or any amount of finance. And yet, even with his slightly fearful reputation, we all flocked with tenders in tow to sell our agency services.

Steen and his team of builders have recently started working on executive apartments in Liverpool's docklands. The land remained derelict until his construction plans were approved, ironically in the same week another's were declined. Rumour has it that the competitors have applied for a judicial appeal, but they haven't a leg to stand on and they know it.

The two apartment blocks will each contain fifteen split-level, two and three-bedroom apartments, fully equipped with mod cons including integrated sound systems, a communal gym, underground parking, twenty-four-hour security. The list goes on. And on. And at a starting price of six-hundred thousand pounds, these state-of-the-art premises clearly aren't for the average Joe.

In truth, I couldn't have prepared more for the meeting had I tried. Many an evening has been spent curled up on the sofa, with the compulsory glass of wine, studying the apartment specifications and exploring the impressive yet fairly short history of Steen Developments Ltd. For a man in his early forties he certainly has some balls and, with what appears to be flawless business-planning and decision-making, I'd say they must be made from crystal.

To say I have drifted off into a fantasy world once or twice is an understatement. What are the chances of me owning one of these luxury dwellings? I could have an L1 docklands postcode. If I thought I was someone now, forget it; I truly would be someone living there. No more queues for the treadmill at Fat Busters with the mandatory fifteen-minute maximum workout. No more purple veins in the water telling tales of vile imbeciles urinating in the pool. No more packing and unpacking of the gym bag with the wet towels and dripping swimsuit all crammed together in an impatient attempt to make them fit in. Sound familiar? Imagine arriving at the gym in sixty seconds. Unstressed and with light hand-luggage containing lip-gloss, hair-bobble and MP3 player. Workout complete, welcome to the power showers of the century. Lather yourself into a frenzy under waterfalls of free-flowing hot water beating down on your body with all the sensations of a sports massage, before getting lost in heated, soft, velvety bathrobes. Next, cleanse, tone and moisturise with complimentary Molton Brown products, leading to the finale: a generous application of whipped body soufflé slathered onto your soft glistening skin. Sounds like heaven, doesn't it? Well, after the workout it does anyway.

My sporadic gym visits consist of leaving with soaking wet hair, venturing into the cold climate of this wonderful country while fumbling for the car keys. Shivering all the way home, you will the dilapidated heater to kick in before you reach your front door and hypothermia sets in. But no need for any of that here if you have wads of cash. Basking in your continuously healthy glow, simply press a button for the lift to be chauffeured back to your door. A smooth, seamless ride to even more luxury. One can dream and, by God, I truly have.

The reality is that my homework has been done both in relation to the properties and their prospective marketing requirements and I know who and what competition I'm up against. But someone has to win the tender and I've already achieved a short listing. It's surprising that Brian Steen himself carries out the interviews – you'd think he'd have an underdog carry out that task for him. Still, I'm delighted with the prospect of meeting him personally and nervous enough to be able to put in a personal best in terms of performance.

I am a trained actress after all!

My hair is sleek, nails are manicured and with the incentive of one-and-a-half-per-cent commission for the sale of every apartment, the stakes have never been so high. Securing this deal has tangible benefits that include settlement of existing bank debts and, with the remaining cash, the ability to open a second office debt-free, potentially doubling my business turnover and keeping me in the lifestyle I've constantly craved. The success of this contract can seriously take Harding Homes to its next level and never has there been a more crucial opportunity to grab this with both hands and turn the dream into reality. It truly is make-or-break time and only destiny knows on which side the coin will land.

Fidgeting rather nervously, I take in the simplistic surroundings of the café bar. I have to admit that it does seem a rather strange place to do business, particularly when the other options include my business premises, Steen's various offices and a multitude of hotels and affluent bars eager for our trade. I find this thought a bit disconcerting as it is vital that I understand what makes Mr Brian Steen tick. But I am confident that I will be able to figure him out. I have always considered myself a perceptive person and pride myself on my ability to tap into people's minds. I suppose I typify the majority of Geminis in that I can be a little spontaneous at times, particularly when I want something, and how to achieve it is irrelevant. In this case, be it through mind-tapping, business acumen, professional flirting or razor-sharp stilettos, I care not. I intend to have him eating out of my hand at first sight.

Today's wardrobe has been given considerable attention and I must say even I am taken aback. I haven't looked this good in ages. There is definitely something to be said about power dressing. Sporting my best Jaeger suit, comprising a straight skirt sitting just above the knee, coupled with a buttoned-up three-quarter-length jacket nipped in at the waist and bearing low enough to expose a deliberate cleavage, I thank God for padded bras. *Thank you, God*. With a head-to-toe coat of natural-looking fake tan, the pale cream suit complements my just-back-from-holiday look, and I feel feminine and sexy from the inside out. The recent addition of blonde and brown hair-tints has added warmth and colour to my complexion and, strangely, even my freckles appear more forgiving than usual, which given how I feel towards them can only be a good thing.

My considered assessment of this place is that he has deliberately chosen a middle-of-the-road establishment. Not too flashy in order to avoid the stuffy, phoney atmosphere synonymous with those high-class types of places, and yet not too basic, simply I imagine for reasons of common courtesy. Yes, that's definitely it. This place is well thought out. I have to give him credit for his analysis – perhaps I've been underestimating him, like I do most men.

How easy would it have been for me to be taken to JC's, Liverpool's most elite private members' bar? He could have easily and deliberately chosen to remain within his own level of comfort, not giving a damn about me. Not that I would allow myself to be distracted by wads of cash being exchanged for bottles of Bollinger and Taittinger. Of course not! The fact that champagne happens to be my favourite drink is purely coincidental. It certainly beats tap water which was all I could afford once upon a time!

"Can I get you something to drink?"

I look up to observe a handsome young man, wearing fitted black trousers with a tight black T-shirt tucked in, accessorised with an eagle-head cowboy buckle. *Yum*. Only a guy with his firm young torso has the ability to wear this worn, slightly faded uniform which would make anyone else appear dowdy and bland. Although the trousers do seem a bit tight though – you know, around the . . .

"Sorry . . . did you want to order a drink?" he muses, shifting uncomfortably. Hardly surprising wearing pants at least a size too small.

Oh my God, snap out of it, Tina. Eye contact above crotch level. Quickly.

I focus my eyes on the brass-and-silver-plated buckle, pretending to have been taken by it.

"Yes, thank you." I put on my best business voice just to show I am not a complete idiot. "I'll have a sparkling water, please." I clear my throat. "Nice belt."

He acknowledges this with a smile, somewhat amused at my lobster-coloured face and neck. I'll bet he wears those pants deliberately. He must rake in the tips. I might just start frequenting this place after investing in a purchase of green compact. I hear it does wonders for hiding blotches of colour and with that bulge just inches from my eye-line, where else is a girl supposed to look?

My papers have been efficiently arranged on the plywood coffee table in front of me. Cleverly enough to allow my eyes to glance down at the material in the event of short-term memory loss, but discreetly enough to hide confidential information which I know Brian would not like to be broadcast. Not at this stage anyway, but soon enough he'll be expecting one of us applicants to shout it from the rooftops. Literally. Let's hope it's me.

Looking around, I reassess my choice of table. Most of the seats are backless brown-leather stools which are fine for a short time, although for longer periods the soft leather chocolate-coloured sofas look incredibly inviting. The problem with those is that you have to sit right back, languishing in their total comfort and running the risk of an element of complacency setting in as you drift into a soporific state. Or you can attempt to stay alert by perching awkwardly on the edge as your knees shake from the exertion of supporting your weight, which you pretend is light as a feather. What a choice!

Attempting to impress Brian Steen with intricate detail, I opt for the stools, placing them opposite each other so we can make clear eye contact, observe each other's body language head on and share our material intimately but professionally.

Oh God, I should have gone for the sofas! Too late now.

My heart thumps heavily and an intemperate dizziness hits me.

I watch him glide across the floor, moving with the natural grace and sophistication of an Arab sheikh, and in one seamless motion he is standing before me with his coat slung casually over his arm. I'm almost breathless, and standing up in anticipation of my impressively firm handshake (another Tina trademark), takes all my energy. *You can do it. You can do it.*

Brian launches his masculine hand in greeting and taking a solid grip of my, by comparison, feeble one, he locks his eyes with mine. The corners of his mouth flicker affably but it is his eyes that carry the weight of his smile, authentic and sincere.

Refusing to be intimidated, I attempt to take control of our first encounter.

"Pleased to meet you," we chorus.

Damn.

Brian laughs, letting go of my hand. "Great minds

think alike, Miss Harding." His eyes sparkle. What a beautiful colour! Neither green nor blue, but crystal clear in the centre and whiter than white on the outside. Almost edible, if you're into that sort of thing? Perhaps they could make sweets just like them, only tasting better of course. Aqua drops. I bet they'd sell quite well.

"You could say idiots never differ, Brian," I offer, already flirting outrageously. "Not that my assessment of you is that of an idiot of course," I add quickly, invisibly smacking my head against the nearest wall. "Although there are plenty of them around." *What am I on?*

Thankfully he appears distracted and I watch him deftly remove his suit jacket, placing it and his overcoat carefully over the stool I had positioned for him, right opposite me. *Great! Where the hell does he think he's going to sit now?*

I watch as he grabs a spare stool from the table behind him, dragging it along the floor to our table, placing it inches away from me. His knees brush against mine as he sits heavily and a bolt of reality hits me. It's him. The man everyone wants to work with. The man with the Midas touch. The god of couture construction. And here is me. A failed actress trying to turn a small business into a high-street brand and completely unqualified to do it, apart from a burning drive so powerful it draws bile to the back of my throat. I suddenly become aware of his masculinity, observing the size of his smooth hands, broad chest and distinguished face, which until now had only been witnessed from a distance. Next to him I feel slight in frame and slightly meek, if I'm honest.

Come on, Tina, you're going to have to do better than this. You never get a second chance to make a first impression.

"I hope you don't mind me sitting here, Tina?" he says plainly.

I shake my head, scared to speak for fear of another faux pas.

"I'm not a great fan of formality – reminds me of the days when I had to beg, borrow and steal from the bank manager!" He shudders and then grins. "If I can avoid putting someone else through that intimidation then I make it my mission."

Cocky bugger. Me? Intimidated? Erm?

I watch him watching me, observing my determined face and clearly witnessing the sharp change in my expression.

"Unless of course you'd *prefer* to be intimidated, Miss Harding?" he mocks outrageously, cocking his head to one side. He looks at me with a mischievous glint in his eyes.

Fascinated for a moment by his ability to be so expressive, I lose myself in his gaze. How could that face intimidate anyone? Yes, he must be in his mid-forties but he really is in immaculate condition and forty is the new thirty after all.

His tanned, smoothly shaven skin emphasises his perfect bone structure and square jaw-line. Full lips protect a set of white teeth which must have seen the benefit of cosmetic dentistry over the years. They look too faultless to be natural. I'm speaking from personal experience, having undergone painful episodes of pulling, filing and refitting myself.

Sitting up straight, I twist around on my stool until my entire body is facing his like for like. It's called mirroring. I learned it at drama school.

"Mr Steen, you couldn't possibly intimidate me," I tease back, raising my eyebrows in a gesture of humour but never losing that vital eye contact.

"Is that so, Miss Harding? In that case I'm beat!" He winks at me. "Then let's get straight down to business."

While I have impressed myself with my ability to appear both fierce and flirtatious, my new positioning has made it impossible for me to see my well-devised notes. *Shit.* Second dilemma of the day. Do I revert back to my pre-rehearsed angle giving him a side profile, albeit a pretty decent one, but potentially displaying signs of retreat, or do I continue to face him head on and wing it?

You couldn't have worked any harder on your preparation, Tina. It's now or never. Wing it!

Smiling confidently but quaking inside, I nod to Brian, giving permission to commence the interview, although I am tempted to return his wink to see if, like me, he finds it patronising yet arousing at the same time. Conscious that I have tucked and untucked my hair from behind my ear twice in the last ten seconds, I place my hands on my lap, neither aggressively nor defensively. Just in a comfortable and relaxed position, allowing my sweaty palms to feel the benefit of the air conditioning.

Brian rests his arm on the table, leaning into its low level and slouching awkwardly.

He's trying to relax me with his body language. I've got you well sussed out, Mr Steen.

"Tina, your firm has been short-listed for this

development," he begins with an assertive seriousness. "Nonetheless the competition is fierce and you're only one of the many agents I'm considering."

"Naturally," I respond.

"Let's not waste time here, Tina. What can Harding Homes provide that no-one else can in terms of marketing these properties?"

Tina off. Actress on. And action!

"Well, Brian, people buy people before they buy into anything else. Both myself and my staff understand the importance of this basic rule and as such the reputation of Harding Homes has gone from strength to strength, simply as a result of our behaviour. An integral part of doing business is building relationships and you and I know this doesn't happen overnight." I watch him nod with interest. "It takes time, you have to sow your seed, nurture it and watch it grow." *I'm on a roll.* "My relationships with local business-owners has gifted me a plethora of opportunity to not only promote my own practice over the years, but to ensure that these advocates can be called upon as and when the need arises."

Brian lifts his glass, pointing towards my barely touched water and with a shaking hand I take a few ladylike sips, basking in its ability to release my tongue from the roof of my mouth and proudly observing the lack of lipstick marks on the glass as I set it down. Every girl should invest in a Magistick.

"These contacts you've built, Tina, how exactly can they help you to help me?" Brian questions bluntly.

"I was just coming to that bit," I reply, feeling much more relaxed and in control now. "Brian, common sense has it that the potential purchasers of these upmarket apartments must be extremely high earners with possible occupations of business-owners or those working within the media or sporting industry and looking for primary or secondary accommodation here." I lean forward with the excitement of my new-found confidence, eager to continue. "My network of contacts includes the best casting and PR agencies in the North West."

Brian, now mirroring my body language, leans towards me nodding.

"I currently have an arrangement, which will be legalised when required, with the majority of these leading agents," my voice breaks with exhilaration, "who have agreed to actively promote the apartments to their A-list celebrities." *It's in the bag.* "I will in return ensure generation of a procuration fee, debited naturally to my own commission."

Brian sits up, arching his back uncomfortably but still nodding. "Well, Tina, of all the pitches I've heard, yours is the first to consider using external contacts. Outsourcing. Impressive." He nods, looking somewhat amused.

I am glowing from the inside out. Slightly sweaty of course but that's only natural in a woollen suit. I ought to have taken my cue from Brian and removed my jacket earlier but never mind. Rosy cheeks and a shiny brow can't stop me now. I wonder if he has bought into it? I guess he must have to some extent already, otherwise I wouldn't have been short-listed. As they say, once you've come this far the only thing you can do is fuck it up! Let's hope I haven't.

His face gives no indication of what he is thinking

although he still has that playful glint in his eyes. *Is it my imagination or is he flirting with me?*

"How do you know these agents, Tina?" he asks after a lengthy pause.

Damn. I was hoping he wouldn't ask this question. Here I am trying to sell my services as a professional estate agent and would much sooner avoid the failed-actress scenario. That part of me died a long time ago although I did just manage to pull off one last Bafta-winning performance! Professional in content, perfect in delivery. Should I prepare my acceptance speech?

"I used to do the odd bit of acting and modelling," I answer coyly, then continue matter-of-factly, "I never lost touch with my agent and it's not about what you know, it's who you know in this life. The rest is history."

"I can't argue with that statement." Brian raises his eyes, taking in the stainless-steel wall clock ahead of him. "Tina, forgive me, but I didn't realise it was that time." He stands abruptly. "I have another appointment to go to. These things are literally back to back." He smiles down at me, looking incredibly sexy. "It truly was a pleasure meeting you."

Did I just catch you looking at my chest?

Hurriedly he throws on his jacket, puts his coat over his arm and extends a hand. "Thanks very much for your time and interesting pitch." He smirks. "I'll be in touch."

Taken aback at the speed of closure, I too stand up – but far too quickly, sending my stool crashing to the floor behind me. Ignoring it coolly but inwardly cringing, I stretch out my hand to meet with Brian's monster grip. He grabs it, bending down to pick up the stool with his other hand.

I wonder if he knows his hair is thinning on top? Best let someone else tell him.

"Thank you, Brian," I say, with a nod in recognition of his gentlemanly skills. "Who said chivalry is dead!"

"You're welcome, Miss Harding." His voice is soft and alluring and he lets go of my hand after what seems to be a lingering grip. Turning on his heel, he walks to the door where he stops half in, half out, and glances back at me. "Tina, what type of modelling did you do then?"

Flustered, I glance down momentarily to collect myself. *Don't tell him whatever you do. You were young and inexperienced.*

I look up to find he has disappeared.

Shit! Nice one, Tina!

3

"Get your monthly horoscope here!" he hollers in an effort to make himself heard over the racket. "See what the coming year has in store for you! Twenty-five pounds is all it'll set you back, people!" He summons a group of young girls standing and watching him in awe. "Come on, ladies! You know you want to."

Holler Man inhabits the very first stand at the exhibition. A prime spot and an advantage if everyone is like me, that is, inclined to hover close to the entrance thus making him appear popular as the crowds gather around the mouth of the room. Although little attention is actually being paid to him. It's more of a meeting place and a chance to stand back and take in the events, before being swallowed up and strangled in its umbilical grip.

I make a mental note to reconsider my positioning for the overseas property exhibition. I'd hate to lose out on prospective buyers. *Well spotted, Tina.*

A group of giddy students stampedes us and I watch as they huddle together, toe-treading and hand-holding and pointing excitedly at the goings-on. The whiff of stale body-odour hangs heavy, but thankfully follows after them as they embark on their flight to revolutionise their final student years through predictive babble. A party of pensioners hobbles through the double doors, released and freed for the day. I observe their more strategic approach as they trudge at a snail's pace into the nucleus of it all, stopping there to take in its outer core and to consider a more utilitarian approach.

I can't help but be amused. You should see them! They're barking mad. All of them. I can't believe I'm actually here rubbing shoulders with these people! Holler Man looks kind of normal which surprises me. Well, if you class a purple velvet Dickensian jacket buttoned up to the neck with long greasy grey hair scraped back into a bird's-nest-cum-ponytail as normal. It's hardly this season's fashion, is it? I can't see his bottom half and have no desire to either. The upper torso is repelling enough and if the view is as gross as it is from the waist up, then no thank you – besides, these days I can't seem look below any man's waistline without getting caught.

I am prepared to spare him some credit for his stand though. Even without his rather vocal pitch it's obvious that his field is Astrology and his stand is impressively decorated with a massive collage of zodiac signs. I spot mine. The twins of Gemini. Tacky key-rings of rats and snakes and other vulgar creatures dangle from metal spinning racks. A line of papier-mâché balls clipped on by washing-pegs spans the length of his stall, each one hand-painted in earthy colours. A celestial feel certainly exudes from it even if his own façade is not in keeping, and a true cosmic sense fills the atmosphere.

"You okay, Miss? You're looking a bit lost." Holler Man stares right at me.

"I'm just waiting for my friend, thanks," I say, adding hastily, "I'm here for her." *Definitely not my cup of tea, Mr Dickens!*

He picks up a scroll held together with an elastic band and, walking away from his stand, hands it to me personally. "Have this with my compliments. You're a good soul. I can tell." He mimes a gentlemanly bow.

Flattery works wonders and a mild flush sweeps across my face. Partly because he actually does smell of horrendous body odour and partly at my ignorance toward him simply because of his staged attire and unsightly hair – oh and just for being here.

"That's very kind, thank you." I unravel the paper to see it is a calendar with a picture of a snake on its cover. *Nice.*

Holler Man, now back behind his stand, witnesses my expression and his thunderous laughter causes me to make reluctant eye contact. "It's the Chinese calendar, Miss. Folklore. They use animals to represent cycles. There are twelve in total."

I nod, feigning interest. Where is the nearest bin?

"I'd offer to tell you what sign you are and what it means, but I could never ask a lady's age."

"Why do you need my age?" I ask, forgetting my rule of engaging with no-one. "Don't you just need to know the month I was born in?"

He looks encouraged by my interest. "Well, the Chinese use a cyclic system featuring twelve animals," he explains. "Each year is represented by an animal. The animals all have different personalities and as such it is believed that as a person you mirror the animal of your year and actually copy its traits and characteristics." He grabs a plastic pig from its stand. "Look at this and tell me what comes to mind?"

I stare at the cheap miniature, wondering what on earth to say. *Where the heck is Chantelle?*

"Erm . . . fat?" I begin to feel under the spotlight as his clever tactics begin to draw attention to us. "Smelly," I add.

"A pigsty!" a voice calls from behind me.

Holler Man grins knowingly. His act is perfectly staged and he is playing the protagonist beautifully. "Contrary to popular belief the pig is kind to a fault and with impeccable manners." He strokes the back of the plastic mould. "He is highly intelligent and in constant need of a challenge." He beams down at it lovingly and thrusts it into my hand. "If you were born in his cycle it means you're likely to be a loyal friend, a loving person and have a heart of gold. Remember, people, things aren't always as they seem." He delivers the last line with a sinister edge to his voice, penetrating the crowd with a 'mystical' gaze. "Dare to come closer?" he teases dramatically, striding back to his stall and standing tall as its intriguing figurehead.

A low hum of activity echoes as people move closer and a sea of hands grabs at various merchandise before Holler Man is flooded with an ocean of questions.

I stuff the freebie into my Radley bag, standing back to let in the more enthusiastic buyers.

Hurry up, Chantelle, for goodness' sake.

I have attended today with no intention whatsoever of handing over my hard-earned cash. Certainly not to hear some spoof impart news of Mars meeting my anus. Let me tell you what my forecast is. Pay the shop rent and utilities. Pay the bank, the staff and then keep whatever is left over for me divided up between necessities and luxuries. It really is that simple. I haven't always been so matter of fact about things. It's only since I've matured, both in years and in approach, that I've become more practical and pragmatic about life. As an actress it was all about being someone else. Taking on their persona, their characteristics and completely losing yourself in them. It was wonderful at the time but it does tend to leave you a little confused about who you really are.

But the strangest thing is that being here today makes me feel strong and focused and well . . . Christina Harding.

Conscious that my attitude has been a little ungracious, I make a determined effort not to write off the day and firmly remind myself that I am here for Chantelle, a loyal friend to whom I owe a plethora of favours. I also make a mental note not to write off most of the participants or exhibitors. Who knows what type of lives these people have had? It is perfectly understandable for an individual of perhaps a lower level of self-esteem to want to be enlightened with news of a windfall or a blooming romance or the job of their dreams. You have to take an empathetic approach and, let's face it, we've all been there. How often have you scoured the out-of-date magazines in your hair salon, reading horoscopes from months before just to see if any of the events have actually transpired? Apparently it's bad luck reading them if they're out of date but sometimes you can't stop yourself. It's the sheer intrigue that grips you. It's the *what-ifs* and *maybes* that keep us going through most of our lives. Having said that, reading a magazine is harmless and it costs next to nothing. Spending six times the minimum hourly wage on some so-called astrologer or psychotic psychic isn't quite the same as prising open the wrinkled pages of *Hello* magazine while dried-up locks collect in your lap, is it?

I try to shift my attitude into positive mode and think only of good things. It's going to be a long day if I clock-watch and I could certainly do without the negative energy blocking my chakra.

There aren't as many new-age hippy guys as I expected. In fact, to my surprise, most of the exhibitors appear so run-of-the-mill that it's almost disappointing. *See, that wasn't hard, Tina. Be nice.*

But where are the theatrics? Where are the flamboyant costumes, the teacups and the gimmicks? Most of these guys are managing to avoid the age-old perception of looking like caricatures – you know, headscarf, hooped earrings – and it's kind of disappointing. Seriously though, they must think we came in on the slow boat if plain clothes are supposed to enhance their normality and have us buy into them as the gifted professionals they're purporting to be. *Well, that lasted long.*

An overpowering aroma hits me and tickles my nostrils before hitting the back of my throat. The scent of joss sticks. And not one either, but a variety of scents travelling from all directions, working inharmoniously and thwarting what could have been a wonderful nasal experience. But there it is again. No communication between the exhibitors. No 'Let's work together' or 'What are you using? Right, I'll do something different then'. It comes down to the same thing. No business skills. These guys are so clearly not business people. Their expertise consists of conning techniques and imagination on demand. Their living is based on one-hit wonders and quick wins and a sea of palms crossed with silver. I almost feel sorry for them.

Feigning interest in the Fayre, I wonder how on God's earth Chantelle is going to make her selection from this lot? We have a Top to Toe tarot reader claiming to be an international psychic and clairvoyant. *Yeah, right.* An aural photographer offering information about your aural field. *Whatever!* And the centre for harmonious living. *Like that's ever going to happen.* Unable to control my amazement at this complete and utter bollocks, my giddiness turns into snuffles and I just stand in The Great Hall sniggering hysterically at the pantomime of events surrounding me. What's even more hilarious is the seriousness of the rest of the visitors. This is brilliant. It get better and better. We have Soul Rescue, Site Planning, Psychic Attack, Colour Therapy, Animal Healing and Spiritual Surgery. Spiritual Surgery? Whoever would have thought a ghostly apparition capable of the removal of one's appendix? Fascinating or what?

I have to say, I am really starting to enjoy myself now and you've got to hand it to them, they're good, bloody good. If only I had their creative skills. Maybe I could learn a thing or two here. But what strikes me as I watch these pathetic folk hand over their money is the complete lack of regulation. I mean, globally this must be a multi-million-pound industry, at least, operating with no authority or governing body like most industries do. Who do you complain to if you get a dud reading? Merlin, Russell Grant, Mystic Meg? Also, how could you prove that the events prophesied didn't actually happen? Their defence is likely to be that while you are of this world, there is still time for these events to present themselves. How can you argue with that? Perhaps on your deathbed with a professional medical assessment of only a few remaining hours you may have a case, but by that stage the collection of a refund less interest is hardly a priority. Still, you could always get your revenge post mortem by rattling a few chains in the middle of the night, assuming of course they don't hit back at you with psychic-presence-clearing or exorcism rituals.

The visit is almost worthwhile simply to be in The Great Hall. Having frequented this place on numerous occasions it occurs to me that I have overlooked its splendour and ambience. Although during those attractions, alcohol has been the star of the show, not the décor. The Royal Fort is distinctive in that part of its structure is early 19th century, a former stately home which suffered a series of bomb attacks during WWII. The property stood as a ruin for decades until a wealthy investor made an application to purchase the land with the intent of demolishing its remains and building a modern hotel in its place. And with the enticement of job creation and a boost to the local economy, permission was granted, providing what was left of the Great Hall was salvaged and made structurally sound with its original fittings preserved. Little else was in a recoverable condition. The Great Hall, given its sheer grandeur, has over the years become the venue to host weddings, seminars and any other type of formal engagement. I can easily see why.

Venetian chandeliers, intricately designed with bronzed leaves and flowers and made from hand-blown glass, hang gracefully from elegant ceiling roses. The chandeliers are indeed a work of art, flawless in brilliance and clarity with each stone cut to precision. Heavily patterned carpets cover the darkly polished floors. Plump-backed ottomans busy with oriental-bird displays clash offensively with silk wallpaper bearing floral designs. The Victorian feel is so heavy on the eye that it's almost blinding, but there is something about this room that can capture your soul and hold it firmly, only releasing it once you begin to appreciate its eclectic values.

The place is steadily filling up and already small queues are forming. I am amazed at the amount of older people here. We're talking fifties upwards. Would you not think at their time of life they'd be fulfilled or at least have learned from their mistakes? And surely their life experience so far would have shown them enough to understand what they do and don't want? You'd think so, wouldn't you?

A smartly dressed pensioner is buying a crystal. She passes it from hand to hand with such care and grace you would think it were a diamond. Her thumb caresses its ragged edges and she holds it to the light for closer inspection. *Why on earth?* The stall sign offers: *Crystals To Lift Your Mood.* Why do they never offer "*Next Week's Lottery Numbers*" or "*How To Lose Weight by Eating More*"? They truly know how to lure us in.

What does occur to me is that while each exhibitor is quite individual in appearance, they all – apart from subject matter of course – have one thing in common. Each and every one of them is smiling. I'm not talking a slight curvature of the mouth here, but a jubilant happiness which seems to exude from the depth of their soul. Could this be as simple as good customer relations? Something we lack in this great country of ours. Or could it be an inner peace they share? Maybe it's the pound signs? But whatever it is, job satisfaction oozes from these weird folk and they certainly know how to put on a show without making it look remotely staged.

A clumsy tap on my left shoulder startles me and, as I turn to look, Chantelle childishly jumps out to my right.

"Gotcha!"

Why do I fall for it every time?

"Chantelle, don't do that to me! I nearly jumped out of my skin," I chide her. "I'm already on tenterhooks in case some other nutter tries to use me as a sales prop!"

"What?"

"Never mind."

She shakes her finger at me in a scolding manner. "Well, if you'd got yourself a reading while you were waiting, Tina, you might have known to expect it. You could have saved yourself from a mini heart attack!"

I snort at the stupidity of it while Chantelle remains straight-faced. *She actually meant it! Crazy girl!*

Today I see a totally different girl to the one I witness during office hours. She really is an immaculate dresser and, with her naturally petite frame, she manages to wear clothes effortlessly. By day she power-dresses in suits, usually wearing tight skirts with sheer legs and high heels. But her extra-curricular attire demonstrates a totally different girl. Skinny jeans in dark denim tucked into brown suede knee-boots wrap themselves around her slim thighs. A low-cut top clings to all the right places and stops at her narrow hips, inches from the curves of her dainty bottom. Her long dark hair falls into loose silky waves and sits halfway down her back and she is without make-up as always. Suddenly, I feel a little frumpy. Don't get me wrong, I still attract my fair share of attention, but unlike Chantelle I can't survive without St Tropez, hair-straighteners and my Urban Decay collection. She is a beauty au naturel while I invoke masses of effort by comparison. But you simply make the best of the hand you were dealt. If Chantelle put on a quick coat of mascara and a dab of lip gloss, I swear she'd be kidnapped and put on the next flight to Hollywood.

"What do you reckon then, Chantelle? Let's have a good look around and make sure we pick a good one for you." *That's a euphemism for let's get the hell out of here.*

The stands are positioned down each side of the massive hall, meeting in a V-shape below the only remaining stained-glass window. Its religious theme bears a host of angels watching over the room with illuminating halos floating high and lighting the floor below as the sun shines through. I can't see them being in favour of this myself. Theory has it that the art of seeing into the future comes from a negative source, a link with Satan. I guess that will be one of those questions that will remain unanswered until we all move on to the angelic realm. Unless Chantelle's gran knows something for sure.

I follow Chantelle's lead, watching with interest the sheer level of concentration on her face. There must be more than fifty to choose from. We pass by Breath Meditation, Metaphysical Healing, Psychic Intuitive Techniques and a whole host of other bizarre stands with fancy names, conveying little indication as to their actual therapies. It would be interesting to learn what some of these are about and where on earth they were invented but I'll leave it to someone else to ask. If I keep my head down, I'll serve my time quicker.

"I'm going to choose this one, Tina." Chantelle stops assertively halfway down the first leg of our tour and points towards a stand decorated with blue curtains covered in yellow moons and stars.

"Meridian Healing," I read aloud. "Don't you want to look at the rest of them first? We haven't even covered more than a dozen."

Moving towards the stand, Chantelle shakes her head. "I like the curtains. Simple as that. Every year I win on the Grand National by picking my favourite jockey outfit. Same rules apply here."

Not a smirk in sight. She is deadly serious. So am I – about getting her to put my bet on next year.

I stand back as she hands over twenty-five pounds to a spotty teenage girl.

"Won't be long, love," she assures her.

'*Love*'? *She's barely in her teens.*

There isn't much to this stand in comparison to the others surrounding it. A long pasting table has been hurriedly covered with blue crêpe paper and messily sellotaped down. Promotional flyers are scattered about, in a deliberate attempt to cover the odd tear here and there, and a clipboard of names sits next to a small metal cashbox with some coins inside, sitting open. How trusting. The cosmic curtains are the only obvious effort and even they don't fully close over, leaving the participant in part view, much like women's changing rooms. Don't you just hate that on a fat day?

The curtain is thrown back and a lady, mid-forties, steps out.

"Mam, this girl is next." The girl gestures towards Chantelle who looks up eagerly. You can tell they are mother and daughter. A double-act. Two con-women for the price of one. The mother, aka Rita, I note from the flyers, is built like a house and is dressed in a pair of jeans which she must have sprayed on, and a thick black polo-neck adding inches she simply can't afford. Rolls of fat protrude over her waistband. Her face, although filled out, is pleasant, with piercing green eyes as the focal point. Her chin plays host to its own family of chins and as the surplus folds become smaller, the baby of the family sits alone, snuggled into her ample bosom. She sweeps her black hair back from her eye-line and looks kindly at Chantelle as she holds the curtain open for her.

"Wish me luck." Chantelle's face is willing and pensive.

I smirk at her. "See you at the other side."

She disappears behind the curtain, leaving me once more companionless amongst these non-starters.

4

"Sam, it's me. How are you?"

Sam is my sister. We don't speak too often these days as she 'lives to work' as a successful criminal barrister. Our sisterly social life has also taken a downturn since she met Tim. A few months ago he moved into her apartment and I have barely seen her since.

"Tina, I was just about to phone you. That's so spooky." She makes a ridiculous ghostly sound.

Perhaps she should be here with Chantelle instead.

"I'm at Mum and Dad's with Tim." There is a moment of silence. "Oh, what the hell, I might as well tell you now!" She screams down the phone with pure elation, "Tim and I are engaged! We're getting married!"

I am speechless. My sister, the girl I used to have all to myself, is leaving me. I will never be her priority again.

"Oh Sam, I am so happy for you I could cry." *Literally.* "Wow!" I struggle for the right words, trying to compose myself. "You guys are fast workers but I'm made up for you, Sam."

"Sometimes you just know, Tina."

I wouldn't, Sam. That's always been my problem.

"I knew straight away but had to keep it quiet until I was sure he felt the same way." She giggles. "That's part of the reason you haven't seen me for ages. I knew I could keep how I was feeling from everyone else," she pauses, "but not you from, Tina. You know me too well."

I swallow hard, hearing such words from my big sister. My aspirational role model. "I'll take that as a compliment."

"It was meant as one. How soon can you get here? I'm desperate to see you!"

"I can't wait to see you too, Sam." *I really can't. It's true.* "Just let me finish up here and I'll meet you at Mum's as soon as I can get there. Don't you dare leave."

"Where are you now?"

"Oh, just out with Chantelle."

Now is not the time for a spiritual debate and, ever the lawyer, Sam likes a darn good debate. And always wins. She was always like that even when we were kids. She was captain of the chess team and leader of the debate team while I shook pom-poms and practised the splits as part of my extra-curricular education. And look what good it did me . . .

"Congratulations again, Sam. I'll see you shortly." I blow kisses down the phone until she hangs up. I stand there, staring at the floor, stunned yet overjoyed, jealous yet swollen with pride, but almost wishing that the phone call had been my imagination.

Sam was the one I would run to if I fell down. It was she who picked me up. Sam was the considerate sort who would buy gifts for our parents, always signing

'*Love, Sam and Tina*', even though I was mostly oblivious to her efforts and was never asked to give a penny. Sam was and still is, the stable, wise daughter that most parents aspire to produce. I wish I were like her, but I'm not. Sam and I have been chalk and cheese our entire lives. She was the brains and I, while not exactly the beauty, was the more attractive of us two. I busied myself delivering all-singing all-dancing shows to family and friends, while Sam tucked herself away like a hermit, studying hard. It was no surprise that she was accepted to read Law and it was no surprise to them that I chose to study Drama (to my mother's delight, admittedly).

Now even my love life has taken second place to Sam's. In reality, it has practically been non-existent for the past two years apart from the odd one-night stand here and there. But even those have diminished lately, through my own choice. How embarrassing would it be to negotiate the property sale for a guy you had bagged after a drunken night out with the girls? No doubt he'd be expecting some type of rate reduction as old pals! *Yeah, right.* As a respectable businesswoman, alleviating the risks to one's reputation has its drawbacks. No sex.

The back of Chantelle appears through the gap in the curtains, snapping me aggressively from my sorry train of thought.

"Thanks very much!" I hear her say. The pitch of her voice is definitely higher than usual. She waves at the mother and daughter with gratitude before pulling me away from the stand with urgency. Her slender fingers grip my arm.

"Oh my God, Tina!" she explodes. "She knew about

my mother! That she had passed on when I was a child! How could she have known that, how, how?" She pulls me further from the stand, her nails almost piercing my skin.

When Chantelle was nine, her mother died of breast cancer.

"You must have given her some indication," I say dismissively. "Did she say your mother specifically or did she simply say a female relative who was dead?"

Chantelle's forehead wrinkles as she frowns intensely. "She said my mother is no longer of this world. They don't actually say *dead*, Tina." Her tone is clipped.

"I'm sorry, Chantelle – that was insensitive."

"It's okay." A watery smile materialises. "She said my mother's spirit is guiding me."

"But you *must* have given her some indication, Chantelle? I don't want to be a party-pooper or anything but she could hardly pluck that information from thin air."

"I didn't, Tina, honestly. I know what you're thinking but I swear I sat there straight-faced and said absolutely nothing. Not a word. I believe it, Tina." Her voice quietens. "She said other stuff she couldn't possibly have guessed." She fondles the gold locket around her neck. "She knew this was my mother's. She said it helped her get a link with her, you know, bringing something that she once wore."

A single tear rolls down her cheek and I reach out and touch her arm lovingly, swallowing hard to be strong for her. My heart aches for her. Of all the people who deserve to be loved, it is her and it's at times like this you do wonder if there is a God and where the hell his logic is. "To know that my mother is around me is the greatest feeling ever." She sniffs like a lost child in much need of motherly tenderness.

"Here." I hand over a tissue. "Good for you. I'm made up for you." I squeeze her tightly, kissing her cheek before releasing her.

It is rather strange though. I mean, you can tell Chantelle is young, too young to guess that at her age she could have lost a parent. I have a suspicion that she gave it away indirectly. How else could the woman have known? Peculiar.

I remember the news. "Oh, you'll never guess what! Our Sam is engaged, can you believe it?" A heaviness hits me once more.

"Wow, that was quick!"

"I know, she probably thought her biological clock was ticking over."

"She's pregnant?"

"God no! She never said."

"I can't really imagine Sam as a mother, no offence meant." Chantelle's eyes regain their mature composure.

"It's okay, none taken. I know what you mean but neither can I imagine myself as a mother. I'd probably go out with the baby and forget to bring him back!"

"What if it's a 'her'?" she teases.

"I'd definitely leave her then!" I snort. "I spent a life time clashing with my own mother. If you think I'm going through that again you've got another think coming!"

We roar with laughter, linking arms, as we make our way to the car park.

Today is a great day for Sam and Chantelle. Sam has the man of her dreams and Chantelle the dream of her mother. But I can't help feeling like the stuffing has been knocked out of me. All this great news has left me feeling rather self-absorbed. I am so happy for Sam even though Tim is not exactly what you might call dynamic, but he is a good man who clearly worships the ground she walks on. I, on the other hand, fall for the bastards every time. It must be wonderful to feel so wanted and so secure, never caring whether the total stranger who just walked past you in the street finds you attractive. It's totally shallow but true, I'm afraid. The day I stop attracting attention is the day I stop leaving the house and curl up to die. It's been a long time since I've felt loved up and I guess it will take a strong man to provide me with that blanket of security and to eradicate the need to be aesthetically appreciated by all.

Most of my ex-boyfriends were the Thespian type, insecure and dramatic. And while there was rarely a dull moment, high-maintenance relationships are bloody hard work. Particularly when it's the bloke who does all the demanding.

Arriving at the car park, Chantelle releases her tight link of my arm and grips me loosely around the neck. Her temporary warmth takes away my internal chilliness and I feel good for supporting her.

"Thanks again, Tina. I'm so glad you were with me. I can't wait to tell Colin, although you know what a cynic he is." Her car bleeps and the lights flash as she presses the key-fob before climbing into her convertible blue Mini. She climbs in with a natural grace that could teach royalty a thing or two. "See you Monday, Tina!" Then she shouts as she pulls away, "And don't forget to tell your Sam I said congratulations!" She waves madly until out of sight.

I make a mental note to stop off at my office on the way to Mum's. I have a few bottles of chilled champagne I keep for special occasions and this is definitely one of those. Plus I need a drink! Visions of Sam gliding up the aisle flood my imagination. A picture of elegance and serenity. I can't wait to see her although I feel like I might cry and I don't want to. Not for all the wrong reasons.

The diesel engine rattles with uncertainty and I wait for it to settle down. I've been thinking about replacing it for ages but any liquid cash, for now, has to be pumped back into the business. At least until it starts to show consistent signs of making profit. My brain ticks over in sync with the noise. A chug here and a groan there. Why are there no guys for me? A good-looking, financially secure professional is not too much to ask for? Surely? You walk past those types every day. I'm not a bad person. I give monthly payments to charities and rarely pass a collection box without digging deep. I buy *The Big Issue* without actually taking it so they can sell it on to somebody else. I know just how they feel and curse those mercenary types who stroll past them with rich arrogance. I even smile at people I've never seen before just to brighten up their day. *When will it be my turn? When? When?*

Switching off the engine, I practically fall out of the car, slam the door shut and sprint up the marble steps of the hotel. My legs run instinctively towards the Great Hall. *Don't do it, Tina, don't do it!* But my feet seemingly run of their own accord. The physical battling the mental and winning fiercely. *And why do I keep attracting the wrong person? Surely I have a soul mate out there? Doesn't everyone?*

I halt abruptly, breathless and panting, staring deep into the Great Hall, willing myself to have the strength to turn and go. Just walk away.

I am my destiny. I hold it. I control it. The words drill into my brain. Repeat after repeat after repeat. I watch Holler Man still singing the same dreary song and using the same pitch. This is clearly a déjà vu.

I gaze at the stained-glass window showering flecks of brilliant light across the room and decorating the walls and floor with a million tiny rainbows. An abundance of colour dances prettily, costumed out and performing to an unappreciative audience, bar one. I feel the tingle of angel dust as it travels through the atmosphere and I inhale its medicinal remedy until dizziness results. It tickles my senses and penetrates my soul and then, with an invisible click, the spell has been lifted and once more I am of this world.

Phew! That was close, Tina, you bloody idiot! What the hell were you thinking?

5

"Place your hands on the crystal ball, my dear, and try to free your mind of any thought," says Gypsy Florence.

Free my mind? How long have you got? It's suffering from a humongous thrashing. Beaten by a pair of legs. I guess it was a case of who got there first, and it well and truly lost. Mind over matter? I don't think so.

I don't expect this to take long. Having said that, I didn't expect to be here to start with. In fact, it's one of those surreal experiences where you keep asking yourself *'Am I really here?'* But here I definitely am. I attempt to eradicate any level of contemplation by exhaling it noisily from my body. In through the nose, out through the mouth.

"Tina," her forehead creases, "can you fix your eyes directly on the crystal ball? Try to erase all thoughts." She frowns once more.

The cubicle is dimly lit and my eyes adjust slowly. The atmosphere is mellow and relaxed and suddenly focusing is easier. But I am feeling a little tired now. The crystal ball is sitting in the centre of a small round table covered with a black velvet cloth trailing to the floor. A foldaway chair bears an open leather briefcase displaying a pack of tarot cards, various crystal rocks and a rag or cloth of some description.

A flicker of light shines into the cubicle and the crystal ball glistens as the light travels across it. Muttering, Florence excuses herself momentarily, awkwardly prising her elderly body from the chair, and fixes the canvas curtains in an attempt to black out any distractions.

"Plays havoc with the magnetism," she fusses. "It's only just been charged up."

I glance down at the crystal ball, curious as to how you might charge a piece of glass. Looking up I catch her surveying my face intently. It feels intimidating.

"You leave it out during a new moon," she tells me. "It makes it more powerful."

My question never moved from my lips. *Freaky.*

Seated once more, she resumes the reading with my hands wrapped securely around the crystal ball, willing it to predict a future of lavishness and love. In any order.

"You have an unusual aura around you," she begins. "A mixture of outspokenness combined with a rare sensitivity."

She is looking around my shoulders from one side to the next. *For what?* I quickly turn my head left to right but can see nothing.

"Does that make sense to you?" She pauses. "That you can be almost confrontational but at the same time have a sensitive side?"

I guess it does really. I'm renowned for my outlandish and outspoken opinions but unravel the layers of hard-nosed Tina and you'll find a purring pussycat lies within.

Determined to give nothing away, I remain without emotion and simply shrug my shoulders.

"I am being drawn to your higher self," she continues. "Your higher self indicates that you have not yet learned to trust your own voice." Leaning into the ball, her eyes strain and she looks at me fixedly. "You need to believe in yourself." Her face softens. "Find a way to forgive yourself."

What is she on? Forgive myself for what?

"I feel that you are battling with a failed past and I must warn you that you must *not* become what you are not truly destined to become." Her face is overflowing with concern and a deep grimace distorts her already heavily lined forehead. Taking a break, she squints and moves her eyes from the ball for a few moments and then questions me directly, seeking affirmation. "Can you identify with any of this, my dear?"

Like I'm going to tell you. How unspecific was that? Doesn't everyone have a past failure that they'd rather not discuss? Feeling ill at ease and somewhat deflated at my lack of willpower, I simply nod. Humour the old dear so you can get out of here, Tina.

I could be with Sam, knocking back champagne.

"Good." She smiles. "I thought you might understand that." Her face lights up excitedly. "Ooh, I am also being shown a ring which indicates a marriage."

I sit up, suddenly interested to learn more, nodding for her to continue.

"I don't feel that this relationship belongs to you, however, although the person who is destined to be *your* soul mate is all around you." Scratching her head, she asks, "Are you in a relationship currently?"

I shake my head, attempting to hide my disappointment. *Aren't you supposed to tell me that?*

"Well, it won't be long for you, my dear. As I say, this person is around you as we speak and your paths are destined to cross very soon if they haven't already." She hesitates. "If you allow it, Tina."

That is the first time my name has been used which in fact was all she asked me for, apart from the thirty pounds of course.

"*If you allow it,*" she repeats, watching me sternly.

Okay, I got the message the first time around.

Fidgeting on the white plastic chair, I cross and uncross my legs impatiently, unable to relax and cursing myself for just being here. My sharp stiletto heel clumsily attaches itself to the draped velvet cloth and I jerk my knee up trying to free myself. *Ouch!* It bangs hard beneath the table top and I freeze in horror as the table rocks with its force. In what seems like slow motion the crystal ball rolls towards me, twisting and turning and heading for the edge of the table.

"Jesus!" I manage to grab it just before it rolls off, clutching it without a millisecond to spare and holding it tightly to my chest.

I watch as her face changes from a ghostly panic to utter relief. It looked like the old dear was a goner for a moment.

She prises the ball from my perspiring hands, frantically examines it and heads to the open case where she pulls out the soft cloth. She wipes the ball with soothing, loving strokes.

"I'm so sorry . . . it . . . it was an accident," I implore. "My heel got caught on the cloth."

But she ignores me, still wiping the ball. Caressing it with affection.

It's a bloody piece of glass, for God's sake. Nothing more than a big marble.

She stares at me. A look of repugnance crosses her face. "This ball is made from quartz crystal," she scolds. "And I simply cannot practice without it."

Okay – once is coincidental. Twice is plain spooky.

I stand to go, no longer feeling the need to hear more. Enough damage has been done for one day.

"I'll leave you to it," I mutter in embarrassment. I turn to go, looking for the break in the canvas drapes. "Again, I'm really sorry."

"Tina." Her voice is lowered and calm as she hobbles towards me, giving the impression of being concerned. "I no longer have a connection to continue." She inhales deeply and with much effort. "But I must warn you that you truly need to learn to trust *yourself*." Her eyes, although worn and bloodshot, are filled with wisdom and compassion. "Only you know who and what is right for you and things are not always as they seem."

I've heard that before.

"Thanks," I reply awkwardly. "I don't know what I'm doing here. Sorry to have wasted your time."

"Everything happens for a reason, my dear," she answers gently.

"Not this," I retort, angry at myself.

"Let this not be a wasted experience for you."

I find the break in the curtains with relief and am as desperate to run back out as I was to run in.

"Tina!" she calls to me and I stop to look back at her

elderly face and stooped posture. Her distorted hands are dry and craggy.

"You know . . ." She pauses. "It is okay to be less than your dreams."

I stand there just staring as her tired red eyes pierce through my soul, washing me out and leaving me with a feeling of great unease.

Maybe. But is it okay to be less than others' dreams for you?

Stopping off at the office, I deactivate the alarm and tear up the stairs to grab a bottle of champagne.

Every year we receive a case of this wonderful stuff from the solicitors across the street. The conveyancing staff over there are so efficient and thorough, and with their close proximity we recommend them whenever we can. Keep it in the community, as they say. It certainly doesn't go unnoticed by them and they reciprocate in any way possible. It's usually on a social level which is right up our street. Chantelle and I get invited to their Christmas bash, and every year we stagger home with enough post-bash gossip to last us through the following year. It's generally who's shagging who, the ongoing sexual-harassment case against the senior partner, and the dirt on underhand transactions and who is doing them. Illegal as they are, they happen, believe me. Alcohol does wonderful things to you, doesn't it? It loosens the tongue, lubricates the imagination and releases all your inhibitions. Oh, and makes you think you can sing karaoke better than anyone else in the universe.

Our office parties are extremely quiet by comparison. Besides Chantelle and myself, I employ Heather, the

SAGE accountant, for two mornings a week, and Trisha, the singing cleaner, or 'domestic' in politically correct terms. She cleans for us three evenings a week. Much as the balance sheet is a glowing indication of Harding Homes' success, the property business is both fluctuating and somewhat seasonal and we get slaughtered by any social or economic downturn. We're just coming out of the mid-winter crisis and very slowly prospective buyers are starting to prise themselves out of hibernation, ready to face the property world and all the sharks in it. Or so they think.

For the time being, the salary overheads are right on their upper limit and an embargo has been placed on recruitment but once the sales pick up in the spring I fully intend to remunerate the staff with some sort of sales incentive. Or commission bonus. I want to keep them and I want them to want to stay with me. Good management is all about satisfying your staff. Reward them with thanks, encouragement and achievable incentives and in return they will serve you unequivocally. And if that doesn't work get them completely pissed and they'll love you forever!

Looking around, I note the odd jobs that need doing, simply to bring the office into mint condition. It's nothing major but it is in need of a little touch-up. It's been three years since the upstairs rooms were painted. Both of them. We use one as the staff-room-cum-storage-room where the stationery, exhibition banners and photocopier live. The other is my office, used also for client interviews, away from the inquisitive ears of snooping folk. With so much identity fraud, it doesn't do to convey your personal details in an open room full of strangers. I wouldn't do it and I certainly don't expect my clients to.

The premises as a whole comprises a large open-plan ground floor, with separate WC and a small storage room to the rear of the building, and the two large rooms upstairs. There is a small back yard scattered with potted marigolds and pansies, which Mum kindly donated to us, in addition to a stained timber bench which was the congratulatory opening gift from my wonderful family.

Talking of whom . . .

Pulling up outside the large white detached house, I witness a driveway overflowing with cars, two of which I recognise, the rest not, but I would certainly like to meet the owners.

My former home is today playing host to a Porsche Carrera and a BMW 5 series with a private plate. You wouldn't get much change from sixty-five grand if you bought that.

Parking on the busy road in front of the house, I adjust the rear-view mirror, quickly applying a dab of Touche Éclat but going completely overboard on the lip gloss. You never know who you're going to meet or when, and yes, I was in the Brownies. You really do have to be prepared.

Hurrying down the long gravelled driveway, I admire the mature gardens and inhale the fresh scent of the recently mown lawn.

Sam and I had some fun playing in the front garden with the other kids in our street. Or *'road'* as Mum would correct. *"A street, darling, is for council houses."* My mother, a snob without any just grounds, is part of the reason for my past shortcomings, or so I feel, rightly or wrongly. It was she who pushed me towards a media career. It was she who was first in line to sign me up for dance lessons and it was she who managed to land me an agent at the hormonally challenged age of fourteen. I guess like a lot of parents they live their dreams through their kids and by God was my mother ever the dreamer.

Talk of the devil!

"Christie. Darling." She smooths down the cashmere sweater, fixing it just below the waistband of her tailored trousers. "Hurry up, sweetie, we're all waiting for you." She is standing at the front door, bouncing excitedly. Her eyes are more alive than I have noticed for years. It's nice to see.

"Hi, Mum." I hand her the champagne. "Sorry I'm late, I had to call in to the office first."

She grabs me, crushing me to her ample bosom, before roughly pushing me back to take in the view. *How subtle.*

"Never mind about that, darling. Isn't the news just wonderful?" She scans me from head to toe. "You look so well, you know, I really don't know why you're still single, Christie. Look at you! You're gorgeous." She squeezes me once more, not noticing my lip-gloss smudge on her beige sweater. "And well done for keeping the weight off, sweetheart. I'm so proud of you."

For crying out loud, it's been ten years since I lost all that weight yet she still talks about it like it was yesterday.

'Christie', incidentally, was my stage name, acquired after my agent suggested that Tina was perhaps a little bland. Charming. Mum still uses it for some bizarre reason.

"Where's Sam?"

Taking my arm, Mum leads me into the living room like a tour guide.

I used to live here, for heaven's sake.

A sea of faces stares at me, each one smiling joyfully with untouched champagne flutes in hand.

They've more willpower than me, that's for sure!

"Tina!" Sam releases her hand from Tim's and rushes over to hold me in a tight embrace.

I can almost smell her happiness. It seeps from her invisibly yet distinctly. I grip tightly onto my big sister, my heroine, tears welling in my eyes. The reality hits me and quite selfishly I wonder if our relationship will ever be the same again.

"Congratulations, Sam!" I offer, not breaking away from her. And I really do mean it. Her happiness is my happiness. "Don't forget about me, will you?" My voice breaks. "Am I still your best friend?"

Sam squeezes me tighter, stroking my head, kissing it with tiny sisterly kisses. "You and Tim are the two most important people in my life," she assures me solidly, disengaging her grip but holding my shoulders firmly. "Don't you ever forget it. Okay?" Her eyes are kind and full of love, sparkling with elation.

"I won't. Thanks, Sam."

I feel a bit better now. We've only ever had each other and the thought of not having her in my life would seriously kill me. I really do think I would die. She understands me so well. We had no cousins and no grandparents on either side so it's always just been the four of us. Our own little family. But for Sam and me, it was just the two of us. No-one else could have penetrated the special bond we shared. And still share.

On her manicured hand sits a cluster of diamonds, dazzling effortlessly, with one massive stone in the centre surrounded by six smaller diamonds each side and encased in a platinum setting. When the sun shines in through the bay window, the walls and ceiling come alive with a scattering of light pockets. Each one a different shape and dancing their own unique celebratory dance.

"Let me introduce you to Tim's family," Sam proposes as Mum thrusts a much-needed glass of champagne in my hand.

I am so tempted to down it in one after my eventful day but, taking in the evidently snooty in-laws, this is neither the time nor the place. But, by God, do I need it right now!

I am introduced to Major Heath-Jones, Mrs Hilary Heath-Jones and the rest of the family comprising Tim, who I know of course, and Simon his younger brother. Looking at his parents, it comes as no surprise that Tim is so dull. He's probably been raised with military precision by an overpowering father and a timid mother too afraid to voice her opinion in a '*Know your place, woman*' milieu.

Simon is actually quite cute and bears no resemblance to the rest of the family with his strawberry-blonde hair and green eyes, compared to their olive skin and brown hair. Hilary, whose hair colour looks wildly confused, is in dire need of a trip to a decent salon. I could recommend a few. I'll get to know her a little first. Simon, unlike the rest of the Heath-Jones, doesn't speak with a mouthful of marbles and, although he is well spoken, it's in an ordinary passable way and not at all snooty.

I wonder which of the cars is his?

My mother is in her element playing the wonderful hostess, while Dad feigns interest in the Major's anecdotes and Hilary nods away with interest, not admitting to have heard them all before. *The obedient wife!* Ordinarily, she might have got away with it, but laughing heartily a split second before every punch-line gives the game away. Comedy acting is all about timing and, Hilary darling, yours needs a little work. *Perhaps I can coach you while we're at the hairdresser's?*

The room is overflowing with energy as Sam and Tim talk giddily about their wedding plans, with frequent interruptions from both the Major and my mother. I think she's found her soul mate and he's definitely met his match. And seems to like it. Hilary is taking a back seat, followed closely by Dad, whose only questions will be "How much?" and "*What?*"

Simon, who until now has been sitting quietly, stands up and excuses himself, returning just moments later looking mildly embarrassed.

"Mrs Harding, where is your bathroom, please?"

My mother, a little more forward with alcohol, links her arm through his and takes him out to the hall, returning on her own. She winks at me tactlessly while I glare back with a '*Don't even go there*' expression. Honestly.

I can see why my mother is so happy though. I mean Tim is the next best thing to royalty. Well spoken with a double-barrelled surname, undoubtedly to be used as a bragging tool to anyone and everyone. I can just imagine my mother at her hospital League of Friends meeting. "Oh, did I mention our Samantha has married a Heath-Jones? I did? Silly me, I must have forgotten." Like hell!

That woman has the memory of an elephant. It's unlikely that there will be any real commonality between the two families, Tim and Sam being the exception of course. But does there really need to be? Gone are the days where families gather together for loved-up Christmases, revelling in the ambience of *The Waltons*, each family member consumed with the virtue of its true meaning both in terms of faith and traditional family values. Christmas is undoubtedly the most stressful time of the year, particularly if you are married or in a serious relationship. Make one family happy and you offend the other. Go home separately and your marriage is in jeopardy! Celebrate at home, just the two of you and you're antisocial. Sometimes you just can't win.

Perhaps being single is easier? But why does the grass always look so much greener on the other side?

Simon joins me on the two-seater fabric after retrieving his glass. *Clink!*

"Cheers – again," he smiles and we drink. "I wish I could stay for longer but I have to go in a few minutes. Still, it's better than a no-show, I guess."

"You're not a bit like your brother," I reply. "Not physically anyway."

"Is that good or bad?" He laughs raucously. "Actually, don't answer that!"

"Indifferent."

He grins and gets up to leave, putting the champagne flute on the mahogany coffee table in front of us, still half full. He notices my look of sacrilege.

"I'd happily drink it all but I'm driving," he remarks. "Usually I don't drink at all if I have the car but today I bent the rules. And quite rightly." He smiles again and his entire face lights up. He looks both young and middle-aged at the same time, with flawless skin, pale but interesting, and a mop of hair conveying that just-out-of-bed look. His green eyes are speckled with a red tiredness and his expensive clothes are in need of a little TLC. I see before me a man who clearly knows his own mind and a man who may be in need of a little TLC himself. Starting with an ironing service.

"Perhaps you might like to have a drink some time, Tina?" he asks, barely audible and looking around shyly. He plays nervously with his key-fob.

I never had him down as the shy type. Quiet, yes, but not shy. Then again, he is in a room full of people, including his own parents. It's not exactly the venue for a blossoming romance.

I feel bad letting him down, but after the ridiculous day I've had it's time to make a decision like an adult. Head on.

A high-pitched bleep sounds and through the bay window I watch the lights flashing on the classy Porsche Carrera, pillar-box red with a private plate.

I don't hesitate. "Okay. That would be nice, thanks."

He looks taken back with the alacrity of my response. It's plain to see he half-expected me to say no.

And I fully expected to say no!

"Oh, well, that's erm . . . splendid."

I open my purse, pull out a business card and hand it to him. "Call me." I glance up at him with Bambi eyes, teasing him skilfully through long eyelashes subtly coated in a single layer of black.

"Most certainly." He is flushed and distracted bidding his gentlemanly farewells.

Escorting him to the door, I watch as he pulls away with caution, edging the car forward inch by inch until the coast is clear.

Nice car. Simple Simon.

6

Chantelle slowly peels back the sticky fold. The envelope shakes in her hands and her face is solemn. I know she is willing the news to be good. Not good but great in fact. Or better even. Rarely does she lose control of her composed façade, but today the entire office knows what is riding on the back of the content of this letter.

She pulls out the folded paper, dropping the envelope to the floor, and opens it out fully, looking up at me for permission to read it.

"Just tell me, Chantelle." My voice trembles. I squeeze my eyes shut and throw my hands over my ears. *I'm too scared to know.* I dare not hear nor see unless the news is worth both hearing and seeing.

"Dear, Miss Harding," she reads slowly. "Further to our recent mee–"

"Yes or no!" I screech.

Her head moves left to right as she speed-reads, talking in fast forward before she yells, "*I am delighted to tell you that Harding Homes has been awarded the contract to –*"

I remove my hands from my ears yet can hear

nothing. My world has fallen into slow motion and my ears ring with the sound of nothing. The weight of my body struggles to balance on quivering legs and I feel as though the breath has been sucked right out of me, leaving me feeling winded and nauseous.

Jumping high, I punch the air as euphoria sets in and my body strength jerks from instability to zip in a microsecond. I kick my legs as high as they will go, skipping from one end of the room to the other until breathless and panting, I force myself to be composed. *Oh, what the hell!*

"*Waahhhh!*" I shriek, doing playground star jumps. "We did it, we did it, we did it!" I can hardly believe it. *This can't be real.* "Will someone pinch me? *Aah!*"

Heather nips me with her stubby fingers, a little harder than desired. I survey the office, clearly wide-awake and definitely not dreaming.

Ever since I was a little girl I had aspirations to be an achiever. Someone who was tenacious and driven, never stopping until success was all mine. Whatever it looked like. But after my initial vocation left me high and dry and flat on my homeless face, it took a long time to shake off the memories of failure. It didn't help that I was reminded each and every time I looked at my mother. But now, unless I'm hallucinating, I swear I have just witnessed my Thespian soul leave my body, floating above me and waving a last goodbye.

The exorcism of a failed past.

The champagne flows easily, poured by hired professionals also offering hand-made, mouth-watering canapés with crab and goats' cheese and other twenty-first-century culinary inventions. *Whatever happened to sausages on sticks or cheese and pineapple?*

Fresh arrangements of flowers protrude from tall glass vases placed with a well-judged precision. They dress the premises beautifully, oozing classiness and a joyous potent scent. The room is crammed with invitees, both business and personal, all celebrating in style at our expense. My mother used to say, "If you're going to throw a party, make it a good one." Hence the expense of the evening, but money well spent in my opinion. Not to mention tax deductible.

Chantelle is on meet-and-greet duty, a perfect role for a woman with her magnetism, and Heather by the look of things is promoting her own accounting services. Trisha, hard-working as ever, is swiftly removing empty glasses and finished plates. She was invited here as a member of the team and she is unable to stop giving and working like a trooper. My role this evening is to network and rub shoulders with the local business-owners and other professionals, from travel agents to insurance brokers. All of whom I intend to make my mark on, predicting that at some point in the near future their services and wisdom will be at my disposal. Similarly, Harding Homes will reciprocate where necessary as is the unspoken rule of any successful business. What goes around comes around as they say. Reciprocity in business. Karma in life.

Through a small gap in people-traffic, I spot Simon listening intently to a lady I recognise from one of the offices on the high street, but I can't quite place her. She poses no threat to me, although for a woman of her mature years she is extremely attractive, and Simon, ever the gentleman, is nodding courteously, his body language evoking interest. *He's probably bored silly.*

Tonight was supposed to be our first encounter but was cancelled in light of the news. So I did the next best thing by inviting him here to join the rest of my family, including Sam and Tim. Until now, I had completely forgotten about him and catching his eye I wave across at him, gesturing that I'll be with him as soon as I can escape from these boring suits.

Why do people never quite grasp the concept of selling? Quit the shop talk where possible, talk about the other person as much as you can by asking them questions about themselves, without being intrusive of course, and never ever underestimate the fact that people buy from people. Business is about relationships and without a fundamental understanding of that simple rule, you are doomed to failure at an accelerated speed.

It becomes apparent that while I have acquired a vast quantity of information about my fellow business folk, very few have sought to ascertain the specifics of this celebration and what this means to us. Each individual is merely consumed by the WIIFM factor – 'What's In It For Me' – as is the case with most serial networkers. They almost make a hobby out if it. You see the same faces at every event and tonight has reminded me why I categorically avoid cold networking events like the plague.

Extricating myself from a group of boring blokes, I squeeze through the crowd, standing on the odd toe here and there, breathing in to fit through barely-there gaps. I pray that a fire doesn't break out as I am undoubtedly in breach of health and safety. But that's what happens when complimentary drinks are up for grabs. Something for nothing works every time.

"Sorry, Simon, it's mad busy – I feel like I've neglected you." I flick my hair back from my shoulders, lifting it off the nape of my neck in an attempt to both cool down and look sexy.

Simon, straight from work, is dressed in his typical lawyer attire. Dark pinstriped suit, loosened sober tie, and tidy hair for once. Quite a contrast to the laid-back impression portrayed last weekend, although he does look a little uncomfortable. His tired gentle eyes convey compassion and loyalty and his hypnotic gaze has thrown me. Standing before me is a man who could converse with his eyes alone, his lips emitting no detail but leaving you with a feeling of wanting to hear more.

"Seriously well done, Tina." He smirks at me playfully. "Or is it Christie?"

Cringing, I shake my head. "Ignore my mother. She's a little eccentric."

"Well, I was worried when she escorted me to the bathroom," he mocks in good humour. "I thought she was never going to leave!"

"I never had my mother down as a serial bathroom-loiterer," I snigger. "Are you sure you weren't fantasising?"

Simon shudders, rather sexily in fact. He looks like he'd quite a good mover – on the dance floor of course!

"Tina, like all men I cannot deny I have many a fantasy, but sharing the evacuation of one's bladder is not top of my list."

The pair of us burst into laughter. How distasteful a conversation for our first encounter, but how nice it is to feel at such ease with a practical stranger soon to be an in-law.

As Simon bids his farewells, I apologise profusely once more for letting him down at such short notice, offering to rearrange very soon. *How can a girl say no to a man with a Porsche?*

The evening has been truly successful although the place looks like a Beirut high street. Discharging Trisha early was clearly not a good idea but in my drunken kindness I sent her home. Lip gloss glistens from half-finished glasses and turned-up sandwich crusts wilt. Flakes of pastry garnish the carpet unattractively and an abundance of cocktail sticks lie scattered on the floor. A copious amount of champagne bottles sit empty and lonely, separated from their corks, still in the fixed position they landed in.

I'm awash with a mixture of alcohol, lack of food, exhilaration, euphoria and the dawning realisation of the task in hand. Contrary to the proposal put to Brian, talking the talk as they say is much easier than walking the walk. The sheer volume of preparation is suddenly overwhelming me as is the anticipation of owning and running a second office, which is now wholly achievable. But it's all I've ever wanted.

My head is splitting. No other drink hurts your head as much as champagne, but still it tastes divine and the bubbles tingle your nose and stimulate your tongue.

The office, now immaculate thanks to a Tina/Chantelle team effort last night and an early-morning effort by Trisha, is ready for business as usual. But a comfy bed, coupled with horse-sized painkillers is what my body is crying out for although there is too much work ahead.

My eyes are sore to touch. The pain emanates from the back of them, drilling its way to the front, and moves up towards my forehead as the morning drags on.

I attempt to outline a scarecrow plan, a prototype of how to drive this project forward, a plan which can be modified where appropriate – but with a head feeling like an out-of-control washing-machine on constant spin cycle, even thinking produces pain.

The presentation needs to be to the point. Catchy and delivered expertly, highlighting the benefits of owning one of these apartments, and brought to a climax by dropping in the percentage up for grabs here for an agent.

Talk about going the extra mile for your clients! Most PR and media agents tend to stick to serving the basics, unless of course they're Max Clifford or other arrogant PR agents keen to be in the face of the bloodthirsty media. Generally, they arrange only the fundamentals from first meetings to auditions and castings – all on your own time and at your own expense, of course – and when you've worked your butt off to get the job, they have the cheek to deduct undeserved commission. Plus, they pay you late every time without fail. Why the payments always have to go through the agent is beyond me. Anyway, I am offering these PR and media agents the opportunity to become realtors to their clients, securing them a place of residence incomparable to anything else on the market right now, and making themselves indispensable to their clients. A one-stop agent. Perfect.

The intention is to keep the brief as simple as possible

as research shows that people's concentration span lasts approximately thirty minutes. That's fine by me, given that the boardroom charges by the hour.

I scribble a note to contact Mark at Commercial Ventures. There's no harm getting a head start and putting the feelers out to see what second premises are available.

Second premises! It sounds wonderful. All achieved by Harding Homes with me at the helm, responsible for my own destiny.

A decision I made long ago, way before we secured this contract, was that I would go it alone and trade as myself, not under the EMA franchise to whom I was initially signed. During our first meeting they had promised a comprehensive training package to include SAGE training, trading standards and trade-description regulations, plus detailed budget-management planning. It was promised that complete support would be given in terms of marketing, advertorials and sales training, but once the early honeymoon months had passed by, I struggled to get any assistance still less the Full Monty they had promised. And I had paid for it – all fifteen grand's worth. My calls weren't returned, emails were left unanswered and it didn't take me long to establish that buying into a franchise probably hadn't been the best idea. I felt robbed, not only of money but of the trust I had placed in them.

After a sharp legal exchange, they were out and Harding Homes was in and it felt good to be left to stand on my own two feet without someone else taking a cut of what was mine.

The phone rings and I answer it, faking eagerness. "Good morning, Harding Homes, Tina speaking."

"Miss Harding. Mr Steen here."

My heart jumps with apprehension.

"Congratulations on your new appointment. I hear I missed a great party last night?"

What's he heard?

"Well, you were invited, Brian," I say, matter of fact. "And again let me thank you for making a decision you will never regret."

"I have faith in you, Tina." He pauses. "I wonder if you would like us to get together?"

"As gratifying as your company is, I have a golden rule of not mixing business with pleasure." I hear Brian exhale calmly.

"Perhaps this is mixing business with business?" he says.

That's a new one!

"I would like to offer you an invitation to dinner, Miss Harding." Clearing his throat. "Purely business."

"What's on the agenda, may I ask?"

"Yes, you may."

There is total silence and more silence and then the penny drops. I get it.

"What is on the agenda, Mr Steen?"

A roar of laughter bellows down the receiver. I join in laughing at the stupidity of two adults behaving like overgrown teenagers but disappointed at my slow response. Although as a sense of humour goes, I wouldn't recommend he gives up his day job. I've definitely heard funnier.

"Sorry, Tina, I apologise for my sense of humour. I couldn't resist it." He sniggers.

How childish! Can I resist the urge to say yes to

dinner? To stare into the aquamarine underworld of his eyes, floating in waves of lust, resuscitated by those puffer-fish lips?

Please don't rescue me. Leave me to drift ashore and come around in my own time, hanging on vividly to every moment.

"You haven't answered yet, Miss Harding."

My loins have.

"When where you thinking? I'm exceptionally busy right now."

"You name the time and the place and I will be there."

"Oh, okay."

I am taken aback and don't have an awful lot of little grey cells today. They've been mutilated by Veuve Clicquot. I flick noisily through the blank pages of my diary, ignoring the Wednesday *'drinks with Simon'* note. I hold the receiver deliberately close so it picks up the sounds of the turning pages, making me appear busy and important.

"Let's see, I can make Friday 7 p.m. at The Merchant," I declare boldly. Too expensive for my existence but pocket-money for him.

"Perfect. I will see you then, Miss Harding."

"Brian," I jest, "don't forget to bring the agenda, will you? After all, it is a business meeting." That'll teach him I'm not up for grabs.

The line is dead. What is it with that man and abrupt goodbyes?

Let's hope his hello is more welcoming.

Chantelle enters the office, looking remarkably well given the after-party party we had last night. My policy was for the staff to hold back on the drink until it was clear that everyone else was relaxed and well catered for. It really is the most professional way. There's nothing worse than the host acting like some drunken lush, slumped in a corner. *Sounds a little too familiar actually.*

Chantelle does look worse for wear but unlike me she recalls arriving home, getting undressed and hitting the sack. My last recollection is sitting in the tiny yard slumped on the bench with my bare, smelly feet draped over Chantelle's cream trousers, dragging on a Silk Cut. *Any wonder my mouth tastes like a dustbin today.* I detest smoking with a passion, even to the ridiculous point that I glare at people smoking in restaurants who light up, even if they are in the designated smoking area, and yet without fail, every time I'm intoxicated, I steal a cigarette from someone, somewhere.

"Thanks for helping me clear up last night, Chantelle. I'll give you the time back when it's a bit more quiet."

She shifts uncomfortably in the guest chair, looking pensive. Chantelle is pretty transparent as people go. What you see is what you get with her. Me? I'm a bit of an enigma to people but I kind of like it that way. Never hand anything to them on a plate. Keep them guessing and on their toes. Not our clients of course – that would just be silly.

"What is it, Chantelle?" I ask. "What's going through that head of yours?" I laugh and a stab of pain compresses my delicate head. "You look pained!" *And I feel it.*

Playing with her pen, she presses down the top, clicking it on, off, on, off. "You know last night you told me how you went back to see that gypsy woman. Gypsy Florence?"

What? I don't recall telling her that. By God, I must have been out of my tree.

"I told you that last night?"

"Yep, when we were in the cab on the way home. You couldn't stop laughing about it, but I knew the name was familiar and then, this morning when I woke up, I remembered it."

"Remembered what?" I sit up straight in the chair, anxious to hear what she has to say.

"I told you that my friend Sophie was going that Saturday, only we didn't bump into her, right?"

"Yeah."

"Well, Sophie rang me on the Sunday to tell me that that woman, Gypsy Florence, knew about her abortion."

I shake my head impatiently. "Chantelle, a huge percentage of women have terminations at some point in their lives. She could have guessed it."

Chantelle bites her bottom lip. Her face is taut as she recalls the details. "I was with her when she went through with it. We were fifteen. She was so unlucky – it was her first time and the two of us were so green in that area it never dawned on us that she could get pregnant. But she did."

I'm not budging here at all. "I do empathise, Chantelle, but so what?"

"So, she told her the baby was a little boy. And it was. She told her that she was just weeks away from her sixteenth birthday when it happened." She pauses while a tear rolls down her face.

I pass a tissue across the desk, squeezing her hand as she takes it.

"She also told her that she can no longer have

children because of the botched operation and it's true. She can't. She couldn't get the money together to get a proper job and her parents would have turfed her out if she'd asked them. Devout Catholics they were."

I snort at the last statement. Bloody religion. It's a curse.

Chantelle blows her nose and dabs her eyes gently. Her tears have soaked her thick eyelashes, elongating them, framing her dark eyes in a perfect snapshot.

I absorb the information. How much is fact and how much is fiction? What is the probability of guessing three specifics as accurately as that? It is rather peculiar. And what a risky statement to make just out of the blue. Surely even those crooks wouldn't risk it?

I drift back to sitting in that darkened make-shift room, my mind working overtime and asking muted questions. I remind myself how within a split second of my every thought, she had answered the very question that had been consuming me. I shudder as my spine tingles and the hairs on my arms stand on end. She had mentioned a failed past, which I agree most of us have experienced. But her single line still haunts me: "*It is okay to be less than your dreams.*" I was, in fact, less than my dreams for a long time. The dream didn't realise. It's a simple as that.

I jump up, standing tall. "Right now I am not less than anything or anybody! I am more than –"

"Who are you talking to, Tina?" Chantelle asks, looking alarmed. "There's only me here and I don't know what you're on about."

I belt out a peal of raucous laughter at the stupidity of even considering Gypsy Florence's words to be true.

"I'm just having a blonde moment – something you know nothing about!" I tease.

"Colin said he's sure I've been dying my hair brown for years and that I must be naturally blonde underneath."

"Cheeky sod. Hey, Chantelle, tell him there's only one way to check! Do the collar and cuff test!"

"Ooh! Naughty girl," she squeals, playing her coy act beautifully.

Colin is one lucky man.

Being serious for a moment, I collect my thoughts so I can file them away in my brain's archive. I so need to write of this experience and even apply logic to what Chantelle told me about her friend. Some guesses work, some don't, and perhaps Gypsy Woman just struck lucky. A failed past, come on? How general is that?

There. Case dismissed. Filing complete.

"Promise me you'll be careful though, Tina . . . about whatever it is she was warning you about."

She really is so caring but it should be me mothering her.

"I will be, I always am." I avoid eye contact, pretending to concentrate on the post so we can end this conversation. I consider telling her of the business meeting at The Merchant, but change my mind. I've said enough lately and don't want her to worry any more than she already does.

You can tell that Chantelle was raised by her grandmother. She is way older than her years in terms of her outlook on life and how much she worries, and for a young woman she should loosen up a little but, as always, she means well.

Your soul mate is all around you. All around you.

But I'm permanently surrounded by men. It could be anyone . . . if it were true, of course. My mind runs through an accelerated list of my male counterparts and dismisses them one by one. My face contorts as I imagine acts of consummation with some of them. Yuck. How gross! *No! It couldn't be. No way.* But then again didn't the crystal ball say not to be surprised at who was about to ask me out? It said he was my destiny, my soul mate and that I probably already knew the person who would shortly cross my path for a more intimate, soulful purpose.

Deliriously, I journey through my married life – perfect children and the sound of laughter emanates from my imagination. The scent of money drips from every orifice . . .

What are you doing, Tina! It's all nonsense – every bit of it. Snap out of it!

Coming to, my logic steals the moment. This is nothing more than pure coincidence. The fact that this date with Brian is the only exception to the business/pleasure rule I have ever made is nothing more than synchronicity.

Isn't it?

7

"Tina, it's Kate." Her voice echoes. "How the hell are you?"

I was thinking of Kate that very second – how bizarre.

"Kate, so great to hear from you. I'm really good, thanks, loads to tell you. Where are you?"

The sound of a loudspeaker reverberates through the handset, forcing me to hold the phone away from my ear.

"I've just come off set – we're filming the sequel to *Family Furores*." Kate's phone bleeps, indicating a low battery. "I'm about to lose you." She coughs from exerting her voice above the background noise. "I'm coming home this weekend – fancy a girly night?"

Do I? Kate works so hard that I barely see her and there is so much to tell right now, from hot date to wedding gossip, that I am in desperate need of someone to confide in. There is nothing that Kate doesn't know about me nor I about her.

"I'm well up for it but it will have to be Saturday," I reply gleefully. "Give me a shout when you're home and we can take it from there."

"Will do." She snorts. "Let's go for glam, yeah?"

"Definitely."

Glam I can certainly do and, after my recent application of fake tan, both Brian and Kate will most certainly be snooping around for my white bits – all one of them in the shape of a perfect landing strip and neater than a Wimbledon tennis lawn.

During our university days, when we were poor students and plied with alcohol, Kate and I would inevitably end up snogging each other. It made good business sense all round. She was damn gorgeous and, given our Thespian nature, we didn't care about anything apart from the male audience kindly providing free pints for an encore. Fortunately, we grew out of it, what with me as a prominent local businesswoman and Kate Symms practically a household pin-up. Don't knock it 'til you've tried it is my motto and I've tried many things in my time. The beauty of being an actress is that you can put it down to research.

Six forty-five p.m.

I scour the wardrobe, willing an outfit to present itself, fly off the hanger and glide over my body, leaving me the simple task of stepping into sexy stilettos before doing the obligatory last-minute twirl in the mirror. *One second, two seconds, three seconds. Nothing's happening. Shit. Shit. Shit.*

I grab an old favourite. A simple black dress, fitted and to the knee. I throw it over my lace bra with matching thong, dragging a pair of sheer stay-ups from the underwear drawer, scanning frantically for ladders and pulls. Straightening the lacy stocking-tops around my thighs, I pull down the dress, loosely tying the fabric belt around my middle and rather dangerously opening an extra button, exposing a sneak preview of what may well be on the cards, providing he lets me deal.

The cab honks its horn impatiently. I grab the house keys while quickly drowning myself in a last-minute dose of perfume, spraying it up into the air, allowing it to fall in invisible sprays over my head and shoulders.

After the office had closed, the urge to catch up with outstanding paperwork had simply consumed me. With a massive backlog, the result of an entire day spent doing practically nothing, suffering from the hangover from hell, I got carried away, immersed in a forest of papers, invoices and SAGE printouts. Driving home like a maniac, I congratulated myself for the forward-thinking lunch-time hair appointment and attempted to soothe my concern at how little time there would be to get ready, by using the 'less is more' argument.

That's the beauty of having an all-year-round tan – you need very little else to complement it. Just a few good coats of mascara, a squirt of high-shine lip gloss and a gentle dusting of shimmered powder to accentuate your cheek-bones and leave you looking radiant and sun-kissed, at minus one degree.

I shudder as the chilled air hits my skin and regret the decision to leave my coat hanging over the white wicker chair at home. Spring is close yet the days are still tinged with a frosted fragrance. The seasonal daffodils have begun to poke up their budding heads but their survival is dependent on spring bringing forth its thawing qualities and this has yet to be in evidence.

The scent of perfume exudes from my hair and neck

and journeys throughout the cab, causing a fracas with its sitting tenant: vomit! The cab reeks of stale sick and, opening the window, I gasp for breath only to be met with a cloud of exhaust fumes. But what's the travelling alternative? *À pied*? *Definitely not!* Feet weren't made for walking. They were made for shoes, the higher the better, bejewelled and dangerous. But this evening I have kept it relatively simple. Glancing down admiringly at the black patent-leather shoes, I rotate my right foot, sexily practising the art of seduction, noting how slender my feet look in the four-inch heels and how toned my ankles appear wrapped in criss-cross straps with a simple diamanté buckle fastened on each side. It's quite a close call between shoes and sex. Sex truly is the physical act, but shoes are the foreplay, a teaser to what's lurking beneath, a metaphor for stimulation. Their uniqueness promises individuality between the sheets and mine tonight declare power, danger and a sense of wildness.

"Just here, thanks," I rattle quickly, sensing the cab is about to drive right past the hotel and at some speed.

Winding up the window, I notice the outline of dried lip-marks on it, the detailed lines on full display like a fingerprint waiting to be traced.

Desperate to escape the filthy vehicle and making a mental note to never use this firm again, I hand over a five-pound note. "Keep the change. Cheers."

"Ta, love." His heavy Liverpudlian accent collides comically with his ethnicity.

The cab door swings open unexpectedly and a smooth pristine-white glove reaches in. Startled, I look up to take in a man dressed in black trousers with long grey tails and a matching top hat. Quickly realising it is the concierge, I take his hand gracefully and swing my legs out, placing both feet flat on the ground, knees together, before allowing him to take my weight and pull me from squalor to splendour. I feel like royalty.

"Good evening, madam." He smiles at me with a happy sincerity. "Will you be dining with us this evening?"

By God, this place is amazing.

"Yes, I will. If you could direct me to The Platform restaurant I would be most grateful." Best behaviour already.

"Let me show you, madam."

Following him up the granite-paved ramp, I am personally escorted to a set of revolving brass doors turning at quite some speed it would appear. Flashbacks of my playground days suddenly engulf me and I recall a single moment of standing alone, watching enviously, as my friends tossed two ropes together, in opposing directions. Squealing with delight, the onlookers jumped into the middle, one maybe two at a time, elevated and spritely, carried along by the high-energy chant of the spectators, clearly demonstrating the skill of tackling two ropes coming at them, one from each side. But I could never master it, much as I tried. One rope was fine but not two. My legs couldn't operate that fast but by God did I try hard!

Kate was the skipping champion. She was tiny and thin and bounced around like a pogo-stick on acid. I was constantly tripping. Isn't it funny how you hold on to certain memories, mostly the bad ones? The ones where that feeling of failure and humiliation never leave you.

"Excuse me?" I turn in the direction of the concierge.

"Madam?"

"Do you have another entrance, please?" I raise my

eyebrows in recognition of the doors. "I'm not too good with these doors at the best of times." Lifting my leg a little, I show the impressive shoe heel to the concierge, seeking a degree of empathy.

He bows slightly in a 'message understood' fashion and personally escorts me through the doors and into the reception area, pointing out a set of stairs displaying a sign for *The Platform. Thank God!* The doors themselves weren't necessarily the issue. It was knowing when to jump and timing the speed they were revolving. I swear I could have been there all night!

This place is absolutely incredible. I've never actually been inside before, although a few months ago Chantelle and I staggered up the main steps trying to sweet talk the doorman into letting us into the private members' bar. We failed fantastically.

But tonight, I am a guest of the hotel, and should a handsome gentleman taking me by the hand be an indication of the total experience, then I'd say I'm definitely in for a good night.

Climbing the stairs, I grip the handrail, already wobbling slightly, thankful that there was no time for the obligatory gin and tonic usually consumed while getting ready. *God, I need to get back to the gym.* Out of breath, I reach the top stair and step onto a small landing area, heavily carpeted. My feet sink into its deep-red shag pile. A huge brass mirror is on the adjacent wall and I risk a quick glance before entering the restaurant.

Throwing my head upside down, I ruffle my hair messily before jerking back up at whiplash speed in an attempt to gain as much height and volume as possible. I love that Mark, my stylist, manages to get it so poker-straight, but it leaves it with no real body and for a hot business date like I have tonight, that simply won't do.

"Upside down, Miss Harding? How novel!" a familiar voice murmurs close to my ear.

I feel the warmth of his minty breath.

Oh God, how long has he been here? It isn't any wonder I didn't spot him, wearing a body of hair over my face like an out-of-control cavewoman. But I had to mess it up in order to fix it. It's a female thing.

"Brian." My face is flushed and I'm suddenly stuck for words. "Hi."

Incapable of anything better, I thrust out my hand to shake his, but Brian clearly spots my awkwardness and simply leans forward, kissing me on the cheek.

"Shall we dine, Miss Harding?"

God, he smells amazing. As he places his masculine palm on the small of my back, I feel his warmth penetrating my body. My spine tingles with the discharge of his energy and my loins work overtime. Guiding me gently, never losing that physical contact, he ushers me to a table marked *Reserved* and graciously pulls out the chair, holding an assertive hand up to the waiter and declining his assistance. Ensuring my comfort takes priority, then Brian takes his place opposite and suddenly I am overcome with emotion. Him, this place, the contract, it's all too much. What the hell is happening in my life for me to be sitting in the Merchant Hotel, listening to the City's most eligible bachelor ordering a bottle of Bollinger's La Grande Année 1997?

Undoubtedly, my success is fast-growing in terms of business performance, particularly for such a young company. But it's certainly not at a level in keeping with this place, although I could really get used to a life like this.

It's typical – after years of being single and having no money, just like the bloody buses, everything seems to come at once. But who's complaining? Right now, it feels like it's a case of frantically grabbing whatever I can and stocking up. You never know, the next bus might break down or the timetables might change without warning.

The waiter deftly removes the foil and wire and firmly grips the cork, twisting only the bottle, expertly. A muted pop sounds and I watch, drooling, as he pours the contents into long slender flutes.

I wait impatiently for the bubbles to die away.

"Here's to us!" I smirk then.

Brian, eyebrow raised, questions me. "Us, Miss Harding?"

Knowing full well the game I'm playing, I feign innocence. "Yes, us. Our business relationship and its success." An angelic expression sweeps across my face but behind it lurks the devil in disguise, working out my next *double entendre*. "What did you think I meant, Brain?" I lean forward into the table, enjoying this game of 'catch me if you can', my breasts perched on the crisp linen tablecloth, my hands and wrists coloured by its stark whiteness.

"I'm not a man of assumption, Miss Harding." He raises his glass towards mine. "Certainly not with a woman of your calibre whose presence flatters me greatly."

Keep talking.

Chink!

Holding the glass by its long delicate stem and eager to display the art of fine dining etiquette, I take a sip of champagne, noting its lavishness, feeling its expense and I roll my eyes with pleasure as it slides down my throat, massaging it as the bubbles explode. Encore! By God, you can tell this stuff cost the earth – it takes you on a return trip to heaven and back in a millisecond. That's what I call value for money. Someone else's money, of course!

"Mmmm . . . exquisite . . . but such extravagance for a simple business meeting," I quip slyly.

"What did you expect? Beer?" he laughs. "I never drink beer."

"Seriously?"

"Never."

Weird. But impressive.

"Brian, haven't you forgotten something?" I ask coyly.

"And what might that be, Tina?"

That's the first time he's used my name this evening.

"The agenda!" I laugh raucously, attracting the attention of affiliated diners. Two sips and I'm already feeling giddy. And horny. *Don't give it to him on a plate, Tina. Make him work for it.*

The view tonight is sensational. Before me I take in this virtual statue of a man, muscular in build and striking in profile. I mentally undress him with my vivid imagination, feeling our lips lock together, longing to feel his manliness vault up against my frame. In short, I'm gagging for it. It's been too long.

"Madam, are you ready to order?"

Shaking as he strokes the soft flesh of my inner thigh, fingers expertly removing my lace . . .

"Tina, do you need a little more time?"

"What? Erm." My face burns with embarrassment. "No, no. I'm ready, thank you."

"Kate," I whisper. "It's me. I'm in his house. Oh my God, you should see it!"

Tucking the phone between my ear and shoulder, I plump up my lips with a dab of collagen crème. "No, I'm not going to sleep with him. Maybe a kiss or something – but by God is he drop-dead gorgeous!" I lift my dress with one hand, checking the stocking tops are in battle position, armed and ready for attack. Or better still, defence. "I'd better go. I'll fill you in tomorrow. Bye!"

Washing my hands, I remove a smudge of lipstick from my teeth and squirt a final measure of Euphoria on my neck and down my cleavage after hoisting it up a little. My stomach feels rather bulging after such a wonderful meal. Divine in taste but lacking a little in quantity, but made up for by copious amounts of alcohol, filling the gap perfectly though leaving me feeling a little bloated. And a little drunk. *Pure indulgence.*

Out of the blue a repeat thought passes through my veins, stopping me cold and numbing my body. Again. *"The person who is destined to be your soul mate is all around you. Your paths will cross soon . . . if they haven't already!"* It's been staring me in the face all along. It was so close to me I was touching it but couldn't see it clearly, until now.

Leaning against the granite sink, I stare at my reflection in the mirror, reminiscing about every time we've met. The tingling, the excitement, that feeling in my solar plexus that makes me hyperventilate until dizziness hits. The physical reaction down south merely at the thought of him.

I think about this evening when his hand was against my back and how desperate I was to spin around, to feel his palm pressed against my breast, to allow his fingers to peel back the black lace, brushing my hardened nipples, squeezing the tips before taking the full breast in his open mouth, feeling its warmth and wetness, surrendering to a languorous tongue-bath. *How could I have been so blind?* The chemistry has been there from the start and it's been reciprocal.

My legs feel a little weak at the prospect of what I am suddenly planning for the rest of the evening, but my reflection staring back reminds me that from head to toe I am perfection, cosmetically that is. There is nothing much I can do about my freckles but, strangely enough, they're not bothering me too much tonight. Not since I was a child have my bare legs been on display, no matter how tanned, and while the thought of their exposure tonight causes me a little insecurity, I can think of plenty of distractions to ease the burden.

Brian sits alone on the white leather sofa holding a champagne flute, watching the fire burn romantically as the rain pelts against the window frame. Operatic tunes sound through the stand-alone speakers, low in volume but loud enough to gauge the passionate but alien words of the singers predictably declaring their undying love. Or rather *dying* as is so often the outcome.

The room is minimalist and typifies every man's perfect bachelor pad. It plays home to a cinema-sized wall-mounted TV sitting above the fireplace, and a compact music system with endless speakers carefully placed in various angles of the room. Real boys' toys! On the solid floor, polished to precision, lies a huge white rug, immaculate and uninviting.

I tip-toe into the lounge, conscious of damaging the floor but determined not to lose my killer heels. I nestle down close to Brian. Very close.

"I won't ask what took you!" He laughs, leaning closer, inhaling deeply.

Oh God, please don't come any closer. Okay, do. Yes, do!

"You smell wonderful, Tina." His head sinks into my hair, inches away from my tingling neck, and he gently takes a handful of it, savouring its boutique like a vintage wine. This is all too much for a girl who hasn't seen more than her Rampant Rabbit for God knows how long.

Brian pulls away, turning to retrieve my drink, and as he hands it over our hands touch and we freeze. With two hands practically clutching the same glass, we stare into each other's eyes – his wild with lust and mine desperate to witness the sight of his muscular chest, to run my fingers over it, stroking it, teasing it and giving a clear indication of the level of expertise awaiting.

"God, you're sexy, Miss Harding!" he pants breathlessly.

"You're not too bad yourself," I wink, taking the glass from him, placing it on the floor away from us.

I sexily kick off my shoes and, lifting my legs, draw my feet onto the sofa. The deliberate motion causes my dress to slide up a little, revealing more thigh.

I take Brian's hand and boldly place it on the soft denier and like a puppet I control his every move. Holding firm, just above his wrist, with my eyes never losing his, I slide his hand up very slowly, inch by inch, teasing him. I let out a loud groan as his fingertips touch my bare flesh and try to stop myself from taking his hand and thrusting it deep inside my pants. *Slowly, Tina. Make him beg for it.*

Brian, unable to control himself any longer, suddenly makes a plunge for my lips. His strength topples me over and, no longer in control, I lie helpless on my back as he regains full authority.

"Are . . . you . . . okay . . . Tina?" His words are broken up between gentle kisses on my neck and I arch my back, feeling the wetness of his tongue flicking expertly, wishing he would make his way down my body with accelerated speed. I feel a wetness ooze below, ready for him, and as his body leans more heavily against mine I note his hardness and the smell of his manliness, desperately wanting to feel him deep inside of me.

Getting carried away, my pelvis rises and falls violently against him as I simulate my eagerness.

"I am going to make you come like never before, Miss Harding," he promises and I almost cry with the anticipation.

"Oh God!" His knee gently presses against my swollen clitoris and I part my legs, allowing added pressure, feeling like I could orgasm like this alone.

"Brian," I mutter.

He continues to tease my neck and earlobes.

"*Brian!*" I say with urgency.

"Tina!" He joins in with the game as I push against him fiercely but his weight suppresses me.

"*Brian!*"

"*Tina!*"

"*Stop!*"

8

Kate clutches onto the pillow, burrowing her head in it deeply, but the muffled sound of raucous laugher still emits from it. Giddy and uncontrollable, she lifts her head with tears rolling down her face. "Oh, Brian!" she mimics. "I'm going . . . to . . . be . . . sss . . ."

Once more she collapses onto the bed, snorting, improvising kissing then vomiting, pretending to wipe her mouth and come back for more, her tongue dancing around foolishly. "No, really, I'm okay," she mimes. "Don't stop now!" Her hips thrust back and forward. "What? Oh, yeah, I'd better brush my teeth!" She's off again, into peals of uncontrollable laughter.

How many times do we have to go through this tonight? I wish I'd never told her now, although I certainly wouldn't be able to share this with anyone else, especially not Chantelle given how often I preach to her about not mixing business with pleasure.

"It's not funny, Kate." I wince, holding my head in shame. "Right in the throes of passion. How the hell am I ever going to look him in the eye again?"

Kate makes an attempt to be serious for a moment,

although in an oversized pair of pink flannelette pyjamas with a Snoopy design it's really not possible. "Look, why don't you just blame him for plying you with drink – tell him you're not used to drinking that much?"

"I was okay until I lay down, but then the room started to spin. That hasn't happened to me in years." I shake my head, groaning. "I ruined his rug, Kate!"

"*Pphwwwrrr!*" Kate is off again, rolling around the bed, beating down on the duvet wildly and gasping for breath. She surfaces. "Just tell him you thought a souvenir of you might be nice!"

"Oh what a wonderful idea! The next time he sees carrots he's going to think of me? Any more intelligent suggestions?"

I really can see no end to this situation, nor the funny side of it, particularly after such a romantic meal followed by the promise of the most spectacular orgasm in years.

Brian was as gentlemanly as usual. He apologised profusely, taking full responsibility for the episode. He, naturally, thought I was calling out his name in lust, hence he didn't move off me. I have to admit, it was rather nice to hear him call my name back. "*Tina! Tina!*" Hhmm . . . I tried my best not to make him feel stupid but he seemed to take it quite hard. Or maybe he was more gutted about his Conran rug then he was prepared to let on.

"Why don't you just call him, Tina. He's rung you three times already and you're giving out all the wrong signals by ignoring him."

"I can't, Kate. I haven't got a bloody clue what to say apart from 'Can I buy you a new rug which incidentally I can't afford!'"

Kate tops up our glasses with red wine and tips the remains of the crisp packet into the glass bowl, placing it in the centre of the king-size bed. Fat lot of use this bed has been to me. It's an investment with a nil return.

I am also feeling guilty for ruining Kate's evening. We haven't had a girls' night out in ages as Kate works on location so frequently, but I simply couldn't face it tonight. Plus my eyes look like they haven't seen sleep in weeks and my body is shaking, although a little less after our hair-of-the-dog exercise. Kate's suggestion, of course.

"Tina, are you happy with estate agency?" Kate asks bluntly.

"Yeah, it's the best achievement of my life, Kate," I answer without hesitation. "Why do you ask?"

"I dunno really. Maybe it's because you keep quizzing me about work and you've talked about your old acting career more than once in the past half hour." Kate shoves a handful of crisps into her mouth, attempting to talk at the same time. "I haven't heard you mention it in years." She chokes deservedly. "Why now?"

That's what I love about Kate, her willingness to challenge you over everything.

"It's not something I'm conscious of doing, Kate, to be honest. I suppose you being here reminds me of the fun we used to have." Our glasses clink together as we down the remainder of their contents in a race to finish first.

"Fun like that," Kate giggles. "Except in our day it was cider and black."

"Do you believe in fate?" I quiz her curiously.

"Yeah. About as much as you do!" She rolls her eyes sarcastically. "What's got into you, Tina? You're a bit of a weirdo tonight. You and I have never believed in fate and all that stuff. We've always said it's about being in the right place at the right time. That and bloody hard grafting."

"I know, Kate, but for some reason I can't help wondering if life is already mapped out for us from the day we're born." I look at her confused expression. "Don't you think?"

Kate lunges forward, grabs a full wine bottle from the bedside unit and unscrews the cap. "I'll tell you what I think." She fills my already half-full glass right to the brim. "You're talking shite and you're not even pissed. Knock that back and at least you'll have an excuse!"

She jumps off the bed and slides open the mirrored wardrobe doors. "Let's have a fashion show like we used to!" she says excitedly while I groan with reluctance.

My body feels like it's glued to the bed and I feel bloated from eating hangover junk all day. "You do it and I'll be the comp," I suggest, rolling over into the warmth left behind by Kate's body.

Exhausted from so much thinking and ill from alcohol poisoning, my eyes close as I await her first little number.

My throat is dry and barren and I clumsily feel about in the dark for water, desperate to replenish some much-needed fluids. Kate is flat out next to me in her pyjamas, snoring gently. I knock back the entire pint glass which I can only assume Kate kindly put there given I don't even remember falling asleep.

My mind races with thoughts of the past few weeks as the alcohol stimulants keep me from sleeping. The psychic, the contract, Simon, Brian, the wedding . . . How much can a girl cope with? I make a note to prioritise and conclude that work and my sister's wedding have to be at the top. Much as a screaming multiple orgasm from Brian would be at the top of my aspirational list, I've made so much of an idiot of myself that it's redemption time. Maybe Kate is right? Maybe there is no such thing as fate. *But how can we really be sure?* Perhaps instead of a guardian angel each one of us is born with a cartographer? Their role being to compile a map for our lives and navigate invisibly, allowing us to go off course from time to time but sitting ready and waiting to clearly signpost the correct turning when we're about to venture into unknown territory, or take the wrong route?

Kate is right about one thing. I do talk some shite. Go back to sleep, Tina.

Still pyjama-clad, Kate and I slump on the sofa watching mindless Sunday TV with mugs of freshly brewed coffee.

"Let me know when you're hungry and I'll make us breakfast," I slur, too tired to talk properly let alone make breakfast. And anyway, just in case I haven't completely blown it with Brian, excuse the pun, I need to feel and look as svelte as possible, without contracting bulimia or visiting the gym, and the loss of a few pounds certainly won't do me any harm.

While I jest about bulimia, during the start of my career and not long after graduating from university, I was signed to a local agency for both acting and modelling jobs. The pressure to remain stick-thin was overwhelming. To say that I have witnessed the sound of countless retching from toilet cubicles is absolutely no exaggeration. Hence the reason I tried it myself and, quite worryingly, found it easy. When Gemma, the director of City Models, suggested I lose a few pounds, I starved myself for a week, surviving on two pieces of toast alone. I felt and looked lighter by the end of the exercise, and I walked like I was floating on air. Which is practically what I was living on. Anyway, I decided that starvation definitely wasn't my thing so I decided to join the rest of them by binge-eating anything and everything from chips to chocolate, relishing the flavours as they teased my mouth but feeling remorse and guilt minutes later as the food hit my stomach making me feel bloated and fat. "*What goes down must come up,*" we used to joke. There was no point hiding it to be honest. Anyone carrying Polo mints was bulimic and it was quite acceptable in the industry. I'm definitely over the whole addiction thing but once you've battled with some form of weight problem, it haunts you for the rest of your life. Consequently, my weight oscillates like a blow-up doll with an irreparable puncture.

Kate's face is green and tight and as the mask dries out it drags at her skin, distorting her face, pulling it in different directions. She catches me smirking at her, wondering how she can pluck her eyebrows at the same time

"It's not easy being an actress," she mumbles, barely moving her lips. "Everyone thinks it's so glam, don't they? It drives me mad." She yanks at her brow fiercely. "Shit, that hurt!"

I laugh at her stressing over the tediousness of earning in excess of two hundred grand a year, walking from job to job, getting her hair and make-up done and having her clothes picked out.

"Get a grip, Kate!" I snap. "Most people would kill to

have your lifestyle. Me included." I stare at Kate, shocked at my comment and the ease with which it slipped out. "I can't believe I've just said that," I declare, somewhat stunned.

"Tina, you're definitely not yourself. I thought you were over all that stuff! In fact, you told me so when you got the contract."

"I was. I am. I don't know why I said it. Maybe I was just thinking generically."

"Why did you say '*me included*' then?" she challenges me, as she prepares to scrub away the green clay, soaking cotton balls in water before wringing them dry.

"God knows," I answer truthfully. "Although maybe it'll never really go away, Kate, even though I'm happier and more stable with the way my life is now." I rest my head on my knees, tucking them into my chest. "Maybe I can't help but wonder if the next audition would have been the big break." I pause. "Perhaps I gave in too early?"

"Tina," Kate says with concerned authority, as she dabs at her face, "when you rang me the other week to tell me about the contract, I hadn't heard you so excited in years. I could almost feel you tingling and, I didn't tell you this, I had tears streaming down my face with pride." Her eyes fill up now at the thought.

"Really?" I am surprised. "Kate, I only ever think I should be proud of you." I hesitate. "For making it right from the start – that's a damn good achievement, you know."

"I know it is, Tina, but although we talk about grafting, a little luck was also on my side. Never forget that. But you, Mrs, have worked your socks off with that business. You put your house at risk for it and if that's not a testament to how much you want it to work," she sighs heavily, "then I don't know what is." Her eyes penetrate me. "But I do know this, Tina. Whatever it is that's got into you, get rid of it, because you're not the strong-minded assertive Tina you were the last time I was home."

What's she on about? I'm no different than I was yesterday, last week, last month. But still, I don't answer her. She only tells it like she sees it.

Perhaps I'm taken aback by the accelerated speed with which my life is progressing. Perhaps it's the male attention or Sam's wedding causing me subtle distractions. I don't know, but I do know that I am determined to prove that stupid old woman wrong for haunting me with past ghosts. Why the hell did I ever go to her?

Cheering up, I think of the contract and how close I am to opening the second Harding Homes. *Yep, that's what I want from life. No doubts about it.*

"Kate, I'm fine honestly. There's just so much going on right now." I polish off the remains of the coffee, setting the empty mug on the floor. "Now pass me that magazine and get off your bloody pedestal." I laugh, cowering as she hurls the magazine towards me like a cricketer bowling to take out his batsman.

Lying back against the cream suede cushions, I glance at the contents and flick through the pages – then stop abruptly. "Ooh. God, that's weird!"

"What's weird?"

"My horoscope. To think I never used to believe in these things but this one might have been written for me!"

Kate shakes her head, grabbing the magazine from me.

"Tina!" She shakes my shoulders roughly. "What have you done with my best friend?"

9

"Hi, can I help you?" Chantelle ventures across to a young couple holding hands, pointing at the various property displays and ooing and aahing excitedly at every detail. "First-time buyers?" she asks cheerily. They look at her, astonished, and nod giddily. "Good for you guys." She shakes hands with them. "I'm Chantelle. Please, have a seat and we can chat about how Harding Homes can help you."

The couple follow her, hands still gripped, eyes aglow with eagerness, clearly delighted at the prospect of their own place with no parents, no rules and no housework if you can't be bothered. I know Chantelle is wondering at what point to discuss the budget planner – outlining utilities, council tax, home insurance, mortgage payments and life insurance – and how best to avoid shattering their illusions about what they envisage to be, simply, a round-the-clock sex den.

The front door chimes as it opens and a uniformed man enters, holding a huge bouquet of flowers across his arm, balancing them with his other hand. Romance is definitely in the air today.

"Excuse me, love," he interrupts Chantelle. "Tina Harding, is she here?"

I step forward. "Yes?"

Chantelle apologises to her clients for the interruption. Making an effort not to be distracted through sheer nosiness, she continues professionally with the young lovers, both of whom are now clearly consumed by curiosity about the flowers.

"Wow! Who are they for?" I ask, mesmerised by the size of the arrangement and desperate to tear them from his hands.

"You're Tina Harding?"

"That's me."

"Here you go then." He thrusts the flowers towards me with a gesture of relief, shaking his arms out, thankful for the release.

A flush of embarrassment sweeps over my face as Chantelle falls silent and the room comes to a standstill, blatantly waiting for news of the sender. Me too. I pull the card from its plastic stand and rip open the envelope, anxious to know who thinks me so important to have purchased the entire florist's.

Miss Harding, You and I have some unfinished business.
Scarlet, I shove the card back into the envelope and risk a glance at Chantelle who winks surreptitiously.

Heaving the flowers from the centre of the floor, I rest them against the wall out of the way, with the card tucked safely in my trouser pocket. The room suddenly looks like it has shrunk in size and smells like the Chelsea Flower Show. My heart is thumping wildly as I recall his message to me and I am desperate to take him up on it sooner rather than later. God, that chemical thing, it's happening again. *Think of your VAT returns, Tina. Anything!*

Chantelle bursts into my office. "Oh – my – God! How big were they? What have you to say for yourself then, boss?"

I really should have been prepared for the Spanish Inquisition but since my mind has been taken over by a vision of me lying naked beneath his six-pack, it's left me little time to concoct a plausible fob-off.

"Simon," I say blandly. "They're from Simon, how sweet."

She looks at me with raised eyebrows, picking up on my lack of enthusiasm. "And what have you done to deserve those? I thought you two hadn't even officially dated yet?"

"We haven't. In fact, the last time I saw him was the other week at our celebration bash. Perhaps he's missing me. Come on, he's only human!" I laugh, fluttering my eyelashes.

"Is there something in your eye, Tina?"

"Aren't you the funny one!"

"So what happens next with you two?" She perches herself on the end of my desk, arms folded and feet crossed. "I really think you should ring him to say thank you and arrange a date. Don't you?" She lifts the phone eagerly. "Call him!" she directs with a masterful glint in her eyes.

"No," I answer without hesitation. "I can't disturb him at work, Chantelle, he's probably with clients or something."

"Well, at least leave a message for him, just so he knows you've received the flowers."

Give me a break. Sometimes with Chantelle it's like knocking to find no one is home. I love her enthusiasm for my love life but, for heavens' sake, this time I would prefer her to keep out. "I'll send him a text then if it keeps you happy." Picking up the mobile I quickly text a short message, holding the phone at an angle away from Chantelle's view. I send it to Brian.

"There, message sent." I flash her the screen face as evidence. "Happy now?"

She nods approvingly. "My gran has always said that, if you're not academic, you should use your social skills and they will get you anywhere you want to go in life. Manners are of vital importance." She stares at the floor pensively, her head tilted to one side, enhancing her perfect jaw-line and profile.

"What are you thinking about?" I enquire, keen to steer the conversation away from me, for once.

"I was just thinking about my mother and how she used to make me repeat a word over and over again until I was able to say it without the Liverpudlian accent." Chantelle shakes her head, smirking. "At the time it used to drive me mad and I thought my mother was such a snob, but the funny thing is that she was right in a way."

"Why do you say that"

"Well, when I dropped out of my A Levels and was trying to get a job, it was so simple. I practically walked every interview I ever attended." She snorts comically, still managing to look angelic and ladylike. "Because I was so well-spoken everyone assumed I was far more intelligent than was the actually the case, so I stood out more." She throws her head back in laughter.

"How stupid were they!" I snort.

"You mean, how stupid were *you*!" she retorts.

"Oh yeah!" I screech. "Oi, you – you posh thicko, you're fired!"

The room is awash with the sound of two laughing hyenas, braying childishly, indeed displaying no evidence of the so-called intelligence we are perceived to have. Although didn't Chantelle just say if you're not academic to use your social skills? *What's that supposed to mean?*

"Well, thank heavens you didn't take those jobs or I wouldn't have you here now." Gesturing to the door, I point rudely. "Now get back to work, you good for nothing phoney!"

"Yes, ma'am." Chantelle salutes me, back straight, chin up, chest out, and marches to the door, turning to bow to me before exiting.

"Bloody hell, Chantelle, don't do that on the sales floor – your knockers nearly fell out!

"Oops!" Chantelle fixes her top, pulling it up by about, erm, a millimetre. "Wouldn't that be terrible for sales?" She winks sexily. "Who needs the likes of Brian Steen when you've other such assets working for you." She pouts dramatically, folding her arms, thus inflating her already ample chest.

"Much as I find you very attractive, the thought of being seduced by *you* doesn't exactly do it for me," I declare, "but if I ever decide to bat for the other side, you'll be the only girl for me!" I roar with laughter as she stares.

But I have misconstrued her reaction.

"Are you saying that you *do* want to be seduced by Brian?" Her eyes are wide with interest.

"God, er, no way!" I fake.

"Phew, for a minute there I thought you were breaking our number-one office rule."

"Not a chance," I answer convincingly and with relief as she stomps heavily down the stairs, ready to professionally seduce her next victim.

"Shit, the projector isn't working." My hands shake nervously as I fumble around with the lead, double-checking it is firmly inserted into the back of the laptop. I could seriously do without this hassle and have just twenty minutes to go before two dozen invitees strut arrogantly through those boardroom doors – venturing out of their world of Casting, Media and PR to hear what I have to say.

Chantelle puts down her flyers and offers assistance, deftly flicking on the switch at the back of the projector and squinting as we're almost blinded by the laser of light piercing our eyes.

She touches my forearm gently. "Tina, don't be nervous." Her dark brows almost meet in the middle as she frowns intensely. "This stuff is a walk in the park to you." Her eyes kind and sincere.

I don't know why I'm so nervous. I usually love doing this kind of thing but today, for some unknown reason, I feel sick. Sick with nerves, sick with excitement and burdened by the sheer amount of potential commission I can make within the next half an hour. It's mind-blowing. And to know that my future business rests on every word that will shortly leave my lips is making me freeze with trepidation.

Just remember that you won the tender fair and square, Tina. You did it then. You can do it now.

"*Fail to prepare. Prepare to fail,*" I repeat aloud,

reminding myself that once again I have truly worked like a trooper for this event. I understand not simply my invitees but their industry, including the types of people they are in touch with. I am also fully aware that apart from the hook of making money, the majority of my guests know little about today's subject matter and, as such, I have prepared a killer presentation that should have the desired effect. *Where do I sign?*

The room is bright and airy, with the temperature set deliberately low to ensure that Chantelle and I aren't pitching to a dozen sets of closed eyes. Simplicity is the key for us today. I guess it's a bit like singing. Stick with the melody because it's what people know and expect and they can join in, but go off-key and bring in the harmony too early and people will get confused with the unpredictability. Make sense?

I have selected three key points for today's discussions: Why? What? How? And the entire delivery will revolve around the answering of those three questions.

Why should they take part?

What is in it for them?

How will we do it?

Taking a deep breath, I survey the room in satisfaction. The refreshments have been delivered to a table positioned at the rear of the room. On each chair sits a pre-printed brochure, designed by Heather, paid for by Brian, providing key features of the apartments, prices and commission fees for the agents. My business card is stapled neatly to the face of each one.

"Tina?" Chantelle asks as she carefully slides the spare brochures into a purple folder. "Where are you hoping to open the next office?"

Good question and I have just the answer. In fact, even before I opened the High Street branch in Little Hutton, I had mapped out the exact locations of twelve Harding Homes branches spread throughout the North West. "In Camberwell Road," I answer promptly. "There are two key players there already which is great news, plus the national stats on census show the surrounding areas to be among Merseyside's most populated." I smile assertively, glad to know that my research has paid off. "Did you know that sixty-nine per cent of households in our region are owner-occupied?" I show off. "Which is slightly higher than the national average for England."

Chantelle cackles like a fishwife, her hands on her hips. "There is more to you than just a pretty face, Tina Harding!" She runs her fingers through her dark locks, sweeping them away from her brow. "I'd love to have the concentration to sit there and digest all that stuff," she shrugs her shoulders, "but I just can't."

"It's certainly not done you any harm, Chantelle – you've done alright for yourself." The truth is, while our relationship is that of employer-employee, in real terms Chantelle could buy and sell me in a flash. I know it but she doesn't. If I can use the analogy of her physical self – hers is natural, raw and untouched – whereas mine is man-made, lightened here, darkened there and high maintenance but with hefty dividend payments.

"I know I've done okay, Tina, but who is the boss here?"

Turning to face her head on, I fall onto my knees, bowing down before her, my nose hitting the floor awkwardly. "You are, oh Mighty One!"

Our laughter explodes through the room as Chantelle fakes her best dominatrix impression, producing a ridiculous sound as she pretends to crack her whip, while I cower down subserviently. "Take that, you good for nothing wench!" she proclaims.

Ever the actress, I throw myself in the brace position with both hands protecting my head as I beg for mercy. "Stop!" I beseech. "I'll do whatever you wish, have mercy on me!" I lift my head pathetically, hands in prayer position and eyes wild with desperation.

"Stay on your knees where you belong, you –" She breaks off abruptly and just gapes.

"Well, well, well!" I hear behind me.

As I recoil in shock Brian Steen steps up to Chantelle. He winks playfully at her as he pretends to take the invisible whip from her hand and throw it across the room, gallantly stretching out his hand to rescue me, practically lifting me from the ground with the strength of a single bicep. "My lady!" He preens. "I am here to rescue you from a terrible fate."

Okay, Tina, you can let go of his hand now.

"Brian Steen." He offers his now freed-up hand to Chantelle who shakes it firmly but shyly, looking up at him as though butter wouldn't melt, with dark eyes portraying innocence and naivety. "Chantelle Hungerford. Delighted to meet you, Mr Steen."

Brian fires me a risqué glance as his eyes quickly scroll up and down my body, telepathically undressing me, leaving me stripped and vulnerable.

Control yourself, Tina.

He leans forward, pretending to kiss me on the cheek, muttering into my ear, "On your knees? Interesting."

"What are you, er, doing here, Brian?" I ask, feigning lack of interest, albeit most unsuccessfully.

"I thought I'd wish you luck."

He stands casually with his hands buried deep in his linen trouser pockets. His matching jacket has a *Miami Vice* look and the open-necked shirt leaks strands of chest hair, dark and lush. What I wouldn't do to run my fingers over his six-pack and knead his firm torso roughly, slowing down the pace and aggression as I reach . . .

"Besides," he grins cockily, "it's in my best interests to ensure all goes well." His mouth remains in a fixed position but his eyes are wicked and laughing from the inside out.

I sense a déjà vu which somehow winds me up. It's not fair, I should be focusing on the task in hand.

"Oh, back to that intimidation thing, are we, Mr Steen?" I purse my lips determinedly, ignoring Chantelle's startled look.

"Miss Harding, any attempts to intimidate you are merely a figment of your imagination."

Don't think you can win this one, buster! I'd sooner spend five grand on a new rug than back down now. How dare you sidetrack me at such an important time. That's just damn cruel. And deliberate!

"Really, Mr Steen. Tell me, what do you know of my imagination?" I confront him, narrowing my eyes, mad at him for turning up five minutes before the curtain rises and throwing me out of character.

"Well . . ." He rubs his chin with a bronzed hand and holds still, mimicking the statue of the thinking man, only a six-foot-tall version. "Actually, Miss Harding, not as much as I'd like to know." He casually walks toward the door, then stops dead and turns in my direction. "But when you're ready to share it with me, you know where I am."

Once again, I am left just standing there, staring at the open door, angry for allowing him to distract me and get right under my skin as always. If I were a betting woman, I'd even say he dressed for the occasion. Unfortunately! Okay, it's only been twice that we've met formally, but surely he doesn't wander around like Don Johnson's double every day of the week? But who the hell knows? And in fact who the hell knows what he's all about? One minute he's the ruthless pig, then he's ever the gentleman, then he's making explicit promises – which he has yet to deliver. But the less said on that the better. I'm confused. But taking in Chantelle's shocked expression, not as much as she is. *Here we go.*

"Tina!" she belts out. "He well fancies you!" Her eyes are so wide with amazement that her whole face has almost become a caricature.

I don't answer. I can't.

"He's gorgeous, Tina! What did he say in your ear?"

Oh shit! "He said . . ." I hesitate, "'You didn't tell me your office manager was so beautiful!'"

Chantelle laughs. "Really?" She turns around to see bodies making their way into the room and adds quickly, "Well, how kind . . . but from where I was standing, I'd say he only had eyes for one woman around here." She heads to the door before winking at me. "And it sure as hell wasn't me!"

"A very good morning to all of you." I smile engagingly at the small but well-apportioned audience. "Before we officially start – you will all have noticed a briefing pack left on each of your chairs." I hold up a sample pack, displaying the deep red and blue Harding Homes colours. I feel a bit like an Air Hostess showing the safety card, about to demonstrate the brace position – or maybe not – I've already been down there once today. "Can I ask you to take these away with you, please, ladies and gentlemen, and refrain from reading the material during today's presentation?" A little bossy but with the attention-span of agents such as these, you need to remove all distractions, trust me.

The sound of zips opening and closing and briefcases clasping shut dies down and I continue once more. "Thank you." I smile radiantly, imagining I'm on a West End stage with the world's most successful talent scout in the audience. "Right then." I take a side-step, putting down the sample briefing pack on an empty chair. "Now that I have everyone's attention, let's start with the introductions. For those who don't know me, my name is Tina Harding and I'm the managing director of Harding Homes."

I open my arm out as rehearsed and Chantelle gracefully steps forward, dazzling as always. *Close your mouths, guys, I can see your bloody tonsils!*

"Morning, ladies and gentlemen." She grins eagerly. "My name is Chantelle Hungerford and I'm the sales manager at Harding Homes."

She switches on the projector and picks up the remote control, pressing the button to commence the slide show. The massive screen shows our professional slides. Their content is deliberately brief so we can ad-lib or at least pretend we're ad-libbing. But in truth, every single word has been carefully put together and rehearsed like a high-budget blockbuster.

Chantelle runs through the content of the agenda, finishing with an explanation of the question and answer session to be held at the end of the presentation. Now over to me.

"It's great to see some of my former agents here today." I nod to them. "I hope my leaving the industry hasn't caused you too much financial hardship!"

They laugh politely.

"But if it has," I gesture, "I may just have a replacement solution for you."

Chantelle and I take turns to deliver each slide, vividly describing the turnkey apartments and creating visualisations of everyday living. I note a few raised eyebrows and brief nods, even a few impressive glances between neighbours. *Go for it, Tina.*

"Ladies and gentlemen," I turn off the projector to grab their full attention, "this is where you come in." My voice is deep and authoritative as I continue. "How many of you offer additional services to your clients over and above the normal contractual arrangement?" I glance quickly at the clock on the back wall. Bang on schedule.

Not a single hand is raised, so I continue.

"How would you feel if I were to show you a way not only to increase your bottom line, but to practically make yourself indispensable to your clients?" Carried away, I find myself pacing up and down, loving every minute of it and knowing damn well that I've got them where I want them.

"What are you saying, Tina?" a voice shouts out.

"Good question," I reply, realising a little too late just how patronising I sounded then. "I'm saying that you have been presented with the opportunity to provide realtor services to your clients in addition to your casting and PR operations."

I stop deliberately, hoping the next comment will be from the open floor. *Bingo*.

"Ladies," a creamy voice speaks up, "great idea, but there aren't enough hours in the day as it is."

He shifts in his seat and I can see who it is now. He's actually one of the bigger agents. "Plus, we're not qualified to do this," he continues.

I nod empathetically and share with the room the fact that he has raised a hugely valid point. "In the hand-out packs, ladies and gentlemen, as you will later see, a supply of marketing letters and pre-printed leaflets have been included and as such –" *God, we're good,* "you need only risk the cost of a stamp and an envelope or, where appropriate, simply hand the material personally to your contacts."

I open up my pack, removing a wad of letters and fan them out, clearly demonstrating volume and attention to detail.

Chantelle steps forward. Her face is more serious than before as she continues. "Tina has significant expertise in your industry, understanding the highs and the lows, and she's fully aware of just how difficult life can be for you."

Oh stop!

Her cheeks are flushed with energy and concentration. "And in terms of alleviating any further stress to you," she gloats, "we have ensured that Harding Homes' telephone numbers are boldly highlighted on every single piece of literature." The room is silent as she goes on. "To simplify it, ladies and gentlemen," she concludes, "you take advantage of your existing networks by committing to a simple task of communication."

"That's right," I add. "And in return, a generous commission fee will be paid upon completion of each sale. You have all the right contacts here, ladies and gentlemen, and only clients of your calibre can afford these executive homes. It's as easy at that."

You could hear a pin drop. The silence is both illuminating and menacing, and although I'm desperate to shout out *'Please say you'll do it!'* I know I can't.

I take a generous sip of carbonated water before carrying on.

"Any questions?" I invite.

A young guy sitting in the front row pipes up.

"Tina," he preens himself, "I come from a sales background myself. And I've always believed that if something sounds too good to be true then it usually is!" He belts out a peal of laughter and the rest of the room follows suit.

I too laugh, intentionally, careful not to appear defensive and alienate myself from the group. "You've had good training," I compliment him jovially, letting him see that I'm just like the rest of them. "Let me put it another way to you . . ." I consider. My hand rests on my chin as I think deeply. "If I were simply to approach Joe Public and ask as many of them as possible if they know of anyone looking to purchase a six-hundred-thousand-pound apartment . . ." I pause, "what are the chances of them knowing such clientèle? And how long do you think it would take me to sell all the apartments?"

Chantelle butts in. "You might never sell them, Tina.

It's a restrictive market at those prices, plus we don't have the resources to undertake such activities."

"I can see why I hired you, Chantelle." I nod in her direction and then look back at my audience, grinning. "Not just a pretty face!" *A little tacky but, trust me, our delivery oozes spontaneity.*

A business card flies in Chantelle's direction and an orange-faced wrinkly shouts out, "Give me a call, love, if you're looking for a change in career!"

Chantelle pretends to be flattered and picks up the card, putting it in her pocket. He looks like she's just accepted his proposal of marriage.

"She's right," I say. "You guys have *all* the contacts we need to sell every single apartment here, without mass advertising and draining resources that we simply don't have." My tone is one of a barrister summing up, proving to the open court that his client is of good standing and not guilty. "It makes perfect sense that I outsource the marketing to people such as yourself." I hold out my arms to the room. "You touch these types of people every single day," I summarise, "We don't, and therefore, in return for your effort, albeit minimal," I wink, "I will pay you a fixed percentage for merely handing out a leaflet or holding a two-minute conversation which results in a sale."

I have nothing further to add, Your Honour.

Determined to put closure on the session and conscious that we are billed by the hour for the boardroom, I assertively hold up the agreement form, kindly drafted by Sam. "On the table behind me you can pick up your agreement form should you wish to avail of this opportunity." *Here they come! Yippee!*

I pick up the forms, handing them out one by one as

the delegates come forward, raising my voice over the buzz. "Please look over it and contact myself or Chantelle should you have any questions."

Chantelle has positioned herself strategically by the door, ensuring no one can exit without having to bypass her first. Or should I say bypass *them*! Her chest is standing to full attention and with one slender leg pushed slightly in front of the other, exiting without making direct physical contact is going to be somewhat of a challenge. We discussed this tactic at length and our objective was to ensure that she shook the hand of every single person before they left, using raw instinct to gauge a feel for the potential inners and leaving me to answer any technical questions from that small percentage who hang around at the end of these events, asking anal and irrelevant questions. *No question is a silly question*, they say. *Bollocks to that!*

I didn't, however, expect Chantelle to take this to such extreme levels but I'm so proud of her. *That's my girl.*

Our glasses chink together as we sip on celebratory Bellinis, cosseting each expensive mouthful. Sitting in the hotel lobby we sink into sumptuous sofas, flagging after all the mental stimulation, yet animated with hopes of prosperity.

"What's your gut reaction then, Tina?"

"I'm not sure to be honest, Chantelle." This is the truth. "I've done so many of these things over the years. Not outside of our own sector though and that's why I can't really say. It's as weird for me as it is for you . . . but I still think it's going to work." My face warps as I swallow a mouthful of cocktail containing more peach syrup than champagne. Why are they never as generous with the bubbly as they are with the mixers? At ten pounds a drink you'd think they might be a little less tight. I run my tongue over my teeth, cleansing the syrup away before a cavity develops. "With no additional work for them and easy money, I do think we're on to a real winner."

Cash flow really is the bane of their industry. No sooner have the producers sent the agency payments due, their clients are banging down the doors to get it, and as an agent if you're left with a fifteen-per-cent cut you're lucky. As an actor, I still haven't been paid for one of my commercials after seven years, and have sob story after sob story to tell, like waiting an average of six months to receive payment for various performances. It was fine while I lived with my parents but, when you're on your own, how many times can you expect your landlord to forgive you because you're on TV? It provided clear evidence that I was working, but in terms of paying the rent – much as I tried – an autographed copy of my headshot didn't really do it for him!

Perhaps now you can understand the industry a little more. It does seem amazingly glamorous on the outside but dig a little deeper and you'll find that most actors are overdrawn right up to their collagen lips, and trying to find an agent who will pay you on time is near impossible. Still, you get loads of freebies. You get to keep most of your costumes, unless it's low budget when you wear them with the tags on so they can be returned for a refund afterwards, and you get invited to most of the film premières, even if it is to make the numbers up.

"You know what, Chantelle?" I declare. "Seeing

those guys today made me realise that I could never go back to that life." I stare into the open room. "Never."

She smiles at me, full of reassurance, like a proud mother watching her child take his first steps. "Good," she says. "I don't know how good you were before, Tina, but I do know how good you are now."

I squeeze her hand fondly. I know that Chantelle is one thing and that's honest. She doesn't tell you what she thinks you want to hear and I find that so refreshing if not a little irritating at times, but I wouldn't have her any other way. Like I have a choice.

"I was good actually," I say shyly. It's not really something we've talked about before. I guess I never wanted her to see me as a failed anything, not in the early days of our employer-employee relationship. The barrier is down a little now. "I was bloody good." I laugh arrogantly. "In fact, I might just get one of those guys to sign me up." I flick my hair around dramatically. "You know, now that I'm more confident and self-assured!"

Chantelle joins in the banter. "Yeah, me too, I could go in for glamour modelling!" She pouts sexily.

"Too right you could," I answer earnestly. "I'd buy a picture of you, Chantelle!"

She looks a little shocked and I forget that she's not Kate who would understand that I was kidding. I guess these lesbian-type jokes can be taken a little seriously. I roll my eyes at her. "Joke."

She looks disappointed for a moment. "Spoilsport!" she says, before falling about with laughter, still trying to pose sexily and not realising she does it every second of every day. Effortlessly.

Joking aside, much as I could no longer bear the

travelling or the fourteen-hour days, I do mean it when I say I have more confidence now. I remember my mother always quoting "*Youth is wasted on the young*" and I used to think she was talking rubbish, which in fact reinforces the point exactly. It is wasted on the young and if I was the same person then that I am now, I'm pretty damn sure I would have walked those auditions. But that's the harsh reality of life, isn't it? You live in constant hindsight, never learning at the time but much later on in life. You wish you could turn back the clock and that you had listened to your parents instead of thinking they were sad losers with a capital L. If only there was an easier way to live! A way to get ahead of the game. You know, see in advance what life holds for you and simply head in that direction. Why go through the aggravation of suffering catastrophically just to write it off as a learning curve, when you could go straight to your destination without passing go? Who the hell needs to fail first just to win second? What's that all about? If we could just get it right from the very beginning . . .

I grab my bag with a fierce spontaneity and swiftly polish off my drink, multi-tasking at fast-forward speed. "Oh no!" I look at my watch dramatically and then at Chantelle. "I forgot I have an appointment." I set the glass on the table clumsily and run out of the lobby, leaving behind a speechless Chantelle. "See you tomorrow!" I yell.

Tina, what are you doing?

Still in speedy motion, I punch the numbers into my mobile phone before I can change my mind. My breath is held as it rings.

"Oh, hi," I pant. "I want to make an appointment, please . . . for as soon as possible." My hands shake. "Brilliant. Thanks."

I flip the phone shut, putting it back in my bag, flooded with guilt for leaving Chantelle behind, but delighted at the prospect of what lies ahead. But it wasn't as if it was all planned. Suddenly the penny just dropped. If Chantelle says that old woman knew stuff she couldn't have known, surely that's it? The key to my future? Why on earth would I want to keep making mistakes and then learning from them when I can simply avoid the bloody mistakes to start with? Why all the pain when it's the pleasure we aspire to achieve? I can't believe the answer has been staring me in the face all along! It's practically genius!

If you guys want to go through life learning the hard way, then that's your prerogative. Just leave me to take smartest shortcut and I'll meet you there!

My body prickles with the anticipation of my future laid out as clear as day and unambiguous, and I relax at the prospect of having life's equivalent of an in-car navigator. Simply hold the wheel and let the route take its course.

How difficult can that be?

10

Stepping into the A-line skirt, I pull up the side zip and turn around, allowing the assistant to tighten the laced corset. Facing the full-length mirror I am speechless.

The strapless design has created curves not previously there and the satin skirt skims my hips elegantly, finishing a centimetre away from the dainty Liz René pumps. The deep wine colour sets my skin alight and the fabric sheen reflects against my softly curled hair, complementing it perfectly.

Pulling the curtain back, I stand there in full regalia, taking in the open mouths of Sam, my mother and Sam's future mother-in-law. Sam just sits and stares at me. She says nothing and I say nothing. We can't. I know what she's thinking and she knows what I'm thinking. The corners of my mouth twitch emotionally as Sam just looks up at me, her eyes so filled with love for her little sister and mine so filled with green envy that I might lose her forever, even though she's promised to never forget me.

"You look incredible, Tina." Her voice breaks. "I'm supposed to be the belle of the ball, not you!" She laughs affectionately and the rest of us follow suit.

"No-one can *ever* show up a bride on her wedding day," I reply firmly. "It's not possible."

"Give us a twirl then, darling," my mother orders and right on cue I take the catwalk, right foot over left, exhibiting myself to the world, stopping at the end of the runway (well, the wall actually but I'm improvising), hand on hip, sultry pout – and hold position! This brings back some memories I tell you. Mostly the ones I mentioned earlier – the merciless the sound of retching.

"Sam, is that how you're going to walk, darling?" my mother asks. *What is she on*? "Just like Christie did then?"

Sam over the years has got used to my mother comparing her rather frumpy façade with my apparent glamour and simply adopts a nonchalant expression.

"Actually, Mum, I thought I'd walk like I have done for the past thirty-six years."

I turn to avoid laughing at her wit in front of the potential mother-in-law. Belittling my own mother wouldn't go down too well, particularly while she is still in the *"I'll act like a phoney to impress the Heath-Joneses'* mode!"

"Well, maybe Christie could give you some lessons," she suggests. "You know, the way people go to classes to practise for their first dance."

Bless her, she really thinks she's helping.

Sam, as blasé as usual, has an answer for everything. Like a typical lawyer and unlike myself who doesn't believe in humouring anyone, she remains cool and unperturbed and never rises to the bait. I'd love to be like that. I'd love to be like Sam. Intellectually.

"Actually, Tim and I aren't going to have a first dance," she announces, deadly serious.

I watch her intently, expecting to see her keel over with laughter at any second and for Jeremy Beadle to jump out to the mothers, shouting *"You've been framed!"* or whatever shoddy line they use. But silence penetrates the air and the shop assistants exchange speedy glances, looking at each other with sheer disbelief.

"You're serious, aren't you, Sam?" I ask, already knowing the answer.

"Yep." Sam stands up and faces the mothers, standing tall while they sit low down, looking up at her. *Clever tactic.* "We're simply not comfortable doing it," she proclaims flatly. "Neither of us wants to be exhibited simply for the purpose of tradition." She stands behind me, lifting the back of the dress and fluffing it up to give it more body.

The assistant rushes over. "Let me do that for you."

"It's okay, thanks," Sam answers dismissively.

She's never been one for much fuss, our Sam. Even today she's turned up in a pair of jeans she's had for years with a baggy polo shirt hanging over them and a pair of flat loafers which do nothing to elongate her five-foot-four body and slightly curvaceous figure. She doesn't really care about the stuff I spend hours and hours each week luxuriating in. Seriously, for all her academia, if you said to Sam your tan was from St Tropez, she really would think you'd been to France. I, on the other hand, was so excited about today that I planned my entire wardrobe days ago. And not because we're meeting up with the men this afternoon, but because you never know who you're going to bump into. If I learned anything from my modelling career, it was to always look your best. Needless to say, I feel both casual yet sophisticated in my new Diesel jeans paired with a casual Versace Jeans couture top, with plunging neckline and three-quarter-length sleeves. A pure silk scarf hangs loosely around my neck, adding an element of class and my camel coat has been carefully hung to stop it from creasing.

"Sam!" I exclaim. "I can't believe you've had the willpower to sit there watching me try on dress after dress when you've tried on nothing." I aim to divert the conversation away from the first-dance saga. To be continued, no doubt.

Sam just laughs. She leans forward, giving me a sisterly kiss on the forehead. Don't worry, there's no danger of her leaving lipstick marks.

"Tina, I knew whatever made you look bigger than a size ten would definitely make me look short and dumpy," she admits affably. "So by having you do all the donkey work, knowing full well you'd love every minute of it," she sniggers, "I've been able to narrow things down to the type of dress I think will suit me!"

What a carry on! Here's me thinking I'm the businesswoman of the two of us and all along I'm perspiring like a woman in labour, whipping clothes on and off at her demand, while we play the Harding sisters version of *Trinny and Susannah*!

"You great big sneakster!" I declare raucously, noticing as Hilary looks from one of us to the next. She hasn't quite realised what her precious Timothy is marrying into. Yet.

That reminds me we're meeting Timothy and Simon for lunch this afternoon to discuss colour schemes so they can get measured up for their morning suits. I'd better think of an excuse and fast. Simon versus Brian. Is there any comparison? I think not.

Sam and I giggle like a pair of overgrown teenagers. Me for letting her get one over on me and her for getting one over on me. Yet again.

In the changing cubicle, Sam helps me undress – for the last time I hope – and I decide this is the right time to question her. "Sam." I pause. "How did you know that Tim was the man you wanted to spend the rest of your life with?" Her eyes light up and her entire face portrays the essence of love. At this very moment, even with her understated attire and cleansed face, to me she looks wonderful and I can clearly see why Tim wants to be with her.

"I can't explain it, Tina, to be honest." She shakes her head at me vacantly and shrugs her petite shoulders. "The day after I met Tim at the Law Clerks Ball I said my goodbyes to him and set off home." She breaks out into another humongous grin, literally reaching from ear to ear. "But I had this weird feeling." She frowns. "You know, like I'd forgotten something."

"What?" I implore, standing nearly naked in the small cubicle. "What had you forgotten, Sam?"

A glow sweeps across her face and for a moment I can see deep into her soul and almost feel her euphoria. "Tim," she declares proudly. "I'd forgotten Tim." She fixes her hair and applies a drop of clear gloss.

God, it must be love.

"And then I realised," she says, screwing the top back on the bottle before putting it back in her bag.

"What?" I ask.

"I realised that Tim belonged to me." She looks down

at her rock of an engagement ring. "And I belonged to him too." She nods with deliberate emphasis. "I felt empty without him, like I didn't belong anywhere."

I take hold of her face with both hands and rub my thumbs against her plump cheeks. "I'm so happy for you, Sam, I . . ."

My voice buckles under the weight of pent-up emotion and I break into a sob, falling into her open arms. Sam holds me tightly, just like she did when I was little or when I couldn't sleep because I was afraid of the dark. I had imagination overdrive (I'm sure that's not too difficult to believe).

"I hope Tim knows how bloody lucky he is," I snuffle. "I'll kill him if he ever hurts you, Sam!" Then I laugh at the ridiculousness of Tim ever hurting anyone. "Although, you know what, I've barely even heard him talk so I can't imagine him hurling a load of insults at you!"

Sam sighs. "He is quiet actually, but never let that put you off a man!" She winks and nudges me in the ribs. "Now hurry up and get dressed. There is another man I don't want *you* to put off!"

Wonderful!

Standing outside the quaint Italian restaurant I watch a cloud seep from my mouth as my hot breath collides with the cold wintry air. I secretly pray for the spring warmth to accelerate its journey, conscious that an event of majestic importance is looming.

Taking a risky peek through the window I spot them all inside, chatting away, menus closed. Grabbing my phone, I search through the directory alphabetically and, finding the number, I quickly press dial, conscious of my rudeness in making this call as the Hardings and Heath-Jones wait patiently. In the warmth.

It's ringing. My heart thumps at double speed, shortening my oxygen supply and I fear I may not be able to speak.

"Hello?" *Here goes.*

"I was just thinking about our last conversation," I whisper without waiting for a response. "I take it I'm going to have to *show you* just how imaginative I am." My voice exudes sex appeal and I mentally plan my seduction wardrobe. "Be at my place at eight o'clock." I press the red key to disconnect the call. *No goodbyes? See how you like it.*

Picking up at the wonderment of an evening filled with multiple orgasms I flip the phone shut, more equipped to deal with the in-laws, now that I have a distraction and someone to think about to alleviate my guilt as I let Simon down as gently as possible.

The smell of garlic belts me as I open the panelled door. My mother waves her arm at me frantically, disgusted at my lack of manners. She's never been good at hiding her emotions.

I reach the table, finally lowering myself to Simon's eye-line as my bottom hits the padded cushion. He grins cheekily, taking in my form from top to toe and not even attempting to hide his obvious gratification at seeing me.

"Sorry about that, everyone," I announce courteously. "It was an important client I needed to speak to."

My face deadpan and assertive, I pick up the menu, holding it in front of me, deliberately blocking out the adjacent view. I bet he kept this seat free on purpose. *Enjoy the view of the menu, Saddo, because that's all you're getting.*

"How are things then, Tina?" Simon breaks the silence from our end of the table, raising his voice over everyone else jarring about the wedding.

I set the menu down on the table. "Really good, thanks, Simon," I answer curtly. "Exceptionally busy but I can't complain."

He grins at me stupidly, his messy hair sticking up in all directions, his rugby shirt creased down the arms and his flawless hands wrapped around a pint.

Pen-pusher!

"Jolly glad to hear it." He nods earnestly, eyes intense with concentration and much more green than I remembered.

"How are you keeping?" I ask.

He doesn't answer me. He just sits and stares. And stares.

"Excellent," he beams after an uncomfortably long delay. "Never been better in fact!"

The waiter suddenly appears to my right, pad positioned, pen poised. *Cute.* I have a terrible penchant for Italian waiters. Sam and I have always had a thing for waiters ever since we were teenagers and our hormones had kicked in. Waiters of any nationality generally, but Italian ones more so. Maybe it's the combination of their olive skin with the mouth-watering aroma from the kitchens, but whatever it is or was, it gets to me every time. Sam and I would usually fall into fits of giggles, spilling out our order between childish snuffles and attempting to flirt competitively. But today, I watch as Sam chats merrily with her future in-laws, paying no attention to the waiter as she delivers her order like a grown-up. A happy sadness consumes me once more. My parents used to get embarrassed by our behaviour. But right now, Sam looks and sounds like Sam, but her memories appear to have been deleted. How can she behave this strangely in an Italian restaurant? We've never been sensible around waiters. It's always been the same for us. Flirting, flattery and free drinks. Well, if love denies us our past, then I'm not sure I want it.

I observe Tim making the occasional shy one-liner and then retreating back to silence, even in the company of his own family. How strange. Quite a contrast from his weirdo brother sitting in front of me and still ogling playfully like a maniac who's been let out for the day.

"So, Tina," a voice bellows from the other end of the table, "when are you going to make wife material? Find a man to take care of?"

It's Major Heath-Jones and my mother joins in on cue. Dad gives me a wink, knowing full well what I'm likely to be thinking. *It ends in 'off'*. This guy really rattles my cage and I can see why Tim is so quiet. I'll bet he was never allowed to voice his own opinion.

"Actually," I challenge obstinately, "I was rather looking for a millennium man who might look after *me*."

I watch as his grin fades away and the penny slowly drops that I am deadly serious. Well, not fully, but I'm damn well not going to let him know that.

"Yes," I continue, "I need a man who can cook, clean, iron and know his place in the home." Okay, perhaps I've taken it a bit too far but, seeing Simon's crumpled face, I am forced to break into a grin and suddenly the two of us snort with laughter as we watch the rest of the table, open-mouthed and deadly silent.

Sam keeps her head down, intent on not getting involved even though I can clearly see she is desperate to laugh.

That ends that conversation.

Simon points to his tufts of messy hair and creased-up clothes. "Well, I can cook!" he declares jovially. "One out of four is a start! And as for making the bed – I simply don't see the point, Tina." He winks. "Do you?"

He really is quite funny but sometimes I don't know whether to feel flattered or plainly insulted by his quips. There is nothing complicated about him from what I can see – he's just Simon, although actually not simple. Someone quick-witted and sincere. Someone who can laugh at himself and take life in its stride. It seems. I make a mental note not to be mean to him anymore. He doesn't deserve it.

His fair skin is flushed by the struggling winter sun breaking through the window, illuminating his face. He carries an aura of youthfulness about him, perhaps more in attitude than anything else but isn't that what counts? I'm still slightly concerned that he is the only member of his family with pale skin and green eyes, but thankful that he is unlikely to end up as arrogant and chauvinistic as his father. *Although why do I care?*

Quite surprisingly, he hasn't asked me about our date yet which is pretty endearing of him. Perhaps he doesn't want to embarrass me which is very gentlemanly.

What he's not, however, is Brian Steen!

Stepping out of the shower I shiver as the warm drops of water turn cold on exit and watch as goose-bumps garnish my torso. Quickly wrapping myself in a towel, I take off the shower cap, checking my hair hasn't frizzed with the steam.

My clothes, if you could call them that, are carefully positioned on the bed, outlining the shape of a woman's body and placed in accordance with the order of dressing.

The music is romantic and scented candles are dotted prettily around the room well away from the curtains and with drip trays underneath. I've made those mistakes before, setting the curtains on fire and scalding the furniture with dripping hot wax.

I look deep into the heart of the full-length mirror. *Wow.* Earlier I had a bellyful of pasta but these wonder-knickers make me look amazingly slender with their high-cut sides elongating my legs. The black seamed stocking are doing their best to hide my scattered freckles and they stop just high enough to expose a few inches of tanned thigh. The push-up bra exposes just enough to tease, with the party piece hidden beneath soft padding.

It's eight o'clock. I look out the window. No sign of him yet.

I take a huge swig of wine followed by a smaller sip, conscious of the need not to relive the late embarrassing episode but too anxious and too excited to be stone-cold sober.

I check my teeth for gloss-marks and feel so grateful towards the cosmetic dentistry sector. How the hell did we survive without it?

I glance out the window again. *Shit, a car! It must be him. Time for another seductive performance! Perhaps this one might even reach third base.*

Once more I stare at the sexy woman staring back at me. The black bra hoists up my chest like two firm, ripe grapefruits. The briefs cover very little as is the point and the home waxing kit has worked a treat. Removing the hair from my buttocks was a little tricky and I'm not sure I would recommend the home Brazilian kit. *Great if you're a contortionist, mind*. My new black lace suspender-belt sits on my hips and the hooks cling tenderly to the lace-topped stockings. Finally my killer black-patent-leather heels allow me to stand tall and dominant.

The bell chimes again and, barely clad, I strut sexily through the candle-lit hall, ruffling my hair.

Standing there exposed in full erotic regalia, I fling open the door as a shadowy figure approaches it, then immediately spin around to expose my pert buttocks as I strut sexily towards the bedroom where I slip on a lacy black eye-mask and lie on the bed in a well-rehearsed pose.

"Close the door behind you!" I call out provocatively as manly footsteps vibrate on the floor.

I dictate my orders. "Don't talk. Just use the scarves to tie me up."

I feel a hot breath cloud over me and the scent of overpowering aftershave.

In silence, my hand is lifted gently over my head and I wince with lust as the silk fabric tickles my wrist, tying it firmly to the bedpost. Taking the other hand, he leans over me – his face brushes mine and I long to snatch at his soft lips. I shudder as my legs are pushed apart, sliding gracefully over the satin sheets, and he gently kisses my ankle before wrapping another scarf, a little too tightly. His teasing fingers run up and down my stomach and I breathe in, arching my back, groaning with pleasure.

I feel my foot being held and listen to the sound of the buckle unclasp, the shoe hitting the floor with a thud as it separates itself from the orgy. Soft lips wrap around my toes and a tongue attempts to penetrate through the stocking fabric, both hitting and missing touch points but driving me wild with restriction. I relish the prospect of the removal of the stockings, imagining my toes being sucked vigorously and wallowing in his eager wet mouth.

"Come up here," I pant, desperate to take in this moment of pent-up longing, well overdue, and yearning to thrust my mouth onto his. I take on his tongue in battle.

Our mouths lock magnetically as his lips bully mine and, for once, I am happy to be bullied. I taste the remnants of beer and note its bitter aftertaste.

My heart stops.

Brian doesn't ever drink beer!

I tear off my blindfold.

"*Simon!*" I screech, my mouth as wide as the Mersey Tunnel. "How the – what the – *get out! Get out now!*"

Simon has leapt to his feet. He just stands there looking bewildered as I struggle to free myself.

"B-but what have I done wrong?" he stutters, apparently as shocked as I am.

Well, not quite.

"Get me out of these things! And don't you *dare* look!" I snap through gritted teeth as he fumbles nervously with my wrists, loosening the fabric.

I break free like a caged animal. Grabbing my dressing gown I frantically wrap it around my body, tying the belt so tightly that I can hardly breathe. Sitting on the end of the bed, not knowing what to do, I just freeze.

"Tina, talk to me, please," Simon says softly, keeping his distance.

I can't. I can't move.

"Tina, you invited me . . . you set all this up . . ."

I continue to stare deep into a corner of the room,

deafened to his pleas and oblivious to all but the sound of my chest thumping.

With no response, he moves towards the bedroom door, picking up his jacket from the floor. "I don't know what I've done wrong," he whispers sadly, "but I'm so sorry."

I can't do this any more. I've made such a fool of myself, again, that I might even have to tell Sam I can't go to her wedding. The tears roll down my face with shame. *What happened?* I grab my phone, scrolling down the directory until I reach the name *Steen* and, shaking my head in disbelief, I see the name *Simon,* sitting before it, as clear as day.

Shit, Tina. Why can't you be like Sam and get things right? Why do you ruin everything?

I knock back the rest of the wine. Grabbing a replacement bottle from the fridge and turning up the music, I slam the bedroom door angrily before clambering into bed. I tear off the outfit from beneath the sheets and throw it across the room, never wanting to see it again. I curse it. I curse me and my inability to succeed in love and most other simple things. Apart from my business.

Downing the second glass in a matter of minutes, a warm fuzziness mellows me and a glimmer of hope appears in my mind's eye. *Well, not for much longer!*

The prospect of my appointment aids my bruised ego. I never need to be degraded again like I was this evening. I'll have someone looking out for me, telling me what to do, pointing me in the right direction.

Bring it on!

11

"Pick five cards and place them face down on the table," she says, shuffling the pack before handing them over.

Pick five good ones, Tina.

Closing my eyes, I will myself to choose wealth, success and anti-ageing cards if they exist. I try to focus on those cards, which appear to be calling out to me, choosing those either sticking out or those almost hiding as if deliberately. I focus on the Law of Attraction, putting out clear signals of the things I want most in life, using my energy to send out the right frequency. I read about this stuff years ago: *The Power of Positive Thinking.* Apparently what you think about, you put out into the universe, causing the universe to transmit it back to you. It's supposed to be practised daily but, sometimes, well, on most days actually, I forget.

I spread the cards out, face down as instructed, and scanning my eyes across the back of them, I wait for my future to be revealed.

Gypsy Rose, close up, looks to be no older than I am although I guess she must be, on the assumption that the young girl Chantelle dealt with at the exhibition is her daughter. She looks different from when I last saw her, but perhaps I'm the one looking differently at her? And maybe with increased anticipation. But today she is simply stunning. Facially, that is. The rest of her lets itself down (without being too blunt about it). What a tragic shame to be so facially attractive but let the rest of you go! Well and truly. I'm sure she'll use childbirth as an excuse like most women I hear venting about excess weight. "*I was a size zero before I had the kids!*" Yeah. Whatever. Although perhaps I should refrain from judging until I've actually been there. *Ouch!*

She attaches an unlit cigarette to the corner of her mouth and, making minimal eye contact with me, turns the cards over one by one, placing them in the pre-marked squares on the black cloth. Some of the cards are placed on top of others but at a different angle so you can still see the images that lie beneath. The cloth clearly dictates where and how each card should lie, providing pre-marked squares and presenting an Idiot's Guide to Tarot. Even I could manage this bit.

Each card is decorated with amazing images and vibrant colours, and an air of mystery and adventure leaps from them. Their façade bears no immediate indication as to their underlying message and a well of confusion overcomes me until my muddled thoughts are interrupted.

"It is important that you don't talk until this part of the reading is over," she says.

I nod.

"It's best that I don't hear your voice and that you pass no comment on what I say to you until I've read every card and tried to explain how it fits into your life."

Once more I nod vigorously, anxious for her to simply get on with it.

She looks up at me smiling and gestures to the first card. "You'll like this one." Her finger touches the card delicately, never losing contact. "This one reveals an exuberant, flamboyant man. A man always in motion and constantly seeking new challenges."

My skin tingles with goose-bumps as thoughts of Brian flood my head. *He's determined and certainly seeking new challenges. Me for instance!*

"This card is the Knight of Wands and it shows us that a male person, who is around you already, craves adventure." She hesitates. "Although he can be a little divorced from reality."

I can cope with that! I don't even watch the news these days it's so depressing. Reality! Who needs it?

"The Knight of Wands is a real charmer – women tend to love him but," she looks at me seriously, "no woman can hold him down."

Whatever! I've got him eating from the palm of my hand.

I try to remain emotionless as the reading goes on. It's so difficult though. Keeping your mouth still is one thing but stopping your eyes from showing signs of life or giving away snippets of information is so hard and, for some reason, particularly today, trying to get my right eyelid to stop quivering on its own is posing a challenge in itself. Funny, it started a few weeks back and whenever I get excited or nervous I can feel it flickering about. I've never managed to look in the mirror while it's been happening but I hope that whatever is going on is from the inside only. I lift my hand to hold it still, pressing down on the eyelid, looking at her through just one eye. *She looks thinner. Half the size in fact.* Once again I try to focus and unblock my mind from the usual rubbish it hoards in an effort to allow her into my psyche.

She draws my attention to a rather hideous card called The Hanged Man. It has a picture of a naked man (naked bar loincloth), shackled in a tortuous position on the face of a cliff. I shift in the chair rather uncomfortably.

Gypsy Rose observes my horrified face and laughs aloud. "It means sacrifice," she explains. "This card shows that you need to sacrifice something in order to acquire something else."

"Like what?" I interrupt, immediately regretting opening my mouth.

"The sacrifice can be one of many." Her tone is clipped and edged with reprimand. "In the case of this card, the hanged man is tortured with an anxiety that his sacrifice might come to nothing, but he is prepared to sit it out and suffer for his cause. But how do I see it fitting into your life . . .?" She tilts her head to one side, pushing her ample chin down so that it practically hangs over her shoulder. "You need to adopt more of a willingness to put your trust in unseen events. Perhaps even take a more . . . you know . . . gambler's approach." She talks directly at me. "Go with your gut reaction a little more and, remember, nothing ventured nothing gained." She shrugs. "You need to learn that putting yourself through your paces, as they say, is a small sacrifice if it opens up new doors for you."

Put so vaguely I'm really struggling to understand what all this stuff means. To me. Tina Harding. It's all very well her telling me the story of each card but, if she can't explain how this is likely to impact on me and my life, then what's the point?

I struggle to comprehend Chantelle and the goose-bumps she had when she left this woman that day. The urgency with which she dragged me to one side. The shaky pitch of her voice as she told all.

Okay, Tina. It's you. You're making it difficult for her. Focus. Focus.

Gypsy Rose, lost in her own world, is scribbling down notes for me to take away. Thoughtful of her if her writing were legible, but they may as well be written in hieroglyphics from what I can see. *I wonder if I can borrow her pen and paper?* I open my mouth to ask and then shut it firmly again as those piercing green eyes hypnotise me.

"I can't seem to get past this card," she frowns, tapping The Hanged Man with a tar-stained finger. "There's a message in it for you but I can't quite get it." She repositions the cigarette that has been quite settled in her mouth for some time now, lighting it without asking and dragging heavily on it. She reaches behind her, picking up an ashtray overflowing with cigarette stubs and places it on the table to the right of her. *Overweight smoker? Does this woman not want to live for much longer?* My sympathy for her pretty face but disproportionate body suddenly disappears.

The air carries a taste of second-hand smoke and already my clothes smell of a night on the town – the only night I've ever come away from sober and financially intact! Although I haven't paid her yet. She blows the smoke to one side, taking a long final drag before stubbing the remains out and placing the ashtray behind her once more. Her façade is more relaxed now and her face less strained.

"This card is telling me that you have made past sacrifices . . ." She pauses. "But you gave in too quickly." Her eyes soften as she regains confidence. "Don't speak but do you understand this?"

I nod in slow motion, my brain working ten to the dozen as the words translate into my own interpretation.

"You have great potential in this area and the self-doubt you carry needs to be removed." Once again she scribbles on the paper, finishing the page and starting a new sheet of indecipherable mush. "In summary, what I'm saying is that you gave up too soon." She points to the card. "There is no reason to be a martyr to any cause like this guy, but only a fool allows a single blow to keep him down."

My heart is beating so fast it's practically in overdrive and I'm pretty sure that, even in her current condition, her cardio-system at this very moment has to be stronger than mine. My chest tightens as I recall that very day I chose to put closure on the only dream I ever had. Was it too soon? Surely I'd tried everything to sustain its life? But that's the weirdest thing, isn't it? Even when you've made agonising decisions based on logic, facts and reality, you still feel torn up about the 'what ifs' and 'what could have beens'. What more could I have done with no fixed abode, no cash, no energy and certainly no fight left in me whatsoever? Oh and no regular work coming in.

Throughout the rest of the reading, I find my mind drifting away as her inability to be specific takes its toll on my concentration. She turns over card after card, talking about cups and pentacles and other such trivia and once again I am forced to question myself about my reasons for being here. I recall them. But things haven't quite transpired as I had imagined.

Rose collects the cards, integrating them back into the rest of the pack. She shuffles them thoroughly like a trained croupier.

"I want you to think about a burning quest –" she coughs suddenly, her cheeks flaring with redness and her chest sounding like it's about to explode, "– question, hhm, sorry!" She croaks painfully, holding her ample bosom (her chest must be under there somewhere). "Keep it in your mind so I can try to answer it."

I wonder if I can speak now? Oh God, she'll think that's my question. It's not, it's not.

"Okay – ready," I reply, keen to show my openness to work with her.

What is my ultimate purpose in life? What is my ultimate purpose in life? I repeat this in my head over and over again, staring her in the eyes, willing her to answer me plain and simple. After a long pause she lights up another cigarette and begins. Her eyes blind me with determination as she stares deep into me and a feeling of sudden relaxation hypnotises me.

"You have a good heart but so far your virtuous deeds have been minimal."

What? I raise my eyebrows defensively.

"You are extremely gifted in terms of being creative and resourceful and I feel these skills could be put to greater use in terms of helping others." Her cough returns once more, bringing with it a cloud of smoke from her open mouth. Her eyes water as she holds her chest, excusing herself from the table. I hear the chink of crockery and the running of a tap, followed by silence and then footsteps. The laminate floor vibrates beneath my chair.

"Are you okay?" I ask, concerned about her general wellbeing.

"Nothing that I don't deserve." She laughs a deep chesty laugh. "Thanks for asking. And, there, didn't I tell you just how kind you were?"

My face lights up. Actually, she did. How nice it is that someone recognises a good point in you. It's usually the negative stuff people are so quick to point out.

"Thanks," I beam, feeling warmed up.

"Now where were we?" She frowns, settling back into the hard chair. "Oh yes, strong links with creativity and helping people are coming through. I see you undertaking some type of charitable deed. You know, Karma is a wonderful thing and it will pay you back for your forthcoming virtue. What goes around comes around as they say." She clears her throat roughly. "Just remember, Tina, that you don't always get it back off the same people you've given to, so don't expect it. Life is full of surprises."

I couldn't agree more about trying to do the best for people when I can fit it in, but in terms of being paid back it doesn't really work like that, does it? How naïve is she? What about the murderer who won the lottery? What about the people who devote their entire lives to helping others only to suffer more misfortune than the rest of us put together? What about those women so desperate to be mothers and bursting with love who are denied the joy of conception? I tut-tut aloud at the unfairness of life.

Taking in my obvious shift in attitude, Gypsy Rose hands me her pages of notes. I stuff them into my bag, thanking her, although I am desperate to flick through them given my mind went a little AWOL for a good part of the session.

"Just remember you have a great heart, Tina, and a creative head. Once your head and your heart are synchronised, you'll know exactly how your life is supposed to be."

"Thank you very much," I say awkwardly but at the same time thinking, *Hang on, isn't that your job? You know, to tell me how my life is supposed to be?*

Glancing around the tiny conservatory, I look for the door. "That was, er, great," I mumble, before leaving and hurrying to my car, conscious of the time and mindful of a series of valuations waiting to be done.

It all feels a bit of an anti-climax really. Why couldn't she have just told me in no uncertain terms what to do? And why do these things have to be so vague? Something more concrete would have been nice. But, still, there were a few real specifics.

Weren't there?

"Hi, Tina!" A cheerful Chantelle grins up at me from the front desk, wafting a wad of forms in the air. "These have all been signed up this morning. Five new properties in the space of half a day."

"Well done, you, that's incredible." I shake my head in amazement at the difference a few hours can make. "Do they need valuations carried out?" I ask, suddenly remembering the increased workload every new property brings with it.

"Only three of them do and they're all local. The other two are switchers from Blenheim Jones – they're sticking with their current valuation figures so it's just a case of getting some photos and getting them on display." She separates the work pile, placing some into the ready-to-go tray and the rest into the pending tray. "Apparently Blenheim Jones haven't marketed these two at all. They've never ever been in the window! And they have the damn cheek to charge commission without actually doing anything!"

I laugh at Chantelle getting so worked up. But I love that she is so organised and reliable. In fact, if I never ask her about those properties again, I can rest assured that they're in the window displays, on the website and more than likely, sold. Case closed.

"What took you so long?" she asks, trying to remove a staple with her long manicured nails.

"I wasn't aware I was out long."

Chantelle looks up at me kindly. "I was just wondering what you were up to really. Nothing more."

"Oh, this and that," I reply vacantly. "Chantelle, do you remember a few months ago when that lady from the charitable trust called around?"

She nods, still picking away at the staple, well and truly immersed in a batch of papers.

"If you get a second, can you dig out her details for me and tell her it's fine for us to display a charity box in here."

"Ah ha!" Chantelle shouts gleefully. "Little sucker!" The staple, now successfully removed, is hurled into the bin. "Of course I will. Charity begins at home, as they say."

Warm-hearted, I dander upstairs to my office. Firstly to reflect on the morning and secondly to clear some work. I'm a little bit behind.

Every now and then, my heart sinks into the pit of my stomach as my thoughts trace back to Saturday night and the humiliation brought with it. Any wonder Simon never asked me about the date. I'd already rung him and arranged it! Once more I missed out on an episode with Brian and can't help wondering if somebody is playing a huge joker card in my life. Like in the film with Jim Carey where his life is a series of events, pre-rehearsed and impressed for all the world to see. *The Tina Show*, that's it, but with me for once as the leading lady.

Simon's touch keeps coming back to me. His soft hands and warm breath. The smell of his unkempt manliness and soft, unshaven facial hair. I recall the sheer horror in his eyes as I yelled for him to get out, and, now that I've had a little time to mellow, I'm fraught with guilt about how he must be feeling. Pretty soon I'll have to face the music. The wedding rehearsal is only a matter of weeks away. But that's just one thing. The obligatory dance is another. Thanks, Sam. *Still, there's nothing like the taming of a handsome man to take my mind off things.*

"Brian, it's Tina here," I announce sexily. "I just want to thank you personally for the flowers and also to apologise for the brief text message."

A raucous laugh booms down the receiver.

"My office staff followed my every move that day so I couldn't even ring you, but thank you," I offer once more. Now enough of the niceties. "This unfinished business . . ."

"Saturday would be good."

"What?"

"Dinner at eight."

"Where?"

"That's a surprise."

"Right . . . okay . . . great. See you then."

This time I don't bother with the goodbyes but hang up and pull out my diary, going straight to next Saturday's page where I mark '*Dinner with BS*'. He has it all planned, it would appear. Hopefully more efficiently than I did last weekend but at least we've spoken and, unless I'm going completely mad, I did ring his number and he did respond when I called his name so things are looking up already. At least my fingers and phone are synchronised this time, if nothing else.

On this occasion we will be mixing business with pleasure, having received the particulars of what might be office number two. By the looks of things, it is in need of some remedial work so I've decided to ask Brian's advice and perhaps even invite him or one of his builders along to the viewing. Not that it has come off yet but even the mention of office number two is an achievement in itself.

For the first eighteen months or so, I managed Harding Homes on my own. Closing the shop for quick comfort breaks, eating behind my computer, coming in early and staying late. To even contemplate that the business generates, or at least will generate, enough revenue to manage the overheads and staff for a second office, is beyond my wildest dreams. The premises in Camberwell Road, although sighted on paper alone, seem to tick every box in terms of what I'm looking for.

The unit is double-fronted, unlike the current single window downstairs, enabling it to hold substantially more property displays. I'd also love to have a window-mounted plasma TV running throughout the night, demonstrating a continual slide show of all the properties on our books. It will increase the electricity bill slightly but being able to sell even with a closed shop has to be money well spent. You have to speculate to accumulate as they say. There is a little interior work required with the removal of an internal wall and re-fitting of sanitary ware and new windows but it shouldn't be too bad in terms of budgeting. The comments of a pen-pusher, however. I'll wait and see what the professionals say. Still, one-and-a-half-per-cent commission on six hundred thousand pounds times fifteen apartments should cover it. Once more, I do the maths on my ancient scientific calculator and again have to pinch myself at the volume of numbers displayed on the keypad. All I need now are for the agency contracts to roll through the front door and for a host of recognisable names and faces to bombard us with viewings. And down payments.

I add a note to my to-do list to call Gerry, my last agent, to get his feedback from the presentation.

Oh sod it, I'll just ring him now and take the bull by the horns.

"Hello, Tina?"

I recognise Chantelle's voice. "Oh, hi, Chantelle, I was just trying to get an outside line."

"A Paul Stewart is on the line from the Northern Art College. He mentioned you'd been enquiring about an art course?" She giggles away.

"Oh. Erm . . . yes. Put him through, thanks." I wince, wondering what on earth to say to this man about my hidden creative talents.

Standing at the enrol table I look around shyly, feeling unprepared yet excited at the thought of a new venture. I was always good at art. Funny that I should have forgotten about it. Okay, I did get a D in my Art and Design O Level but that was only through lack of application. The talent is all there. It just needs a little development.

A tall, skinny woman wearing a tight black-and-white-striped top, with a matching red belt and red beads, appears before me. She introduces herself as Elizabeth Wren, one of the art tutors, and begins to explain the various courses available.

"Actually," I whisper, a little embarrassed, "I haven't done any artwork since school and I've just taken a notion for it." I'm being honest. Well, almost.

Her striking shoulder-length bob is well and truly glued down. As she moves from side to side, collecting the various leaflets, her hair remains in a fixed position but her beads sashay from left to right jingling away like a wooden xylophone. She exudes an air of artistic eccentricity.

I'm definitely in the right place.

"Here are details of classes for artists of any level," she offers. "Most of them are Still classes so you can work at your own pace." She smiles at me with those scarlet lips that match her colourful accessories.

She glances behind me and I take that as my cue to stand aside, noting the small gathering that has formed.

Thanking her, I collect the flyers and perch myself on a plastic chair in a quiet corner of the registration-room-cum-gym-hall, pondering which of the classes will realise my artistic ability.

Fifty pounds lighter, I follow my new classmates into a small studio kitted out with free-standing easels, hard wooden stools and walls that are decorated with an amateur exhibition of what I assume to be current pieces. Nervously, I choose my stand. My home for the next ten weeks.

Removing the sheet of paper from its elastic band, I unroll it and deftly attach it to the easel, securing it in place like an expert. I pick up the only battered pencil I could grab from the office, poised and ready to go.

I hear the door open and close. My nerves kick in and I stay hidden and out of sight. I don't want to attract unnecessary attention just to find out I can't quite bring it together. My school days are long over. *You can't hide forever, Tina!* Holding my breath, I step out slowly from behind the easel and take in the full view. But not of the teacher as I had expected.

Oh my God!

It's not a plant, nor a bowl of fruit or even a vase of flowers. It's a man! A very very naked man at that, who is now sitting down on the carefully positioned chair with one leg resting on the floor and the other hunched into his pale and rather bald-looking chest. In all its glory his man-piece just hangs there, protected by masses of unruly pubic hair jutting out in all directions and looking like the after-effects of an electric shock.

A loud gasp escapes from my mouth, followed by a childish giggle as I point to his bits, looking around the room open-mouthed. A sea of blank faces greets me and I can hear a few tutting sounds from the back.

"Hhmm . . ." I clear my throat, trying to control myself.

The model looks to be in his early twenties and my guess is that he's a student. A scruffiness hangs over him and from his greasy hair to uncut toenails he looks in need of a good scrub. Settled in a position of maximum exposure, he averts his eyes from the audience, seemingly focusing his attention elsewhere and probably thinking, *"There's always one!"*

I finally compose myself and touch the paper with the blunt pencil, making a small spot at the top of the *page. It's a start.* I seem to remain in this fixed position for some time. My hand has no idea in which direction to take me and I look from him to paper, from paper to him, wondering just where the hell to begin. I've only drawn in Pictionary over the last decade and even then it was matchstick men and crap ones at that.

Woah! I'm off the starting-block and am attempting to trace the outline of his head. Not quite the exact same shape as his, but it's trickier than it looks. I make a mental note to add his hair in later and, in fact, his entire face will have to wait for now. Maybe I could interpret mine as the faceless man? You know, give it that modern, contemporary feel? I clumsily mark out the shape of his unshaven jaw-line and rather pointed chin and allow my pencil to imagine it is tracing the wide line of his neck down to his broad shoulders. I let my hand wobble with bizarre unsteadiness. Okay, he's a little long and giraffe-like but I'm getting there. *What's the hurry?* Concentrating hard, my hand attempts to sketch his bony shoulders, trying to gauge at what point to slope them down so they blend into a pair of arms, but I lose that vital hand-eye contact and get carried away as my drawing leaves the width of the page, spilling out on to the wooden easel. *Damn. I was doing so well. Perhaps he can have really short arms?*

Refusing to give in, I stand back to evaluate my work of art. Staring back at me is a rather large head with an incredibly long neck and seriously distorted arms, not to mention no eyes or ears. But still, I try simply to rectify my error and move on.

"Excuse me. Do you have a rubber?" I whisper to the older lady next to me, gesturing to my quite obvious mistake.

Again, I am greeted by her deadpan face while those within earshot continue to cast me distasteful looks.

"I seem to have made a cock-up," I add genuinely.

Quite suddenly the inappropriate choice of vocabulary hits me and I quickly dart back behind the safety of the easel, fiercely trying to repress my hysterics. Naked man, rubber, cock-up! I stare at the picture with the tears streaming down my face, snorting at the ridiculousness of the situation I have found myself in.

Throwing the pencil down, I grab the page and crumple it up, throwing it in the nearest bin, and through stifled bursts of laughter grab my bag, mouthing my apologies to the rather sheepish model as I exit.

Who the hell are you trying to kid, Tina?

I run through the exit into the car park letting it all out, screeching with laughter.

Tina Harding, the only artist you'll ever be, my girl, is a piss artist!

12

"For those of you who have just joined us at *WNW* we have an action-packed show that will literally Wake the North West!!" she sings cheerily.

But I swear I detected a slight cringe as she delivered those last four words. As usual I'm always looking out for flaws. Ever the critic.

Lying propped up against the pillows, I slurp huge mouthfuls of strong coffee in an attempt to wake myself up and muster the energy for another day at the office. Last night I struggled getting to sleep, whereas usually I'm out for the count as soon as my head touches the pillow, but I found myself thinking about what she had said. You know, giving in too soon and all that stuff.

"Coming up next we have Kate Simms," she reads from the auto-cue. "Dishing the dirt on her co-stars and giving us a sneak preview of the second series of *Family Furores*." She smiles directly at me. "I do hope you'll join us after the break."

Almost choking on my coffee, I sit bolt upright, grabbing the remote control, turning the volume up in anticipation of seeing my best friend on *WNW*. She never told me she was going to be on this morning. Normally Kate lets me know so I can tape these things for her. She says she's collating as much footage as she can so that when she's old and wrinkly and her kids are calling her a sad loser who knows nothing, she can show them that she was once a familiar face to our nation. Not to mention wrinkle-free and well toned.

Good idea actually. I must make sure I keep hold of my modelling photographs. Some of them.

Jumping out of bed, I knock back the last of the coffee, grimacing at its tarlike strength. I give myself sixty seconds in the shower, which is probably all the time I have left before I see my best friend on air. I so need to watch this and in fact I never miss it when Kate is on TV. Maybe it's the pride factor or maybe it's because every time I see her I wonder if she's going to mention me. Her best friend. The one who didn't make it.

Barely wet, I'm out of the shower and running back into the bedroom where I perch myself on the end of the bed just in time to hear that awful jingle of the *Wake the North West* tune.

"Welcome back." Anna Peters grins delightedly as she gestures to her next guest. "Kate Simms is here as promised by *WNW* and looking as stunning as ever." She turns her body in Kate's direction and the camera closes in on my friend who is sitting on the florescent pink guest chair, leaning back and looking extremely relaxed. Not to mention extremely stunning.

"Good morning, Kate, and thank you for joining us at this early hour."

"Early hour?" Kate laughs. "I haven't been to bed yet. This is just a late night for me!"

They both laugh right on cue and Anna continues with the previously researched set of questions and I can tell that Kate is loving every minute of her air time.

"So, Kate, firstly congratulations on the success of *Family Furores*."

Kate nods appreciatively.

"And, secondly, can you tell our *WNW* viewers what we can expect from your character in the second series?"

Kate takes a sip of water and places the glass delicately on the smoked-glass table in front of her. "Well, Anna, my character Scarlett has been somewhat colourful, hence the name!" She grins, raising her eyebrows. "And I'm sorry to disappoint you, gentlemen, but I'm afraid you won't be seeing her in quite as much lingerie during the next series. She's taken on a whole new role." She laughs, shaking her head. "Although it's not easy for a girl like Scarlett. Let's just say she'll never be a nun!"

Anna looks slightly shocked for a moment, probably wondering if they're likely to receive a host of complaint letters from convents up and down the country. But she says nothing that isn't part of the auto cue and continues on professionally. My feeling is that she hasn't the brain power to ad-lib. There's no-one home, if you know what I mean.

"In the final episode you walked out on Harry saying, I quote: '*One ex is a mistake, Harry, but two is just careless.*'"

Her reading of Kate's line was hideous. Don't give up the day job, love. "Can you tell us what that was about?"

Kate sits forward in the neon chair and, as she does so, her miniskirt slides further up her cellulite-free thighs. She crosses her legs sexily, creating further enhanced visibility of the thighs, practically showing the curve of her bottom cheek.

I screech at the TV screen, knowing full well that Kate has this move well and truly practised. I yell loudly to her, "You big tease, Kate!" *Like she can hear me!*

"What's that all about then, Kate?" asks Anna, quickly looking away from Kate's exposed flesh.

Too late – caught you!

"Well, Anna, naturally I can't divulge too much, but I can say that his ex and I get *very* friendly."

The camera jolts slightly, unless it was my imagination but I don't think so. There's only so much a hot-blooded male can take this early in the morning.

"And let's face it, we already have something in common. A lying, cheating Harry who is enough to put any woman off men for life!"

Here we have one of the UK's most popular actress practically announcing to the country that she's embarking on a lesbian affair on national television. That ought to do it for the ratings, Kate. *Go, girl!*

The rest of the interview goes smoothly for Kate but not as well, it would appear, for Anna, who seems to find herself a little embarrassed at Kate's openness about girl-on-girl action.

My thoughts drift back to one particular night. Skint as usual but glammed up to the nines, Kate and I came up with a plan as to how we could get trashed on the guts of a fiver each, and as usual this plan revolved around us flirting outrageously in front of whichever guys looked the most cash-rich. We would play it coy as though we'd never done it before but, for a free round of drinks, perhaps we could try a little kiss . . . but only because they'd put the idea into our heads. We would literally down our drinks, the more expensive the content the better, and give each other a soft kiss on the lips, lingering just a little too long for it to be platonic but not long enough so they got their money's worth. *Perhaps another drink might help us loosen up? You're buying? Great!*

Anyway, one night we were out celebrating our mate Lauren's twentieth birthday. After being plied with alcohol from a group of pompous barristers in the Courthouse bar, Lauren came staggering towards us doped off her head and whinging that we always left her out. Given it was her birthday she too wanted a piece of the action. The next thing I recall was the three of us fighting over tongues, eating the faces off each other as the entire bar came to a stand-still. You could almost hear the conflicting opinions of our fellow-drinkers. The blokes loved it but their girlfriends detested us for manipulating the attention. Rightly or wrongly. It was one of those surreal moments where I knew we'd overstepped the line, but I was so pissed that I didn't actually care what I did. I do remember feeling a little awkward though when Kate and Lauren's mouths were glued together. I felt redundant, but not giving up I tried to make room for a third mouth, squeezing my head in between theirs, gate-crashing their private party. The only thing I remember after that is drinking pink champagne and making up stories about my sex life with Kate simply to keep the bubbles free-flowing! Naturally, that was in the days where Kate wasn't a recognisable face. If we ever fall out, which is highly unlikely, but if it did happen I could seriously make a small fortune by selling stories to the *Sun* and other such newspapers. I doubt I'd ever have to work again! *Now there's a thought.*

An offering of spring has arrived, bringing with it the

lingering scent of freshly cut grass. But still the air carries a mild chill and I silently pray that the temperature will lift in time for Sam's wedding. Unlike your typical Monday morning, where it pours down and you arrive at work just to find your hair-straighteners have disappeared, this morning the air is perfectly crisp and scented with apples. A sheet of silky blue floats high with not a cloud in sight.

I pull up directly outside the office, removing the orange traffic cone placed there deliberately. The rates are high enough so why shouldn't I get my own space? Shoving the key into the front door, I twist it twice to the right and once back to the left, pulling it out roughly before using my hip to force the door open. That's another item for my to-do list. *Fix front door.* There is a pile of post and junk mail lying messily on the floor and I gently move some of it with my foot so that the door can close behind me.

I love coming into work this early and having the office to myself. There are no phones ringing, no clients dropping by, no solicitors asking where the damn house keys are. It's quiet and tranquil which contagiously affects my mood as I fly through the pending tray, making an impressive dent in the pile.

Chantelle will be delighted with the removal of this time-consuming work and it will certainly free up time for her to do just what it is she's best at: selling.

Collecting the post from the grey carpet-tiled floor, I scan through it quickly, sorting the more official-looking letters from the less important items, like promotional flyers, endless stationery catalogues and the Makro Mail which seems to arrive on a daily basis. Don't get me wrong, I'm a big fan of it, but there are only so many toilet-roll deals a girl can cope with.

I tear open a letter marked for my attention. "*Private and Confidential.*" At long last. *Yippee!* It's the contract from Brian Steen. I make a note to ask Sam to cast her eyes over it before I sign it. I'm not one for signing anything unless every clause has been explained and clarified. I know she has a lot on her plate right now, not to mention her future in-laws but she won't let me down and, apart from Simon (the less said on him the better) she is the only lawyer I know outside of my usual conveyancing contacts.

This contract is like gold dust. I'm reluctant to put it down in case it gets damaged or I lose it. How many other opportunities am I ever likely to get where I can earn so much money in one transaction? Probably none. It's practically been handed to me on a plate and, while it is true that I worked hard for the pitch, it was immensely enjoyable so it really didn't feel too much like work. Play is a far better description for Mr Steen. But on a more serious note, the transactional value of this is truly overwhelming and is a life-changing sum of money which, spent wisely, could fulfil all my short-term business ambitions.

"Morning, Tina! How was your weekend?" Chantelle bounces through the front door balancing a wad of files on her arm. She smiles at me as brightly as she does at five o'clock on a sunny Friday afternoon.

I decide to say nothing about Gypsy Rose or my ridiculous stint at the art college.

"Great, thanks, Chantelle. Pretty quiet really but so relaxing," I lie, thankful for the ease with which it comes, but guilty as hell for doing it. "And yours?"

"Wild! You wouldn't believe how drunk Colin was

on Saturday night." She throws the files on her desk, shaking her arms out with relief. "He doesn't even remember getting home!"

"Were you at a party?"

"My aunt's seventieth!" She screeches with laughter. "I feel awful saying it but it was just so dull that we stayed at the bar all night."

She takes out a mirror and examines her eyes, pushing down gently on their slight puffiness with perfectly polished nails. Flipping the cover shut, she shakes her head, wincing. "Never again! I really do mean it this time."

"Yeah, right!" I laugh. "Oh, great stuff, Chantelle, you've just reminded me I have to do something."

"What's that then?" She dabs a crème of some sort beneath her dark alluring eyes.

"I need to set up a direct debit for Age Concern." I notice how she is looking at me suspiciously. "No, really, Chantelle. Do you know how hard it is for these people to manage on the measly state pension this country gives? So many die every year from hypothermia just because they can't afford to put the heating on in the winter. It's an absolute disgrace and unless members of the general public like you and I do something to help, they'll continue to suffer in silence." *Crikey, where did that come from?* I stand down from my soapbox.

Chantelle looks chastened. "I'm sorry, Tina, you're so right, forgive me." She bends down under her desk, picks up her handbag again, removing her purse and pulling out a folded note. Chantelle pushes the note into the charity box and looks at me gratefully. "Thanks for reminding me, Tina. It really is a privilege to work for someone so caring and honest." She grabs me in a tight embrace.

Well, one out of two isn't bad.

"Kate, it's me!" I yell in the direction of the hands-free kit. "I saw you this morning – you were brilliant!" The line crackles rudely.

"Hello, you!" Kate echoes back. "How are things?"

"Oh you know, same old, same old. Trying to bag the sexiest man I've seen in years, possibly opening a second office, chief bridesmaid duties in a few weeks." I beam at the phone proudly. "Usual stuff, Kate."

"As busy as ever then." Kate raises her voice over the interference which seems to have become louder. These hands-free kits are a nightmare but still it's better than three points on your licence. "I meant to call you about this morning," Kate shouts. "But it was such short notice. Stewart Heart was supposed to be on the show but he got the flu last minute so they asked me to stand in for him. Great or what?" She snorts. "Apart from dealing with that Anna woman, bloody great plank of wood!"

I screech with laughter at Kate's honesty. And perception.

"You were great but she was totally shite. Why the hell is she still hosting that show?"

"Rumour has it that she's shagging the director Sam Jenkins." A retching sounds booms down through the speaker. "He is so gross she must be desperate! Here, Tina, I've got a few weeks at the end of next month. Fancy getting away somewhere? I was thinking we could go back to Crete. You know, old times' sake and all that stuff?"

"Oh definitely, Kate, I so need a break!" I call back excitedly.

During our second year at Uni, Kate and I spent the entire summer travelling around Crete, stopping to work at various resorts when we'd run out of money, throwing back ouzo like it was going out of fashion and learning just about every Greek speciality possible – if you know what I mean. Okay, at the time we didn't realise half the men teaching us these local specialities were married but, looking back, we were a little naïve. Any wonder we were so popular.

Kate and I chose Crete as we'd spent a week holidaying there the year before and we'd got to know the place quite well. We needed somewhere with endless bars and night life to ensure that we'd have no issues getting work. Plus we made great friends with many a bar-owner who promised us jobs if we returned the following season. They didn't let us down although we learned very quickly that they always wanted some kind of favour in return.

"Tina, I have to go now," Kate whispers. "I've just been chased out of the green room to go on set. Call you later about the holiday. Bye." She blows kisses down the phone before the line goes dead and my car radio kicks back in.

A holiday is just what I could do with. Lying on a deserted beach allowing the calmness of the sea to send me into a deep state of relaxation, Piña Colada in one hand, Marian Keyes in the other. Well, not Ms Keyes herself naturally although I am a big fan of hers. Just not in that way.

At least for now I've got my date with Mr Steen to look forward to. Who needs to wait for sex on the beach when it's already in the diary for Saturday night?

Without the sand, of course, but that's definitely a plus – that stuff gets everywhere.

"*A man in motion always seeking new challenges.*"

By the time I've finished with you, Mr Steen, motion sickness will be the only challenge you'll be facing.

"Damn!"

Someone has parked in my space right in front of the shop. I glare at the car as if that's going to help matters and notice that, a few cars up, someone is pulling away. The lines are double yellow but I'm only popping in to collect messages and check the office is still intact. I quickly reverse into the space, thankful of rear parking-sensors and wondering what the hell I ever did without them. A few months ago, however, I did reverse into a bollard. There was no damage done apart from a small scratch to the silver A6 bumper. But when I told my dad he roared with laughter. "Tina! You're the only person I know who can ignore as loud a warning as that bloody car sensor of yours!" I guess I must have been reversing a little too quickly because before I knew it I heard a high-pitched bleeping noise followed directly by a bang. And then a four-letter expletive.

Glancing up and down the street now, it appears safe enough. There are no obvious signs of traffic wardens so I abandon the car and run towards the office, popping my head around the door. The office is dead. No foot traffic in sight. I guess that's what a sunny day does for you.

"Any messages for me, Chantelle?"

Her head appears from behind the flat-screened monitor and she smiles at me, removing her black-framed glasses which make her look damned intelligent and even more sexy than usual.

"Hi, Tina." A radiant smile lights up her face and her eyes twinkle responsively. "Nothing urgent for a Monday and certainly nothing I couldn't take care off." She stands up, pushing her skirt down, ironing out the creases, and flicks her dark shiny hair over to one side.

"I can't stop," I rattle quickly. "Some cheeky sod is in my parking space and I can't afford to get another ticket."

"Okay but I want to run something by you so I'll come outside with you."

She steps out of the office and perches herself on the white-painted windowsill, squinting as the sun practically blinds her.

She looks preoccupied for a moment and I feel my heart pounding, preparing for the worst. *Please don't leave. Please don't leave.*

"What you said this morning, Tina, is so right and I can't believe I've been so neglectful towards those less fortunate than myself." She shakes her head in disgust. "My mother would be turning in her grave . . . It's just that sometimes . . ." She pauses sadly. "Sometimes I feel like I've had my own fair share of bad luck and yet I've had no choice but to get on with it. But you made me realise this morning that there are always people worse off." She grabs my hand tightly. "And for that I am truly grateful."

I feel so bad I could cry for her. I have no idea where that soap-box lecture came from but I sure as hell didn't mean for Chantelle to be at the receiving end of it.

"Don't be so stupid, Chantelle!" I perch myself next to her, shielding my eyes from the sun. "Take no notice of me! God knows what I was on this morning, honest

161

gov. You know me – Queen of Crap!" I laugh, trying to win her over.

She turns to face me, beaming away. "It's okay though because guess what I'm doing on Saturday?"

"What?"

"I'm going to help supervise a group of disadvantaged kids," she declares joyously. "St Stephen's Church are taking them to an open farm for the day so I've put myself forward as a volunteer."

Well, that's not so bad. I thought for a minute she was going to sign a life-long contract to the Mormons or join some religious cult like the Mooneys.

"Yeah, my gran mentioned it the other day, said I might find it fulfilling and all that."

"And I'm sure you will." Relieved, I am resting my head against the warm glass, stretching out my legs to even out the weight on both feet when Chantelle bolts up, jumping in front of me, blocking the sun completely with her size-eight frame.

You're blocking the sun!

"Why don't you come with me?" she cries. "The two of us will have a blast, Tina!" She grabs my hands, shaking my arms up and down like I'm a puppet incapable of moving on my own. "Animals aren't really my thing, Chantelle." I try to hide the panic in my voice. *Neither are kids for that matter.* And besides, I have my Saturday nicely planned. Pampering, more pampering and sex, sex, sex!

"Mine neither but think of the kids, Tina. We'll be doing it for them." She looks down on me with those brown puppy-dog eyes, gentle but deceivingly disobedient. "Imagine their little faces. This might be their only day out all year, poor kids!" She looks as though she's about to cry. *God, she's wasted.*

Suddenly, flashes of those heartrending TV commercials flood my mind. The ones where they show you orphaned and emaciated kids with filthy flies landing on them and yet they still manage to smile graciously. It puts me to shame. I always mean to call the number and make a donation. But then it goes out of my head.

"Come on, Tina. We'll have a ball."

"I'm not that great with kids." I wince. It's true. I've never been around them.

"You only need to supervise them, Tina. They'll be so distracted with their annual day out they won't notice how you're being."

"I guess."

I mean, what harm can it do? It's just a few hours for heaven's sake with farm animals and a few small kids. A doddle, in fact.

"Okay, you're on, Mrs," I declare jovially. "It's a date."

I feel good about the decision. It really is the right thing to do and, besides, won't Mr Steen be impressed when he asks about my weekend so far? *Oh, you know, the usual stuff, Brian, charity work, blah blah.* I just need to make sure I get back early so that I can get ready without a mad rush, although thanks to my harsh waxing the other weekend I'm still in pretty good shape. In fact, you know what? I'm quite looking forward to Saturday now. Cute little animals and the warming sound of children's laughter. A little TLC, that's all they need.

Poor things. Auntie Tina's here.

13

My legs wobble as I clutch the loose handrail, trying to stop myself from falling down the stairs head first. From the virtual-web-images the property looked to be in much better condition than it is in reality, and the list of potential, not to mention, costly jobs is getting longer by the minute. The stairway itself is a liability. Every stair is uneven. The handrail is practically hanging off and the carpet is so threadbare it might as well be renamed underlay. Relieved as my feet touch the ground, I look back up to the top of the stairs, wondering if it would be safe to bring Brian or one of his guys with me next time, assuming I get out of here alive. Perhaps I might suggest some steel-capped boots and hard hats just in case. *Now we're talking!*

Downstairs looks to be in better condition which is unusual given this is where the hive of activity would have been. The building, previously an ice-cream parlour, is currently sitting in vacant possession and evidences very little of its former life apart from a tantalising sweetness which I pray will never leave. It is much larger than our existing High Street branch but then again most of the units here in Camberwell Road are double-fronted which is one of the primary reasons for choosing this location. Not to mention the other two other estate agents who are extremely well established in this area. Most of us these days are so shrewd when it comes to parting with our cash, that I think it's safe to say that the punters are likely to shop around all of us before deciding which one is going to sell their home. And Harding Home's strike rate is over eighty per cent, mainly down to Chantelle given I spend so much time out of the office these days. If or when the next shop is opened, I intend to transfer Chantelle up here where she can manage this plus the staff, leaving me to manage the High Street branch. My baby. I'll need to recruit someone else to take on the valuations for us. I'd much prefer to spend time working in the business than going out price-tagging.

The openness of the ground floor is vast and, better still, there are two small office rooms which could be used as interview rooms. *Fantastic!* So far we've been referring our mortgage business to a neighbouring Independent Financial Advisor for a small kickback in commission, but for the new office I'll most definitely be looking to recruit a qualified mortgage advisor who will be office-based. Paid no salary but then again charged no rent. They can't lose either way and neither can we. The majority of clients who come through our doors need some form of borrowing and if we can't service their requirements then somebody else will. Missing out on such a moneymaking opportunity would simply be foolish. A one-stop shop. That's what this office is going to be all about. A moneymaking empire.

"Mark will be with you in just a few minutes now, Tina," she says politely. "Can I get you a coffee while you're waiting?"

I put down the magazine, bored of reading the *Weight Loss for Wimps* column, nodding gratefully. "Thanks, Jo, white no sugar, please."

I originally had my hair booked in for Saturday but had to bring it forward on account of the agenda change. It's not an issue though as Mark pulls it so straight that I could leave it for a week and it still wouldn't look any different. Not that I'd do that, of course. It's so time-consuming, straightening my own hair. Firstly blowing it as straight as I can get it, secondly taking the irons through it piece by piece and, lastly, wondering where on earth the last three hours went to, that I gladly hand over twenty quid each week now just to spare myself the pain.

"Hello, gorgeous!" Mark chirps at me excitedly as he removes the wet towel, roughly drying my hair and kissing the air noisily. "You look faaab! Dish the dirt then, darling!"

Catching a glimpse of myself in the mirror I cringe. My hair has started to frizz already and splashes of black mascara garnish my cheeks. *Gorgeous! Is he blind or what?*

"Nothing to tell," I shrug. "Although ask me next week and there might well be." A dirty laugh escapes, followed by a squeal of delight from Mark as he clasps his hands together.

"Well, remember me when you're married off to this rich tycoon, won't you?" He empties his pockets, pulling out the lining, and purses his bottom lip, looking truly pathetic. "The lowly skint hairdresser you once confided in."

"Mark, if I ever had enough money you know I'd hire you to be my personal stylist. I wouldn't hesitate." *I'm deadly serious.* "You'd have to come on holiday with me though, maybe to the Maldives or the Caribbean so it wouldn't be too cushy a number! And let's face it, you'd pose no threat to my future husband so I can't see him objecting."

He squeezes the melon-scented serum from its container and smooths it through my hair right down to the very tips.

"Don't be sooo cheeky, Miss Thing!" he snorts effeminately. "A man like me could turn the even straightest of men gay! *You* might be the one who needs to look out!"

I guess I never thought of it that way before, although it's a chance I'd be prepared to take. Having a blonde Swedish au-pair however, isn't. *What am I talking about? I haven't even got a boyfriend and I'm talking husband, kids and nanny!* Usually I confide in Mark over everything, but the utter embarrassment of the Simon issue is simply too much. Although he'd love it. Vomiting on a white rug has some degree of humour to it, assuming you're not the owner of the rug or the vomittee of course, but exposing your body in agent provocateur lingerie to the wrong man, I simply can't see the funny side of that personally.

"What are we doing today, my lovely?" Mark asks, standing back, assessing his options. "I'm thinking Farah Fawcett?"

"I was just thinking poker-straight actually, Mark."

He looks disappointed.

"My date isn't until tomorrow and I doubt those flicks would survive overnight!" I laugh.

"Have it your way then." He sighs. Ever the Drama

Queen. "Straight it is." He pouts sulkily. "And boring."
Prima donna!

The Sunshine Coach pulls up outside of Noah's Animal Farm. Chantelle and I watch eagerly, standing by ready to assist.

A dozen young faces pressed up against the glass grin excitedly and the vehicle gasps loudly to a complete standstill.

As the children frantically collect their belongings, desperate to disembark, the bus rocks from side to side with the commotion. The doors open with a loud hiss and one by one each child is assisted and lowered to safety.

Chantelle and I exchange grins at the sound of the children's voices, excitable and giddy. Tittering girls and boisterous boys huddle together as they're rounded up like cattle.

A stern-faced, robust woman marches towards us, holding out her right hand. "Hello, ladies, I'm Pat Donnelly. Chairperson of the Church for Children group." We exchange formal handshakes. "Jolly delighted to meet you," she announces confidently.

Actually, speaking with a mouth full of marbles would be a more accurate description. There aren't many of her type left in Liverpool. She must be from old stock.

"I hope you know you've your work cut out today, ladies?" She raises an eyebrow, gesturing towards the group of children who are now lined up two by two, holding hands and looking particularly angelic. *How cute are they!*

"We've come prepared!" I reply cheerfully, lifting my leg to demonstrate my commitment to practicality and showing her my rather clean-looking Caterpillar boots.

Chantelle follows suit, pointing to her pink wellies. She looks suitably unimpressed but we both ignore her sternness and continue to smile broadly at the children.

Nothing can dampen my exhilaration today. I'm so desperate to get stuck in and I just can't wait to hold their chubby little hands and watch their innocent faces as they experience a little farm life and benefit from a dose of good clean air. I want to experience that maternal bond everyone talks about and imagine for just one moment that I have my own children. I yearn to feel that sense of a love that's so strong and so unbreakable that it takes my breath away and sends my heart into emotional overload.

"It's going to take a little more than footwear to protect yourselves from some of these little monkeys," Pat replies coolly, winking at me in particular. "They bite, you know."

My face drops momentarily and then I realise she's joking. I laugh, relieved. Although I notice she doesn't.

"Tina," she takes my arm, "let me introduce you to Charlie and Jake. You'll be looking after these two boys today."

Excitedly, I follow her lead towards the group of children, waving as they wave back at me, and suddenly I am overcome with the pleasure of guarding someone else's child. It has to be one of the highest privileges.

Walking down the line, I become aware that my face is fixed in a joker-like grin. But it feels as good as it does natural. I make a point of saying hello to each and every child and momentarily feel like a member of the Royal Family at the end of a Royal Variety Show. I decide to omit the small talk. Stopping dead, Pat roughly taps the shoulders of two small boys about six years old, standing tall and intimidating them. I immediately stoop down to their level to introduce myself properly, conscious not to do the same as she does. I watched it on *Supernanny*. She says to always come down to the child's eye level and that way you won't be bullying them by looming over them.

"Hello, Charlie. Hello, Jake, I'm Tina," I say affectionately, keen to strike an instant rapport with my two boys. I stretch my arm past Charlie towards Jake and ruffle his hair in a playful gesture. "*Aaaahh!*" A piercing scream escapes from my lips in a pained knee-jerk response.

"Charlie – no," Pat says calmly. "Let go right now."

"*Aaaah*! Get him off me!" I screech as his teeth sink deeper into my arm.

Charlie releases his grip and I pull away in a state of shock. A perfect cast of milk teeth stares up at me and I watch in horror as the blood surfaces and my arm begins to throb. Really throb.

Pat coolly whips out an antiseptic wipe from her bulging canvas bag and roughly scrubs my arm before speed-wrapping a small bandage around the wounded area and taping it down with a large plaster.

"There now – all sorted," she dismisses the incident as I continue to gape at the two boys in horror. "I did warn you, Tina." She smirks knowingly. "I told you they bite."

Yes but . . .

Marching the group through the main entrance like a captain leading his troops into battle, she turns every now and then to check we're all in tow. Chantelle, a few rows up, casts me a apologetic glance as I hold my arm up to her, showing the damage done. She winces sympathetically.

Feeling wounded, although more emotionally than physically, I watch as the other assistants take the hands of their perfectly behaved children and wonder for a split second if I should try to do the same. *Think like an adult, Tina. They're only children.* I tell myself that they're only little and perhaps I scared them off by making physical contact too soon?

I quickly decide to write off the biting incident as an isolated case although I am definitely in favour of adopting a more cautious approach.

"Jake, Charlie, would you like to hold my hand?" I ask with firm authority. The boys nod at me obediently, lifting up their little arms to show me grubby hands with dirty fingernails. I take hold of each small hand gently and with relief at their apparent eagerness. Thankful for their apparent change in temperament. *Wasn't a good start for any of us but still there's plenty of time for a happy ending.*

The group comes to an abrupt halt as Pat stops suddenly in front of a large cattle shed.

"It's five minutes to eleven, troops!" she shouts. "We're going to take a seat inside here just in time to feed the goats at eleven o'clock."

The children squeal excitedly, rushing towards the shed, and my arms are almost pulled out of their sockets by the two boys swinging from them. We follow Pat into the large open shed and take a seat on the low wooden benches provided. Perfectly lined up, row by row.

Placing myself in between Jake and Charlie, I point to a staff member wearing a rather trendy head microphone and dressed in a royal-blue polo shirt embroidered with the Noah's Farm logo.

"That lady is watching us so we'd all better behave really really well." I smile down at them positively. "Can you do that for me, boys?"

"If that stupid goat comes near me I'm gonna punch him!" Jake replies violently. His clasped hand smacks the air as he mimics the action.

"Yeah and I'm going to – eh – kick him!" Charlie joins in.

I'm horrified. Kicking! Biting! How aggressive are children today?

I hear a faint bleating as the goats are led into the shed by what look like teenage volunteers – probably local children earning some pocket money.

"Absolutely *no* kicking allowed!" I lecture, shocked at how Pat-like I sound. Repulsed even. *I'm so glad I haven't eaten yet.* I point to the supervisor who has started to tell us about a Nubian-type goat. "Charlie. Jake. Look!" A tiny goat is trying desperately to extricate itself from her tight grip. The lead is free from slack to keep the creature close and she pokes and prods it in various parts of its anatomy, lifting its ears and allowing them to flop down.

"Sometimes we call them Lop-Eared Goats," she explains passionately. This makes the children laugh hysterically. *Why do children laugh at the most ridiculous things?* "It is also known for its high-quality butterfat and milk production."

"*Uuurrghh!*" yells Charlie. "Milk is so gross!"

"Yeah, it's like puke!" adds Jake.

"Boys!" I snap. "That lady is in charge here and she

will ask you to leave if you continue to be so rude and naughty." The firmness in my voice settles them and for a moment they look as cute and as run-of-the-mill as the other kids here.

Their little necks strain as they try to see over the top of people's heads, frantically following the direction of the bleating. As the noise becomes louder, a baby goat appears at the top end of our bench, sucking vigorously on a milk bottle held in place by one of the teenagers. He gives the bottle to the first child to hold while the tiny goat simply follows the scent of milk, supping on its teat pleasurably. One by one, each child takes a turn of holding the bottle upside down as the goat follows obediently with its head tilted up, eager to take the bottle from anyone prepared to feed it. It really is a beautiful sight. This little white creature, all innocent and trusting, sucking away on the rubber teat without a care in the world.

Why isn't my life so uncomplicated and immaterial? Maybe I'll come back as an animal.

"Look, boys, it's nearly your turn," I tell them excitedly. I'm really starting to enjoy myself now. *Aren't kids great when they do as they're told!*

As the goat wobbles towards us I keep a mindful eye on the children's feet, ready to grab them just in case they deliver their threat. And why wouldn't they?

"Here it is!" Charlie yells, pulling on my sleeve with excitement. "Look, look!"

I note his sparkling eyes, wide and amazed. His bottom barely touches the bench as he shifts about with uncontrollable exuberance. His face is quite angelic, albeit a little dirty and a good scrub wouldn't go amiss. I don't know what the history is behind these kids and neither do

I want to, but I hear that many of them are pretty disadvantaged. Suddenly I'm grateful for the head-start I've had.

"Now be careful not to scare him, Charlie. He's very little." I grin proudly at the teenage boy, taking the bottle from him and carefully passing it on to Charlie. I watch as Charlie holds the bottle high, taking it way out of the animal's reach and his face begins to look a little scared.

"Hold it lower, Charlie – he can't reach it."

The goat's neck is practically distorted as it jumps up to reach the teat, frustrated at it being given and then taken so rudely away.

"Quickly, Charlie." I apply a little weight to his arm, lowering it to a height where the creature can reach it without suffering from goat-induced whiplash. But Charlie whimpers in fear, holding it up high again in a fit of panic.

The goat suddenly takes remedial action and jumps onto its hind legs, reaching up impatiently and bleating with aggression.

"He's jumping on me!" Charlie screams. "Help! Help!"

In reaction his hand flies into the air even higher, taking the bottle with it, while a hungry and frustrated baby goat cries out with distressed anxiety.

Once more it jumps up, balancing on its back legs, and lands with its two hooves on Charlie's lap, where it stresses and strains to reach the milk. Almost eye to eye with Charlie, his bleating sounds become more and more agitated and the teenage volunteer quickly attempts to control the situation. He leans towards Charlie, ready to take the bottle from him, but now tired and angry, the goat resorts to violence and roughly head-butts Charlie causing the bottle to spin from his grip. It catapults through the cattle shed, travelling backwards, and I reluctantly turn to assess the damage, hearing a thud followed by a yelp.

Oh my God. It's hit a child.

The injured child bawls, nursing her head and a frenzy of attention gathers around her.

"Calm down, Charlie, he's not going to hurt you," I say slowly and with a firm reassurance. I watch the young guy running across the shed to retrieve the milk and hope the goat will follow suit. Not a chance. I hear the teenager shout for a first-aid kit, pointing down to the injured child. Her muffled cries fill me with horror and I stand to witness her holding her injured head which has an already impressive swelling. The poor mite must have taken the full force.

Charlie is sitting there deadly still with his eyes firmly shut and his breath sucked in. He's practically turning blue. Quickly – *do something.*

I place my hands beneath the goat's stomach, slowly lifting it from Charlie's lap and holding it close to me. I grimace at the feel of its coarse hair and try counting to ten in a distraction bid. A warm sensation hits my legs followed immediately by a strong putrid smell and I glance down to see drops of urine trickle from him, falling onto jeans that are already soaking wet.

"*Aagghh!*"

In utter horror I release my grip. The goat falls from mid-air, hitting the floor clumsily and yelping as it tries to regain balance. Its hind legs lash out with aggressive punishment and I shriek as my shins take the full force of his assault. Not once, but twice. "*Oouch!*" I bend, doubled over, to rub the throbbing pain and, thrusting my hand up the inside of my jeans, I feel an immediate swelling. A fresh waft of goat's urine rockets up my nose. I suddenly feel ill.

Abandoning the boys I rush outside, gasping for fresh air, desperately trying to remove the taste of urine from the back of my throat by swallowing repeatedly. The burning sensation eases a little but my head is still light and floaty from drawing too many short breaths and the stench is overpowering.

Feeling a little more composed and reluctant to give in to the circus of events, I turn to recommence my childcare duties but the full force of the weight placed on my legs makes me wince and I hobble a little further before stopping dead. My jeans are soaked through. The Caterpillar boots are for the bin. And I stink. My legs hurt beyond belief and my arm is probably in need of a tetanus injection if the inside of Charlie's mouth is as dirty as the outside.

Oh God! *I can't do it. I can't go back in.*

Half-running, half-limping, I rush back to the car and grab my handbag. Scribbling on a blank cheque, I sign it shakily before rushing across to the Sunshine minibus. I glance around, quickly lift the wiper blade and leave the cheque safely underneath it, praying that it won't rain. *Prayers! What use are they?*

That's it. Enough is enough. I've given all I can give and taken all I can take. It's a generous donation and isn't that what these places are crying out for? Money. Bloody army training wouldn't even prepare you for a day like that so it's easier to admit when you're out of your depth and simply surrender. *I surrender.*

I climb into the car and tear away like a joy-rider,

feeling guilty for not saying goodbye to Chantelle but nobody else.

Of all the bloody days! I have the date of my life tonight.

I fight hard with myself not to feel bad about yet another ludicrous episode. What control did I have over it? I did nothing wrong and, as for running off like that, what else could I have done? I've no change of clothes, I stink to high heaven and there was no way on God's earth I was going to perform mouth to mouth on Charlie even if it did look like he needed it. And as for knowing how to handle animals, do I seem like that type of girl?

Working with animals and children definitely isn't my ultimate purpose in life . . . *but as for studs . . . now we're talking . . .*

14

Absolute heaven!

Immersed in a deep warm bath, the water laps around me as my body shuts down into a state of relaxation. A towel is wrapped tightly around my head to stop the humidity from curling my hair, although given how dirty I feel from the inside out it's killing me not washing it. But I just don't have the inclination nor the arm-power right now.

A single injured leg hangs over the side of the bath, nursed by a bag of frozen peas. It's not a bad bump but it's a lot worse than the left which looks unscathed by comparison. It is, however, obvious enough that a change in outfit from skirt to trousers is now required. And for that alone, I'm not happy.

I lean forward, grabbing the loofah, desperate to scrub away the goat's pee which seems to have penetrated my skin. I scrub ferociously. My legs are red and tender but thankfully now rather sweet-smelling so who cares about a little pain? Although self-inflicted pain is much easier to swallow. Being bitten by a human and urinated on by an animal is much less forgiving in my book.

Once again today was a Tina write-off. Why me? Why couldn't I have been given the little girls that Chantelle had dancing and skipping around her with joy and affection? A child who would have looked up to me and decided early on that she wants to be just like me when she grows up. Instead I got the all-biting all-kicking kids from hell.

I must ask Sam if she's planning to start a family after she's married. I've got a few parental tips for her.

Thank goodness I've got this evening to look forward to. I've no idea where Brian is taking me which makes it all the more exciting. And alluring. He sent me a text last night to advise that he will now be picking me up and to dress smart casual. *Whatever!* Once more I'll be going for the kill, starting with the underwear. The better I feel physically, the more easily I can ignore the burning red thighs, bruised shins and bite-marks on my arm, and the choice of a classy cream trouser suit will cover my limbs adequately, giving little away. Perhaps later in the evening things will be a little different. But after a few drinks and dimmed lights, all he will see is the lust in my eyes.

"Hi, Chantelle." I answer the phone reluctantly.

"Tina, where did you get to?"

She's annoyed, I can tell.

"Sorry but I'd had enough, Chantelle! I got bitten, kicked and pissed on in the space of a few hours and I just threw the towel in!"

A howl of laughter vibrates through the receiver and I wait patiently for her to calm down.

"What?" Her voice jumps up an octave. "I saw you with wet jeans but I thought someone had spilled a drink on you or something." She snorts. "Did one of the boys pee on you?" *Here we go.*

"Actually . . . it was the goat," I reply, immediately wishing I had lied to her. "Chantelle. Are you still there?" I can hear muffled noises in the background and someone clearing their throat.

"Yes . . . I'm erm . . . still here." Her voice breaks. "Tina, how did you manage to *phwwrr* . . ."

Once again Chantelle is off but this time there's no stopping her. At least that clipped tone has disappeared. I hate it when she's cross with me because I know I usually deserve it, but on this occasion I think not. I smelled worse than any of the animals there. It would have been a danger to stay any longer, I could have been jumped on or anything. You never know. Don't some animals cover themselves with urine to attract the opposite sex? My escape was both practical and necessary. I shudder at the thought of getting launched on by a horny four-legged creature. Works for some people though! *Yuk!*

I go on to tell Chantelle the whole story, omitting no detail. It seemed no-one knew exactly what had happened given the speed with which I left. Naturally the tight-lipped boys had given nothing away.

I enquire about the little girl with the injured head and am pleased to hear it was nothing serious, just a minor scrape and a swollen forehead. I should really ask if Charlie has started to breathe yet but I'm afraid to.

"Pat was furious when you'd gone, Tina. She said it wasn't any wonder she'd not seen you in church and that girls like you have no staying power for anything, let alone a lifelong relationship with God!" She giggles.

"Cheeky cow," I say angrily. "I've a good mind to stop that bloody cheque."

"I told her you must have been ill or something but I'll ring her to fill her in if you don't mind. I don't want her bad-mouthing you to my grandmother on Sunday."

"You tell her I said she needs a darn good seeing to!" I snap. "That'll bring a smile to that sour old face of hers!"

"Tina, that woman is an MBE on account of the endless charity work she does," Chantelle retorts. "She probably hasn't time for a love life she's so busy putting everybody else before herself."

"Okay, okay, I get your point, Chantelle! But I can't be like her. I tried and it wasn't me. I can't apologise for who I am, or who I'm not, more like."

"Nobody's asking you to apologise, Tina." Chantelle's tone softens. "You're great the way you are, just try not to knock anyone else for being the way *they* are."

"You're right, as always. Cow!" I sigh, conceding to her insightful maturity. "I did try, though, I really did, but it went so wrong from the beginning to the end that I swear I'm jinxed. I'm serious – I have this terrible feeling hanging over me."

"Yes, Tina." Her tone is nonchalant. "It's called guilt."

There is a rap on the door and I take one last glimpse in the mirror. I'm not overly satisfied but I do feel pretty good. Underneath, however, is a different story. My shins are still swollen and after endless scrubbing my legs are patchy and a little raw. The once all-over golden tan has transformed into white thighs decorated with red blotches. On a positive note, the rest of my legs are still bronzed. I did consider scrubbing my entire body so the colour would be consistent but I'd sooner have two pale thighs than an all-over pasty bod.

I grab my clutch bag and open the door nervously.

"Good evening, Miss Harding." Brian bows gently. "Your chariot awaits." He holds out his arm to escort me to the car.

Oh my God. It's a Bentley.

I try to feign little interest as he leads me courteously to the car, before opening the passenger door and standing back with gentlemanly effect as I climb in, thankful of the trouser choice. The door glides silently shut and, as he walks around to the driver's seat, I take in the walnut dashboard and stroke the soft leather interior, wondering just how much this set him back.

Brian catches my look of wonderment. "Do you like it?" he asks nonchalantly.

"Like it? It's amazing!" I retort ecstatically. "What speed can a car like this get up to?"

"A GTC can do up to one hundred and ninety-eight miles per hour and nought to sixty in four point seven seconds."

Holy shit.

The engine starts with quiet sophistication, purring like a thoroughbred cat. *Where's the key?*

I lean to my right a little, checking out the ignition. *Wow. Keyless entry. That would be perfect for me. I'm always losing my car keys.*

Brian presses a button and I look up to see the roof folding back rather elegantly. All I need now is a headscarf and a pair of Jackie O' sunglasses.

"Ready, Miss Harding?"

God, you smell good.

"Ready, Mr Steen," I pant, strapping my seat-belt in place, breathless with exhilaration.

"Hold tight," he teases.

As we pull up on what looks to be a piece of waste land close to the sea, I glance around, wondering where the hell we are and searching for the restaurant while my stomach rumbles away. I could desperately do with a drink! I suddenly remember that I haven't eaten all day and the sweet smell of the dusk air suddenly fuels my appetite.

It's just starting to get dark but the air is still warm and light with a tender, romantic breeze floating through. My stomach churns with excitement as I think of a summer filled with sex, champagne and the wind sweeping through my hair in the open-top Bentley. *Can life get any better?*

As we walk down a bumpy road filled with potholes and loose gravel, I curse my choice of typically impractical shoes as my ankle almost gives for the third time. I look up at Brian quizzically.

"It's over there." He points towards a dimly lit building before taking my arm once again to steady me. "Shackleton's. Heard of it?"

"I can't say I have," I reply truthfully. There's no point lying to him to impress.

"Thought not." He grins.

He takes my hand spontaneously as I stumble again.

A small white villa oozing with Mediterranean charm comes into sight and I sigh with relief at the prospect of sitting down but simultaneously almost cry with disappointment as Brian's soft but manly hand slips from mine.

Inside, a tiny wooden bar filled with every drink imaginable greets us and a rotund balding man scurries around comically. *Where are the other customers? The place is empty.* The dwarf-sized pot-bellied man grabs Brian's hand, shaking it vigorously, slapping him on his lower back with his other hand before reaching up to kiss him on both cheeks. Brian stoops down kindly to allow easy reach and returns the back pat, but not the kisses.

"Tina, this is Serge." Brian rests his hand on Serge's shoulder. "One of the finest chefs in the country who has kindly agreed to come out of retirement for the evening." He looks at me intently. "Just for you."

I'm speechless. What on earth can I say to that? I lunge forward towards Serge in an act of appreciation and kiss him on both cheeks. Manners are manners.

"*Enchanté, Mademoiselle. Vous êtes très belle!*" Serge takes hold of me, pushing me away at arm's length to cast his squinting eyes over me. His hands slide down my arms and clasp my hands once more.

I wince with the friction as the bite wound throbs.

"Mademoiselle, what 'as 'appened?" His face is a picture of genuine concern.

Like hell I'm going to tell either of these two about my day's events.

"Oh nothing, I have a slight bruise on my arm, that's all."

"Allow me to distract you with my culinary delights, my daahhling!" Serge laughs a deep hearty laugh more appropriate to a rugby player than a midget.

He takes us through a set of doors onto a candlelit

patio and I take in the sea view. The tide is out but the potent scent of salt and seaweed still linger heavily and the breeze dances around us, a little more up-tempo than earlier.

A single table is set for two.

A multitude of candles protected by colourful glass bulbs hang from timber beams. The flames shimmy energetically, taunting the wind as it tries to seek out their hiding places but to no avail. Speckles of colour flash across Brian's face and I notice he is just staring at me. But it doesn't feel uncomfortable.

"What is this place, Brian?" I whisper, bewildered by a day which is becoming more bizarre by the minute.

"It's his home," he replies matter of factly. "Serge had a chain of London restaurants but sold them all about ten years ago. He retired early but still cooks for a select few on demand." He grins. "And I, Miss Harding, appear to be one of the select few!" His cockiness for once is endearing.

"He's probably heard of Harding Homes," I say, tongue in cheek. "I reckon he wants to sell this place and is looking for reduced fees!"

"Talking about work for a moment, how are you getting on with the contracts?"

Since the first day we met I haven't seen him look so serious. The twinkle in his aqua eyes has disappeared. Just like that.

"Actually, Brian, that's on my to-do list for Monday morning." *I'm not lying, honestly.* "I know how those guys work and not to give them a good couple of weeks to put the feelers out would only put them under a level of pressure they're not capable of handling."

That playful sparkle is back, only sexier than ever. Brian just nods and smiles at me affectionately. His prominent cheekbones are just to die for and he looks like he's done something different to his hair this evening although I can't quite pinpoint what it is. Looks good though and by God does he smell amazing!

My groin aches with desperation as I stare at his large manly hands with perfectly manicured nails, wondering just how they're going to feel later on as they wander around my body, exploring every bit of it. Inside and out.

No no no! Simon's smooth touch floods my thoughts and I groan loudly as I recall his knee pressing up against the crotch of the silk lingerie.

"What is it, Tina?"

Oh, well, actually, Brian, there's this other guy who was supposed to be you but . . . !

"I have a bruise on my leg. I just knocked it," I lie convincingly. I'm beginning to sound like a victim of domestic violence.

"I'll kiss it better for you later if you like?"

Serge flies through the doors before I have the chance to reply which is possibly a good thing given we're out in public. Almost. His arms are laden with brightly coloured plates and he sets them down in front of us.

"Meze," he points, "you like?"

"I love." I smile at him appreciatively. *I love? I've only been around him five minutes!* Now this is my type of food.

He runs back and forth delivering more and more sumptuous dishes before the long-awaited wine arrives.

Brian notices my eyes light up as I catch sight of the

bottle and he casts me a cautious glance. I screw my nose up at him, trying to look cute, but at the same time letting him know that a repeat performance simply won't happen. But God knows after the day I've had, I really do need a bottle of wine to calm me down.

We tuck into the appetizers and I think back to our first date where I barely touched the meal because I was so nervous and almost too shy to eat in front of him, but tonight something feels different. I'm not sure if it's because I've already made a complete idiot of myself or if it's because you can never truly recapture that first date magic. Although this is a very close call.

My teeth plunge into a tightly wrapped stuffed vine-leaf and fragments of rice fall from my lips and bounce down on to the plate in front of me. I glance across at Brian to see if he has noticed and his face is in a fixed grin, demonstrating once again the art of perfect dentistry. He is all but laughing at me as he bites neatly on a piece of toasted pitta bread loaded with chilli-flavoured hummus. Not even a smidgen remains in the corners of his mouth. *How can anyone be so perfect?* Embarrassed, I delicately dab my lips with the napkin before replacing it back on my lap. *Stop grinning at me.*

Shifting uncomfortably in the hard wicker chair, I look away, momentarily unsure of what to do or say right now, particularly to a man who gives so little away and is not someone I've fully managed to suss out. Mentally. Nor physically for that matter.

I hear him cough gently and take this as my cue to make eye contact. But instead Brian's eyes are glued to a small parcel in the centre of the table. *I didn't notice that before.*

"It's for you. Open it." He pushes it towards me, weaving it expertly between the plates laden with olives and freshly caught mussels.

"What is it?" I finally manage, staring at the box and wondering what the hell is in there and in fact *why*?

Lifting it, I pull gently on the gold satin ribbon, watching as it falls on to my plate. Pulling back the taped-down flaps, the thick gold paper tears loudly, echoing noisily in the stillness around us. A racing-green box reveals itself and I quickly remove it from the remaining paper. *Oh my God!* I gently lift the heavy lid, desperate to make contact with its contents, and gasp for breath on beholding the exclusive gift.

It dazzles effortlessly. The mother-of-pearl face is surrounded by ten small diamonds and a heavy platinum bracelet secures it together. It gleams up at me, yelling expense, and I simply stare at it dumbstruck. I don't even notice what time it says. Shaking my head, I look up at Brian, gob-smacked, and wonder if I should consider giving it back. *Over my dead body! This is the stuff you dream of!*

"I don't know what to say." I'm speechless for once. "You really shouldn't have. Honestly." *But am I glad you did!*

Brian gazes back at me fondly, lifting his wineglass and holding it towards mine. "I wasn't sure if the Rolex was the right choice. I was torn between a Cartier and that one."

"It's perfect, Brian. Thank you so much."

Chink. His glass delicately touches off mine.

"Don't worry." He winks provocatively. "You can make it up to me in other ways."

"You make me sound like a high-class hooker!" I retort, suddenly feeling a little cheap.

"Here's hoping."

I shudder with cold, tightly wrapping my cream jacket around me as far as it will stretch. One of my arms is stinging like hell (not the human-bite-decorated one) and I've spent the last hour with my hand up my sleeve scratching away violently. My head is fuzzy and flu-like and, although I'm shivering, my body feels like it's on fire.

Knocking back the rest of the wine I attempt to drown out this horrible feeling, determined to let nothing get in the way of this night of passion. But my body is aching, my glands feel sore and my arm is burning away.

Brian returns from the bathroom and I stand shakily to greet him and to embrace Serge with true thanks for a wonderful evening. Not a hint of French cuisine but wonderful all the same. The floor rises to meet me and I slowly put one foot over the other as the room starts to spin around in slow motion.

We make our way towards the door but I grab hold of the bar, steadying myself as a heavy faintness kicks in.

"Tina, what's wrong?"

I can't answer. My throat is dry and my face feels numb as I clutch onto the uneven wood before my knees give way beneath me and everything turns dark.

"Tina!" A distant voice echoes. "Wake up, dear!"

I try to move but my body is weak and lifeless.

"Can you hear me, Tina?"

My eyes flicker involuntarily, weighed down under the heavy lids hell-bent on keeping themselves closed. I feel like a sheet of lead has been laid over me, pinning me down from head to foot. But, with an overwhelming dryness in my mouth, I force myself to come to. At least I know I'm not dead. Although the lights are very bright. Even with my eyes closed I can feel them burning down on me.

Prising my eyes apart, I squint up at the light and quickly lower my vision for comfort. That was a little too bright.

A pale blue curtain separates me from the rest of the world and through a small gap I take in another bed opposite mine with another body. Lying still. Little else appears to be happening until a woman looking to be well past retirement age leans over me, smiling reassuringly.

"Hello, Tina."

"Where am I?" I croak. "Who are you?"

God, do I need water!

"I am Sister Hayes. You're in the Royal Hospital, dear, but you're alright." She pats my hand sympathetically. "You've had quite a nasty reaction to an insect bite though," she explains, picking up the case notes hanging over the end of the bed.

I lift my head up to observe the seriousness of the situation and glance down at my arm. It's swollen and covered in blisters with some form of revolting liquid seeping from them. A needle is in my hand, taped down with a transparent plaster. I trace the plastic tubing to an IV drip and gape up at the drip chamber, wondering what the hell it's administering.

I shriek hysterically.

"It's not as bad as it appears, dear," she soothes. "We've covered your arm in an antiseptic cream called Crotamiton and the drip in your hand is dosing you with a mixture of antihistamine and steroids which will get you well in no time."

What?

My head slumps back, hitting the pillow hard, and my cheeks warm as wet tears slide down them running behind my ears, nesting in the nape of my neck. *This can't be happening to me.*

"My sister gets married in a week," I begin to sob. "How long will it take for these things to go away?"

Sister Hayes thrusts a wad of tissues in my hand before patting it in a motherly fashion. "They should be gone in a couple of weeks providing you keep using the cream and take the full course of antibiotics." She leans closer to me, examining my face, just inches away. "The rash on your face should be gone within a few days though." She beams. "Lucky we got you here in time, otherwise you would have looked much worse."

Please, God, not my face! Oh no! Please!

"D-do you have a mirror, p-p-please?" My voice breaks with terror as I prepare to take a magnified look at myself. "*Aaahh!*"

The taxi pulls up outside the family home late the following afternoon and a familiar comfort relaxes me to the point of tears. Again.

I hand over the cash drearily and prise myself out of the seat, slowly walking down the gravelled driveway, swaying from side to side. The front door flings open and my dad rushes out.

"Tina, love, you should have called me to get you."
He puts his fatherly arm around my shoulder and helps
me into the house.

I shrug weakly. "I'm fine, Dad," I lie.

He steadies me as we cross the threshold.

Mum appears and stares in horror.

"Tina!" she exclaims. "Your face!"

She rushes over to me for closer inspection. "But the
wedding is next week! Will it be gone by then?"

"Veronica!" Dad snaps angrily as he leads me into the
living room. "Don't you think she feels bad enough
without you adding to it?" He shakes his head at her as
he sits me down and fixes cushions behind my back.
"Why does everything you bloody-well say or do revolve
around appearance?"

My mum is shocked. As am I. Dad rarely flips but
sadly he speaks the truth. My mother is the primary
reason for my obsessiveness about my own façade. Not
that she's ever made me feel like I needed to make such
efforts but she has always maintained that looking good
on the outside is the key to feeling good on the inside.
Any well-balanced person, however, will tell you it's the
other way around.

Chastised and forlorn, Mum brings in a tray of tea
and toast – comfort food. I gratefully tuck in.

"What happened to your date, darling?" Mum asks
sweetly after a long pause.

I slurp the tea noisily, staring into a corner of the
room, feeling extremely tired. And sore. And itchy. "I
told the nurses to send him home. There was no way I
was going to let him see me like that, Mum," I answer
her nonchalantly.

"But Christie, darling, hadn't he already seen you by that stage?" she questions me gently.

I ignore her. I don't want to think about that.

"Don't you think that was a little mean?" she persists. "I'm sure he was rather worried about you?"

Suddenly, the enormity of the situation grabs me and my head sinks into my hands as long-drawn-out sobs come out. I think about the ridiculousness of this hateful day. I was only trying to help people – you know, put a little back into the community but look what it's damned well got me. A human bite, smelly abuse from a goat and a gruesome insect attack. Plus a second bloody ruined night with Brian. How many times can a man like that wait? He's a human being, for God's sake.

"Why me, Mum?" I wail, sinking my head onto her shoulder as she pulls me towards her tenderly, stroking my hair. "I – won't – even – be – ab – le – to – go – to Sam's – w-wedding now!" I cry relentlessly as Mum and Dad continue to pass positive comments in soothing tones best kept for babies. Right now I want to be babied and held tight and secure.

"Nonsense, love!" Dad chirps positively. "Look on the bright side – you'll have that lovely Simon bloke to look after you."

Then he just stares at me open-mouthed as the wails reach maximum decibels.

"Was it something I said, dear?"

15

"Tina! Tina!" Chantelle screeches loudly as the stairs thunder with her ascent.

I'm spending the day tucked away in the upstairs office until my leprosy disfigurement has died down and I'm so not in the mood for small talk. The door is unusually closed today, given how I feel about having an open-door management policy, but Chantelle flies through it at breakneck speed, sending it crashing into the wall behind.

"Calm down, Chantelle," I say abruptly. "Otherwise you'll be the next one in hospital." I don't actually mean for that to sound so threatening! She stands in the middle of the floor, panting and waving a collection of papers in her hand.

"They're in!" she cries. "They've come in, Tina!"

"What are you on about?"

I push myself out of the chair and go over to her, placing my hand on her forehead. She is a bit warm.

"The contracts!" she screams, thrusting the letters in my face. Literally.

"What?" I snatch them from her before they

suffocate me. My eyes scan them one by one and suddenly the tears slowly run down my face. I can only put it down to a mixture of sheer fatigue and anxiety, but of late crying seems to have become a normal part of everyday life. I don't know what's been happening to me these days but I can't seem to put a foot right.

I reread the letters and then pass them to Chantelle to read again. And again. Just to make sure.

"Tina, do you realise that's eight of the fifteen apartments sold?" She holds out her hand with the palm faced up, pretending to use it as a calculator, and presses invisible buttons. "Erm, yes," she taps away, "that's erm . . . loads of money! Huge amounts of money!" She squeals, running around to the other side of the desk, throwing her tiny frame down heavily in the black leather chair, using her feet to spin herself around and around.

I feel sick just watching her.

"God, Chantelle, that's so weird. I had this on my to-do list today. I was going to phone every agent from the contact list just this morning as it happens. Spooky."

Chantelle stops spinning and slumps further down into the chair, looking a little green. "Well, isn't it a good job I beat you to it?" she boasts, tongue in cheek. "You seem to have been a bit preoccupied lately, Tina, so when you were out last week viewing the new premises I thought I'd take some pressure off you and do it myself. *Et voilà*!" She gestures to the post once more, grinning proudly.

I rush over to her and fling my face and body on hers, squeezing her tightly. Partly with relief and partly with pure adoration.

"I so don't know what I'd do without you, Chantelle," I tell her earnestly.

"Can I make a suggestion?"

"Yeah, what is it?"

"Take you're scabby face off mine," she says seriously. "This face has seven more apartments to sell and if the pair of us look like lepers we might as well just shut up shop now!"

Things are starting to come together and my mood lifts like a balloon, light and floaty but still a little vulnerable. I leave Chantelle in charge of contacting the remaining agents with a deliberate hook of advising them that, in just a matter of weeks, more than half of these prestigious homes have been sold. They snooze, they lose! Okay, so no deposits have been paid yet but eight of the signed contracts are in from the agents and accompanying each of these is the specific name of the person they already have lined up to make the purchase.

Steen Developments' reputation has certainly made light work for us and coupled with the docklands location, only two out of the eight buyers actually want to bother with viewings. The rest of them have simply turned the pages of the rich, glossy brochure, sighted the location and turnkey specifics and hey presto, case closed. *Sold*.

The only drawback now is that I need to ring Brian to both thank him and apologise for Saturday night, again, and to ask for his advice about the new office given we're well on our way to affording it now. I certainly don't want to lose it. The rent is reasonable, location perfect and the floor space is double what we're used to.

Once again I'm racked with guilt about my treatment of Brian. Never in my entire life have I treated a guy so sought-after so badly. But then again, never have I puked over a guy on one occasion and passed out on him the next and, if I didn't know better, I'd be questioning just how destined we were to be together. I've heard of someone '*constantly seeking new challenges*' but this has to take the biscuit.

Pulling up into the church car park my stomach sinks down into my feet and I drag them heavily from the car, sluggishly walking towards the entrance. A host of other cars including my parents' are already parked up and I glance at my watch to check I'm not late. I guess everyone else is just early.

The church where the wedding will take place is St Martin's, the oldest church in Liverpool. Built in 1856 of red sandstone, its huge stone pillars dominate the entrance like a wide-open mouth sitting, ready to devour you. I shudder as I pass through, expecting a set of teeth to come gnashing down on me, shouting '*Heathen!*'. Weddings, funerals, christenings, that's about all I seem to manage when it comes to religion although in years gone by I was an avid churchgoer, but found that hangovers and Sunday mornings simply weren't that harmonious.

Inside the church it is breathtakingly beautiful and the fourteenth-century Gothic design feels both eerie and yet calming at the same time. The aisle elongates itself into an Oscar-winning red carpet leading up to an altar overshadowed by a thirty-foot stained-glass window. Flickers of rainbow-coloured light shadow the stone walls and the font water glows with a still florescent joy. The intricately carved pulpit stands at the passage to the choir vestry where rows of solid pews sit in silent symmetry. On the opposite side, the church organ boldly commands its position, armoured with endless brass pipes extending into orbit.

I stop dead as I see both families sitting in the first few rows, chatting away. Bravely putting one foot in front of the other, I slowly walk towards them, wondering what the hell to say to Simon when he arrives. The walk seems to go on forever and for the first time I can truly empathise with nervous brides. It looks so easy when someone else does it but keeping your poise, balance and getting the speed right is more tricky than it looks. Not that I'm practising of course. My snail's pace is down to sheer reluctance, nothing more.

"Tina!" A radiant Sam rushes over to me, hugging me tightly. Her bright eyes sparkle and her happy soul oozes a hypnotic charm.

"You look wonderful, Sam," I tell her with sincerity.

"Mum's only just told me about you, Tina." She frowns. "Why didn't you ring me?"

I shrug my shoulders. "Didn't think, to be honest. I just wanted out of there, Sam, and the less people that saw me in that state the better."

She inspects me closely. "Your face looks okay. Let's have a look at your arm." I roll my sleeve up to show her the burst blisters, lifting the stretchy bandage so she can peek underneath. She shudders.

"What are you like!" she laughs softly. "That type of thing normally happens to me." Her face suddenly turns serious and she steps back. "Is it contagious?"

"Very," I smirk, lurching towards her, pulling monster-like faces, pretending to smite her.

"Suits you," a voice murmurs in my ear.

Oh God, he's arrived.

Sam belts out a raucous laugh before kissing Simon on the cheek. She links him tenderly, leading him up to where it's all happening as I follow gingerly two paces behind, frantically waiting for the lobster face to die down.

Why is my timing always so very wrong?

"Okay, *go!*" the vicar shouts excitedly.

He extends his right leg, followed inevitably by his left, and marches down the aisle comically, looking like John Cleese on a bad day. He glances behind him to check we are in tow but then stops abruptly. Sam and Dad's close proximity to him almost causes a pile-up.

"No, no, no!" he tuts, throwing his arms around. He gestures for the organist to stop playing. "It's step together, step together." He gives a six-foot-four lanky demonstration of his expectations. "Sam, if you walk that fast you'll not give anyone the chance to see what you look like. This is your day to relish in the attention – so take as long as you want."

"You know you want to, Sam," I say.

"Whatever," she retorts giddily.

Manhandled into position, we go back to the very basics of mastering this simple yet seemingly complicated part of the ceremony. The walk.

Standing at the very back of the church, I observe Timothy rubbing shoulders with Simon as they stand close together at the top. Both men are angled side-on for the best view of the bride. The two mothers and Major Heath Jones are sitting in the same pew. Although that won't happen on the day. The vicar is at the front entrance, a few feet before me and bible-armed, and my dad and Sam are safely tucked in the middle, linked arm in arm, poised and ready for action.

"Okay?" The vicar checks behind him.

Sam and my dad nod in concentration.

"*Go!*" yells the vicar and I watch as my dad practically yanks Sam's arm from her socket, dragging her down the aisle at full speed.

A giggle escapes from my mouth, followed by a frustrated squeal by Sam. We reach the altar in what seems like a millisecond.

My dad shuffles uncomfortably. "Sorry, love." He turns to Sam, white as a ghost. "I'm just a bit nervous. I'll be fine on the day."

"Don't worry, Dad." She leans forward to kiss his cheek. "You'll be great on the day."

Who's the one getting married here!

"Dad, if you drag *me* down the aisle that fast on *my* wedding day," I say, "I'll make you parade the entire church!"

"Tina, you'll be so concerned about people looking at you, poor dad will have shackles on his feet!" Sam blurts through stifled giggles.

"Hey, thanks, Sam, I never thought of that."

We high-five each other.

The rest of the rehearsal runs smoothly and Simon manages to effortlessly relieve the tension by pretending to have forgotten the wedding rings. *Highly original.* The entire party cracks up, grateful for the excuse to laugh and to rid themselves of that pent-up emotion only a family affair can bring. Before that, you could have cut the air with a knife.

The obligatory all-hugging all-kissing '*see you on the day*' farewells come to an end and Simon leans forward to kiss me on the cheek. I wait for the repercussions of our last encounter.

"I didn't recognise you with your clothes on," he whispers in my ear.

Here we go!

Stunned and beetroot (at least from the chest up), I look away, mortified, but he laughs a kind and forgiving laugh so I risk making eye contact with him. It's clear to see he is trying to make light of the situation.

"Fancy a swift one?"

"A what one?" I stutter. Still scarlet.

"A drink? I want to talk to you about decorating the bridal suite." His voice is low and slightly husky.

"Oh right." I nod in slow motion, deliberately stalling my decision while I quickly think of a get out clause. "A drink?" I repeat dumbly.

"That's right, Tina." Simon raises his eyebrows. "Comes in a glass, you swallow it!" He roars with laughter. "Actually, that does sound rather rude, doesn't it?"

Shaking my head and observing his ludicrous grin and slightly impish face, I find myself laughing at his stupidity and sense of humour. Although it is alarmingly vulgar. There is something about Simon that tells me he'll be in student mode until his retirement.

A drink? With a proper agenda? What harm could that do?

I don't have a problem in conceding. It's for a good cause and let's face it there'll be no avoiding him now, what with the wedding taking place next week and us being in-laws. Almost. We'll have to walk down the aisle together at the end of the marriage ceremony and we, and our parents, have been instructed to carry out the first dance. Have you ever heard the likes of it? Sam reckons it will take the pressure off her and Tim doing it. *Hello?* Like no-one's going to notice the bride and groom are missing from the dance floor. For someone so intelligent, she can be bloody dopey at times.

"Okay, just a quick one."

Simon extends a friendly arm for me to link and we march down the aisle together, worryingly in synch and without a smidgen of rehearsal. We couldn't have carried out the real thing with such ease of expertise.

"A quick one, eh?" he snorts. "Never had you down as that type of girl!"

Slap!

"Ouch."

The engine revs loudly as we pull away from the churchyard. Simon eases gently through the wrought-iron gates before joining the main road and flooring it.

"Slow down, Simon. It's a forty zone," I lecture, gripping the door handle tightly.

"I'm only doing forty-five – it just feels faster because you're sitting so low down."

I take a sneaky peek at the speed count. He's right.

"This car is so old now but I can't bear to get rid of her." He strokes the leather steering wheel. "Plus the insurance has only just become affordable! Turning thirty has some benefits, don't you find?"

"How do you know I'm even thirty?" *Cheeky boy.*

"I asked your sister." He grins. "She told me all about you."

"Really? What else did she tell you?"

202

"She told me that you've yet to meet your match, but when you do you won't like it and you'll fight it." His grin drops momentarily. "And so you'll probably stuff up like you always do."

"How dare you, Simon! You don't even kno–"

"I'm quoting your sister. That's what Sam said about you," he interrupts calmly.

"Well, that's where she's wrong," I snap coldly. "I've already met him. I know it and I like it and I'm not *stuffing up!*" I glance down at the sparking Rolex, wondering how on earth no-one has noticed it. "I have well and truly met him."

The rest of the evening goes reasonably well and Simon keeps me entertained by leaking the secrets of his office politics. A euphemism for who is shagging whom. I'm dying to ask about his past or even present girlfriends while we're on the subject but I dare not. Not directly.

"So are you bringing a guest to the wedding?" I enquire, risking it.

"Nope. You?"

I shake my head without hesitation. "You know what, Simon, this day is so important to me that I simply wouldn't want any distractions. My role that day is to indulge my sister and give her all the attention she deserves. Nothing less." I mean it hand on heart. Even Brian doesn't come close to Sam.

"You and Sam are pretty close, aren't you?" Simon's face turns pensive for the first time all evening. "I'd love for Tim and me to have been like that, or even to be like that. But he was always the Goody Two Shoes while I was the rebel." He smiles. "But with a cause!"

My gut reaction is to laugh in agreement. With his

overbearing father and a wife who can't hold her own, I understand how rebelling might have been the answer. But I don't laugh. They're still someone else's parents. Not mine thankfully, but I would hate to offend by commenting on his unfortunate biological makers.

"Your mother is pretty quiet, isn't she?" I venture.

Simon scratches his stubbly chin. His nails are jagged and uneven unlike Brian's perfectly manicured smooth hands. "She's always been quiet," he says pensively. "She's quite the comedian after a few drinks though." He grins. "Usually when she has centre stage." He pauses, stone-faced. "Which is only when my dad is not around."

I sense a degree of frustration around his father and can't help but compare him to my own. My dad was a real hands-on dad who taught us to ride our bikes, put up a tent and catch tadpoles with a home-made fishing rod made from a twig and a pair of laddered tights. Not his tights of course! He's a man's man, is my dad. He was and still is a warm and caring man who would whistle while leaving for work in the morning and sing coming home at night no matter how long or tiresome his day was. It was he who paid for all my dance and drama lessons although my mother took the credit for it and still does. My dad has never asked for even so much as a thank-you. He has no expectations whatsoever apart from that old cliché called happiness.

"What was it like growing up with your dad? He can be quite overpowering, can't he?" I chance.

"You mean he *is* overpowering? And overbearing, obnoxious, chauvinistic and loud?" He laughs a half laugh and I wonder where the other half went to.

"Are you mad about it?" I probe him with genuine concern.

"Not for me." He stiffens. "But for my mother. I . . ." He stops talking.

"What is it, Simon?"

"I always thought she deserved better than him." His body relaxes and his pale skins flushes with warmth. "She's such a beautiful woman and I just want her to have whatever it is that makes her happy."

"Hey, maybe we should match my mother with your dad!" I chortle. "She'd sort him out in no time. She's nobody's fool."

Simon's face drops. "My mother is certainly no fool, Tina," he says coolly.

"Oh God, no. Erm, I really didn't mean it like that . . . I just mean that . . ."

Simon smirks at me from ear to ear. That same cheeky grin he wears whenever he scores a point against me. "Gotcha!"

Whatever!

"Thanks for coming, Brian," I say sheepishly as we survey my potential new premises. "And thanks again for looking after me on Saturday."

"Any gentleman would have done the same, Tina, although you should have called me to take you home."

I don't answer him. The explanation is far too obvious to leave my lips.

"What a shock we got!" he says. "You were fine one minute and on the floor the next. Poor Serge nearly had a heart attack. He thought he had poisoned you!" His hand reaches out touching my shoulder and I shudder at his gentle touch, longing to reach up and charge into battle with his slightly parted lips.

"Nothing to the shock I got waking up in hospital! And how did you not notice? Did you not see my face . . . erm . . . changing colour as the night went on?"

"It was so dark on that veranda, I could barely see you as it was! As the night wore on, I caught the odd snippet over a flicker of candlelight but that was it."

"Well, Mr Steen, I'd usually say aren't you unlucky! But given my facial attack I'm quite relieved to hear that."

"You look fine now though, Miss Harding." He takes a step closer to me until our bodies are inches apart. *It's awfully hot in here.* "More than fine. Delicious in fact."

"I feel fine . . . now . . . thanks." *Not here, no way!*

The place reeks of stale ice cream and the neglected tables, crippled with damp, look set to crumble should even a feather land on them, never mind two bodies. And besides I'm not prepared. Not physically nor mentally. *Is my underwear even matching?* Absolutely not here! No way.

Brian's soft lips thrust onto mine and the pressure of his lunging tongue forces me backwards step by step until I'm pressed up against the wall behind. Trapped. His manly hands grip my waist, tickling me just below the ribcage, and I long for them to move lower down.

Oh what the hell!

I manoeuvre us into the back of the building where we can't be seen through the filthy glass windows. Unlikely, given the state of them, but I'm taking no chances. Our feet shuffle together clumsily as our lips remain firmly locked together, unwilling to do anything else. His grunts become louder and louder and I feel his manliness twitching away beneath his tailored trouser suit. My hand feels for it over the expensive material, getting the bearings of where it starts and finishes and I slowly rub it from base to tip, almost sending him over the edge. I can't believe my actions and I do feel like some type of two-bit hooker subconsciously repaying him for the Rolex as he suggested. But it's not that. It's just that no matter how carefully these romantic dates have been planned, they haven't worked out, so I'm going to darn-well grab this opportunity while I can.

His kisses become more frantic and he pulls my hand away, grabbing my wrist and holding it firmly away from his anatomy. As I try to wrestle free he takes hold of my other wrist and pushes them both above my head, pinning them against the wall with a single hand as his tongue continues its attack. But I don't bother with the defence. He uses his foot to push my legs apart before thrusting his knee up against my crotch, teasing it with tiny knee-lifts, increasing the pressure with each jolt. His free hand brushes over my nipple and I yelp with delight, feeling it harden instantly. His hand thrusts up beneath the camisole top and he roughly lifts up my bra, pushing it up to expose both breasts, soft with throbbing blood-filled nipples. He lets go of my hands, leaving his own free to cup both breasts before taking one of them into his mouth. He kisses it like he kissed me on the lips, flicking his tongue around, sucking it, biting it. All a little rougher than I imagined but who's complaining? My back arches in spasm and I pull at his trouser belt, yanking it aggressively before releasing the buckle.

Then, as my hands journey back to undo his trousers, he stops me dead.

Don't stop!

I reach up to resume our kiss, frustrated at the interval. The only interval where I so don't need a comfort break.

"Sshh!"

I look up at him vacantly, conscious that my breasts are hanging alone and throbbing. In fact they're feeling rather neglected.

"Did you hear something?" he whispers.

I listen for a microsecond before throwing myself onto him once more, biting his bottom lip like a Jack Russell. There's no escape from this grip.

Suddenly, the door slams and I freeze. I hear the sound of voices and footsteps travel across the worn flooring.

Shit shit shit. I must have booked a viewing for this time! Or Chantelle did and I didn't check!

Frantically, I pull the bra down followed by the camisole top, straightening my skirt back to its traditional knee length while Brian speedily fixes his belt and flattens down his hair.

"What shall we do?" I whisper inaudibly.

Brian coughs loudly. "This wall is a partition wall so it's easy enough to come down." His voice is formal and assertive. "You'll definitely need to look at rewiring though and refitting the kitchen upstairs is a must if you want to maximise all of the available floor space downstairs."

I join in the game with utter reluctance but the situation calls for it. "Right. Right." I nod, catching sight of two people out of the corner of my eye. "Can I leave you to come back to me with quotes for the work, please? As soon as possible if you don't mind."

"Consider it done," he replies before turning to leave.

"Hello!" He gestures to the suited guys standing in the way of our exit. "We've got company, it appears." His voice is wooden and unconvincing.

"Hello there!" I chirp. "We've finished the viewing now, it's all yours."

We brush past the guys with our sharp exit.

Outside, Brian lets out a frustrated moan while I stifle giggles at his pathetic attempts at acting.

"Tina, come back with me," he groans.

"To where?"

"My place."

I hesitate for a moment but shake my head reluctantly.

"Brian, I can't. I really can't." My diary has scheduled valuations on the hour for the rest of the afternoon. Unlike him, I can't afford to pay someone else to do the job, not yet anyway, so it's all hands on deck.

He throws his jacket across his arm, pulling his car keys from his trouser pocket. "You know something, Miss Harding?" he protests. "If I didn't know better I'd think we were jinxed!"

He shakes his keys, clearly agitated and dispirited. "You don't have some sort of bad curse hanging over me, do you?"

"Not over you!" I answer brusquely. "But I'm bloody well beginning to wonder if there's a curse over me!"

16

Chink!

Our glasses slam together as we toast the bride once more.

"To Sam!" we cheer.

"To the girl we thought was still a virgin!" Jessie squeals.

Sam rolls her eyes, as reluctant as ever to be dragged into any conversation concerning her personal life. "Just because I didn't put myself about, Jess!" she retorts boldly.

"You didn't put yourself anywhere, Sam, apart from in a bloody library!"

We laugh in chorus.

"Now, now, children." I step in to protect my sister even though I know Jess is right. "Look at Kate and me – we put out with everyone going in our student days but our Sam is the only non-singleton amongst us. She must be doing something right." I pat her hand patronisingly. "Exactly what are we doing wrong, Sam?" I ask, only half-joking. She's one step closer to passing *Go* than I am. Funny, after all these years when I always thought Sam was the complete nerd who would be stuck on the shelf while I would be married to some handsome tycoon, carrying our beautiful children on my slender hips while handing out autographs. It never dawned on me that she would have the high-flying career, retro apartment and be married first. The fact that she's carrying a little extra weight and has no fashion sense hardly seems relevant now. Life has a funny way of working out.

"Your problem, Tina, is that you expect too much," she replies, slightly slurred in speech. She's only had three drinks.

It was a rhetorical question actually, Sam.

"You want the fairytale and it doesn't exist."

Will someone please steer the conversation away from my love life and quick?

"*Pretty Woman* was a film," she continues. "That crap doesn't happen in real life!" She takes a gulp of wine, placing the glass clumsily on the wooden floor. *Crack!* The stem breaks in two and the glass falls on its side with the red content spilling out across the beech-laminate flooring. "Oops!" she hiccups.

"Don't move." Jess uses her long nails to collect the large pieces of glass followed by the smaller fragments while I run into the kitchen to grab the kitchen roll and duster-buster. These wet and dry things are a godsend. How did our parents cope with such a lack of appliances and gadgets? And Rabbits?

Kate follows me in. "How much has she had?" she says under her breath.

"Not enough, Kate! It's her hen night and if she remembers it then we've let her down!"

Kate claps her hands together with spiteful glee. She

can be such a bitch sometimes. "Oh, you're so mean!" she says, sending the blame back to me with a boomerang effect. "But I've never seen Sam drunk before so I'm in for it!" We high-five each other before returning to the lounge to clean up the mess.

I'm so glad Kate has made it. She has always been a major part of my life, and Sam's, that it would seem strange giving my sister a send-off without my side-kick next to me. When we were nearing sixteen Mum and Dad let us go out into town one night with Sam. I remember it like it was yesterday. She took us to a bar where you had to be twenty-one to enter. But in we walked with Sam and Jason, one of her past dorky boyfriends. We couldn't believe it, the bouncers just let us glide right past them. Inside, Kate and I stood there feeling so grown-up, gulping cider and black until our pocket money had dissipated. We were plastered in Constance Carroll make-up, with hair six feet high permeated with a full can of Insette hair spray. I swear it was us who damaged the ozone layer. Shortly after the gap in the ozone was announced, the hairspray was reinvented with a CFC-friendly logo on it. It never worked as well. How strange. Looking back we must have been a hilarious sight with our theatrical make-up and granny boots. But that was the fashion in the eighties and like all teenagers, experimenting is all a part of growing up. Sam just let us get on with it and no matter what we got up to, or who we got off with more like, she never said anything to our parents and she kept everything we did top secret. We thought she was the coolest big sister in the universe. In some ways, I still do.

"I know, let's play Fuzzy Duck!" Kate suddenly screams, jumping up from the floor, giving us a flash of her underwear from beneath a skirt that barely covers her bottom. She grabs two more bottles from the kitchen and quickly returns and refills our glasses to the brim.

"How do you play that?" Sam asks.

She really is clueless.

Kate explains the rules of the game where we each take turns to say 'Fuzzy Duck' until someone stuffs up and gets it wrong. But it's clear to see that Sam can't quite see the humour in its simple repetition; not in theory anyway.

"Sam, stop asking questions and just play, will you?" Kate chides, never one to mince her words. "Just remember that when someone says 'Does he?' the game reverses and you have to say 'ducky fuzz', which is the reverse to 'fuzzy duck'. Get it?" She snorts loudly, winking at me. She and I are experts at this game – we learned it on our first Club Eighteen to Thirty holiday. We were just eighteen and it was our first holiday away together. We made a pact that when we had graduated we would return to become holiday reps. That way we could party day and night and get paid for it. Perfect!

"You start, Tina," Kate orders.

"Fuzzy duck," I say, looking to Jess.

"Fuzzy duck!" Jess belts out, clapping with excitement.

"Fuzzy duck," Sam joins in with monotone boredom.

A wickedness breaks across Kate's face.

"Does he?" she says, and turns back to Sam.

Sam looks at Kate. "Does he fuck," she says deadpan.

We keel over with laughter, screaming and pointing at her drink while she sits there oblivious and we wait for the penny to drop. This makes the situation all the more comical as she hasn't a bloody clue that she's said it wrong. But that's the beauty of such a stupidly simple game. "In one – in one – in one!" we cry, thrusting her wineglass at her.

"Oh no!" Sam's hands clasp her face as the realisation of what she said becomes clear. "I got it wrong! I said 'does he fuck' instead of 'fuck he does' . . . oh God . . . what is it again?"

"Now do you see the humour in the game, you great big square?" Jess ridicules.

Unable to answer, Sam's wineglass covers her face as she knocks back the Rioja in one impressive swoop, leaving a red moustache decorating her mouth.

"This game's brilliant. Let's play again," she slurs. "I'll start." She clears her throat and musters up some concentration. "Fucky duck!"

Sam rushes to the toilet for the third time as Mark waits impatiently, brush in one hand, hair dryer in the other, ready to create the trial hairdos.

"What did you do to her, you naughty girls?"

Kate and I shrug innocently.

"We just stayed in and played a few games, Mark," I say. Kate nods in agreement. "She's not a drinker," I add sympathetically.

"Doesn't that show."

Sam returns, pale and shaking, and sinks into the chair as Mark gets to work like a man on a mission. I catch him glancing in the mirror, taking in the clock on the wall behind, and smile at him kindly, knowing full well we've kept him late. He doesn't smile back but I know Mark well enough to say that he'll be loving every second of the drama.

He blasts and flat-brushes Sam's hair until it's dry before scooping it up and rolling it into an immaculate French pleat. He gently teases out some of the underneath strands, wrapping them around his fingers in an attempt to add some curl and softness to her look.

"You're wasting your time, Mark," I tell him. "Sam's hair hasn't a kink to it. Has it, Sam?" Her eyes are closed and she doesn't answer. "Sam!" No answer. I give up. "Try the tongs but don't burn the back of her neck like you did that poor girl. Remember?"

Sam's eyes fly open.

"Just kidding, Sam, go back to sleep," I taunt wickedly.

A young whippet of a girl, dressed in the black salon uniform, taps Mark on the shoulder and whispers in his ear before walking away. "That's one of my juniors." He motions to Kate. "She says can she please have your autograph before you leave."

Kate swivels around on the stool, gloating at me. She loves this bit of her job, who wouldn't? "*I'm so famous, I'm so famous!*" she sings to me, grinning like a two-year-old, deliberately preening her long blonde hair in the mirror. "*La la la la!*"

"And modest with it, you vain cow!"

For the most part I've felt remarkably renewed, given the copious amounts of wine we put away, the remnants of which have discoloured my teeth and left a black line running across my bottom lip. But now I'm really flagging and, lying back against the basin, I feel my eyes blinking rapidly, fighting to stay awake. That's the trouble with these seats, they're just too damn comfortable.

Mark opened his salon just over a year ago, after spending the past decade or so as a mobile hairdresser. The location is amazing, slap-bang in the middle of the city centre but with amazing rent and rates thrown in for good measure. The décor is state-of-the-art with low-level triangular basins and red-leather reclining chairs with built-in foot rests. I swear I'm practically horizontal but it sure as hell beats sitting upright with your neck at an awkward angle, cursing as the water gushes down your face attacking the fake tan and non-waterproof mascara. *Never again!* I'd sooner pay a few quid more and enjoy the experience.

Keith, Mark's second junior, is massaging the conditioner through my hair with his fingertips and, while my head is still slightly tender, each application of pressure is sending my body into a deep state of relaxation. As his hands knead my scalp from base to crown, I feel all the impurities and late stress escaping from my pores.

Mark thrusts a pile of magazines onto the glass shelf in front of me before sending orders for more coffee. White, no sugar. *Perfect.*

"Pity Sam couldn't have stuck around to give her tuppence' worth," he says, spraying my hair with much-needed detangler. "Did she say how she wants your hair to look, Tina?"

I put the magazine on my lap and look at him through the mirror. "She said it was up to me, Mark." *That's the truth.* "Just do something bridesmaidy and nothing that will take the shine from her."

He sniggers cruelly. "You sooo don't mean that, my girl!"

"I *so do* mean that, Mark." I'm totally offended. "She's my sister and this day is about her and no-one else and I'll be damned if anyone or anything gets in the way of that."

I'm shocked at my little outburst.

"Okay," he yields cheerfully.

"Ooh!" Keith leans over my shoulder, pointing to the back page of the glossy magazine. "I've always wanted to see one of them."

I think you mean 'one of those', darling.

I look across to the opposite page from the one I'm reading and just stare while Mark bends forward nosily. I feel his warm breath on the back of my exposed neck.

"Destiny calling!" he reads aloud. "Density more bloody like. Bunch of con-merchants, the lot of them!" I'm tempted to jump in, telling him he's wrong, but on what grounds? What solid evidence do I really have that the predictions given to me weren't derived from a quick imagination and a penchant for a fast buck? Although at the last reading she did describe Brian to a tee. Okay, she added that he's a hard man to tie down and so far that hasn't surfaced. In fact, he's keeps coming back for more. Well, maybe not more given that 'more' implies something having happened in the first instance.

My skin develops goose-bumps as I recall the old lady at the Psychic Fayre telling me of my failed past and advising me to trust myself. *Only you know who and what is right for you.* I thought I did. I think I do. But sometimes life throws so many balls at you that you catch the ones closest to you, dropping the others without a moment's thought and you never think to pick them up the next time your hands become free. It sometimes feels like a game of bingo. You wait excitedly for your numbers to be called out, but when they're not, you never think to make the most of those numbers you were given. You know, make them work for you. You spend the rest of your life mourning over the numbers that could have been. They could have been yours.

"Thank you for calling Psychic Readings by phone," the pre-recorded message continues. *"You can talk to a live psychic right now. Phone calls cost one pound fifty per minute from standard landlines. You must be over eighteen to use this service. Press one to continue."*

I hang up quickly. One pound fifty a minute does seem rather steep. Tapping the desk in agitation, I shove a pile of paperwork out of the way, allowing me to think with no added distractions. *Why are you doing this, Tina?*

I wait for an answer. Nothing happens.

Why? *Why?*

I'll tell you why. Because my love life sucks and always has done, the only career I ever wanted passed me by in a flash leaving me with only what I stood up in and now the opportunity for me to change the quality of my life has practically been handed on a plate and I damn well want to make sure I don't stuff up like before! That's why. That's bloody well why!

Satisfied that my decision is purely logical and pragmatic, I redial with more confidence holding the receiver pressed between my ear and shoulder while I fumble for a credit card. I listen impatiently to the same message before pressing option two.

"If you wish to speak to Alexia, select Pin 1076. If

you wish to speak to Dario, select pin 1295, if you wish t–" I punch in the numbers of the first option given. What's the point of waiting? I don't know them from Adam. *"Please key in your credit-card number followed by the hash key."* After what feels like an eternity a real voice transmits through the receiver. "Hello, caller, this is Alexia, who am I speaking to?"

"Oh hi." I feel like hanging up but it's too late now. "I'm Tina."

"Hello, Tina, have you had a reading by telephone before?"

"No." *This is my first and last.*

"Okay. Let me explain to you what is going to happen. You may choose two topics for me to link into and I will try to be as thorough as possible around those areas." She sounds like she's reading from a script. She probably is. "You can choose from 'Finding Love', 'Finding Happiness', 'Career and Success', 'Pet Psychic Zone' and 'Live Astrology'."

Pet Psychic Zone?

"'Finding Love', and 'Career and Success', please." These seem the most appropriate to my situation. I don't want anything airy-fairy. Just stick to the key issues.

"Okay, Tina, please try not to think of anything. This will allow me to pick up psychic images from you. I will then translate those images back into psychic messages."

I perch myself on the edge of the seat, pen poised to record every word.

"I see a relationship doomed to failure," she begins. "Although this relationship is about to be moved to its next level, it really shouldn't be. One person is turning the water into wine but the other is drinking it."

What?

"I see a ring linked to this relationship but feel that, if it goes ahead, failure is imminent."

A ring? I've had a few dates with Brian and been given a Rolex but slow down with the wedding business – we haven't even passed first base yet . . . well, that is debatable after the skirmish in the ice-cream parlour but . . .

"Now I'm not sure if this person has even proposed yet but, regardless, this relationship should be stopped."

What? My whirlwind romance halted in its tracks?

She goes on to talk about my career, telling me how successful and innovative I am and how I like to be in control but adds that I should cut myself a bit of slack and not be hard on myself for not achieving perfection one hundred per cent of the time. How general is that? True admittedly, but a very generic statement. Most women are hard on themselves. We've created a millennium version of ourselves which is damn hard to live up to. Sometimes I think we're our own worst enemy and those women who choose to stay at home while the husbands go out to work have clearly got it right, unlike the ones who try to balance everything and wonder why they're constantly stressed and unhappy.

She carries on without waiting for any reply from me. "Your career and success are not linked, which is unusual. I feel that your career sits in isolation from what you deem to be success but for most people they go hand in hand. Just not you."

"What do you mean?" *I'm baffled.*

"Success to most people means a good job or career with a decent income but from you I'm picking up vibes in my solar plexus that your success still awaits you and is not related to your present career."

I'm feeling butterflies in my stomach – maybe that's what she's picking up from me. *It's called hunger.*

"Your success won't necessarily come in the form of your job or money," she goes on. "I can't tell you where it will come from but a link with study keeps flashing before me. Have you been considering any studying lately?"

"No, and I haven't the time," I tell her flatly.

"Well, maybe it's past studying, maybe it's future studying, but whatever it is, it will help you." Then she repeats, "Help you."

I'm close to running two estate agent's and you're telling me to go out and study? Get real.

"You've a real healing quality about you and the colours white and blue surround your aura." *I've a telephone aura now?*

"White for your caring, healing side, and blue for its health implications. Now there's nothing to worry about, but often the colour blue can represent certain conditions which need attention, such as backache or looking after your immune system better or it can even relate to your mental health, such as looking out for obsessive or addictive behaviours."

Oh my God, I'm an addict. I could only be an alcoholic though. I can't think of any other addictive downfalls. Then again, alcoholism runs in my mother's side of the family.

"I sense you get a little stressed sometimes and would suggest that you carry around some stone or quartz crystals with you. These should help during tense times.

I would recommend rock crystal – this has a natural affinity with the earth and all things spiritual. Just be careful sometimes, though, as the energy these things have can be so powerful you may be prone to the odd small electric shock."

Laughter bursts from my mouth, belting down the phone, but I recompose myself quickly. I thought something had to be live to be electric? *Yes, I can change a plug, thank you.*

She ignores my laughter. "For healing yourself, why not try blue agate? We can arrange to send you samples of these pure rock crystals, all one-hundred-per-cent genuine, and simply charge it to your card." There is a silence. "Shall I arrange for these to be sent to you with notes of your reading?"

Anything for an easy life, Tina.

The reading finishes shortly after, much to my relief given the cost of the call. Maybe my relationship with Brian is doomed although one could hardly call it a relationship at these early stages. Doomed to failure before it's even begun. But hang on a minute, aren't I supposed to be taming him? Isn't he my soul mate, my destiny?

Is it any wonder I'm confused?

17

The hive of activity at Mum's is frantic as we all rally around, bumping into each other, giving over-the-top apologies and other phoney niceties. In reality, it's a stress bomb waiting to go *bang!*

Sam is sitting in her bedroom with her feet up on a small glass-topped table slurping on what appears to be her tenth cup of coffee this morning. I take it she wants to be awake to consummate her wedding but at this rate she'll not be sleeping her entire honeymoon.

"Come and get ready, Sam. You've only got an hour before the cars get here!" My voice is high-pitched. I'm starting to feel the Matron of Honour pressure.

Sam sets the cup down on the table and smiles at me with a peaceful serenity. "Tina." She pats the empty seat next to her. "Take a load off."

"Have you been smoking dope?" I ask her suspiciously, examining her pupils.

She just grins at me. "No, silly. But try to relax, Tina." She tightens the belt of the towelling robe. "My hair and nails are done so all I have left to do is to put a little make-up on and get dressed. How can that take an hour?"

"Am I still allowed to do your make-up?"

"Yes, but make me look like a Barbie doll and I'll kill you."

"*Au naturel*, big sis, I promise. And no offence, Sam, but a Barbie doll is something you'll never be!"

"That's the best compliment you've ever given me, Tina." She smirks. "Although don't think I haven't noticed you trying to turn me into a Barbie over the years!"

I gasp with incredulous innocence. "Me?"

"You indeed!" Sam shakes her finger at me chidingly. "Remember that time I asked you to book me in for a dry trim but when I got to the hairdresser's they had me down for a peroxide blonde rinse?"

I forgot about that one!

"And the other time I *let* you come when I had the personal shopper for the day and you took her to the side, telling her I was really a rock chick but too embarrassed to admit it – and that my outfit should mirror how I felt inside!" Sam laughs with hearty ease.

"Yes, but the clothes she was picking out for you were so frumpy and middle-aged."

"Tina." She stares at me through freshly tinted lashes and perfectly plucked eyebrows. "I was going to a wedding!" We fall into peals of laughter and suddenly I can see just how trying I must have been for all those years. All thirty-one of them, in fact!

But God bless Sam for never trying to change me.

"Tina, Kate's here!" I hear my mother yell up the stairs. "Go on up, darling."

Mum is relishing the hustle of the day and blossoming into the mother-of-the-bride role effortlessly.

Kate pops her head around the bedroom door. "Is it

safe to come in?" she says, pushing the door back and slowly entering like her theatrical curtain has just risen. God, does she look amazing!

"Wow, look at you!" I say.

"You look beautiful, Kate," Sam agrees.

"I'm supposed to say *that* to you!" Kate laughs, taking in Sam's head-to-toe exterior. "Although I'm not sure about the towelling dress. Perhaps something a little more traditional might be more appropriate?"

Sam picks up a lilac satin cushion from the bed and hurls it towards Kate who ducks with impressive speed. Kate picks the cushion up and puts it back on the pillow. Kate's fingers run across the gold embroidered lettering *SH*.

"I know what you're thinking," I say to Kate quick as a flash.

During our first year at secondary school we attended mandatory needlework classes with a head-case of a teacher called Mrs Pringle, often referred to as Mrs Prickle. Or Mrs Pric on a really bad day. At the start of our very first class, she gave us the option of making a rather kinky-looking nightdress or a decorative satin cushion. Given that neither Kate nor I could see the fun in doing either, we opted for the cushion, thinking we were taking the easy option so we could finish it quickly and skive for the rest of the term's classes. You take a piece of square material, stick some sort of stuffing filler inside of it and then sew it together so it doesn't fall out. Right? Well, that was the height of our experience at the age of twelve anyway. Horrified, we discovered that each cushion had to have a specific design on its cover and the bulk of our assessment score would be judged on its decorative complexity.

Kate chose to weave a simple cross in the centre of her cushion on the basis that it would win her Brownie points. And given we were in one of the most strict Church of England schools in the county I could understand the merits of her choice, but I decided that my cushion was to be a gift to my big sister who was in fifth year at the same school. I would often see her in the playground, hanging around with her friends and I truly thought she was the coolest sister in the world. Every now and then she would come and check on me or give me money for sweets on the way home and so I dedicated my cushion to her with hand-stitched *SH* gold lettering and a series of woven kisses in each of the four corners. The innocence of a twelve-year-old!

She loved it and hence has never parted with it.

While Sam escapes to the bathroom to inspect her freshly made-up face, I confide in Kate about my escapade with Brian. I've been conscious of a cheapness hanging over me ever since.

"I feel like a cheap old slapper, Kate," I moan. "Fancy getting them out like that in the middle of the afternoon!"

"Stop being so bloody prudish, Tina," she dismisses me bluntly, retouching her lip gloss in the hand-held mirror. "You'd had enough failed attempts by that stage and you guys must have been like dogs on heat!" She tilts her head back and gives a canine yelp. "*Oow oow!*"

"Kate, you sound like that girl they called Lassie from the *Porky's* films. Remember?"

"Maybe I could audition if they ever do a British remake?" she suggests, coming down onto all fours. "*Oow oow oow!*"

My mother comes into the room and stares at Kate

on her hands and knees, howling away. "Whatever are you doing, Kate dear?"

Very little that Kate or I do shocks my mother. In fact, I'd almost go as far as to say that she's encouraged us to be bold, outspoken and slightly deranged individuals.

"Just practising for my next role, Roni," she replies deadpan.

"Good, good." My mother surveys the mess of the room before retreating. "I suppose you do have to be versatile these days." She smiles fondly at Kate before leaving and closing the door tightly behind her. The door reopens a millisecond later. "Sorry, girls, I knew I came up for something . . . would you like a glass of champagne?"

Kate jumps up and hugs my mother. "Yes, please, lovely Mrs Harding!"

"Just a little for me, Mum, thanks but make it a double for our Sam – it might perk her up – she's far too chilled."

"Just a little, Tina? What are you on?" Kate takes the piss.

Although I don't drink too much midweek, I certainly make up for it at the weekends and I'm suddenly becoming conscious of my health for some reason. I would hate to turn into one of those people with that obsessive-compulsive-disorder syndrome and given that alcoholism practically runs in my family, I've decided that these things need to be nipped in the bud before they spiral out of control.

"I'm trying to be more health-conscious."

"Why? You've got no kids or anyone else to consider so who gives a shit?"

As blunt as ever but she does have a point.

"You're right!" I concede. "My teetotalling didn't last too long but I feel healthier already."

The organist hammers out the wedding march and the hairs on my arms stand on end as I stare at the back of my dad and Sam. I watch as they exchange proud glances. Sam turns back to wink at me before embarking on the most important walk of her life.

I grab the small train of her dress for the last time, fluffing it up and allowing it to fall into a perfect pool of shimmering silk. They're off. And slowly. I had no idea Sam would be this calm or that I would be this nervous. I've done endless runway shows and filmed with cameras just inches from my face and not been remotely perturbed but right now walking down this aisle behind two of the most important people in my life, I feel so privileged that it's humbling. My eyes well with pride as sporadic gasps exude from the appreciative congregation. Sam's shoulders are back and her poise is amazing although I'm sure the dress is helping keep her upright.

The cream strapless bodice falls into an empire line from just under her bust, skimming flawlessly over her curvy hips. She's kept it simple but not too basic and the bodice is decorated with crystal beading and small sequins which also feature on the back of the semi-cathedral train. The scent of iris intoxicates the air, oozing from the massive arrangements displayed at the altar and our small hand-tied bouquets waft smells of sweet peas and lily of the valley, which I did think was a strange choice but Sam said she wanted typical spring flowers given it was a spring wedding.

Throughout the ceremony, I avoid eye contact with Mum. I just know that if I look at her I'll start crying and I didn't think to bring any tissues. Not that I would have anywhere to put them anyway and gone are the days of shoving bits of tissue paper down my bra now that they've invented wonder, push-up, chicken-fillet things.

Jess finishes off her reading called *Soul Mates*, which she chose specifically for Sam and Tim and I swear I see Simon wipe a tear from his eye.

The formalities of the ceremony continue gracefully. *"If anyone knows of any lawful impediment as to why these two may not be joined together in holy matrimony, speak now or forever hold your peace."*

I turn to look back at the church, grinning proudly at Jess and Kate as we serve the obligatory spell of silence.

Failure is imminent. Failure is imminent. What? *This relationship should be stopped.* My head hurts as the voices echo loudly, thumping and pounding inside while I try to suppress them. *I see a relationship doomed to failure* . . . Oh God! Why didn't I realise she might have been talking about Sam, not me!

What if this wedding isn't meant to go ahead? Okay, they look happy right now but doesn't everyone when they're standing at the altar? How often do you see the bride or groom in the midst of their wedding vows saying "I'm sorry, love, but I've changed my mind!" It happens in films and TV but not usually in real life. Maybe Sam has reservations and she's desperate to share them with someone.

Don't even go there, Tina!

"Ppsst!"

Simon swings around, looking at me strangely.

Not you, dopey!

"Psst, Sam!"

Sam casts me a quick glance. Her face is filled with inquisitive curiosity. "What?" she whispers, looking around to check her dress isn't tucked into her knickers or that she's popped out of the bodice. "What is it, Tina?"

"Can I have a quick word?" I whisper close in her ear. It's all very tactful.

"Tina," she says calmly but in a clipped tone, "I'm in the middle of getting married." Her body shifts position as she turns from facing Tim to facing the stained-glass window for privacy, turning her back on the guests as we speak.

"I know it is but I just want to make sure you know what you're doing. Is this really what you want?"

Simon whispers across to me. "Not now, Tina."

The wedding rings jingle in his hand as he shifts around nervously. I'm suddenly nervous that he's going to come over and drag me away. The guests, in their turn, shift around nervously as the silence is prolonged.

"Is everything okay here?" the vicar intervenes, smiling uncertainly at Sam and Tim.

"Yes, please continue," Sam instructs, throwing me a swift dagger before swivelling side-on to face Tim once more.

"Sam!" I beseech with quiet urgency. "Maybe just think about it for a minute, take a bit of time out."

I hear my mother's voice asking my dad what's going on. I mouth to her that everything is okay. Either that or she'll be rushing over to see what's going on for herself, and that we don't want. Everything needs to remain calm and collected.

Sam roughly grabs my wrist, pulling me towards her. It hurts.

"Tina!" she spits. "I don't need to think about how much I want to marry Tim. I damn well wouldn't be standing here otherwise." She lets go of me and I rub my wrist to improve the blood supply. She's stronger than she looks. "This is the only time in my entire life that I've ever been the centre of attention over you." Her voice breaks and Tim puts his arm around her waist. "But you just can't bear it, can you, Tina? I never had you down as jealous but by God was I wrong!" Her face is filled with a burning fury. Nothing I've ever seen before.

Jealous? No way.

"Sam, I swear I was only trying to protect you. I promise – on my life," I sniff. *What have I done?* "I only want what's best for you, it's the truth," I beseech, still in urgent whispering tones.

Sam coolly gestures for the vicar to continue and she and Tim once again face each other, this time clutching each other's hands and standing as close to each other as possible, letting nothing or no-one get in the way.

The rest of the wedding nuptials go ahead as pre-rehearsed only without the nervous giggling that Sam broke into on the rehearsal night. She looks a little more relaxed now and, as the vicar announces them to be husband and wife, her lips dive towards Tim's and they exchange a passionate and lingering kiss. The congregation claps and cheers and occasional foot-stamping echoes acoustically through the centuries-old monument.

The vicar beckons us to follow him into the vestry where the register needs to be signed. Both sets of parents follow and all of a sudden I pray that they won't ask about the earlier hold-up. It really was out of genuine concern.

"Sam, darling!" My mother rushes in. "What on earth was that all about?" She looks from me to Sam to Tim while Simon simply stares around the room, avoiding the conversation at all costs. For the first time since the event, Sam looks straight at me and my stomach sinks heavily. My eyes well up as I take in the sight of my beautiful sister, now a married woman in her own right, and I realise how things must have seemed. I shake my head at her, my eyes heavy with remorse. How could failure be imminent for these two? They're made for each other.

I was only checking. Isn't it better to be safe than sorry?

"I just felt a little faint, Mum," Sam tells her, still glaring at me.

My shoulders relax with utter relief and the tension in my body eases slightly. "Congratulations, Sam and Tim." I dare myself to speak for the first time, although these few simple words have been sounded in my mind over and over again just to make sure that nothing else can be taken out of context. Nobody replies. "I hope you two will be very happy together," I add, overcome with emotion, as the realisation of just how hurt they must be washes over me. "You both deserve it." I stare out of the window, praying for something to distract me and remove the impending tears or maybe even remove me. From everyone.

"I thought you were being more health conscious?" Kate skits as I down yet another glass of champagne. "Slow down or you'll be rat-arsed on an empty stomach."

Thankfully the weather has remained dry and bright, enabling us to use the gardens of Stapleton Manor. Pure white gazebos are scattered across the freshly mown lawn and black-and-white attired waitresses carry trays of complimentary drinks. I grab another glass as one of them walks past. Each gulp sends me further into relaxation.

"Is that you done with the photos then?" Kate eyes the fresh glass suspiciously.

"Yep. It's just Sam and Tim now. Although I'm shocked at Sam – she hates having her photo taken but she's going for it today." I watch her and Tim as they're manhandled into position around a huge tree trunk. She's at one side of it and Tim's at the other and the photographer has them pretending to peep around at each other seductively. If I didn't know better I'd think they were filming a sequence from *Lady Chatterley's Lover*.

"Isn't it better to get loads of photos?" Kate adjusts her cleavage on the off-chance that nobody's looking at her, which is so not the case. After Sam she's the belle of the ball and a very recognisable face. And body. "Regret is one thing you don't want on your wedding day, isn't it?" Kate states firmly while I cringe with crippling pain.

"Absolutely."

Absolutely!

"Ladies and gentlemen, will you please be upstanding for the bride and groom!"

The room applauds raucously. The effects of alcohol have clearly kicked in and the air is relaxed and charged with exhilaration. Sam and Tim glide in hand in hand, taking their seats in the middle of the top table while Simon shifts around, nervously flicking through his cue cards as he prepares to make the best-man speech. His untouched champagne sits next to a glass of orange juice and beads of sweat gather across his forehead.

"Nearly there," I whisper to him. "Break a leg!" I watch the colour drain from his face as he is announced as the next speaker. He stands up, slowly pushing away the chair behind him and clutching onto the cards as though his life depended on it.

"When Tim told he'd met a woman that he described as *'something else'*, I really thought she would be *something else* literally, based on his past girlfriends anyway." The room laughs effortlessly. "So you can imagine my surprise when I met Sam to find that she was *normal*, good-looking and professional." He clearly starts to relax a little as he hears giddy murmurs from the floor. "Hell, I told him, *bag her before she finds out that you're a total freak!*"

Snorts from Tim's friends echo loudly and Sam is giggling away. She squeezes Tim's arm before leaning forward to kiss him on the cheek. Tim is taking it rather well but I guess growing up with a joker in the family has led him to expect little else from his best man. Maybe Simon and I are well matched, given I'm the joke of my own family right now. And a jealous one at that it would seem. But that's not true and that's what is killing me right now. I've never been more proud and pleased for Sam.

"When Tim decided to ask Sam to marry him, after just five months, he came to me for some brotherly advice which was "*Sod the one-knee thing and just show her your inheritance!*" Works for me!" Simon laughs out loud, checking the reaction of his parents at the other end of the top table. Hilary looks a little embarrassed but Major Heath-Jones belts out a hearty laugh, taking it on the chin. Nothing else for a Forces man to do, I guess. "Funnily enough," Simon continues with added confidence, "she said yes straight away, without hesitation – well, that's what Tim said anyway but I reckon my dad used torture tactics in getting her to agree! Why else would a good catch like that marry a Heath-Jones?" He clears his throat for comical effect. "Present self excluded, of course." He surveys the room dramatically. "Did I mention I'm single?" He tuts jovially, picking up his glass of untouched champagne and downing half of it. "God, that's better!"

I had my eye on that!

I find myself slowly forgetting the episode in the church with the distraction of this hilarious speech. Surveying the room, it's clear to see that this guy knows how to capture an audience and keep them there. He's reeled me in hook line and sinker although I'd still love to give his hair a damn good comb. He continues to demand the attention of the well-watered guests for the next fifteen minutes and sits down to rapturous applause and a standing ovation from some of the younger guests. To give Tim his credit, he took it very well. Very well indeed.

"Tina, can't you stand up a little more?" Simon whispers. "I'm practically carrying you."

Our bodies sway around the floor amidst our parents in the obligatory first dance that Sam, true to her word, has avoided like the plague. I quickly scour the room for her and spot her in the corner with Tim, up close and personal.

Releasing Simon's firm grip of my hand, I wave across to her and she waves back to me, but not with her usual enthusiasm unless I'm drunk and paranoid. And I'm certainly one of those right now – I just can't make up my mind as to which it is.

"Perhaps we ought to move from the spot," Simon teases, once more pulling me closer to him to stop me from falling. "I'm at risk of contracting deep-vein thrombosis if don't shift from this position."

"Don be ridiculous, S'mon," I slur. "You af to be onaerplane first." I snuggle into his neck sleepily, inhaling the scent of his aftershave. The effects of binge-drinking and eating very little appear to have taken their toll and bed is the only place I want to be right now. I fight to stay awake. "You arr nicesky, S'mon." I hiccup loudly. "Oops! How you mange to be normal one in your fameelee?" *Hiccup!*

"Just am, I guess."

He leans back to take in my face, looking at me with grave concern. "Although I wish I could say the same about you. What's got into you?"

"Nofin, sno me, s'everyone else," I tell him matter of factly.

All I was trying to do was look out for my sister and give her the chance to take a moment out to reflect on the day. It was hardly an act of evilness. So why won't anyone believe that my heart was in the right place when I did it?

"Fink maybe shou gobed now."

Simon leads me from the dance floor, his arm gripped tightly around my waist, the other under my armpit. Kate rushes over to join him and the two of them carry me upstairs.

My head hits the pillow and the room spins around like an out-of-control fair ride. I try to move but my body is pinned down. I can hear the voices of Kate and Simon but can't make out what they're saying or doing, which for some reason disturbs me. I try to call them but my mouth is glued together and a coma-like state sweeps over me, taking me with it deep into the night.

Why couldn't I have just kept my mouth shut . . .

The light practically blinds me as the curtains are roughly pulled back and my eyes squint with discomfort. The open window allows some much-needed fresh air to ventilate the stuffy room and a light wind wafts around me, its tender whispers slowly easing the throbs in my pounding head. *Why are hotel rooms always so bloody overheated?*

"Coffee?" Simon chirps.

What the . . . ?

He's fully clothed and definitely showered. I can smell a sweet wetness seeping from the bathroom. I struggle to push myself up after being dormant for so long. I muster my strength, using my elbows as props, until inch by inch I'm upright against the rock-hard pillows. *Maybe they're the reason for my aching head!*

"What the hell are you doing here?" I growl, pulling the covers around my chest and surveying the room for signs of any untoward business. I spot the bridesmaid dress in a heap on the floor and my stomach heaves as I shake my head in sheer disbelief. "No. No way." My voice breaks as I stare at the dress staring back at me but giving nothing away.

Simon takes a noisy slurp from his cup before setting

my coffee on the bedside table next to me. He looks at the dress and grins at me, winking.

"You gave me no option, Tina." He holds up his hands in a position of surrender. "I tried to fight you off but your advances were just too much for a single guy. But don't worry," he goes on, deadpan. "Your secret is safe with me. Or should I say *secrets*!"

"Secrets?"

"Yeah, secrets. Don't you remember telling me how much you liked me last night? In fact, you were all over me on the dance floor." His voice breaks with laughter. "Literally!"

I peer under the covers to see that my underwear in still intact and my stay-ups have done their job wonderfully and stayed up, although being horizontal for the guts of eleven hours they were unlikely to do anything else. Holding the duvet back to my chest with a protective hand, I roll down each stocking one by one, tackling it as far as my arm will extend – then, using my feet, I scrape at them carelessly until freed. Each thigh has deep indentations from the tight elastic and my legs look like a series of crop circles have been drawn on them. I give them a vigorous rub to improve the blood flow but know that getting out of bed is the only practical remedy.

"It's nothing you haven't seen before," I bark at Simon, throwing the covers back, revealing my scantily clad body and mottled thighs.

This bold move was supposed to intimidate him and have him make gentlemanly apologies, quickly turning to allow a lady a little modesty. But Simon just watches with obvious pleasure, refusing to budge. I feel his eyes scanning every part of me and my ploy to rattle him has pretty much backfired. I'm the one left feeling shy and flustered.

"Here!" he reluctantly concedes, throwing a heavy towelling bathrobe over to me before collapsing on the bed, fresh coffee on the bedside table and the remote control at the ready. "Let me know if you need a hand with showering, won't you!" he calls as I slam the bathroom door, locking it and yanking down the handle to ensure I'm safe.

"My Rolex!" I yell through the door. "Where is it?" No answer. I yank the door open to confront him. "Where is my Rolex, please?" I ask as sweetly as I'm capable of right now.

"Tina, I wouldn't know a Rolex from a Timex!" Simon sniggers. "You're talking to the wrong man there." He lies back on the bed, no doubt fuelled with impure thoughts and throbbing loins for the second time.

"To Mr and Mrs Heath-Jones!"

We salute the happy couple as they at long last join us for a farewell lunch before jetting off to Bali on a three-week honeymoon. What I wouldn't give to lie on a beach for three weeks, drinking cocktails and soaking up the sun! Pure heaven!

Apparently Kate and I talked about reliving our holiday in Crete last night. Naturally, I have no recollection of it but am still up for it and right now I could do with getting away. Although there are a few things I need to put to bed first.

My dad puts his arm around me tenderly. "What happened to you last night, Tina? You're normally first on and last off the dance floor." He shakes his hips in jest, waving his arms in the air, mimicking me. He's in good form today.

"Are you still drunk, Dad? And someone please tell me I don't dance like I'm about to take off?"

"You dance, Tina?" Simon joins in. "I thought you just clung to strange men on the dance floor?"

My dad looks at Simon and laughs. He's very fond of Simon – at least my mother said so. Not that he'd ever try the matchmaking thing with me, he knows better, and to be honest my own taste in men is so inconsistent that most people gave up trying to help me years ago.

"You two did look pretty intimate with that first dance," Dad braves it.

"*Dad!*"

"I was holding her up, Martin, that's why!" Simon chortles and my dad joins in.

I glare at the pair of them, holding my head in pain and trying to catch Sam's attention out of the corner of my eye. She sees me staring at her and her eyes soften instantly, making mine water with remorse. We need no words to make conversation right now. She knows how sorry I am and I know she's slowly coming around. *Thank you, God.*

18

"Pleased to meet you," I say for the fourth time in the space of a few minutes. "It looks like everybody's here so let's press on. Feel free to interrupt me at any point with your questions." I smile sincerely at the small but very lucrative group of viewers all anxious to put holding fees on the apartment of their choice but not without the opportunity for closer inspection. This show apartment will have them eating out of my hands. "Each apartment is a minimum of two thousand square feet spread over split levels."

I put the key card in the door of the impressive prototype, stepping back to allow them to enter while I follow. "As you can see the open-plan spacing is ideal for both family living and social gatherings, and with a view like that," I gesture to the full-length glass windows overlooking the river Mersey, "you need never leave the comfort of your own home."

"It's hardly the Caribbean!" someone pipes up.

"Not quite," I agree amiably. "But does the Caribbean house the world's most famous yellow submarine?"

He laughs and the rest join in.

We move around the show apartment while I talk them through the hand-made kitchen with built-in appliances and granite worktops. The fully tiled oyster bathroom with mini-bar and plasma TV goes down a storm.

"Each room contains one or more speakers discreetly placed, allowing you to control the sound level from that room or from the master keypad, which is located in the master bedroom." *God, I'm envious.*

Reaching behind the heavy silk curtains, I pull out a slim remote from its walled bracket. Clicking a single button, I stand back to watch a piece of automated heaven as the cyber home cinema screen rolls into place. Pure silence. "The screen is six feet wide and seventy-seven inches diagonally," I tell them excitedly. "This room has four speakers to maximise the surround-sound field and a sub-woofer to help with those lower frequencies."

I haven't a clue what it means but I imagine most of the blokes here will find it impressive.

We finish with the communal gym in the basement and it is clear to see the guys are totally impressed.

"What did you say the ground rent was?" I recognise the lady speaking but I just can't pinpoint where. Somewhere on the television though.

"It's twelve hundred and sixty pounds a year," I reply. "Which isn't bad considering the level of maintenance required." She nods, giving nothing away.

A recognisable voice pipes up breathlessly. "Am I too late for the viewing?"

"Kate?"

Kate marches up to the rest of the group, recognising

some of them. She exchanges polite kisses on both cheeks with a number of them.

"We're just finishing up here but if you give me five minutes I'll show you around," I tell her formally.

"Okay."

We finish up with the obligatory question and answer session and all the while my fingers remain crossed behind my back.

This morning has gone well. Really well, in fact. I'm a great one for intuition when it comes to business and I'd safely say that three out of the four will buy in. The moaning guy I'm not too sure about, he may have been along for the ride. Who was he anyway? Nobody I recognised.

As the last of the guests leave, Kate turns into the Kate I know and gives me a great big bear hug accompanied by a sloppy kiss.

"You're a bad girl, Tina!" she says, wincing.

"What did I do?"

"You got so pissed at your sister's wedding you missed half of it, you dope!" She wanders off into the kitchen area, opening and closing every door before nosily shoving her head inside for microscopic inspection. "Simon and I had to carry you upstairs." She presses the ice machine to see if it works and pieces of crushed ice fly past her onto the floor below.

"Here, I'll clean that up." I'm glad of the distraction.

"He's a nice guy," she adds dismissively, running her hand along the smooth surface of black granite. "Not your usual type, Tina, but he's definitely got the hots for you."

I carry on drying the floor although I'm keen to hear

more about what they talked about while I was slipping under.

"Kate, he's practically my brother-in-law and besides," I push myself up from the floor, "he's a scruffy little sod who doesn't know the difference between a Timex and a Rolex!" I laugh, remembering how stupid his comment was. And possibly how deliberate it was. The guy drives a Porsche for heaven's sake! Bloody hypocrite.

"Stop being so shallow." Kate stares at me harshly. "I know you too well, Tina Harding. Now where do I sign?"

"Sign?"

"I'll take one." Kate beams at me proudly as she pulls her cheque book from her very real Gucci bag.

"What?" I stand back, flabbergasted. "I thought you were here to give me a lecture?"

"I am but I also need a place to live when I come home." She shrugs, matter of fact. "I'm sick of hotels and my mother wants to fatten me up when I stay with her and my dad. It's about time I had my own place here."

I don't know what to say for once. "Don't you want the full tour?"

Kate shakes her head. "My agent sent me a brochure and I've read the spec list a thousand times."

"Wow, Kate, I had no idea you were doing so well," I say quietly. "I'm made up for you." Kate takes in my pensive expression and grips me tightly. "Tina, I'm paid a shitload of money for being blonde and thin. I was in the right place at the right time and the minute I gain a few pounds or start to age I'll be coming to you for a job!"

We burst out in laughter, knowing full well that Kate and administration don't go very well together.

"I did the right thing, didn't I, Kate?" My bottom lip begins to quiver. "It's just that sometimes, lately, I feel like a total failure. I'm all over the place."

"*You* are the real worker of us, Tina, not me. You have it all." Kate's voice is pure and sincere. "You're gorgeous, clever, determined and a great friend."

I stare at the floor for a moment before looking up with deliberate puppy eyes. "Is that it?"

Kate slaps me on the arm. "Stop being so bloody insecure!"

Now I have a reason to be jealous!

Chantelle is deep in conversation with a middle-aged couple, showing them a series of executive properties on the laptop. They look extremely wealthy but then again, with Chantelle's aristocratic looks, so does she. I notice a bling ring on the woman's finger and am desperate to ask if it's real but they're deep in conversation. Chantelle sits back, waiting patiently for them to decide which of the properties they'd like to view. I smile at her, tilting my head, gesturing for her to come over as soon as she's finished. I can't wait to tell her the good news. *All four of the guys this morning want the properties.* My mobile phone rang incessantly within an hour of them leaving but the fifth contender, now that was a surprise, but Kate swears she told me on Saturday night that she was interested. She currently has a one-bedroom flat in London which has seen a significant rise in value since she bought it five years ago but she now wants a base in her home town. I can't help thinking it should be me! *It should bloody well be me!* I would kill for one. Literally. But even though I've turned a shade of envious green, I am pleased for Kate. She does deserve it. She words hard, looks after her parents and is a loyal and honest best friend. She's slightly disturbed at times but that's what I love about her. On the bright side, consider the parties we can have when she comes home! We can invite the celebrity neighbours and their rich friends across. We can sup on mini-bottles of Veuve Clicquot with little black straws and order in caterers to deliver fancy hors d'oeuvres. Or 'horses' hooves' as Kate and I call them. I pick up a little at the thought of fun-filled nights in the docklands followed by healthy mornings in the gym. A lifestyle one can only dream about because so few are rewarded with such benefits from life. I think about the amount of money I used to make from various acting and modelling jobs. It was exorbitant but the problem was it was just like the buses where all the work came together and you spent the following six months surviving on it while you worked your butt off desperately hoping for your next big break. Sometimes I miss it, sometimes I don't, but as for having a real opportunity to get cash rich, unless I get my skates on and open a dozen Harding Homes over the next few years, which is unlikely, I'm beginning to think I'm in the wrong job.

My chest feels a little tight and I suddenly feel lightheaded and woozy. I've worked so hard both in and on this business. It's my livelihood, my baby.

Is it ever going to keep you in the life of luxury that you crave?

I'm working at my own pace and doing very well, thank you. Our reputation is growing thick and fast and, with the second shop only months away, I really couldn't ask for much more.

"You gave in too quickly . . . the self-doubt you carry needs to be removed!"

"No, no, no!" I shout out loud. My head is beginning to throb as I try to erase the voices from it. "Leave me alone!"

"You have great potential in this area . . ."

"Just shut up!"

"Put your trust in unseen events . . ."

"Go away!"

"You are battling with a failed past!"

"Because you won't bloody let me forget it!"

Chantelle twists the bottle, holding the cork firmly. It hisses seductively as it separates from the neck of the bottle and mini-bubbles surface to say hello before disappearing as quickly as they came.

"You've done that before, Chantelle. Good bit of wrist action there, Mrs!"

Chantelle just winks at me.

"Not a drop wasted – although wouldn't you like to just shake it everywhere like they do on TV?" Heather snorts as she holds up her glass to join ours. "But it would be such a waste."

"Just keep it away from my hair," I order. We salute each other warmly, toasting to health, wealth and happiness. Not necessarily in that order.

"I've loaded all the figures on to SAGE and filed the VAT returns, Tina." Heather hands me a tape marked *Q1 2009*. "It's all backed up on here and even without Steen Developments we're looking good. Damn good. The sales are up, overheads are minimal and with a pipeline of pending sales of the docklands properties in tow plus close completion of more than two dozen here, Tina, I'd say you could consider opening two more shops." Heather takes a rough swig of champagne, leaving her glass almost empty.

Her words are music to my ears but it's still a little ambitious . . . although I do feel myself tingling with excitement, the same type of excitement I got when my first business loan was approved. I guess it's like having your first child, nothing can beat the experience. From what I hear!

"Just one will do for now, Heather," I tell her wisely. Unless you're actually running the business, it's easy to forget that there are other considerations apart from the financial. "Don't forget that I'd have the salary overheads as well as the running costs for two more offices, and until at least one of the two new offices was paying for itself, this one here would be carrying the cost for three Harding Homes. We're not quite ready for that yet. Oh, that reminds me – I'm expecting the building quote in any day now." I feel my face redden at the thought of my last encounter with Brian and almost groan out loud as I recall his soft hands openly massaging my breasts, and my nipples harden instantly. Thank heavens for the protection of padded bras. I had to turn down his invitation for dinner last weekend what with Sam's wedding and all, but this weekend come hell or high water I'll be there by his side (though preferably underneath him), only this time I will be able to tell him that we've sold them all. Every last one of his amazing apartments and in a short space of time that has impressed even me. I suddenly feel the urge to hear his dulcet tones and find out the plans for the weekend. It's never too early to organise your wardrobe and in light of our recent success, I might even consider treating myself to something new and totally seductive.

Excusing myself from Chantelle and Heather, I run upstairs to use the phone in complete privacy and, dialling his number, I notice my hands are shaking. *Damn! Bloody voice mail.* Still, I did say I'd ring him and the purpose is legitimate.

"Hi, Brian, it's Tina here," I say professionally. "As promised I'm just ringing to confirm arrangements for this weekend. Talk soon. Bye."

I hang up, wondering if I sounded too disinterested and a little too standoffish. Why the hell is a post mortem necessary after every conversation I have with the guy?

My phone bleeps with a new text message. **Pick u up Sat 6pm. Pak overnite bag. BS**

I'm not sure whether to be excited or insulted that he's made the decision for me to stay with him and, after our last episode, I doubt very much we'll be in separate rooms. *God, I hope not!* I'm so tempted to text him back to ask where we're going. What's the harm?

Where u taking me? I text before I can stop myself.

4 me to no'n'u 2 find out! he replies.

I give up. He's not going to tell me but God only knows how I'm going to get through the rest of the week. The suspense is killing me already. Flicking through the diary, I notice a blank space where I quickly type in *No Appointments Please.* This will allow me time to go shopping for a new outfit but I'm not sure I can afford the Lejaby underwear I've had my eye on . . . after spending a fortune on the last lot for it to be sampled by a middle-aged student. Tragic waste! I really ought to consider wearing that again, given neither myself nor anyone else has had their money's worth. I'm so excited that I want to tell someone. It's hard keeping this under wraps but I've preached for so long about the business-and-pleasure rule that I'll appear a complete hypocrite if I even mention it to Chantelle. She did tell me ages ago that she thought he fancied me but still I think the less said the better. I need to continue to lead by example. I could consider telling Kate, given she knows the history so far, but after her comments yesterday she seems intent on fixing me up with Simon, and if I tell my mother she'll start planning the next wedding and knitting baby booties. Well, the former possibly as like myself she can't thread a needle yet alone knit and, besides, her acrylic nails would only get in the way.

I laugh out loud as my memory skips back some years, reminding me of a comical night of bowling with Mum, Dad and Sam. My mother truly had no idea what she was letting herself in for and we had to explain to her that the three holes in each ball were designed to fit three fingers. Easy? She nearly hit the roof. "But my nails!" she whinged in a mild tantrum. "You can't expect me to run the risk of losing them! Do you know how much these things cost?" Dad rolled his eyes as usual as if to say 'just humour your mother' but Sam and I could do nothing but laugh. I did hear him say something under his breath about him paying for them. Sam disappeared for a few minutes and then re-appeared pushing a metal stand shaped like a ski-slope with a flat shelf on top. She grabbed a ball, curving her hands around it to demonstrate the *no-nails-required* technique, and placed it on the flat part of the metal stand which she had positioned just on the red line of our bowling lane.

"Mum, just point the stand in the direction of wherever you think the ball is likely to hit the skittles best." She snorted. "And when you're ready, just push the ball down the slope and let it roll away!"

Needless to say it worked a treat and my mother scored the highest both in terms of bowling scores and best entertainer. All the other kids were staring at her as she held the ball clumsily, blatantly refusing to take her turn unless the sides were up, no matter how much of a cheat we called her. She always maintained that it was the winning that counted and how you actually played the game was irrelevant!

Perhaps she and the competitive Mr Steen would get on after all! *But perhaps it's a little too soon to think of that right now. Still . . . it's food for thought.*

I send one final text to Brian, purely for work purposes. Seriously. **"Pls don't 4get 2 bring bldg quote need 2 org internal work asap. Thx."**

His reply comes thick and fast: **"Internal wk Ms Harding! Nthg a quik lick wont fix!"**

OMG! Roll on Saturday!

19

"This is Golden Aura. Who is my caller today?" Her dulcet tones drool seductively.

"Tina," I tell her, offering no more. I refuse to give my surname or any other information which might help her quest to find my chosen path.

"Hello, Tina. Welcome to Golden Aura," she salivates. "I hope you enjoy your reading today." I remain tight-lipped, focusing on the art of will power and clearing my mind as blank as a sheet. "I'm going to use tarot cards to tap into your psyche today. I find the cards have an uncanny knack of allowing me to tune into you and your situation and I let the cards tell me the topics I need to discuss." She draws breath. "As opposed to me asking you and not really feeling a connection with your chosen topics. How is that for you? "

"That's fine as long as your cards show my love life and career path," I retort. I'm not paying two pound a minute for her to harp on about what she can see or what suits her mood today. Beside, I've one thing on my mind. And only one.

"Let's see what we can do," she answers in smooth

tones. "I've chosen eight cards and one by one I'm turning them face up." The silence is unnerving. It continues.

"Well, now . . . you are an unusual one. Your aura is very yellow. There's no doubt about that. You are very much a free spirit." Her voice brightens with floral tones. "Your psychic energy is produced by your life force and yours is truly joyful. You're generous and lively and a teacher of good behaviours."

Wow. How cool is that!

"You are mentally optimistic and always seeking to learn new skills in order to gain wisdom which may be shared with others." She pauses. "You do play your cards pretty close to your chest. You might like to consider sharing your skills with people a little more?"

I remain tight-lipped.

"I also see some specks of silver," she goes on, "which is a sign of immense creativity. Do you have creative involvement of any sort in your life?"

"Erm." I think at accelerated speed. *Is she trying to extract information? Don't give anything away.* "I was creative but not now," I state in neutral monotone.

"Nonsense!" she bounces back. "You are creative beyond belief although some of your silver aura has weakened a little."

"Weakened?"

"It's quite common. This can be down to any negative thoughts or habits. A poor diet, alcohol, drugs, etcetera."

"I don't do drugs!" I blurt suddenly, feeling paranoid. Oh my God, that's one of the key symptoms of drug-takers! Paranoia. "Okay, maybe at uni I had a few spliffs. And some poppers but that was it." I suddenly remember the speed episode but decide to keep it to myself. I discount the ecstasy tablets. They were only half a tablet each time. We couldn't afford a whole one so that doesn't really count.

"I'm talking about bad habits in general," she soothes me with a hint of humour. "But anything that damages the body is also damaging for the soul. You can strengthen your aura with a healthy diet, fresh air and sunlight. Meditation is also a great way of strengthening your aura."

Tried it. Couldn't concentrate for long enough.

"Your key weakness is your indecisiveness, Tina. Why is this, do you think?"

"I'm not indecisive. At least, I don't think I am." *Am I?*

"Hhm. I still feel this is an area which needs development and this in itself is key to your success. I feel, however, that you are struggling to maintain power in a business or personal relationship. Does this mean something?"

Cheeky cow. I'm about to open a second office and am being courted by Liverpool's most eligible bachelor.

"Nope," I reply, glancing at my watch. "Nothing at all. My relationships are great, thank you very much."

"Yes, of course they are." Her tone is subtle and easy. "But they could be better and it does no harm to seek to improve them. Always remember, Tina, that life is nothing more than a series of relationships."

Yes! And this relationship is going to be bloody expensive if you don't get to the point.

As if my frustrations have been felt, she does get to the point.

"Who is Richard?"

"Richard?"

"Richard," she repeats. "I keep getting this name when I look at the Sword of Cups."

"I've no idea." I tingle with apprehension. *Richard and Tina*. That sounds quite nice actually.

"Well, I want you to look out for him. He's going to come into your life soon and I see a relationship developing here . . . although I can't see how long it will last."

Ooh! Some news of my love life at last. Not quite the name I was looking for though.

"Go on," I urge her.

"There is nothing more emanating from this name apart from what I've told you. Your paths will cross and there will be some type of relationship . . ."

"Business or personal?" I demand.

"I'm getting nothing more than what I've told you about this individual, but what you make of it when it happens is down to you." Her candy softness hardens. "Everything you do in life is about choices. Just make the right ones, Tina."

Well, I'm choosing to end this bloody call right now!

"Fine. Point taken," I snap with gut-wrenching disappointment. "Oh and erm . . ." I whisper in embarrassment. "Can you please send me the dowsing pendulum you have on your website?"

"Pardon me?"

"The brass medium pendulum. Please add it to my bill, thank you."

I hang up rather rudely. I do this every time yet I don't like doing it. It seems I just get so tense and hyper before these readings, almost holding my breath with the anticipation of clarity handed on a plate. But it never seems to happen. *Why? Why? Why?* How bloody hard can it be? And indecisive? I've never heard anything so ridiculous in my life. I stick by all my decisions thank you very much. Like deciding I wanted to order that pendulum the moment I saw it. I didn't hesitate.

"Tina, what on earth is in here?" Brian lifts the bag which almost fills the impractically sized sports boot. (That'll have to go when the kids come along.)

I squirm with embarrassment. It's been packed and repacked over a dozen times and is at its lightest point right now.

"It serves you right, Mr Steen," I scold him. "You wouldn't tell me where we're going so I've packed all but the kitchen sink."

"You're telling me!" He grins, closing the boot and opening the passenger door for me. "Top on or off?"

"What?"

He grins, pointing to the roof. "Would you like the roof top on or off, madam?"

I narrow my eyes at him for making such a deliberate *double entendre* but hope it looks sexy at the same time. I should ease off the pouting a little though.

"Off please. Unless it starts raining of course."

The journey is crammed with provocative comments and suggestive remarks and at this rate I'm wondering whether we'll manage to hold out until we make it to the room or wherever it is we're heading. It's certainly in the opposite direction to his place which is quite a relief. I'm not in a hurry to see the orange-tinted rug.

Brian goes to speak but hesitates. It's not typical for him to do this and it stands out like a sore thumb.

"What is it?" I look across at him holding the wheel of a car which is driving itself. His tanned arms are muscular and toned and his square jaw-line juts out with perfect symmetry. He shifts position and lowers the music slightly.

"I was just wondering how you felt about sharing a room with me this evening?"

Aaha! So it's a hotel we're going to? He sounds more anxious than I've ever heard him.

"But I've reserved two rooms," he adds quickly. "Just in case you thought it a little forward of me."

Forward? Are you for real. I'm gagging for it! Isn't that why we're here? Fulfilment and all that stuff? We've tried and failed on enough occasions that if he has to bind and gag me I'm not leaving this weekend until I've had a screaming multiple orgasm. And not the cocktail type. My weekend's single aim is to finally consummate this relationship.

"It's fine, Brian," I reassure him. "We've passed first base already. More than once!" I giggle. "But thanks for asking."

I turn away to catch a glimpse of anything which will remove the giddiness of how I feel right now. What if I had set *yes* to separate rooms? I should have, just to see his reaction. It would have gone down like a lead balloon. Brian and Tina in separate rooms – I think not.

'Richard? Who is Richard?'

Not now, Tina!

'I keep getting his name when I look at the Sword of Cups?'

Not now, I said!

"Do you, erm, have a middle name, Brian?"

"Sorry?"

"I was just wondering what your full name was, that's all," I say in as normal a tone as possible, shrugging my shoulders to downplay the randomness of my remarks.

"Brian Henry Steen."

I nod, taking in his reply. "Nice. Nice name."

As he continues to concentrate on the road ahead, I see the corners of his mouth curl up ever so slightly and his cheeks puff out with suppressed humour. I do feel a little embarrassed now but it was just a question. Don't they say no question is a silly question?

"Did your parents ever consider calling you 'Richard'?"

Brian hurls a puzzled look in my direction. "No. Why?"

"No reason. It's just that 'Richard' is a nice name too."

Brian looks bewildered but makes no response.

Now that the discomfort of our earlier exchange has passed, I begin to relax a little, consuming myself with lascivious thoughts of what's to come. I check out Brian's slightly parted legs, longing to run my hand up and down them feeling for his manliness while he sits back enjoying the scenery, suddenly wallowing in the deep-throated sucks of my warm mouth as I plunge on him in a surprise attack. My mind races as images of me straddling him come alive and I moisten immediately as I imagine how we gently rock on the verge of coming. Together. This time there will be no excuses. No distractions. Nothing. *And as for that internal, I'm open. For business, of course!*

The rain stays off for the remainder of our thirty-minute journey although heavy clouds are starting to gather above us with colours of concrete grey and charcoal. A typical day in the North West. Ridiculous as it sounds, I carry a shower cap around with me wherever I go. I once made the mistake of going out in a pair of jeans and a black backless top and carrying a tiny purse big enough to hold only a lipstick and money. The forecast was for a dry bright evening hence the reason my jacket remained on the comfort of its purple-scented hanger, which incidentally, faced the same way as every other hanger in the wardrobe. But during a walk between bars the heavens opened and I mean literally. The rain lashed down, beating us brutally, and my scalp was soaked to its core within a few short minutes of exposure. The make-up I could fix, but my hair, well, that had a life of its own. It dried neither straight nor curly. In fact, to say it resembled a Brillo pad would not be an exaggeration. The night was as short-lived, needless to say, as my sleek, smooth locks.

Brian notices my head tilted to the sky and glances up. He deftly pulls into the inside lane, slowing right down as the roof glides overhead, protecting us with a soundless motion.

"We're almost there." He glances at the clock. "Perfect timing."

"I know we're in Manchester." I laugh, pointing at the blue motorway signs. "But where in Manchester are we going?" *Apart from to a hotel where I'm going to bonk your brains out.* Brian follows the signs for the city centre, steering away from the familiar airport route I'd usually be taking if I were headed in this direction. The airport sign fills me with anticipation of another holiday with Kate. It's been years since we've been away together and a sense of nostalgia rushes through me. Just seeing the sign sends a gush of excitement through my veins.

The scent of coconut sun oil, the lapping of the sea and the taste of ice-cold beer served from a chilled glass. New bikinis with matching sarongs and manicured feet. Oh and a face full of freckles thrown in for good measure. I must get back to her about dates although I do recall her mentioning she'd be in a position to tell me next week after some audition or other.

We pull up outside an impressive glass structure which I can only compare to the Sydney Opera House. Its angular dome shape juts out prominently from the more traditional lime and sandstone neighbouring buildings but for some reason it works. The old versus the new. The concierge, kitted in top and tail, opens the car door for me before assisting Brian and deftly removing the key card from the ignition. In a smooth series of events our luggage is removed from the boot by his minions and the car is driven off with immaculate control, leaving us to walk freely and lightly into the impressive open gallery. It seemed to happen in the blink of an eye.

Inside, the air conditioning controls the temperature to perfection and the polished marble flooring glimmers like a pool of perfectly still water. Fully grown trees stand erect in gigantic pots, pointing towards the domed glass ceiling. The tinted sky peers through like a painting, a replica, and staring up at it I'm no longer sure if it's the real thing or a massive kaleidoscope of blues that dazzle your eyes with beautiful confusion.

"Impressive, isn't it?" Brian joins me in looking up. "Although I wouldn't fancy cleaning the windows here."

"It's incredible," I answer, awestruck. "How do these living things survive indoors?" I point to the lush gardens packed with exotic plants and listen as the waterfall gushes in ecstasy, slapping noisily as it hits the pool below. A little piece of the Caribbean here in Manchester, who'd have thought it?

"There's enough light coming through for the plant life to survive," Brian explains. "The glass is anti-reflective which means it only reflects a small amount of light back outside. It sends back the excess light, but only just enough to stop the building from overheating on the inside. The same stuff is used in air-traffic control towers."

I sense an air of passion as Brian talks about the architecture of the building. It really is quite sexy listening to him talk so technically. Most of our conversations lack depth, which suited me in the early days. But suddenly I'm keen to learn more about him – what turns him on, how his career started, past relationships. (*Or maybe not the last one, given I'm not prepared to share my series of failed lovers with him.*

"I can see you're in the right trade."

His eyes scan the reception area. "I'm not quite in this league. Not yet," he says absently. "Give me time though." His face is serious and it's clear to see that he means it.

"Does that mean I'll get free overnight stays when you build your chain of hotels?" I ask cheekily, fluttering my eyelashes alluringly. *I probably look like a complete idiot with a squinting habit.*

Brian leans forward unexpectedly, kissing me softly on the lips and taking me by complete surprise. "Only if I can stay with you."

He kisses me again and my lips tingle with the friction. I long to throw myself at him, starting with gentle pecks, working up to full-blown tongue action, but in the reception area of a five-star hotel it's hardly appropriate.

I suddenly feel nervous about going up to the room and frantically look around for a place to freshen up. Excusing myself, I follow the sign for the restrooms, holding on as a moving steel floor transports me to the next level. A blast of pandemonium hits me as I derail and the volume of a rowdy gathering stings my ears. Men, women and children of all ages stand in orderly lines, supervised by folk with CB radios and prominently displayed security ID tags.

I stop at the top of the escalator to take in the scene that charges me with immediate familiarity and I sense the nervous tension in the air. *What's going on?* A group of teenagers burst out from the ladies' room, heavily made up and clearly flustered as they join the back of the shortest queue before being handed stickers with boldly printed numbers. Their hands flap about excitedly and I watch as one of the girls starts taking deep breaths in an attempt to calm herself down. The others waft sheets of paper in front of her to provide air until a CB guy brings a chair over, forcing her to sit in it, placing her head between her knees. A middle-aged woman wearing a doleful expression returns her number to the nearest attendant, shaking her head at another man queuing patiently. She shrugs her shoulders at him before slumping into a chair at an empty table and downing a glass of water with trembling hands.

"Next!" a young woman shouts, clipboard in hand.

No way. This is all too familiar.

I rush over to one of the attendants, fixing my hair on the way. "Excuse me, what's happening here?" I ask politely. You never know just who you're speaking to.

"We're casting for *Stiffs*," he answers without looking at me. "Move along, move along, please!" he calls to the queue. His sharp tone works and the shuffling sound of trembling feet seems to satisfy him.

"Who do you–" I begin.

He points to a woman with wild wiry hair sitting at a large table and chewing the end of a pen. Without allowing time for logic, I dash to her table, smiling graciously.

"Am I too late to register?" *Tina, what are you doing?*

She looks back at me warmly and points to the three long queues which don't seem to be going down. "Not at all, hon." She pushes a pen and paper towards me. "The wait is about an hour I'd say. Fill in this sheet for me, love." I take the pre-printed sheet to a quiet table and stare down at it.

You don't even know what you're casting for!

Does it matter?

But why when you've a business to run? Practically two!

It's just harmless fun.

It's dangerous.

Shut up!

The multi-tasking continues as I complete the ever-so-familiar paperwork in between arguments with myself over the what, whys and hows of it all. Glancing at my watch, I hand the form to the lady, explaining that I'll be back soon.

"No problem, babe." She chews heavily on her gum.

The escalator down to reception seems to take forever. I spot Brian, a porter and our luggage already loaded onto the brass trolley.

"I'm so sorry, Brian," I pant. "I bumped into a girl I used to go to school with and couldn't get away!"

He looks at the porter with a raised eyebrow. "Women!"

We follow the porter in silence as he leads the way to our room. Brian casts me the occasional lustful smirk which amuses me. While his behaviour is generally unpredictable, although certainly not erratic, it is kept very much under wraps. But right now he is as transparent as they come and his eyes are fuelled with a dangerous desire. His hands twitch nervously in his pockets as he plays around with the loose change, jangling it tunefully like a xylophone being lightly tapped.

"Who was she then?" he asks as the elevator moves upwards.

The porter remains focused and faced away from us as we stand at the back of the lift with our backs to the immaculately polished mirrors.

"Who was who?"

"The girl you went to school with?"

I catch him taking a sneaky peek at his side profile in the mirrored reflection.

"I wonder if she'd like to join us later?" he whispers in my ear, tickling me with the flow of his breath.

"Oh, erm, just a girl I went to school with." *Think of a name. Quick!* "Hazel. Hazel Topping," I add a second later. "Yep, that's it. Slipped my mind for a moment." Brian throws his head back, laughing hysterically until his eyes glaze over with tears.

"Hazel Topping! She definitely sounds good enough to eat. Did you get her room number?"

"Ha ha. And, erm, *no!*"

"Well, did you give her ours?"

I kick myself mentally for coming up with such a bloody stupid name. Hazel Topping! I did go to school with a girl named Hazel but God only knows what her surname was – it certainly wasn't Topping.

"I bet she'd be up for a good whipping!" Brian continues in full flow.

You asked for it, Tina. I coolly ignore his continued gestures and silly but actually funny quips as my mind plays the scene of the first floor over and over again. And again. The sheer buzz of it, the thrill of the familiarity, the tingling sensation as you await your turn to demonstrate your natural ability in front of the camera, pushing yourself as the next amazing talent yet to be discovered. The anticipation that it could be you. You've as much chance as anyone else in the room. Haven't you? But sadly, the harsh reality of it all is simply this: *does your face fit?* As I said, in the years I spent as an aspiring actress, I often starved myself for days on end, once surviving on nothing more than two pieces of toast in a whole week. My hair was died a peroxide blonde and every casting saw me turned out to perfection. My young, naïve mindset advised me that you had to be some type of *Baywatch* pin-up to make it and even when I'd hung up my cloak I agonised over whether I'd failed due to carrying that extra few pounds during certain times of the month or whether it was the cursed freckles my ancestors unkindly donated. The inherited freckle gene. Why me? Only as the years have passed and I've become more mature and secure in my own skin has the penny dropped, just a few years too late. Why, in casting, is it necessary to look like anyone other than yourself? Why turn out like a blonde bombshell when they could be casting for the girl next door? Why put your body at the risk of infertility by eating tissues and shoving fingers down your throat when they might be looking for a girl mirroring the national average size fourteen? Why feel the need to go blonde and sexy, spending a fortune on dying every last strand, not to mention matching eyebrows when they could be looking for a Plain Jane brunette? It's simple logic, isn't it? But at the time that degree of lateral thinking bypasses you. You feel the constant pressure of younger, thinner girls pipping you at the post, leaving you standing alone in the cold to once again analyse the very thing to which no reply ever comes. *Why not me?*

Whatever is going on in the casting suite must be high budget because of the massive turnout, not to mention the choice of casting location. It also means it's likely to be a production filmed in the North West. Castings don't generally hit the road unless they are for some sad talent show – they're usually carried out within close proximity to the filming location. Instantaneously, I think about the contract and the speed of our success, the pending value of its impressive commission and the second office we're *this* close to securing. I envisage myself driving past a Harding Homes office beaming with pride as I pass yet another and another and am in Tina heaven with my very own empire at my size-six feet. I fantasize about living next door to Kate, rubbing shoulders with anyone who's anyone, popping in for a latte with television's latest sensations and meeting and greeting in the gym for a mild workout followed by cocktails galore, my competent management team subconsciously forcing me to down yet another as I sit back in the comfort and thought of sleeping in the next day, afforded by the luxury of well paid and highly motivated staff. *How many years from now though, Tina? It might never happen.*

I'm well on my way already. It is happening.

A successful TV series would bring this level of comfort overnight.

And then what? A quick win, then back to estate agency, or sell the business and back to door-knocking? No, thanks.

"Your success won't necessarily come in the form of your job or money." Her voice rings in my ears. But what is success to me? Is it purely financial? Or is it a sense of achieving the unachievable? I wish I knew. I thought I knew.

"Your career sits in isolation from what you deem to be success."

Stupid woman, repeating herself! You've made your point already.

What have you got to lose? It's just an audition!

It's pure regression, I've moved on.

Isn't it strange that you're here while they're here? It's meant to be, Tina. Go for it!

Life is full of coincidences. That door was closed a long time ago and it was the right decision. I've achieved great things since then and my life is exactly where I want it to be.

Who are you trying to kid?

Ah, shut up!

20

The tip of his tongue teases my bottom lip, flicking it roughly, teasing with its sharp edge. I part my lips, desperate to feel it in my eager mouth but he continues on the outside only, making my tongue redundant. I surrender to his overpowering strength, resting and preserving my energy for when I'm invited to join in the exertion. He expertly worms his way into my mouth, writhing and slippery, exploring it with vigour and a fiery passion. *My turn at last.* Locked in a head-on collision, our mouths launch in simultaneous attack as we thrust and bite, with the intensity rising second by second, and my hips thrust against him in a reflex action. Brian slides his fingers through my hair, grabbing it with a rough tenderness and clenching his fists around it while pulling my head back. He pounces on my open neck, licking it from bottom to top, his tongue simulating the lascivious actions of lapping dripping ice-cream, and my neck feels the skilful touch of his warm sweetness applied with a delicate touch. He leads me to the bed, still in oral embrace, and we perch on the end awkwardly. My hands slowly clasp his thick, firm waist, kneading it aggressively to get a true feel for his well-toned body before sliding up his torso towards his impressive pectorals. He groans with pleasure as I feel around for his nipples, scratching them with manicured nails over protective clothing which has outlived its welcome. Slowly, I unbutton his shirt to the waist, pushing it away on each side to reveal his tanned chest and perfectly proportioned body hair, blonde and appetising. I nuzzle into it, inhaling its rich fragrance, hyperventilating with each draw of short, sporadic breath. Single-handed, he expertly opens the buttons of my shirt and my nipples tingle with apprehension but he takes it slowly, kissing my chest with tiny pecks, stopping at the impressive cleavage, a creation credited to the push-up bra only. I breathe in, lifting my ribcage, ballooning my chest in the process, emphasising that it's ready and waiting.

Rising to my knees, I straddle him, gaining an air of dominatrix confidence as I look down at him. *He's still thinning on top.* Grabbing his shoulders, I push him so forcibly that he tumbles into a perfect horizontal position and I wallow in my new level of control. Shuffling clumsily, my knees move up inch by inch until my hips are in line with his crotch and with aggressive movements I push against his hard bulge, simulating sex without the actual penetration. He groans, grabbing my hips, adding pressure to the friction with the weight of his grip and an immediate wetness gushes through me, giving me sunstroke symptoms with the intense heat. As his hand travels up to my open neck, his watch brushes my skin, cold and sterile, and I glance down at its expensive face. *Don't look at the time. Don't look at the time.* The remaining few shirt buttons come undone and Brian pulls back the flesh of my see-through bra to reveal a single pert C-cup. My nipples harden with insane speed and I'm caught on the verge of an orgasm without actual sex. It's just too much!

Your hour is nearly up, Tina! Don't miss the opportunity.

Once again I'm in the throes of passion with one of the Mersey's best catches but this time, come hell or high water, we'll damn well get it on.

Just make an excuse. Tell him you've got business to take care off. Improvise, it's what you do best!

N. O.

I plunge down onto Brian, our bare skin touches, releasing an immediate stickiness. My mouth clasps his for planned distraction and he takes the opportunity to yank the shirt from my shoulders, pulling it down from my arms and throwing it across the king-size bed before un-clipping the ludicrously expensive bra.

Tina, your chance is slipping away.

Then it's not mean to be, is it?

For some reason, flashes of the old woman at the Psychic Fayre penetrate my thoughts and unwittingly I cease the oral fanfare with Brian. The intensity of her ageing eyes, the questions she answered that I didn't ask, the concern she held for my regard. "*You have not yet learned to trust your inner voice . . . believe in yourself . . . find a way to forgive yourself.*" Maybe I haven't forgiven myself? Maybe my mother hasn't forgive me for her lifelong investment which realised no return. Why can't I simply accept the past for what it was? For what it is. "*I feel that you are battling with a failed past . . .*" Maybe she was right. Why would she spoof at her age? Surely she's a bit long in the tooth to go around telling porkies? And she did look genuine. And caring. She practically read my mind! *"Trust your inner voice."*

I am your inner voice. Trust me. Just do it!

I leap from the bed with the aid of a bolt of electricity, an inner current created momentarily. Brian stares at me in wonderment like a dog with its juicy bone taken away. "Tina, what are you doing?" He watches as I grab my bra and shirt before disappearing into the bathroom, dressing at breakneck speed, grabbing my carelessly tossed shoes from each side of the room. My face is flushed and I need a cold shower but there is no time. No time at all.

"Tina, what's going on?" Brian stands there, naked from the waist up, but clearly dressed with a look of pent-up frustration.

"I am so sorry," I lie with ease. "I forgot I have a telephone appointment and I'm late for it!" I inject a tone of urgency to my voice to convince him. "It's a deal I can't afford to lose," I add quickly, flinging my bag over my shoulder.

"But . . ."

His hand thrusts into the air, open and questioning as the exasperation kicks in but I'm already out of the door, running to the elevator at top speed with the aid of the lush shag pile helping to bounce me that little bit further with every step. I'm sprinting like my life depends on it. Maybe it does?

The first floor is eerily quiet by earlier comparison and the lingering disappointment of many stings the climate-controlled air. Scrunched-up numbers lie angrily tossed, refusing to hide their disappointment and sulking for all the world to see. The administration table is still manned by the same person but as I make my way towards her my stomach sinks with a deep fear that I may be too late. The place is empty. Beads of sweat sit on my upper lip and I dare not lift up my arms for fear of wet patches. Talking of which I truly do need a thorough wash everywhere, but acting is acting and I'll have to make do and think myself clean. In my mind's eye, I see Brian standing in the plush executive suite, alone, wondering what the hell just happened – this time. Will he blame me? Will he take it personally? My excuse is pretty valid though – he can hardly expect me to lose out on a lucrative opportunity because of heightened libido! How selfish would that be? And it's nothing we can't take up from where we left off. And let's face it, it's starting to become a habit. I'm sure he expects little else.

"Sorry I'm late," I pant. "I had to go back to work and I barely made it out." My words are short and clipped as the nerves kick in and I'm out of breath. My vital signs feel like they're shutting down and the backs of my knees wobble slightly.

She looks up at me with the same friendly face and down-to-earth expression.

"Boss trouble?"

I nod emotionally.

"No worries, love. There's a girl in there now who had a scheduled meeting with the director but she should be out in a minute or two."

I wipe the sweat from my lip and waft the neckline of my shirt to let in some much-needed air. "Get yourself a glass of water. Looks like you need it!" She grins, exposing a perfect set of white teeth. Her only immaculate feature apart from her empathetic temperament.

At the back of the room I find a table and quickly grab a clean glass, filling it with water before knocking it back, sloshing the remnants around in my mouth to cleanse my palate and rid it of the taste of Brian. *Nothing personal, Brian. It's all very short term.* Flicking open the silver clasp, I peer in my small mirror, horrified at the person looking back at me. My lips are like a blow-up doll's, puffy and red with lipstick as far up as my nose. My cheeks are red and hot and any evidence of cheekbones is long gone. My eyes aren't too bad although they are a little bloodshot but nothing that a squirt of eye-drops won't sort out. With impressive speed, I cleanse my face with a tissue dabbed in water before dotting tinted moisturiser around and rubbing it in, quickly but gently. A second coat of mascara opens up my eyes and I apply a layer of clear lip gloss to my reformed mouth before finishing with a light sweep of blusher on each cheek. *That's better. I wonder if I've time to nip to the loo?*

The casting door opens and I freeze as I hear the distinct sound of a recognisable voice. *No, it can't be.* I listen again to the man and woman holding the conversation. *It is. Oh shit! Think, Tina, think!* Darting behind the nearest pillar, I hold my breath and stand rigid like a wooden soldier, pinning my arms to my side. The voice becomes louder and I pray I won't be seen. I can't risk it. I make a dive towards the table behind me, scrambling underneath it and curling into a ball. A five-foot-seven-sized ball. *Damn.* My handbag is left on the table next to the water jug. The door closes with a bang and the voices continue.

"Thanks, Kate. We'll be in touch."

"No worries, Larry. Great to see you again."

I hear the artificial smacking of lips and picture the Thespian air kisses synonymous with the industry.

"Larry, there's one last girl then it's a wrap," I hear the admin lady say.

"Where is she?"

"Oh. She was here a minute ago." But I can't move in case Kate sees me. Maybe she's gone? I don't hear her voice but I can't risk it. She'd kill me if she knew I'd even contemplated coming here and although her success has been without question from the day she graduated, she has warned me frequently to steer clear and to focus on my business. *"It's where you belong,"* she told me. *"I'm surrounded by coke heads and wankers for a living but you don't need to be."*

The sound of soft footsteps pricks my ears and my fingers and toes cross together as I pray for it not to be Kate.

"Her bag's here!" the admin woman calls to Larry. "Maybe she's gone to the loo?"

"We're about to wrap, Karly – tell her she's got two minutes."

Okay, Tina, hide and you miss your chance. Come out and you risk confrontation with Kate. Take your pick.

It really is the lesser of two evils but I can only make one decision.

I make deliberate noises under the table, grunting loudly and sighing impatiently. A soft padding sound heads in my direction and its volume increases with close proximity. I lift my head an inch to see two feet in rather worn shoes eyeing me up, peering underneath the table. Unshaven ankles bare themselves from beneath a three-quarter-length A-line skirt and a scattering of varicose veins lie exposed without a care.

"Found it!" I cry in exhilaration.

Backing out from beneath the table, bottom first and most unladylike, my eye squints effectively as I hold down my eyelid dramatically while clambering to my feet. No sign of Kate. Grabbing a tissue, I dab the corner gently and roll my eyes around the back of my head before settling and composing myself. *A couple more squints and that should satisfy her.* Admin Woman stares at me strangely but still with that kind expression, although she does look a little confused.

"Contact lens," I tell her. "Little sucker fell out, took me ages to find it."

I'm desperate to laugh at the ludicrousness of it all. Leaving Brian partially naked with a massive hard-on. Casting for a production I know nothing about. Well overdue a shower in terms of cleanliness, and hiding under a table to avoid conflict with my best friend. And to top it all, my vision is twenty twenty – but she doesn't need to know that.

"I couldn't audition without it," I explain with utmost seriousness. "I wouldn't be able to read the script." I laugh a little too hysterically. "How bad would that look?"

"I know how you feel. You should consider getting that laser treatment done," she tells me excitedly. "My friend said it changed her life!"

"Wow!" I can't think of anything further to add so I simply gesture to the door. "Shall I go in?"

"Yes, go ahead," She smiles at me. "And good luck!"

"Thanks."

"Oh wait!" she calls after me.

I freeze. She knows I'm a phoney and that I'm here under false pretences. And a false pretence it is. Let's face it, I'm never going to get a part in a high-budget production. If I couldn't do it then, straight from university when I was young and wrinkle-free, I'm never going to have success now, am I? Besides, even if in a bizarre twist of fate I actually landed a part, I wouldn't take it anyway. I've a business to run.

Why are you here then?

For the same reason that you go shopping. You don't have to buy anything, you can just browse. That's why.

Not convinced!

Who cares. It's a practical experiment. Nothing more.

I turn to see why she called me to a halt with such authority.

"Your form." She wafts the sheet of paper at me. "The director won't see you without this."

The room is bare but for a camera perched on its tripod and a piece of tape stuck to the floor. I walk confidently towards the two guys, extending my hand, dazzling them with my smile. Unbeknown to them a smile of combined salivation, a smile that was just moments ago in the throes of passion.

"Thanks for seeing me."

I was about to apologise for keeping them but my business skills quickly reacted and thank heavens. Never use negative words. I could easily have put the idea into their head that I'd kept them waiting or that my timekeeping lacks just that: keeping time. Instead, I've turned a negative into a positive attempt to display an immaculate set of manners for our first encounter.

"I'm Tina." *Not Christie. She's history.*

"How did your phone call go then?" Brian asks with

friendly concern. He's fully dressed and possibly even showered by the looks of things.

"Really well, thanks, Brian." I've almost convinced myself I'm telling the truth. "Sorry for rushing off like that." I look up at him with my best Bambi eyes, hoping to win him over. "I clean forgot about the teleconference. I simply couldn't let him down – he was expecting my call."

Brian nods with quiet understanding. "Quite," he says absentmindedly. "Quite." He walks over to the bed, pulling open the top draw of the bedside table. "Your mobile bill must be worse than mine, Miss Harding."

"It's astronomical," I tell him, relieved that he's coming round and even smiling at me now.

"Do tell me then how on earth you managed to spend over twenty minutes on a phone conference?" He pulls out an object from the drawer, holding it up before thrusting it towards me. "Without a damn phone!"

Oh shit.

"It fell out of your bag when you snatched it so quickly. I shouted after you but you'd gone." His piercing blue eyes show hurt and anger and once again my careless spontaneity has caused a situation.

I never used to be like this.

"Tell me the truth, Tina, what were you doing?" He sits on the bed. His body language is defensive and his arms are folded tightly across his chest, exaggerating his pumped-up biceps. "What can be so bad that you have to lie to me?"

What do I say? Do I tell the guy who is paying for office number two the truth, and risk the ruin of my reputation? *You're doing a good enough job of that yourself, Tina!* Do I tell him I used the payphone? I've a great head for figures, his number is in my head actually, Brian. Do I quickly think of another lie? Well, I was trying to find my old school pal, Hazel Topping, to see if she wanted to join us for a ménage a trois! *Where is she then? On top of some bloody trifle?* Don't tell the truth. You'll open a can of worms and you don't know him well enough yet. I say nothing. I can think of nothing to say. What about 'I'm on drugs'? Okay, not drugs as such, more medication. I lost my inhaler? I'm insulin dependant? I've got women's problems. Liverpool are playing at home – come on, you Reds, and all that! I'm on Prozac? Now *that* he would believe.

I join him on the bed, sitting close but giving him a degree of space. *Take one.* My head hangs low and I snuffle with remorse. My shoulders stoop with embarrassment and my eyes well with artificial tears. To the untrained eye I am disconsolate. Dejection hangs from the tip of my tongue and each time I go to speak, I halt deliberately as though it's just too difficult.

Pull yourself together, Tina!

It's not real, you fool!

"I am so sorry, Brian." I dab the corner of my eye with my sleeve. "I panicked." I risk a fleeting glance at him. His eyes have softened a little, giving me the confidence to continue. "I've ruined it so many times for us. Firstly with the rug, then the hospital trip, then double booking the viewing and giving us unwanted intruders." I begin to snivel and reach out, touching his hand gently before retreating with shame. "I just panicked under the pressure of getting it right this time . . . so much so it overwhelmed me."

You're doing great, Tina.

I do feel like such a wimp that it's killing me. Any type of admission is not my thing, so, to fabricate this makes me cringe so much I could curl up in a ball and die. But needs must. I have to get out of this unscathed.

"Can you forgive me?" I sniff dramatically, maintaining eye-contact with the floor, waiting for Brian to make the next move. And he does. *Bingo!*

"You fool!" he laughs. "I have to hand it to you though, Tina. Trouble seems to follow you around, doesn't it?" That impish grin returns once more and a flicker of wickedness adorns his eyes. "You have to be one of the most fallible people I've ever met." He shakes his head in disbelief. "But for some reason," he leans forward, planting his soft full lips on mine, "I can't get enough of you."

It worked. It worked. Fallible? What? He really is gullible for a business tycoon.

"I was beginning to think you were a bad omen!" he adds.

Okay, that does it. That woman was so right. He is a little divorced from reality but tame him I will!

"Do you believe in soul mates, Brian?" *Did I say that out loud?* Christ, I did!

"What?" He looks at me quizzically.

"Nothing." I jump up quickly, ignoring him and silently kicking myself for thinking out loud. Me and my big gob. "Come on." I grab his hand, yanking him off the bed. "I need a drink." He raises his eyebrows.

"I said *a* drink, Mr Steen!" Tutting with disgust, I take my phone from him, shoving it deep into my Radley bag. "'A' means singular! Honestly, Brian, oh ye of little faith!"

I'll have a magnum of champers with one straw, please. What? It's still 'a' drink . . . just in a big bottle!

As expected, the restaurant is exquisite. It truly underlines the term *'fine dining'* and belongs in a league of its own. I take a sneaky peek around, spotting a few familiar faces. A bloke from *Coronation Street* and a group of guys I recognise from a reality TV series. A blonde tanned bimbo type from *Footballers' Wives* with an actual footballer, not the acting type. Brian, however, is the main focus of my attention this evening. After what I put him through this afternoon, the least I can do is give him my undivided devotion. I think about our first date, where I drank too much and played around with my food. Tonight feels so far removed from that night but good, bad or indifferent I can't decide. To Brian, it's probably been fun and games from the start with my theatrics and unfortunate series of ridiculous events. Perhaps he even thinks me moronic and a bad omen as he clearly said earlier. Or maybe he just likes a challenge and is tired of pretty girls eager to please.

"Are you ready to order, Tina?" he asks, closing his menu. The choice is not extensive but the mouth-watering recipes are causing frequent mind changes. *It's a woman's prerogative!*

"I think so." I laugh. "Do you think they'll give me a little bit of everything?"

"If you really want that, I'll ask for you."

He's serious. Really, his face is deadpan.

"You'd do that. For me?" I feign appreciation but for some reason I just want to laugh. *"What would Madam care to eat this evening?"*

"Oh, *just chuck a bit of everything on a plate for us, mate. Ta!*"

He sips from the elegant flute, holding the stem to stop the content suffering the warmth of his hand. Champagne should simply be chilled and served in frosted glasses.

"If that's what you want, then yes."

I laugh. "Of course not!"

He beckons to the waiter.

The waiter glides to the table like a puck floating on an air-hockey table, lightweight and effortless, although his journey is a little less erratic and he manages to avoid banging into the other tables quite successfully. His black attire has been pressed with immaculate precision and his sleeves and trousers carry symmetrically perfect creases.

"Sir?" He bows slightly, tilting his head with humble subservience. "What can I get for you this evening?"

Brian conveys his order with ease.

Isn't it ladies first?

Frantically opening the menu, again, I scan the content to remind myself which dishes I chose. *Was it the beef or the fish? Oh God, I can't decide.* My eyes run up and down as both men wait patiently for me to choose. It's so difficult and the pressure of their attention isn't helping.

Aha! Rummaging in my bag I quickly pull out an aid. A tool for easy decision-making. Holding the string at the top, I swing the brass ring around waiting for it to decide its clockwise or anti-clockwise direction, while muttering under my breath. *Clockwise, beef. Anti-clockwise, fish.* Looking up, I take in the startled faces of Brian and the waiter.

"Nearly there," I pacify them, watching the speed of the string slow down to tiny circular motions. It almost hypnotises you.

Brian swiftly glances around our neighbouring tables, the occupants of which appear to be keeping themselves to themselves. It suddenly dawns on me that he looks a little embarrassed. *What's he like!*

"Fish," I conclude. "I'll have the fish, please."

There. How easy was that? I put the dowsing pendulum back into my bag. "You should get one of those, Brian," I advise him. "It really makes decision-making so simple."

21

Brian picks up his camel-coloured, leather holdall and opens the door. I don't understand it. Things are going so well yet he's leaving.

"Please keep the room on, Tina. I'll send my driver to collect you tomorrow." He points to the sideboard. "His card is there. Just phone him when you're ready to check out."

I can't believe it. He's leaving me. Me. Here, alone at a five-star hotel. *Why?*

"Why?" I ask him with incredulous disbelief. "Why on earth are you leaving? And at this time of night?"

Brian, still hovering by the door, just sighs. He sets down the holdall, using it as a door prop, and steps inside the room.

"I'm confused, Tina. I thought I knew this passionate, ambitious and slightly quirky girl with a fierce reputation for success, but I'm not sure I got you quite right if I'm honest. I'm not sure who you are."

I want to jump up and down on the bed shouting, *"You do, you do, I'm here, the same girl you interviewed not too long ago – remember the chemistry?"* but

I continue to allow him the courtesy of no interruptions.

"Your disappearance today, that ring thing at dinner, the crystals on the bed, asking me if my parents thought of calling me 'Richard' . . . And why on earth you need to know my horoscope is beyond me." He picks the bag up once more, edging his way out of the door. "Things just don't seem to add up here. I'm not sure who you are, Tina, but let's just call it a day." He pauses. "I'm sorry. This is not what I wanted."

The door closes silently. No bang, no creak. Pure silence. And the reality kicks in. I'm here in Manchester Alone. No man. No sex. Again. Brian was pretty quiet throughout dinner. I kept asking if he was okay, and he simply nodded each time. His eyes lost their lascivious glint, which in turn made them appear bland and coloured with a very ordinary shade of blue. The flash of his pearly whites lessened and, towards the end of the night, I could clearly see he no longer wanted to be in my company. In fact, I'd go as far as to say he looked like he didn't want to be in the same room as me.

I still can't understand it. What's his problem? So what if I disappeared? I have a perfectly valid excuse. So what if I used the dowsing ring? Millions of people do it, it served its purpose perfectly. So what if I might have mentioned my acting career once or twice? *I didn't know shop talk was the only item on our agenda, Mr Steen!*

I make myself a much-needed gin and tonic from the mini-bar, ignoring the price menu. I'm not paying and what else is there for me to do right now? I long to call Kate but I can't tell her where I am. Although maybe I should – she must be close by if she was here early this evening. But I do nothing. I'm in a state of shock and not sure whether to laugh or cry. But I can't cry. For some reason my mind is so consumed by the earlier audition, I can feel no emotion other than sheer excitement. More than that, exhilaration, even a touch of euphoria, and the walking out of a rich tycoon isn't enough to get those tear ducts into flowing motion. I'm on a high, well and truly, and can't come down. I don't want to. I reassure myself that Brian will come around. *He's your soul mate, your destiny. Of course he'll come around.* It's just a temporary setback. Life is full of them and once he's realised his behaviour is a little irrational, he'll be on his knees begging for forgiveness. I pick up at the thought of our reunion. The strength of feeling carries me through as I imagine the intertwining of our bodies, the passion of our souls as we rekindle that pent-up sexual energy. But regardless of how we come together again, we simply will. We're soul mates destined to be together and if we have to suffer a few ups and downs in the meantime then it means our relationship will grow and develop. What's meant to be is meant to be and no matter how ridiculous his behaviour, fate has thrown us together and it's far stronger than anything either he or I can do or say to each other. It won't allow a relationship to be tampered with to the point of closure. In fact, we're practically invincible.

The blackout curtains do their best to cast an eerie bleakness across the room. My eyes dart as I try to make out shadows and varying colours of black, just for something to do. Sleep appears not to be an option tonight. The same could be said for sex. I try to turn but struggle to move under the weight of a million tiny feathers which seem intent on crushing me and punishing me for simply being me. I try to cry, once more reminding myself that I'm lost in this king-size bed, alone.

Flashbacks of days gone by overpower my thoughts and insomnia jeers at me, telling me I deserve a sleepless night, and a strange feeling of nostalgia sweeps over me as I suddenly recall the very day I hung up my acting cloak. A day that still remains crystal clear no matter how hard I try to erase it.

As an aspiring actor I'd spent years struggling to make it, to get somewhere, battling against the crème de la crème who unfortunately included Kate Goodwin, my best friend. Kate and I had been friends since our first day at school and even as children we never wanted to do anything other than an act. Although physically we were chalk and cheese, as opposing personalities went we were perfectly suited. Kate had long flowing blonde hair which hung heavily against her slight frame, in keeping however with her lack of height. "That girl is a ballerina in the making," my mother used to say. I, on the other hand, was five feet seven by the age of fourteen, carrying a mop of frizzy auburn hair and a face full of freckles, each one carrying years of history. History of taunts from teabag to beans-on-toast-face, from ugly to sun-kissed. None of which I embraced emphatically, although neither did I bother to shed a tear for something I could do absolutely nothing about, apart from avoid scorching hot days and wearing baseball caps and applying the thickest foundation available, removable only with paint-stripper and a trowel! Beauty is pain as they say and believe me, my pain started young.

As talent goes, all probability indicated that mine was natural whereas Kate's was bought from years at dancing school, private singing tuition and elocution lessons, the latter being necessary living in Liverpool with its strange vernacular, not to mention its bizarre pronunciation that seemingly requires master classes from Spit the Dog. I never understood that about Scousers and still don't. A sense of humour, wit, humility and generosity typifies the average Liverpudlian, but where on earth the phlegm throat-clearing accent came from I have no idea. Needless to say, neither Kate nor I had this – deliberately and as aspiring actors, our accents were universal.

As a child I found it hard to promote myself and my artistic ambitions and had reclusive tendencies, albeit sporadic. The concern of forgetting lines, being out-performed or singing a dud note was often enough to stop me from auditioning for school plays or roles in my local youth theatre, whereas Kate quite rightly breezed through life without my deep and insecure analysis, which ensured her insecurities, if any, remained truly hidden, while mine sat exposed and vulnerable. Kate made it long before we had even left secondary school. She landed a small role in a local TV series which basically set her up in terms of equity membership and ink on her CV. I longed to follow in Kate's footsteps and to achieve her certainty and status. We attended the same castings, auditioned for the same principal roles and every time I came a close second. I'll let you guess to whom.

The entertainment industry was cut-throat. It simply wasn't enough to go in guns blazing, smile dazzling, and charisma screaming; the industry was almost more about luck than talent.

Countless times I watched the finished commercial I had auditioned for, critical of the casting decision, mocking the poor quality of the actor, convinced that had they picked me, I would have been the selling point behind their marketing aspiration. I could have had orders flooding in for broadband, trebled the foot traffic at the Quayside shopping centre and every household fridge would have contained Dairy Gate butter supplies in abundance. It should have been me. I remember Dad throwing his head back in laughter when I told him about my casting for Dairy Gate butter. Giggling, as we reminisced about the previous advert with the talking cows, Dad wittily asked me, "Are you auditioning for the back end of it, love?" Charming. If my own parents couldn't take me seriously as an actor who the hell could?

The most memorable audition I recall was flying over to Dublin for the role of a young mother promoting the calming effects of Eazi Tea. My agent had advised that, based on the profile shots, they were able to match me with two young children, a boy and a girl. I would simply meet them in the casting room.

After a hair-raising flight over the Irish Sea, less stressful if you're a swimmer I'm sure, I arrived at Dublin airport. Still nauseous from the flight, I decided I was unable to cope with public transport and would risk the cost of a cab. But instead of the enjoyment of a leisurely journey learning Gaelic and finding out Michael Flatley's innermost secrets, I found myself being thrown around the cab like a rag doll. Holding onto the car door with white knuckles, I prayed silently for my safe arrival, using a whole host of Hail Marys. Where the hell are a bunch of rosary beads when you need them? I mean, this is the Catholic capital of the world, isn't it? Aren't they supposed to be dangling from the street lights all year round like Christmas decorations? Not that I'm Catholic incidentally but still, you know, when in Ireland . . .

Anyway, arriving at the Courthouse studios looking wonderfully green, I scanned my casting brief and silently reminded myself that I could act my way out of nausea, mind over matter.

Entering the studio, which to my astonishment was nothing more than a glorified shed with, get this, a hole in the fence as the entrance, no kidding either, I was greeted by the noise of hundreds of children, yelling excitedly, their innocent facial features enhanced by soft make-up portraying the barely there effect; and that was just the boys! Each child was scrubbed and preened to their parents' individual standards, some in school uniform, some looking chilled and unassuming in jeans and tee-shirts, while others had donned costly Irish dancing dresses decorated with ribbons and a million hand-sewn tiny mirrors. How a poker-like poise and unnecessarily tight ringlets was going to help sell tea, I don't know. Honestly, parents, all it takes is a bit of common sense.

The heat was unbearable on one of the hottest days Ireland had ever known. The humidity filled the air with a light smoke effect and fresh pre-pubescent perspiration soaked into the atmosphere, the remains of any fresh air disintegrating rapidly by pure intimidation. Thank heavens the money was good, otherwise I wouldn't have lasted more than five minutes and my hair was in severe danger of making Crystal Tips look smooth and sleek and very closely related to John Frieda.

As is typical at these events, the registration form was

completed documenting height, weight, eye/hair colour, dress size, body-mass index and latest TV exposure. These things were so repetitive but at three thousand euro, plus expenses, it wasn't to be sniffed at.

I spotted the casting agent looking somewhat flustered, drowned out by the wannabe kids, completely deafened by the pushy parents gleaming with pride at their child on the verge of rising stardom.

"Christie Harding, Christie Harding!" he called, voice strained.

Christ, that's me! Jumping up, I followed the rather lanky Irishman into the casting room, watching his bony shoulder blades jut out from beneath his soaked shirt, noticing his narrow waist and shapeless hips, which on a dry day would no doubt be hidden beneath his baggy attire. Painfully thin, obviously not enough Guinness. Catching sight of the camera and boom (or 'dead squirrel' as Kate and I call it), reminded me why I was there. I loved the thrill of it, the buzz, that feeling of undeniable euphoria, the desperate propulsion to be someone else, surrendering to its dominance.

At the back of the room, three guys hunched around what was no more than a glorified camping table, squashed into the corner to make room for the plethora of filming equipment. The director, creative director and producer introduced themselves briefly, very briefly; time is money in this industry as they say. Just as my agent had promised, my newly adopted children were there and were already in place. Quite painless really, the agony of childbirth is so exaggerated.

I studied them closely. My little girl, Cloada, had light-brown hair swept back into a single ponytail landing just on the nape of her neck – she was dressed in a denim pinafore to the knee with a baby-pink top underneath, matching ankle socks and black patent-leather shoes. My guess would be that she was no more than four and she really was so cute, particularly with her tiny gold-rimmed specs. She was paler-skinned than I but with a nose full of tiny freckles, and I could clearly see why they'd put us together. My son, an older boy, Kieran, was half-hidden beneath his baseball cap and had 'attitude alert' oozing from him. Personally, I struggled to see the resemblance. I'm no English rose but, please, someone tell me my own son will be better-looking. They took their turn first and, with the camera running, proceeded to communicate who they were, their ages and their agent details. Cloada decided she didn't possess a surname, which sent my newly found son into a fit of uncontrollable giggles. The poor child was looking around frantically for her mother to help her, but her mother, oblivious to the stress put on her tiny child, was probably already replacing her bathroom and kitchen with the fee and royalties. Selfish cow. This is not an industry for keeping kids stable or sane. Nor adults for that matter.

"Cloada," the producer asked gently, "do you think you could remove your glasses for me?"

"I can't! I go a bit cross-eyed and me mammy won't let me take 'em off," she squeaked in embarrassment. Bless her, I just wanted to get hold of her and squeeze her, even though our chances of portraying the aspirational family were reducing dramatically.

Anyway, mocking her with the sarcasm of an eight-year-old, Kieran confidently stated his name, age and agent, gloating at Cloada. For God's sake, she was only a baby and if he were my son I'd have him adopted by now.

Under orders, suddenly looking rather sheepish, he reluctantly removed his baseball cap for the profile shots, only to reveal a mass of shocking-pink spiky hair. I couldn't believe it! Come on, what type of respectable mother allows a child to dye his hair? And pink, what on earth was going on there? I'm not suggesting the Irish are homophobic but how on earth his head wasn't kicked in I've no idea. The baseball cap, the scruffy hooded sweatshirt, baggy jeans hanging below his underwear I could cope with, but surely it's against the law to inject dye into a minor's hair?

Needless to say, after a pathetic attempt to be taken seriously as the young, overstressed mother of these two mismatches, I didn't secure that casting, nor the next, nor the next and so it was that after years of door-knocking, with the odd opening, just not enough to pay the rent, I gave up.

I left my tiny bedsit after being evicted, with barely enough time to pack my belongings before I was turfed out and spent days on the streets, frightened, cold and lonely. My Thespian ambition had been tried and tested, and I had come to a point where enough was enough. I had to put closure on the insanity of chasing fame and fortune and, oddly, it felt right. I was tired of the travelling and the rejection and I knew there was something else that life had in store for me. Another purpose. Another pathway. My new life was out there somewhere and I didn't know what or even how it would manifest itself, but I did know I was taking back control.

I bolt upright, sending my feathered enemy, the duvet, flying. Beads of sweat surface on my forehead and I swallow hard.

Why then? Why on earth am I even thinking about the past? *A failed past!* It was put to bed when my business opened. It was firmly put to bed when we won the contract. I witnessed it floating away. I waved it goodbye. Farewell forever. *Have I gone mad?*

I became an estate agent by a fluke.

When I eventually plucked up the courage to go home and tell my family that after years of trying I had only what I stood up in, I signed up with a local temping agency looking for work. Any work.

"What skills do you have?" they had asked me.

Skills? Well, I can recite you Helena from *A Midsummer Night's Dream*? Not what you're looking for? Okay.

It was established with impressive speed that I was useless. I couldn't type. I knew nothing about bookkeeping. I'd only ever used a mobile phone and had no idea how to operate a switchboard. My data-input scores were rock bottom and, as for words per minute, remove the plural and I'd say I did quite well. I waited for the phone to ring. But it didn't. So I rang them. I rang them every day, reminding them that I wanted, needed to work. More for the sanity than the actual monetary factor although I fully intended to repay my family for the abundance of Western Union transfers. One day I begged them, I told them I'd do anything. Anything at all just to get me out of the house and to avoid looking in the mirror at the useless, pathetic effort of a human being I had become.

"Well, there is one post. It's an office junior role – but they usually hire teenagers," she told me.

"I'll do it," I answered without hesitation. "When do I start?"

And there it was. The irony of helping people buy and sell homes when just weeks before I was homeless. I loved it. I loved the social aspect of getting to talk to new people every day. I loved the importance of being given a task and completing it with alacrity. I loved the working relationship with my colleagues, sharing gossip about the management and other such immature sentiments. But most of all I loved the certainty of it, the stability of a meagre but regular income and the consistency of having purpose and a central focus in my life. It was after a few years of hard grafting and a brain full of appropriate subject matter that I took the opportunity to buy into the franchise and I've never looked back.

Until now. But I just can't figure out why I've changed.

22

"Chantelle, do you know where the holiday chart is?"

She lifts her head from a mountain of paperwork. "I moved it to the kitchen – it's taped to the back of the door."

"Thanks."

The office is empty. Generally, the early morning is our quietest time but it gives us the opportunity to tackle the mass of paperwork we're hit with every day.

From the kitchen, I shout to Chantelle. "Kate and I are going away in a few weeks," I tell her excitedly. "We're going back to Stalis in Crete to relive some old memories." I take the whiteboard marker and mark crosses on the chart right through the days I need to take as leave.

It's worked out perfectly. Chantelle and Heather won't be off until July and August which is a great time for them and for me. People typically want to move in the summer but in terms of viewings or putting their own property on the market, they tend to do this months earlier, some even at the start of the new year, so peak holiday weeks are a perfect opportunity for the girls to get a much-needed break. I'm taking mine earlier to fit in with Kate's filming, plus I can't do extreme sun with the curse of fair skin so it suits me fine.

"Good for you!" Chantelle shouts back. "You really deserve it, Tina. How long has it been?"

I push the lid firmly on the marker, placing it back on its plastic shelf and wander onto the sales floor.

"Three years it's been," I answer, shaking my head in disbelief. "But it's been so busy I just didn't realise it was that long."

Chantelle is still working away. Her black-framed glasses complement her black tailored suit, nipped at the waist and classic in style. Her dark hair has been recently cut and sits just on her shoulders in a contemporary-style bob, curling under ever so slightly towards her perfect jaw-line and touching her flawless, velvety skin. I've often wondered what it would be like to be so beautiful. And to be so unaware of it. I tell her constantly she's gorgeous as I'm sure does Colin. But the best endorsement has to be the head-turning and general reactions from the opposite sex. Even my dad fancies her though he wouldn't say so, but he did manage to get flustered when I ask him what he thought of her. "Very nice. Erm, very nice," was all he managed. And then his face and neck turn a wonderful shade of scarlet.

"Are you and Colin going to get away this year?" I ask her.

"Nope."

"Why not?" I probe nosily, perching on the end of her desk and invading her space. She hates it when I do that.

Chantelle continues to look down, deliberately evasive. I know her so well. Something is going on.

"We're saving up." She looks up at me. "So unless you want to double my salary, we'll be going to our gate and back."

"God, I haven't heard that expression in years!" I laugh. "You know full well that as soon as some of this commission starts coming in you are *so* set for a pay rise. I give you my word."

"Ooh!" She chews the end of her pen.

Please don't do that when the punters are in. It looks obscene.

"What are you saving for then?" *There's no stopping me today.*

Her eyes peer over the glasses, their blackness challenged by even blacker eyelashes and plucked-to-precision eyebrows.

"We thought we might get married." She says this with total nonchalance and a complete lack of excitement.

What?

"What?" I pull the pen from her hand and shove the paperwork to one side to get her full attention. "Hello? Is anybody home?"

She simply shrugs her shoulders. "It's all very low key. I don't even want an engagement ring and we just want a small wedding."

I catch a fleeting glimpse of a sparkle in her eye.

"That way we can put more down on a house." As usual, her practical and pragmatic approach sums her up beautifully and predictably. What a bride she'll make! Me, I'd go for the full shebang! The best of the best. A no-expense-spared truly lavish ceremony and I don't mind admitting that I'd be at the heart of it all. It really would be all about me!

"Get up, you fool!" I stand in front of her, pulling at her arms, but she remains firmly put. "I can't hug you while you're sitting down! Chantelle, if I didn't know you better I'd think you were playing hard to get!" I tease, knowing this will create a reaction.

She dives up from the chair, shuddering, and allows me to give her what I class as half a hug.

"Thanks, Tina." Her smile is serene and calm and I can see how happy she is even if it is being kept under wraps.

"Hey, I usually charge for such physicality but, given it's you, let's call it a freebie." I smack her cheek with my bare lips, watching her look of repugnance.

"Don't be so homophobic," I tell her sternly. "That's your only downside, Mrs."

"Yep, that and working with you!" she giggles.

The phone shrills and I grab it in a millisecond, crossing my fingers as I answer.

"Hello?"

"Tina, there's someone here to see you," Chantelle says. "Are you free to come downstairs?"

"On my way."

It wasn't the call I was hoping for but maybe this is even better? I slam the phone down and rush to the small mirror hanging on a piece of string, held in place by a badly hammered-in nail. My version of do-it-yourself. I give my face the once-over and smooth down my skirt.

I know it's just got to be Brian. I knew he'd come around. I'm not after an apology or anything but it was a bit silly him leaving like that. I don't know what came over him. Perhaps it's a touch of the old mid-life crisis.

Satisfied with my appearance and grateful that Touche Éclair has taken away the sleep-deprivation look I had just seconds ago, I make my way downstairs slowly and calmly, collecting my thoughts as I travel and catching my breath before I come face to face with Brian.

He is standing there with the usual grin from ear to ear and he waves at me as I make my way onto the sales floor.

Simon!

"Simon?"

"Well done," he smirks. "You remembered my name. Not just a pretty face."

I try to be short with him but his impish grin and usual wit loosens me up and I decide not to give him a hard time. He doesn't deserve it.

"Ha ha, very funny." I smile at him. What have I got to be cross about? "To what do I owe this unexpected pleasure, Mr Heath-Jones?" It's quite safe to be friendly towards him – once I drop in Brian's name once or twice, he'll know I'm definitely no longer on the market.

"Pleasure? What type of a guy do you think I am, Tina?" he replies straight-faced. "I'm here in a professional capacity only."

Chantelle looks from Simon across to me and I know what she's thinking. It's not true. A mild flush sweeps over me as I relive the embarrassing memory of our single, intimate encounter.

"I need a favour," Simon tells me with sincerity.

"Okay. Have you time for a coffee?"

He raises his eyebrows. "Do you say that to all the boys or am I special?"

She's giving me that look again.

"You're special alright, Simon," I snort, ignoring Chantelle's look of accusation. "More like a special case!"

We take a detour through the poky kitchen where I make us a coffee and then head upstairs. I move my chair to his side of the desk so it doesn't feel like I'm interviewing him. I do that quite a lot in fact. It can be quite intimidating sitting opposite someone as they fire question after question at you so, where possible, I try to sit on the same side as my clients to relax them more. It works every time and they never feel like they're being sold anything. After all, we're on the same side.

Simon slurps the coffee, dipping his biscuit heartily and cramming it into his mouth in its entirety. My mother taught me never to dunk anything. "*It's so common, darling,*" she told me as a child and as such I don't do it. Neither a biscuit nor a bread roll goes anywhere near liquid form. I take in his demeanour. His pinstriped suit is perfectly tailored but for some reason it looks like it belongs on somebody else. Somebody more prim, more proper. Like Brian. I glance at a stain on the knee of his trousers and observe his scuffed shoes.

"Mayonnaise."

"Huh?"

"A blob of mayo fell on my trousers yesterday," he explains. "Haven't had a chance to put it in the dry-cleaner's yet. Darn good sandwich though!" He licks his lips.

A tingle runs right down my spine as I recall how that same tongue teased my feet and bathed my toes in its moist home. While I've made a damn good job of blocking out the sad state of affairs, every now and then

I'm reminded of how good it felt and just how in control he was. *He* who I thought was Brian. *He* who I thought would be Brian today.

I glance down at the Rolex, a reminder of a special night together. Special until I ended up in the Accident and Emergency department. Maybe he was right. Maybe I am a curse? But I never used to be. Over the past number of years I have prided myself on being in complete control of my life, both business and personal, but looking back over the last couple of months I've done nothing but mess up. Big time. I'm beginning to wonder where it all went wrong. But then again very soon I'll know whether a certain turn of events is capable of fixing it.

"Hhmm." Simon clears his throat.

I look up at him to see him wearing that ridiculous smile. Honestly, he looks so silly. "Welcome back," he says.

I smile at him with sarcasm. "What's the favour then, Simon?" I ask, cringing, waiting for the innuendos.

"My car is knackered," he tells me sadly.

His bottom lip juts out for sympathetic effect but all I can do is laugh. He looks so funny. *And cute. Tina!*

"It's nearly ready for car heaven which means I can't pick Tim and Sam up from the airport on Wednesday. Can you do it?"

My eyes lower with embarrassment as I think about the absolute dagger Sam gave to me when I rudely interrupted her wedding nuptials. We parted on okay terms but I'm not sure my face is the first she'll want to see. But I have to face the music at some point. At least she didn't tell Mum or Dad. I knew she wouldn't.

"Sure, it's no problem. I'd love to, and if that's all you want, then I'm quite relieved," I snort.

"What else could I want?" he asks.

His face is a picture of innocence and, as so often with him, I'm confused. I wonder if he jests so professionally to mask his true feelings or perhaps it's simply that he doesn't fancy me and like a lot of things it's all in my head. I'm never sure with him because it's just like being around a friend. Someone you want to swing from platonically or have a pint with or watch a crap DVD with. Or just be with. Effortlessly. His hair juts out in a multitude of bizarre directions. You can tell that some type of attempt has been made to normalise it, albeit in a mad rush by the looks of things. His shirt collars have been given the once-over and I silently laugh as I imagine Simon removing his jacket to reveal a smoothly pressed front, where the material is visible to the eye, but crumpled sleeves, back and sides. What I can't do is ask him to remove his jacket although I'd love to prove myself right. You just get a feeling for some people but the mere mention of clothing removal and I'll be powdering my face in green compact for days to come.

Clambering up the wonky stairwell I curse the decrepit building for its lack of elevation facilities and pant my way up to the third floor. A single door, half-glass, half-wood-panelled greets me and the words *Tarotscope* are boldly displayed. The floor comprises a small reception area with a single plastic chair and a tatty wicker magazine-rack housing horoscope magazines. It is tight for space and I'm glad I am alone. The single door is closed tight and I'm not sure whether to knock or simply sit tight. In fact, I'm not sure that I should even be here, but needs must. I can't wait for the call to hear of my fate, I need to be doing something more. I need to push on with my life and come out of limbo zone and the outcome has to be accelerated in order for me to do just that. Waiting is not an option when you can short-cut.

The door flies open and a skinny man, mid-fifties at a guess, comes out to greet me.

Inside the small office I sit opposite him, nervous and excited. My fingers and toes are crossed for good luck and I nod, giving him permission to tape-record the reading. None of the others have taped them so I take it as a good sign that he's not a spoof. A reliable source and a psychic obviously proud of his work. Perfect.

He stares at me from head to toe. "Your aura can tell me your biggest secrets." He avoids eye contact with me. "Its colours don't lie and your aura quite clearly throws out the colours of indigo and violet. And black." He fidgets excitedly. "Do you know what that means?"

I shake my head.

How would I? I thought my aura was yellow? Or silver?

"It means you have some degree of psychic ability."

I shuffle closer to the desk and the chair screeches as its legs are dragged in tow.

"You have some extrasensory perception, Tina, but you don't know how to use it. For starters try to write down your dreams each morning and then make an attempt to interpret what they're telling you."

He leans forward, flicking a button, and a whirling fan comes to life, bringing much-needed ventilation into the small, stuffy room. The smell of male perspiration increases. "By associating more with your aura and your

303

spirituality you will be able to uncover the unknown more easily."

Wow! That's exactly why I'm here.

"How do I do that?" I implore, leaning forward in wonderment, ignoring the voice in the back of my mind telling me it's nonsense.

He twists the body of the fan towards him, directing the light breeze further away from me. I decide to remove my jacket before it sticks to me. With a small window and no other means of ventilation the room closes in and a feeling of claustrophobia hits me but the exhilaration of unravelling my own future is a great distraction.

"Try to connect with the free spirit in your life."

His hands wave through the air gracefully as he demonstrates the physical art of opening up to the higher powers. He sways from left to right and his hands resemble a pair of trees caught in a mild storm, whose direction is ever-changing and uncertain. His nostrils flare as he inhales deeply and his breathing becomes deeper and louder. As he exhales, the contents of his mouth splay out and I glance down to see splashes of saliva on my cream shirt. *Wonderful!* He composes himself, focusing once more on staring me out, quite oblivious to his extensive salivation skills.

"Your black aura is quite strong right now which means you can be a little sensitive during certain cycles in your life, the current cycle particularly. Black also suggests negativity and doubt so try to be more positive about circumstances and allow your ebb and flow to live a little." He sways from side to side as he goes on. "Black is the only coloured aura you can actually live without because of its negative associations."

I open my mouth to ask him about ebb and flow but he continues and his eyes lower to my shoulders and chest. I shift uncomfortably, wishing my jacket was now on me and not on the back of my chair.

"You're very tense and I sense some type of family dispute." He makes eye contact for the first time since his initial introduction.

I try to look normal and nonchalant, forcing the Sam scenario to leave me, perhaps a little too late.

"Yes, that's right," he confirms, studying my face. "But there's more to come, I'm afraid. I can see a storm approaching." He pauses dramatically. "And with every storm there is damage . . . but nothing that can't be healed in the course of time."

I don't like the sound of that.

"Your solar plexus tells me of two romances." He smirks knowingly. "One who you will part with and the other who you will grow with, but this decision will not be yours for the making." *Hang on, I make the choices about my love life, thanks.*

Clutching his midriff, his face contorts. "How is your mother's health?" he asks with grave concern and I feel the hairs on my arms stand on end.

"It's good . . . I think." My voice breaks with the anticipation of bad news.

"I sense some type of stomach condition. Nothing overly serious but something that needs to be kept an eye on." He rubs his stomach in an anti-clockwise direction.

Next he'll be patting his head at the same time.

"Your mother would be best to seek medical advice. It could be irritable bowel syndrome, kidney stones or maybe even appendicitis but I definitely feel that she'll suffer from such a condition within the next twelve months so just keep an eye on her."

"Okay. Definitely." *Oh God, I've so neglected her lately.*

"Finally . . ." He clutches his forehead with feigned exhaustion. "I'm losing my signal so I'll be quick. Expect the unexpected, Tina."

"Meaning what?" I butt in, anxious that we're running out of time and disturbed that he hasn't answered the very question that brought me here.

"Meaning don't try to imagine the outcome of events too soon."

Okay, now that was good! He's warming up.

"Just sit back and let nature take its course."

Hang on a minute . . .

"I thought you told me to practise uncovering the unknown or something," I challenge him head on. I truly need to know where I stand at this rather strange juncture. It's vital in fact. He clears his throat. "Yes, I did, but that means understanding what and why certain things are happening to you. It means taking baby steps, not trying to find a conclusion too soon or before you even have an understanding of something." He looks satisfied and his index finger hangs over the tape-recorder keys.

"But I have something I need to know." I lunge forward, almost falling off the edge of the chair, closing in on him, and he sits back a little startled. "There is news I'm waiting for and I need to know if it's a yes or a no!" My voice is raised and frustrated.

"Tina, I can't predict the future . . ."

"Then what's the bloody point in me being here?

What am I paying you for?" I challenge him hysterically. The repressed emotion releases itself without edit.

"I can tell you what I see through the psychic images shown to me but –"

"By whom?" I ask, looking around the empty room.

"By my guide, my spirit guide." He stops the tape recorder. "Our work is done now." He pulls out the tape, handing it over to me. "Fortune-tellers don't exist, Tina, and if you think they do then you're in for disappointment."

"What are you then? A con-artist?" I snap.

"A spiritualist," he corrects. "I get spiritual messages from those in the spirit world."

He stands up, offering me the door. "Use your own ability, Tina, to decide what you really want out of life but be careful what you wish for." His face is solemn and disturbing. "Sometimes when wishes come true it teaches us that what we thought we wanted isn't quite what we wanted after all."

"Yeah, like being here!" I shout, glaring at him while grabbing my jacket. I slam the door behind me. I'm angry. Angry at myself. Angry at him and pissed off that I've just spent thirty pounds in the space of ten minutes without a shopping bag in sight.

I stomp out of the building, throwing my weight huffily behind every step and the noise of my heels rings around me. *Stupid man. Stupid girl!* Why can't they tell it like it is? Why the skirting? Why such ambiguity?

Why do you insist on coming to these things then, Tina?

I'm waiting for a true reading, a glaringly honest prediction of what my life will look like.

It looks like what you want it to look like!

What if I don't know what I want it to look like?

Well, that's what life is about. Learning, experiencing and moving away from what you don't like and closer to what you do.

I sit at the bottom of the stairs, not quite ready to exit and face the world, still cross at myself for another failed attempt at a crystal-clear forecast. I'm beginning to think he was right about me learning to uncover the unknown. I mean, I couldn't be worse than him, could I? But psychic? Me?

Surely not?

"Chantelle, it's just me checking for any messages." The hands-free crackles with interference.

"Rymer Black want you to sign a lease for the new premises so maybe you could give them a call!" Chantelle shouts to be heard over the poor signal. "Oh and we're still missing some holding fees for the dockland apartments. You need to get some of the agents to pull their finger out and earn their commission!"

"Okay, thanks, Chantelle, I'll get on to those right away."

"Where are you?" She sounds frustrated. "It's mad busy here and your diary is empty so I was expecting you here. I've had to bring Heather in to answer the phone so I can deal with the foot traffic and stuff."

Shit.

"I've just had a meeting with Brian Steen," I lie quickly. "To talk about starting the building work."

"That's great, Tina, but next time can we make sure the office is fully manned?" she scolds me. "Did you forget I had a meeting with Hamilton Pyper Solicitors this morning?"

"Oh Chantelle, I did, I'm so sorry." I give myself a mental kick. "I truly did, forgive me."

"Mmm, bad girl," she chides. "I've rescheduled for tomorrow. You've never done it before so I'll let you off this time. Was it the distraction of Mr Steen that caused this short-term memory loss?"

"No, of course not, I just double-booked. Sorry again, Mrs."

"Don't worry – just come in as soon as you can – it really is heaving today."

It pops into my head. "Oh, Chantelle, there is one more thing. The new uniforms we were talking about, I was thinking maybe they could be indigo or violet, you know . . . erm . . . some type of purple colour?"

"What about traditional black?" Chantelle suggests. "You can't go wrong with that."

"No! No black. Absolutely not."

23

The phone rings for the second time but I can't reach it and at seventy miles per hour I'm not even going to try. My handbag vibrates with each ring and I'm desperate to answer it but the floor of the passenger seat seems so far away. To make matters worse, I have a male passenger on board and sitting in that very passenger seat, so speed or no speed I'm not bending down there unless I want to get myself arrested.

"Are you going to answer that?" Simon asks me sarcastically, glancing down at the bag and then back to me. He kicks the bag to one side, allowing for easy reach.

I glare at him, wondering why he hasn't the common sense to simply pick up the bag and hand it to me or better still, retrieve the phone for me. Once more he looks down at the ringing bag, smirking like a fool. His face emits provocation.

"Don't even go there," I growl, weighing up his body language. "I am not bending down there with my head inches away from your crotch! You're lucky I let you come along for the ride."

"Ride? Now we're talking." He slaps his thigh hard. "Tina, you're my kinda girl!" Deliberately ignoring him, I wonder what on earth possessed me to give in and bring him along. I can't argue against the fact that they're expecting to see him but surely the sight of me on my own wouldn't have been too repugnant for them? I gave in on the grounds of having company for the journey but as usual all he's done is grin his way through the past twenty miles. I scan my brain frantically, wondering if once again I've sent him alluring text messages or extended some sort of invitation. In error, of course. The phone shrills for the third time. *Someone must really want to speak to me! Oh no! Maybe it's my mother? Perhaps she's ill!*

"Simon, the phone's in my bag – answer it quick," I order.

He rummages through the bag, still wearing that ridiculous face.

How I wish the wind would change!

"Hello, this is Tina Harding's phone," he says politely. "Okay, just a minute, please." He holds the phone out to me.

What if she really is ill? *He could have got his prediction wrong and she might have something more serious, like cancer!* I shake my head. It's too much for me. I can't bear to listen.

Simon looks back at me with a puzzled expression but merely shrugs his shoulders. "I'm sorry but she's driving right now. Can I take a message?" He seeks affirmation from me. I nod. "Tina, he says it's urgent and he must speak to you." Simon looks uncomfortably compromised.

"Alright," I croak. "Who is it?"

"He didn't say."

"Put him on hands-free, please, Simon." I sense his discomfort. "Thanks." I smile at him warmly. I just might need a shoulder to cry on shortly and he's all I've got right now. The phone clicks into the hands-free cradle, leaving me free to drive safely, and I set the cruise control so all I have to do is steer. A precautionary measure just in case the news is devastatingly bad. Only at that point does it strike me it could be Brian. *Oh no! Not with Smirking Simon listening!*

"Hello, this is Tina Harding."

"Christie, it's Gerry McCann here."

"Oh my God – Gerry!" I exhale with relief. "Thank God it's you!" I nearly cry with gratitude but sharply pull myself together, remembering that this call is business-related. Two of his clients are buying docklands apartments. "Thank you for coming back to me so soon, Gerry. I was ringing you to chase the holding fee for plots eight and twelve."

Simon stares out of the window, pretending not to listen. *I'll show him how to conduct a business call.*

"Christie," Gerry continues as Simon looks at me mouthing, "*Christie?*" before sniggering quietly. "You'll never believe it."

"Don't tell me they've pulled out?" My heart sinks.

"No, no!" he shrieks. "You got the part! You did it!"

"What?"

"*Stiffs* – you got the part you auditioned for. Even though you didn't bother to tell me you were going to audition, you bad girl."

"*No!*"

"Yes."

"Gerry, this isn't funny." My voice shakes. "Stop winding me up!"

"I swear I'm not. Why would I do that to you? And with the budget this production has we're expecting it to be big – massive, in fact – so all the more well done to you."

I don't believe him. I really don't. I've waited a decade to hear this kind of news and now that it has arrived I'm in denial. It can't be true. I burst into tears. The same degree of tears I shed when I was homeless – fast-flowing and uncontrollable – the same degree of tears I wept when I told my mother I could no longer fulfil her dream for me, and the same degree of tears I wept every time I looked at the failure looking back at me for a long time after.

"I did it!" I burst out. "I actually did it – me!" I hear the words but they don't ring true. "I made it! I made it!" I yell out loud, oblivious to the rest of the universe. My nose starts to run but I don't care. "Thank you, Gerry." I find myself weeping with sheer elation. I'm intoxicated but numb at the same time. Fuelled with energy but weak with total disbelief. Electrified and terrified in equal measures.

"Tina, pull over."

Simon checks the inside lane before pushing the indicator down and gently taking the wheel, tilting it and veering us off the motorway on to the hard shoulder. "Brake," he commands. "Brake, Tina." As the car skids to an abrupt halt a mass of grey powder rises. Dried-out earth rains down on the bonnet and light particles of dust stick to the windows. "Switch the engine off." He puts on the hazard lights and unbuckles his seatbelt, turning to face me.

I sense a softness in his approach, a quiet calmness in his eyes and he takes hold of my hand.

"I don't know what just happened there but if you don't mind I'd like to drive the rest of the way!"

A watery smile surfaces and I pull the keys out of the ignition, handing them over to him. I'm not safe to drive right now, not unless my eyes are fitted with a pair of optical wipers.

"I guess I should be congratulating you then, Tina." He winks at me. "Or is it 'Christie'? Although I'll be damned if I know what I'm congratulating you for!" His usual boisterous laughter is somehow quietened as he waits for me to reply. Can I tell him? Shall I tell him? *Hang on, he's already heard the news loud and clear and straight from the horse's mouth.*

I pull out a small packet of tissues kept in the car door and blow my nose loudly, not caring how unattractive I look right now. You know why? Because I've done it! I've achieved what appeared for so long to be the unachievable and, by God, does it feel good!

For the first time in years I open up to someone. To Simon, exposing my inadequacies and my instability. Explaining my ongoing battle to truly believe I could be something other than what I was born to be. Destined to be. Like an estate agent. Simon just listens intently. He says nothing – his eyes shower me with congratulatory affection yet his mouth remains motionless and indifferent. He reaches out and touches my cheek, cupping it with his pen-pushing hand and a fresh tear escapes which he wipes away tenderly. Instinctively, I allow my face to sink deep into his touch and close my eyes, melting in the safeness and security of him. And then I feel his lips on mine, gentle and beautiful and . . . *gone!*

"I'm really proud of you, Tina." He pulls back. "So very well done to you." My hand is released from his grip. "I swear I'll say nothing to no-one. Cross my heart." He crosses his chest dramatically and mimics his Scout's-Honour salute.

"I was thrown out of the Girl Guides!" I tell him in truth, wiping the running make-up from beneath my eyes.

"For what? Burning the camp down!"

"Ha ha. I wouldn't make a cup of tea to get a badge. I told them not to be so sexist and they asked me to leave. They said there was no place in the Girl Guides for a young feminist."

Simon snorts, throwing his head back, belting out rapturous laughter. "Good for you, Tina! So you've always been your own woman!"

Now that's where you are wrong . . . but it is work in progress.

I stand back sheepishly to assess Sam's body language and facial expression before making a decision on my next move. Ordinarily I would have sprinted towards her, throwing myself against her, wrapping her in a great big sisterly hug. But today, needs must, and I tread cautiously. Hand in hand they walk, gazing at each other, all tanned and glowing. Who am I to think that right now I'm even important in Sam's life? I mean, look at her, she's practically oozing with adoration for Tim. Who am I but her little sister who almost trashed her wedding day? I doubt she'll even notice I'm here.

"Hello, trouble." Sam winks at me and releases her hold from Tim's bronzed hand to embrace me.

He actually looks quite handsome with a tan. I glance

at across at Simon's sandy-coloured hair and fair skin and once again wonder where they got him from.

"Sam . . . I'm so so sorry. Again!" I start to cry with relief that she's actually speaking to me. "I really don't know what came over me."

Sam squeezes me tight and then dishes me a sneaky dig in the arm. "I'm sure you had my best interests at heart, Tina. Besides, I've had a few weeks to get over it – with plenty of distractions!"

I nod through watery eyes, oblivious to her innuendo.

"Come here, you fool."

She hugs me again and I long to tell her my news but I know I can't. Sam helped me with all the legalities of setting up Harding Homes and she too invested time and energy in aiding my success and I'm not prepared to upset her again so soon. Besides, I'm simply getting this out of my system once and for all. No-one needs to know about it. It's a bit of harmless fun.

Pulling up outside Mum and Dad's I shudder at the thought of Mum ever becoming ill. Not before I've made her proud, that is. We've clashed over the years but as they say *'you only have one mother'* and while mine is a little eccentric, I wouldn't change a thing about her apart from her unusual fashion sense, her five-foot-long fingernails, her extraordinary ability to expand the truth and her extraordinary inability to hold her own water (that is, hold her tongue).

"What's bothering you, darling?" Mum sets the flowery printed mug on the mahogany table and looks at me. For a woman so modern in her approach to life, the house is still a sad eighties throwback with a concoction of depressing furniture.

I shift uncomfortably on the leather sofa, plumping up the cushion behind me for distraction. "Nothing, Mum," I lie. "I'm fine, thanks. Are you fine?"

"Yes, dear, I am, thank you."

"Are you sure, Mum, because you would tell me, wouldn't you?" I rattle.

"Tell you what?"

"If you weren't fine."

"I've just told you I am fine, darling." My mother looks confused.

"I know that but if you weren't, I mean."

"But I am, dear." My mother frowns, somewhat distracted. "Christie, don't do that with the cushions, darling, they're from Laura Ashley."

She's right. She's perfectly well!

I pick up the receiver and leave another message for Brian. For some strange reason, he's not returning my calls which in itself doesn't worry me, but I do need to speak to him about the Camberwell Road office. We're close to completion for almost all the docklands apartments which has provided me the liquid cash to pay for the work outright and without dipping into the reserves of the business account. The quote from Brian was incredibly reasonable and I half-wonder if he's subsidising it and paying one of his men the balance as a backhander. It's small change to him, of course. The work is due to start next week and I've settled on a neutral colour theme in terms of the walls and ceilings with strong bold purple uniforms, paired with lilac accessories. It definitely beats black and Chantelle as usual looks stunning in those colours, particularly with her sultry skin. The walls are to be decorated with a mass of canvases in varying sizes and in earthy colours to create a relaxed homely feel and the hardwearing laminate floor will add a more clean and contemporary look. The two downstairs offices are to be plastered and repainted and the doors will be replaced with panelled glass set in maple frames with chrome handles.

I think back to the day where Brian and I made it past first base – in fact, up against the only wall which is to be knocked down and, if I didn't know better, I might think that its demolition was a metaphor of our relationship. I feel a little frustrated at the time he's taken to respond to me and actually feel that he should have apologised for leaving me so abruptly like that. Okay, so I lied about the phone call. And so what if I lied about Hazel Topping or tried to teach him how to use the dowsing ring and read his palm for him and asked why no woman could tame him, at which he looked a little confused?

"A man in motion always seeking new challenges . . ." I quoted to him, which he vehemently denied, but his reluctance was merely down to a playful coyness. I'm sure about that. Still, every man likes a challenging woman and I'm sure he wouldn't have me any other way. But there's only one way to find out.

I dial the number before I can change my mind, my credit card poised for payment. And maybe the odd purchase.

"Hello, is this Spiritual Steve?"

I listen to the message again, trembling with excitement but bitter with disappointment that the filming schedule coincides with my holiday. I was so looking forward to reliving some mad moments and will have to find a way to let Kate down gently.

318

'*By the way, Kate, you didn't see me because I was hiding under the table but as it happens . . .*' or '*I can't get the time off work we're so short staffed . . .*' or '*I have my lobotomy booked in for that week*'? I'll also need to take a few more days than I've marked down on the holiday planner. *Now what shall I say to Chantelle?* First things first.

"Gerry, it's Tina." I talk quietly to avoid being overheard. "I got it, thanks . . . all the dates are fine. I was wondering what local accommodation is available to save me commuting every day?" What I really mean is that both work and my family will think I'm on holiday and of course won't be expecting to see me. And so they won't. I'll tell them when I have to but now is not the time. It only seems like yesterday that I was bailed out as my family rallied around to save me from the depths of despair and I had to suffer a mother who couldn't bear to tell her friends that I'd given up. But give up I never do. I just didn't make it. "*She's taking time out,*" she told them all. A long time out. I guess if or rather when she does find out, she can hold her head up high again. There now, she wasn't lying.

Gerry arranges to email me the script for *Stiffs* and a treatment for the series. I can't believe I'm about to sign a contract for a series I know so little about and, in fact, had Gerry not volunteered the information, I would have had no idea what the fee was. *Just turn up and give it your best.* That's what I keep telling myself and for once I'm doing it for the achievement, the satisfaction and for permanent closure. And not the permanent closure I once thought I had. A different permanent. A life-long one. After that it will be business as usual.

"Kate, I am so sorry but I can't get the time off work for

this holiday of ours." My voice is shaky and I feel so pathetically transparent. "It only leaves Chantelle here and I can't get any other cover for that week."

Kate is gutted. "Maybe we could go away later on in the year?"

We agree to check our diaries for another week towards the end of the summer which really means that I need to fit in with Kate's filming schedule, something I'm used to doing and completely understand although I'm not sure she would understand fitting around mine.

I can't quite get my head around the fact that I got the part but I was in the right place at the right time and there is a lot to be said for that.

"*Everything happens for a reason,*" she had said, the old dear at the Mind Body and Soul exhibition. The one I went to with Chantelle. The one I was embarrassed to be seen at. How things have changed. It's not that I'm a convert but I keep hoping, wishing, that the next reading will be *The Real One*. Something that tells me loud and clear where I'm supposed to be, at what time and with whom, so I need only turn up and await instruction. And with every reading, I swear it will be the last one. But it never is.

I change the holiday chart on the back of the kitchen door and leave a note for Chantelle to advise of the few extra days, asking her to contact Heather to arrange additional manpower.

How easy was that? Kate thinks I'm working and Chantelle and my family think I'm on holiday.

Nice one, Tina, covered from all angles!

24

I hold my hair up as Sam stands behind me tying a knot in the black necklace. She straightens the pendant, flipping it around so it faces the right way. It sits perfectly at the bottom of my neckline although it is tied a little too tight. *Should I be concerned?*

I jump up, checking it out in the mirror. *What a weird-shaped little man!*

"Thanks, Sam, it's lovely." Sam always brings gifts back from her holidays, as does my mother. Personally, I can't see the fun in the exertion of hunting for presents when you're on holiday to get away from it all. It's just added stress.

"What is it?" I ask her cheekily.

"It's a fertility pendant. I got it in one of the markets in Bali," she snorts. "Couldn't resist it, sorry!"

"Why?"

"It's supposed to help you become more fertile the longer you wear it. I thought it might help with your sex life!" She belts out hoydenish laughter and Tim looks a little embarrassed by the content of our conversation.

"What sex life?"

"Exactly!"

I pick up the cushion and belt her over the head with it, laughing too. She never used to be this funny. I guess it's that euphoric happiness that she's found with Tim.

"Just because you're getting some, at long last, doesn't mean you can be so cheeky!" I point my finger at her scoldingly. "You were the oldest virgin I ever knew of, Sam!"

"*Tina!*" She glares at me and this time Tim chortles, stopping dead as Sam slaps him hard on the arm. He winces playfully.

"Not any more, my love!" he proudly declares.

"*Tim!*"

Let them think I've got no sex life. Little do they know of the handsome tycoon. My best-kept secret.

Sam changes the subject rapidly. "Do you need a lift to the airport, Tina?"

I stand up, collecting the coffee cups, banging them together noisily. "It's all sorted, Sam, thanks." I hate lying to Sam but needs must. I leave the room and busy myself rinsing the cups in the kitchen sink. Anything to avoid looking at her with barefaced lies.

"Why don't you put those in the dishwasher, Tina?" Sam is standing at the kitchen door leaning against the frame, looking cool and casual and slimmer if I'm not mistaken. Must be all that honeymoon exercise. I'm beginning to feel like the ugly sister by comparison.

"I'm saving energy." *It's the first thing that comes to mind. 'I'm keeping busy to avoid lying to you, Sam!'*

"Not your own obviously," she laughs. She screws up her lightly freckled nose (something she has done since we were kids), her small flat button nose now peeling from too much sun exposure.

Tim's hands appear from behind her, grabbing her waist, and she jumps, letting out a startled scream. She twists around to face him head-on, rubbing her nose against his with Eskimo affection.

"Guys!" I hold a glass of cold water in their direction. "Am I going to have to use this?"

I read through the script once more, almost retching. It truly is abhorrent. My character, Balmy, is dating a necrophiliac but doesn't know it. She works as an embalmer for a local funeral home and her fiancé, Craig, who has only recently proposed, has done so to ensure continued access to the corpses, hence the title. It appears his journey begins with pure fantasy but progresses rapidly to regular necrophilia as the series develops. As his behaviour becomes more sinister he resorts to necrophiliac homicide, that is, murder to obtain a corpse. Little does Balmy know that her mounting work pressures are the vile result of her very own fiancé's behaviour and she continues her relationship with him, innocent and loved up.

I shudder at the real-life prospect of it. This type of thing actually goes on, I hear. I spoke with the director, Larry, who told me of cases where gravediggers and other such folk with access to stiffs have embarked on bizarre journeys of repulsive sexual pleasure, often starting by touching the bodies and then pleasuring themselves, but very quickly moving towards the act of full violation. Unsurprisingly, the majority of these psychos are men but I was told of one case where a woman devised some sort of pump, putting it under the skin of the corpse's penis so she could pleasure herself with full penetrative sex. Thanks for that, Larry! I've yet to meet the writer, but I'll have a few questions when I do. *Sick!*

The room is sparse with no window and poor lighting, and looking around I wonder if it's deliberate – that way I can't see the flea-invested shithole for what it really is. I asked my agent to arrange clean but basic accommodation not too far from the filming location and, after nearly breaking my neck on the stairs and tripping over on the worn carpet, I'd say that 'basic' is a massive understatement.

Throwing the holdall on the floor, I flop on to the bed as the tiredness takes over. Staring at the stained ceiling I wonder if I missed any last-minute office jobs before I locked up. I intended to set off just after seven so I could arrive here chilled and mentally unwound but instead I found a plethora of jobs to do, jobs I actually thought I'd done, but thank heavens I found them all before Chantelle did. I'm not in her good books lately. She told me I've appeared a bit lost recently and for once I couldn't deny it. I used to be so efficient, too efficient it was once said, and when it came to having a clear desk policy, mine was literally that, clear and orderly and completely organised behind the scenes. As of late I keep finding bits and pieces of work that I swear I've already done or messages on bits of paper that I meant to give to Chantelle or Heather, but didn't.

Don't be too hard on yourself. You've had a business to run and lines to learn.

That's why I'm glad of this break. I need time away from the office and am so determined to enjoy this experience like no other. After all, it will be my last. A few episodes and it will all be over and at least I can say I did it! I lived the dream that so many others allow to fizzle out. *Not me.*

"How are you feeling, Tina? It's been a long time." Gerry kisses me on both cheeks and I relax immediately. A friendly face. I'm so glad he's met me here, given I know no-one else. I feel like the new girl joining school mid-term when everyone else is in their cliques with already established friendships while she stands back praying someone will invite her to join their gang. Usually the nerds. No-one picks a freckled face to be in the coolest gang. At least they never did.

"Like a wet rag, Gerry." I arch my back with discomfort.

I spent the night fidgeting and shifting around to avoid being impaled by a ferocious mattress spring. My body feels tender and delicate and my head feels like it's taken a blow. It has, from a rock-hard pillow.

"Do you have the call sheet for this week?" I enquire.

"I want to introduce you to the assistant director first. He's organised a read-through for this morning and then some of you will be going off-site to do some practical training." Gerry scans the room, waving across at a tall, stocky guy who waves back.

Sounds exciting!

"What sort of practical training?"

"I'm not sure, Tina. But you can ask him yourself."

He leads me over to the AD and introduces me.

"Nice to meet you, Tina." Nick Hand smiles warmly. "Sorry I didn't get to meet you at the casting. I must have just missed you."

He seems to be a decent enough guy and not at all intimidating like some directors can be. "Yes, I nearly never made it," I explain earnestly.

"Well, I'm glad you did," he replies absently, striding off with those long legs of his.

"Oh." I watch him disappear. "I'll ask him about the practical stuff later."

"The contract, Tina, I need you to sign it." Gerry removes a plastic wallet from his briefcase and pulls out two typed contracts. "I've checked it over and there's nothing too onerous in there but you might want to fax it to your lawyer for the once-over."

My imaginary lawyer on my imaginary holiday. Erm . . . no, thanks.

"It's okay, thanks, Gerry, I trust you!" I laugh, eyeing him suspiciously. My instinct tells me this is not a good move and normally this contract would be scrutinised with a fine eye but what choice do I have? He's never let me down before and right now I don't have anyone I can ask to check this over. This entire project needs to remain top secret until I find the right moment to announce it, preferably before it's aired. In fact, if I thought I could get away with it, I'd never tell a soul. This is about me, achieving my dreams and putting closure on them.

Before the read-through I take time out to digest the characteristics of Balmy. I must have looked rough on the day of the audition because they've cast me as a dowdy, frumpy, late-twenties weirdo whose wardrobe consists of charity-shop cast-offs and freebies. Her outlook on life is pretty disturbed for a relatively young woman – she refuses to spend money on clothes or luxuries and her motto is '*You go out the way you came in'*. With nothing! I can see her point entirely but surely witnessing just how short life is she'd want to make the most of it, and of herself. That's one thing we don't have in common. I've come to terms with the necrophiliac theme (to a degree), and now the more I read the more excited I become at the prospect of playing Balmy. It's a total challenge for me, plus I get to practise applying make-up to dummies and reliving my Girl's World 'Styling Head' days. How fantastic is that?

"Okay, everyone, can I have your attention, please!" Nick shouts assertively. "Tina, Raymond, Hattie and Cyril, your car is outside waiting to take you to the funeral home."

What? "What?" It leaves my lips in horror.

"It's part of the practical." Nick shrugs. "How can you learn to embalm without firsthand experience?"

The hairs on my arms stand on end and a shiver runs down my spine.

Raymond, my onscreen fiancé, whispers in my ear. "It's in the contract."

I glare at him, cursing inwardly that I've actually got to kiss him. *Nobody likes a know-it-all.*

The reception is bright and airy with pale wooden flooring and bright red walls. It bears no resemblance to my perception of a funeral home: black, dark and foul-smelling. Vases of fresh flowers emit a tingling scent and mellow pipe music plays soothingly in the background. Walled art hangs here and there, with marked prices displayed beneath each picture – the work is truly beautiful and as I move in to take a closer look it becomes apparent that the artists are deceased. Their names and dates of death are clearly marked below, leaving only a legacy of talent, a reflection of their thoughts captured in a montage of colour. I swallow hard. I'm no good with death. In fact, I think I'd go so far as to say I have a phobia about it. So often I'll lie awake at night wondering how I'll cope if any of my family or Kate dies and countless times I have cried myself to sleep with morose fatigue. On the rare occasions I have lost somebody, like my grandma, I didn't sleep for fear she might pay me a visit. Much as I loved her, I wouldn't want to see her as a ghost or anything other than what she was when she was alive and well. I've lost aunts, uncles and grandparents on both sides and on every occasion I swear a picture has moved or a piece of jewellery I'd lost suddenly turns up.

Hattie and Cyril play the directors of the funeral parlour and, like their characters, they're both in their early sixties and extremely pleasant to talk to.

"How come you guys are so calm?" I ask them, nervously shuffling from one leg to the other as we wait for the real business owner to introduce himself.

Hattie sweeps back her dark brown hair, lifting it away from her face to reveal silvery white roots. "You get hardened to it." She shrugs. "By the time you reach our ages you've lost relatives, friends, friends of friends and neighbours." She gives a half-smile. "Besides, death is the only thing in life that really is inevitable."

Thanks for that depressing note.

A door in the back wall opens and a grey-haired gentleman rushes towards us with his hand extended. "Frank Bolton. I'm so sorry to have kept you waiting," he apologises before shaking our hands one by one. Except for mine.

I pull back and stare at his hand, refusing to shake it. I'm sorry but I just can't.

"Has it . . . you know . . . touched one of them?"

Thankfully he's not offended and simply nods. His face is kind and sincere, almost sympathetic.

"Well, yes, it has, but I've washed my hands thoroughly." He offers them for close inspection.

"Don't be offended if I don't, will you?" I look up at him through my long eyelashes trying to win him over, ensuring he knows not to take it personally.

"In this game you learn not to be easily offended, Miss." He opens the door to take us through to the back where it all happens. "But if you won't touch my hand, Miss, I do wonder how are you going to cope as the day progresses."

"I'm going to kill you, Gerry," I mutter under my breath as I step cautiously through the door. "*Nothing onerous*"? *Bloody idiot.*

Frank Bolton carves the path and we follow him down a corridor with doors leading off it to each side. For some reason I'm holding my breath but I'm not sure how long I can sustain it. He turns around. "Are you okay, Miss?"

I refuse to breathe out in case I get possessed when I breathe in again. I've seen it happen in horror films. The dead bodies manifest themselves into apparitions and find a way to draw strength by possessing any living human and sapping away their energies.

"Mmm," I nod, but my head feels light and my chest tightens. *Breathe, Tina, breathe!* I exhale what little air I have left and, in a microsecond, draw a short breath of new air.

329

We stop outside a white door which Frank opens with a key from his pocket and my legs turn to jelly at the thought of my worst nightmare realising itself. I feel physically ill.

"Is there . . . anyone . . . in there?" I ask trembling.

Frank turns to answer, half in and half out of the doorway, keeping it ajar with his foot. "There is someone resting in here, Miss."

He pushes the door wide open and the others make their way inside. He waits like a gentleman for me to pass by him but I freeze, incapable of moving, and the art of putting one foot in front of the other seems to have been deleted from my motor skills.

"I'm sorry, Miss but I'm simply doing what I have been briefed to do with you all." He looks a little uncomfortable.

I nod. I know, and that's all very well if you don't mind being around dead people but it's not exactly natural. Who would want to be in a place like this? They're dead, discoloured and damn scary and much as I love the thrill of Touche Éclait and Urban Decay, applying them to a bunch of stiffs is not quite what I had in mind – it's sacrilege, never mind totally sick.

You have to do it, Tina, or you'll be axed on your first day. It's all in the name of art, remember.

But I can't breathe, never mind make up a stiff!

Put it down to research and get on with it!

I bolt upright as the potent scent hits me and I taste its odour in my mouth as it travels through my open airways. I scan the room for a reminder of where I am and what I'm doing lying flat on this brightly coloured carpet. *Oh Jesus!* Then the penny drops and the reality hits me once more. I saw it. Him. A dead person lying there. Cold and stiff. I don't remember much after that.

"Smelling salts." Frank shows me the sachet which brought me around so abruptly.

He bends down to assist me to stand up but I can't bear for him nor anyone associated with this place to touch me.

My bare hands are in contact with the carpet and I draw them up in a flash. Who knows its previous occupants? It might well have provided a temporary resting place while the steel beds were being prepared. I try to get up touching nothing or no-one but my legs don't have the strength to act with such muscular isolation and I'm beginning to feel faint once more. I attempt to repress the feeling of retching by grabbing the salts from his hand, trying to avoid any direct contact with his skin, and I shove them under my nose for distraction. *Stay calm. Breathe. No! Don't breathe!* I don't know whether to hold my breath and pass out again, putting a temporary end to this nightmare, or take enough of a breath to lend me time to escape from this hellhole. I'm an actress and am all for research but this is totally crazy and unnecessary – they're dead, for Christ's sake – what use are they to any of us?

Frank and my fellow cast members stand around, peering down at me doing nothing and saying nothing. *Bloody idiots. Help me up or something.* I stretch out a shaky hand to Raymond, inviting him to pull me up, I only hope that he hasn't been near it while I've been in La La Land. He pulls me up, placing his arm around my waist while I steady myself, perhaps a little too tightly but I can't tell him to ease off unless I open my mouth and that just isn't going to happen and neither do I have the co-ordination to slap him.

"It's okay, I've got you." His other arm sweeps across my stomach sitting high on my ribcage where it stays firmly put and I'm propped safely from both sides.

Pervert.

"Would you like to try again, Miss?" Frank asks awkwardly. "Perhaps you could watch your colleagues and take on a more, erm, observing role?"

"Hhmm." My head moves from side to side in a 'no' action although the muffled sound comes across as more of a yes.

"I'm sorry, Miss, was that a yes or a no?"

That's it. There's nothing for it but to run as fast as my legs will take me. I can no longer spend another second sharing this toxic and polluted air. My legs sprint with Olympic speed towards the exit and I imagine I'm being chased by a poltergeist to spur me on – I could be for all I know. It can happen to people with psychic abilities.

Bolting through the corridor, past the reception area and straight out of the front door, I dart through the busy streets oblivious to the strange looks, yelling apologies to those I bump into like an out-of-control dodgem. I run and run until the oxygen supply is cut off from my legs and I collapse to the ground, gasping for breath and panting uncontrollably. Of all the situations to be faced with, of all the parts to land it had to include a bloody trip to a funeral parlour! My worst nightmare.

I shudder as I relive the moment where the body was unveiled, its blue protective blanket pulled back to expose a man that once was. Don't get me wrong, I'm not without my sympathy for him and his family but there is something not quite right about associating with people once they're dead.

I'll tell you one thing for certain, I am never going to one of those places again. *Not even when I'm dead!*

"Silence on set, please!" Nicks yells. "Roll camera . . . and sound!"

The clapper-board slams together.

"Take three . . . Action!"

Raymond as Craig goes down on bended knee, pulling a box from his pocket. His made-up face is menacing and dark circles are painted beneath his eyes but his smart work attire steers you away from thinking he's anything more than menacing.

"Balmy . . ." He looks up at me innocently. "I love you . . . will you marry me?" He opens the box, displaying its contents in the rehearsed direction of the camera, angled for a head-on view. I gasp with amazement and hold the position, trying not to blink or show any indicative emotion. The viewing public must have no idea what the answer is as we end episode one with this magnificent cliffhanger.

"Cut!" Nick claps his hands. "Well done, you guys. Only three takes."

I pull Raymond to his feet, grateful to him for not grassing me up to Nick. Neither Hattie nor Cyril have mentioned my little episode and fingers crossed that all three of them will continue on their silent journey.

Raymond and I wander across to the green room which is laid out with catering-sized flasks of tea, coffee and calorific snacks galore. In fact, every production I

333

have ever worked on has had catering facilities which go for overkill – it's a wonder that any actors are slim. I cast my eyes over the pastries, wondering whether to risk it. Just one perhaps? Although if I'm not careful I could very well end up massive by the end of our shoot. Balmy could transform from being dowdy and frumpy, to dowdy, frumpy and fat.

"Where are you staying then, Tina?" Raymond piles his plate with an assortment of biscuits.

"The Anchor." I squirm with embarrassment. "It's the pits."

"Poor you!" He tuts with genuine concern, dunking a biscuit into his tea.

How common.

"Most of us are at the Ambassador – why don't you join us?"

I suppose I could. I barely slept a wink last night fighting off mattress coil after mattress coil and even after a long shower I feel like I'm still wearing the mattress and carrying its plague on my skin. "How much is it?" I chance a plain biscuit, nibbling at it to make it last.

"Sixty quid including breakfast – it's a concessionary rate for the cast and crew and it's within walking distance of here and staggering distance of the pub!" He wipes his mouth with his sleeve to remove the damp crumbs and I watch as they splay on to the studio floor.

"That's not too bad actually. I'm paying forty to be in Fawlty Towers."

My hand hovers over the machine as I wait to punch in the pin code. It sounds four high-pitched bleeps as I hit the keys.

Packed and eager to leave, I sit with my holdall at my feet and I drift into a daydream of lying in a hot soapy bath, ridding my skin of its filthy tarnish, bathing the coil marks with a moisturising glove of steaming water.

"Sorry, love, but this card has been declined."

"Pardon?"

"This says declined – do you have another card?"

Her hair is greasy and scraped back from her face in a style much too young for a woman of her ageing years and heavy facial lines. Her eyes narrow with an uncomfortable tightness.

"Can you please try again? I'm nowhere near my credit limit."

These machines are so temperamental. I keep the credit limit fairly low to avoid the temptation of going spend-happy, but generally I'm pretty constrained. I got my fingers burnt with credit-card debt as a student and I've managed to avoid a repeat scenario since. As a matter of course, I carry only a single credit card at any one time. It's safer that way.

I take a seat and wait patiently while she tries the card once more.

She shakes her head. "Same again."

Huffing with a tiredness made worse by this twelve-hour day, I part with what cash I have in my purse, dialling the credit-card company as I turn to leave.

Some holiday this is turning out to be. Day one and I'm wrecked!

25

The streets are littered and dirty with gangs of teenagers hanging from street corners, hooded and armed with attitude. With no remaining cash for a cab, I've been forced to walked to the Ambassador. My back is aching from the weight of the holdall and my shoulder is bruised from yesterday's passing-out episode (a familiar occurrence at the funeral parlour, it seems).

My hair is frizzy and dry, suffering from alienation and the damp north-west air.

I spot an off-licence and cross over to the other side of the road, desperate for a drink. With less than a fiver to spend, I opt for a cheap bottle of German white with a screw cap and the temptation not to swig it on the journey is killing me, especially after the news I've just had. I'm still in a state of shock. I had a three-thousand-pound limit on that card. I can't understand it. The adviser was extremely pleasant as she read out to me the list of transactions and I swear I detected a degree of humour in her voice. Okay, so I went to see those guys a couple of times and had one or two telephone readings, from memory, but I never expected the bills to add up to this. Twenty minutes here, half an hour there and you're talking hundreds. And hundreds. And more.

I squeeze the wine bottle into the holdall, giving myself a mental bollocking as I relay the list of items read out to me. Crystals, sleep-inducing water, tarot cards, a library of books, the medium pendulum, daily horoscope text messages, a crystal ball . . . oh and calls charged at one pound fifty a minute! Stupid, stupid cow.

This is not turning out how I imagined. None of it is.

I battle with myself for the remainder of the journey, something I haven't done for years – apart from of late. There are so many things to deliberate, the business which is starting to become extremely successful, my love life which appears to have taken a nosedive and my absolute inability to be me, like I used to be. I miss myself.

Message after message has been left for Brian and not once has he returned my calls or texts. Good enough, he's kept to his word and one of his men is carrying out the building work for the new shop as we speak, but in terms of contact with him, it's non-existent and for the first time I'm beginning to wonder whether in fact he isn't my soul mate after all. Maybe she was right in that *"no woman can tame him"*? I certainly don't appear to have succeeded. Or maybe she was wrong? Wrong in her vocation, wrong in her message and wrong for telling me something she couldn't possibly have known without knowing me? Although what feels right is as clear as mud these days and once again I feel compelled to ask for some help. But it's those very words that provide the clarity I need to remind myself just how the debts ran so high. *I need help!* Every time I've been required to make any type of decision, no matter how small, I've called one of them, whatever they answer to – psychic, fortune-teller, clairvoyant, spiritualist – but I've ended up more confused than ever. I'm no longer capable of making choices or sticking with a simple decision and I'm stuck in a strange zone from which I can't escape. It's almost like being an addict. *Just one more,* I tell myself. *Okay but this will definitely be the last.* But it never is.

I frantically scroll through my phone's address book, speed-dialling the number while grabbing my purse for my bank card.

"Look, I'm in a desperate hurry and I need help fast." The words sprint from my mouth.

This one is definitely the last. I really mean it.

"What else have you been in then, Tina?" Craig enquires, knocking back the remainder of his drink. At the rate he's downing Jack Daniels there's going to be a sore head amongst us tomorrow.

"I haven't been in anything for years," I tell him, slightly embarrassed. "I left acting a while back to set up my own business."

"Cool. What do you do?" He rattles the ice around, swigging back any watery remnants.

"I'm an estate agent," I tell him proudly. "I'm just about to open my second office."

He looks suitably impressed. "Wow. How are you managing to juggle the business and *Stiffs* without a nervous breakdown?"

"I have the most amazing office manager," I gloat. "She'll have the place ticking over nicely."

"I've always fancied being my own boss, you know,

when I get bored of this stuff." He gestures to the waiter for more drinks. "Maybe owning a restaurant or a bar or something."

"That's what my best friend wants to do, open a restaurant but serving fat-free food." I giggle. "Kate is as thin as they come but she won't eat more than twenty grams of fat per day as she says the camera puts too much weight on her." I wince as another glass of white wine is placed in front of me. I'm exhausted.

"Kate," he repeats. "She's in the business then?"

"Kate Symms," I boast. "She's my best friend."

He grins at me, chinking his glass against mine. "Every man's perfect pin-up."

"Yes, she'd be mine too!" I think out loud.

He looks dramatically shocked and raises an eyebrow. "Are you two . . .?"

"God, no!" I squeal. "We're way past that stuff now!"

I wobble to my feet, thanking Raymond for his kindness and promising to pay him back tomorrow night. Despite the insistent offers, I decide to call it a night and decline to join the others on their quest for absolute drunkenness. I hardly know my lines for tomorrow's scenes. For those folk who do only this for a living it's easier, but for me, trying to run a business between burying my head in pages of scripts, it isn't easy.

Thankfully Balmy is more of a thinker than a talker but she says enough, and it's what she doesn't say that makes those scenes all the more difficult. In addition, I need to know most of Raymond's lines so I know what I have to do or say once he's finished, and the timing has to be to absolute precision. Do something too fast or too slow and the entire scene has to be reshot, stand an inch too far to the left or right and you're out of range. What looks so natural on television is about as natural as an albino with a sun tan. There's so much to remember but all I can think about right now is getting a good night's sleep.

The room is pitch black and I flick the bedside lamp on to check the time. *Damn*. It's four a.m. and I've been out for the count, fully clothed. The script sheets are crumpled where I've rolled on to them and I gather them, putting them under the heavy mattress to straighten out. I wriggle out of my jeans and T-shirt before diving back into bed with only two more hours of sleep before the alarm goes off.

The set is awesome today, a little too awesome really. It looks like a replica of the funeral home and I did hear that Frank Bolton played some part in its design. Metal tables are lined up in the middle of the room with clinical white sheets draped over them. Some of the extras have been painted pale grey with blue lips and are lying partially naked beneath the thin white cloths, the hard surfaces no doubt aiding their pained expression and as they lie there, breath held.

The camera films a shot of the empty room. The scene is shot from inside the room and the camera zooms in on the door. The sound of a key turning can be heard amidst the absolute silence of death. The door creaks open and the camera closes in on a pair of black shoes entering mutely. As it travels north, it stops at the neck of the intruder, leaving us guessing just who it is. It continues its journey of intrigue by capturing a shot of the person from behind. We see him remove the plastic sheet from a resting female before he begins to fondle her breasts. His other hand disappears to crotch level and a gesticulating action is clearly evidenced, the deliberate sound effects make clear to the viewer exactly what is happening but without the graphic imagery.

My stomach is turned but good on Raymond for his performance – he's amazing as is the poor model lying there allowing her tits to be fondled by someone earning ten times her daily sum.

"*Cut!*"

Raymond fumbles with his fly, apologising to the actress for his cold hands.

"You've done that before!" I tease him.

"Not without a pulse, I haven't!" He laughs dirtily. "Do you want to run over our next scenes?"

"Yeah, that would be good." I rummage through my bag for the script, removing its entire contents but coming up empty-handed. I curse under my breath. "It's under the bed."

"Whose bed?"

"My bed."

"What are you on about?"

"The script is under my bed in the hotel. I slept on it last night and put it under the mattress to straighten it out." I feel like such an amateur right now. "I forgot to get it this morning. Can I share yours?"

"You can share my bed any time, Tina!"

Five missed calls and three voice mails.

I listen to the messages and my heart sinks into the pit

341

of my stomach. Chantelle sounds more and more irate
with each message and while she has apologised for
ringing me when I'm on holiday, it appears there is some
sort of mistake she needs to talk to me about. Apparently we
were supposed to complete on a purchase for a young
couple yesterday but the bank have refused to release the
funds until all offer conditions have been fully met. It seems
the title deeds, which where sent to me, have disappeared. I
do recall receiving them but I swear I sent them on to the
clients' solicitors.

I think frantically before returning her call. The name
sounds familiar and I can almost, if I try hard, recall
putting the deeds in an envelope and into the external
post tray. I dial the office, praying that no-one answers.
I can't lie to Chantelle usually but today I'll have to.

"Good afternoon, Harding Homes, Chantelle speaking."

She answered. Damn. "How are you coping?"

"Fine, Tina, thanks, apart from this hiccup." She sounds
calm which is good. "About 87 Roundhay Gardens. The
vendors' solicitors say they posted the title deeds to you.
They know this was in error and have apologised,
blaming it on a trainee conveyancer but her file clearly
shows they were sent for your attention two weeks ago."
She pauses. "Do you have them?"

I rack my brains again to recall such a rare thing
happening.

"I'll be honest, Chantelle, I do recall seeing some title
deeds but I could have sworn I posted them back with a
compliment slip, noting the error made. But I'd be lying
if I said I could recall the full details."

"The Barkers moved out of their flat yesterday and
have had to move in with family until the bank releases

the money." She sounds empathetic if a little fraught. "I wonder how quickly we can get another copy?"

"Get back on to the vendors' solicitors, and get them to explain to Planning what has happened. They should be able to request duplicate copies for a fee." I sigh heavily and wish I was there to sort this out myself. "One thing's for sure, the bank won't release any mortgage funds until every single offer condition has been met." I sigh heavily. "Wouldn't you think their solicitor would have realised this one condition was still outstanding?" I tut. "Plus we need that commission so I'm keen to get it wrapped up, Chantelle."

"Absolutely." She sounds a little guilty. "Sorry for bothering you on holiday by the way. How is it?"

"It's great, thanks. The usual sun, sea and sangria." I laugh. Suddenly remembering that I'm supposed to be in Greece where they don't drink sangria. It's raki or ouzo. Thankfully she doesn't twig.

"Well, enjoy it and I'll send you a text to let you know the outcome. Oh and sorry for all the messages. There were other problems I had to sort out but they're done and dusted now."

Historically, we have made few mistakes at Harding Homes, but I can't help but think that a few more and Chantelle might gain some much-needed experience in learning to put them right. On her own.

Raymond and I run through our lines once more before going on set. I take my position by the corpse while he stands close behind me on a clearly marked spot. As usual I'm dressed in loose-fitting trousers and a blue linen overall, showing nothing of the figure I've worked so hard to maintain. The make-up is pale and uninteresting, giving me that barely there look. A look I detest in anybody.

"*Action.*"

Raymond as Craig removes his suit jacket and loosens his tie before opening the top button of his shirt. He looks stressed and agitated.

"What's gotten into you, Craig?" I ask blandly in my Balmy role as I apply concealer to the corpse's painted blue lips like it's the most natural thing in the world.

He looks uncomfortable and shifts nervously about the room.

"These places give me the creeps," he tells me. "I don't know how you can work here, Balmy." His words quite clearly speak a different language to his body and a look of lust is evident to all but Balmy who is engrossed in her work of art. "But I love you for it."

His hands grasp my shoulders from behind, massaging them roughly, using his thumbs. He fumbles with the belt of his trousers, dropping them to the floor and bites my neck with sexual vigour.

"Craig!"

I try to duck away from his hungry mouth but his hands wrap themselves around my waist, pulling me close and holding me firmly in place, face down. "I'm working! Stop it!" He clumsily grabs hold of my breasts with one hand, pulling my elasticated trousers down with the other and we simulate the act of full penetration. He thrusts rhythmically, holding onto my hips, staring at the corpse in front of him while I remain bent over with my back to him. "What do you do to their bodies, Balmy?" he pants excitedly.

"We put – moisturiser – on them – to keeeep – their

skiiin – sssoft . . ." My words break as I'm jerked forward with each intense thrust.

"Where do you put it?" he shrieks.

"Ev – ery – where!"

He yells with orgasmic pleasure.

"*Cut!*"

We're into the eleventh hour and my knees are starting to buckle. In between breaks I've been checking the office is running as smoothly as can be with so few staff and my eyes are blinking like mad as the continued fight to stay awake becomes more difficult with each passing moment. This is supposed to be fun and, while I am enjoying being on set, the fatigue of almost twelve hours, day in day out, is beginning to take its toll. The rest of the cast look as fresh as the first day, but me, I'm slowly starting to look like I need some serious embalming.

Every night I've been falling into bed, often without my usual beauty regime, which is a clear indication of my low energy levels and I'm out cold before my head hits the pillow. Up at the crack of dawn, I shove a few spoonfuls of breakfast down with very strong coffee and bury my head in the day's call sheet while refamiliarising myself with the lines. But it's getting harder with every scene and I've noticed a few extra takes here and there which isn't helping. This lie really feels like a lie now, a big fat one at that and I so wish I was sunbathing on a beach with my best friend, laughing at her childish quips and drinking ice-cold beer while planning my evening attire.

I can't believe I've kept this from everyone. My mum, my sister, my best friend, my colleagues and even the man I thought I was courting. Obviously not. I'm lonely and isolated and don't ever remember working so hard for something I can't even share with those I love. Living a lie is no fun and neither is living a double life. I can't, however, regret getting this out of my system. It must have been meant to be because, although I still feel like I belong in front of the camera, I feel more like I belong as Christina Harding, the businesswoman and honest citizen I am, or once was. Reliable, trustworthy and family-loving.

Acting is definitely not all it's cracked up to be and I can see why Kate speaks so harshly of it but, as she often says, she's incapable of doing anything else so they're stuck with her.

Well, they're not stuck with me. Good riddance! Almost.

26

The blasted phone hasn't stopped ringing and I'm too tired to answer it after one of the hardest weeks of my life. I switch it off and thrust it deep into my bag.

It's the wrap party tonight and I'm determined to be the belle of the ball and show my fellow cast that beneath the baggy linen overcoat is a woman with curves in all the right places, although less after the physicality of this week. Raymond has been a complete flirt and I'm looking forward to making a grand entrance now that it appears I might be temporarily single. The ironic thing is that I can't even pretend I'm overly sad about Brian although I am a little mixed up. We were doing so well together and the chemistry was there in bucketloads. For it to have ended so abruptly, with no warning and as far as I can see with no valid reason, is a blow. I feel more cross towards him than anything else. A simple sorry would have sufficed.

I cast my eye over the Rolex, wondering whether I should give it back. *No chance, matey!* I miss the cars, the expensive meals and the prospects of what could have been, but it's the what-could-have-beens that have landed me in so much trouble lately. *It should have been me. It could have been me. Maybe he's my soul mate. Maybe it's meant to be. Perhaps I'm supposed to take this path . . .*

I perk up as I take in the view of myself in the mirror, glamorous and sexy on the outside and absolutely wasted on the inside. My limbs ache, my head hurts and my mind would be happy not to think of anything else for all eternity, but as usual I'm incapable of switching off. In fact, I'm surprised I even sleep at all.

The fitted black satin trousers sit just on my hips, revealing an inch of toned stomach, and the boned bodice pulls in my waist and pushes up my boobs with an impressive hoist. My hair has been curled and then fluffed out, giving it that full-bodied but natural look. I curse that I forgot my straighteners but I left in such a hurry after working on at the office that I just had to grab my bag and go.

As a character Balmy was great to play, a far cry from the usual roles I've experienced, and as for the subject matter, that's definitely a first for my CV. The show will be pitched as a black satirical drama and black it is. The strangest thing for me is the realisation that this is no longer what I want to do. I thought I wanted it and now I truly know that, quite simply, I don't. I really don't. The lifestyle, the money, the parties, it's all so glamorous yet at the same time it's a complete joke. The industry is crippled with insecure wrecks who survive by feeding off compliments or by having people rally around after them massaging their egos and providing them with an air of injected self-importance. It's become clear to me that so few of these people are happy, stable individuals. I know because I've been at both ends of it and still within reason I too can be a little self-obsessed with my external appearance but that I doubt I'll ever shake off. One thing I can be sure of is that I want to go home and see my family, concentrate on my business and make the most of my life by moving forward now that this episode is almost out of the way. I will come clean once a plausible rationale has been devised and then move on with my life. And at least I can say '*I did it*' whatever my motive was. Although in hindsight I'm not sure the motive was mine.

But I still did it wherever the idea came from!

Boom boom boom!

The music pounds and I shout to make myself heard.

No expense has been spared for this wrap party and anyone who's anyone has turned up and in typical red-carpet style. I'm definitely not the belle of the ball but I'm confident I can hold my own and Raymond hasn't taken his eyes off me since I walked in.

Nick struts over to me, kissing me on both cheeks. "I didn't recognise you, Tina." He stands back, taking in the full view. "You look fabulous. We'll have to give Balmy a makeover if she survives."

"Survives what?" I shout.

"The cruel hand of her fiancé." Nick pulls a comedic face and pats me on the shoulder. "Thanks for your hard work, Tina." He moves on, mingling sociably with the other guests.

I'm desperate to dance. The DJ is playing eighties music and it's so reminiscent of my happiest years that I yearn to let rip on the dance floor and just release the anxiety which has been building up for some time now.

It's over and a weight has been lifted from my shoulders.

I find Raymond and grab his hand, pulling him roughly onto the hard floor directly beneath the mirrored disco ball. His shirt sparkles with flecks of light.

"*Re-light my fire ...*" I screech at the top of my voice. My hips gyrate like a piece of elastic as I dance provocatively with my legs slightly apart. It's the same old dance I've done since school. The only issue is that the older you get, the less you can get away with it.

Raymond closes in, placing his hand on the small of my back, and pulls me towards him. Our groins are practically touching. *Loser! What are you doing?*

I spin around, escaping his grip and break into my own dance once more, wild and free and light. *You did it, Tina! It's over now but you made it, my girl!*

I fling my arms in the air to the *'hey'* in the song. How can a girl survive without Take That?

Raymond continues to make his advances by dancing towards me. He evidently has two left feet and I'm not sure whether to burst out laughing or call an ambulance. I've never seen anyone take a fit before but this must be the closest thing to it. *Perhaps he has epilepsy?* As he reaches me his hands crudely grip my hips and he sways them rhythmically from side to side. I take hold of them in an attempt to remove them from my person but their grasp is firm and I struggle to wrestle free from his superbly glued fingers. Without warning he pounces on me, throwing his lips onto mine, and I feel his clumsy tongue forcing its way into my mouth. Horrified, the strength to remove him comes to me rapidly.

"What the hell are you doing?" I yell, tempted to slap his face.

He looks shocked and then embarrassed with rejection.

"It's nothing we haven't been doing all week!" he barks back as I lipread him.

"We were acting, you dickhead!"

I storm off the dance floor.

He runs after me and yanks my arm. "Tina, I'm sorry." He looks forlorn. "I picked up the wrong signals."

"Understatement of the year!" I snap.

"It's just that . . . well . . . you looked like you were coming onto me the way you were dancing."

"That's how I dance, Raymond." I throw my arms up in frustration. "What do you want me to do? Stay glued to the same bloody spot? Look – just piss off!"

"I said I'm sorry." He turns to walk away but hesitates and twists back around, offering his hand out for peace sake. "At least let's be friends if we're going to work together, Tina."

"Raymond, I hope I never see you again after tonight."

"There's not much chance of that."

I'm tired of this argument now and just want to pack my bags and think about my own bed and getting a much-needed fatherly hug from my dad. And I'm suddenly desperate to ring my mum or Kate and tell them how hard yet how necessary this week has been and how I've hated lying to them. I'm ready to come clean.

Raymond tuts. "Now you're just being silly, Tina. At least let's put this behind us for professional purposes."

"What are you on about?" I fumble in my clutch bag for the hotel key card. "We're finished. The series is finished. I won't ever have to work with you again."

"Finished?" He looks genuinely astonished. "What do you mean? We're signed up for three series – we're going to have to work together, Tina."

"*What?*"

The room seems to have turned silent and my mouth dries up. I no longer hear the thumping music nor the hum of strained voices shouting over it. My ears ring hollowly and my stomach folds into itself, contorting and twisted.

"It's in the contract." He laughs sarcastically. "Did you even read it, Tina?" He turns and walks away, leaving me standing there, open-mouthed and gasping for breath.

"Wait," I pant after him. "I don't understand – it's not even been aired yet."

Raymond shakes his head cockily. "A pilot episode was put out to tender before we were even on the scene." He remarks knowingly. "It was snapped up by a private investor who coughed up the rest of the production funds. Where have you been, Tina? This thing is going to be massive!" He glares at me as I stand there, gaping. "What planet are you on?"

I have no idea how I got back to the hotel. I must have floated or had the aid of an out-of-body experience because I'm definitely here sitting on the hotel bed, only I can't recall the journey. "*It's in the contract. Did you even read it?*" The contempt in his voice was bitter, his tone bore all the arrogance of a man with the leading role, a principal with a prima-donna personality to match it. *"We're signed up for three series!"*

I've a business to run. A new shop to open. A staff member to console and a relationship to resurrect, plus I'm still in the process of carrying out remedial work on my sister after nearly ruining her wedding day. This really can't be happening. I delve deep to find an answer that will help me unscramble what's going on in my head, a logical solution to put an end to this illogical episode. I need to phone somebody even if it is midnight, I need to hear a friendly voice. Someone who I know and who knows me. I've been alienated from everyone and everything I love for the past seven days and I'm lonely, exhausted and confused. *And tied into two more series!*

I grab the phone but don't switch it on. *Think, Tina. Don't be hasty. You need a strategy. Fail to prepare, prepare to fail!*

Kate! I'll ring Kate. She has no idea I've taken the holiday I was too busy to go on, she thinks I've been working hard at the office.

I switch on the phone, ignoring the abundance of missed calls and dial Kate's number, desperate to hear her cheery tones.

"Who the hell have you been talking to?" she snarls.

"Kate, is that you?" I must have misdialled.

"Of course it's me!" she spits. "Now explain to me why the hell I'm on the front page of three tabloid newspapers labelled an anorexic lesbian!"

What?

"What?" I rack my brains but come back with nothing. Someone tell me this isn't happening.

"Who have you been talking to, Tina?"

"No-one, Kate! You're my best friend! I'd never betray you." A feeling of paranoia sweeps over me. *Who have I been talking to?*

"Well, isn't it funny how the papers have quoted *you*, Tina."

"Me?"

"Yes, you! It reads '*My Perfect Pin-up*'!"

"Uuh?"

"Don't play stupid, Tina. It quotes you saying '*We're way past all that now*'! Who the hell were you talking to?" Her voice breaks and she stops mid-sentence. She is upset, painfully upset. And then the penny drops.

"Oh God, Kate." I shudder. "I know who it was."

I tell Kate about Raymond, omitting how we came to meet, explaining the innocence behind the misinterpreted remarks, describing how we agreed unanimously about her beauty.

"That bastard!" she yells. "I turned him down for a date last year and he's trying to get back at me! He is a conceited sly little prick who was looking for an opportunity like this!"

Kate blows her nose loudly and a single tear runs down my face. I've humiliated her. Embarrassed her in front of her family and work colleagues and all because of a sly little man whose path should never have crossed with mine.

"And you set it up nicely for him, Tina."

"Kate, it was all so innocent! I swear on my life!"

I start to cry as the weight of everything lands on my shoulders with an almighty thud. "Of all the people to have bumped into, it just had to be him . . . I didn't know who he was or what he would do . . . it was innocent, Kate."

Kate clears her throat. "Where did you meet him?"

"What?"

"Where did you meet him?" she repeats coldly. "He usually hangs out at strip joints and seedy places and I can't see you at one of those."

Think, Tina.

"I was at a seminar in Manchester, with, erm, work," I lie. "I went into the hotel bar for a drink afterwards and he was there."

This seems to satisfy Kate but her distance tells me that she is totally overwhelmed by the exposure and not quite with us. This happens to other celebrities but Kate keeps herself squeaky-clean to avoid any negative headlines – she says it upsets her parents too much.

"Kate," I whisper, "are you okay?"

"Mmhh." She sounds emotionally drained. "My agent had a go at me yesterday over this. He had asked me if I had any skeletons in the closet and of course I said no . . ."

"But you haven't!" I shout in defence.

"I know that, Tina," she snaps. "But to have a quote from your best friend doesn't look good, does it? I just pray he doesn't drop me."

Oh God!

"I am sorry from the bottom of my heart, Kate. I'd never do anything to hurt you." My voice breaks. "You know that, don't you?"

The silence prolongs and my stomach cyclones.

"Yes," she sighs after a lengthy pause. "I know that, Tina . . ." Then she adds almost absently before hanging up, "But I could still kill you . . ."

My head is pounding. I knew I'd regret that extra bottle of wine I had sent up to the room, but in light of the devastating news I so needed it. Once upon a time, in fact, little over a week ago, the news of a long-running series would have been met with absolute euphoria, but after having a taste of the long days and a blatant reminder of that feeling of isolation and not quite belonging, I no longer want it or need it. Neither do I wish to work alongside sly, sneaky individuals who will sell a story for the guts of a few quid. Maybe Kate was right? It wasn't the money for him, it was the revenge – how dare she knock him back, doesn't she know who he is? And I handed it to him on a plate which wouldn't have happened if I was on holiday or working at the office where I belong or doing something with didn't involve a pack of lies. It's taken this experience to appreciate just what it is I have and what it is I want out of life but it's all a little too late now. I'm tied into two more series, I'm ruined for good. It could be months before I'm freed up and there is no way I can expect Chantelle to keep the business going and who else would I get to manage the new shop? The work has already started. I'm completely ruined and it's all my own doing. *Stupid, stupid girl!*

I consider the potential damage to Kate's career. They're clamping down hard on actors who have eating disorders in an attempt to promote responsibility within the industry. A friend of Kate's was turned down just for being too thin, so determined were they to promote healthy eating. She doesn't have an eating disorder, she watches what she eats, that's all. Don't we all?

The tears roll down my face and my shoulders tighten as I try to suppress them but it's impossible. I'm killing my business, I've alienated my chances of marrying the aspirational man, I am going to be stuck working twelve-hour shifts for God knows how long, my sister has only just come around to forgiving me and my best friend is consumed with saving her career while our relationship may have suffered permanent damage. And after a lifetime of dreaming about this very juncture, I find myself in the rare position of trying to give my acting career away.

I break into a sob, a heartbroken uncontrollable sob. I don't ever recall feeling such a failure, not even when I was on the streets. I knew then that I'd worked as hard as I could have, turned up on time for every audition and gave it one hundred per cent with consistency. But this present comedy of events, this ridiculous method of existing, is all down to me. I can't blame anyone but myself for the dangerous position I'm left in. There really is no such thing as having it all and I curse myself for always learning just a little too late.

My hand scans the bed for the remote control and, eyes still closed, I feel the soft rubbery buttons and make a stab at guessing the power key. This one feels bigger than the rest. *Bingo. God, it's so loud.*

I can't believe it's eleven o'clock. The room needs to be vacated by twelve o'clock but at this rate I can't even see me being out by twelve tomorrow.

I force myself to roll out of bed, literally, and I crawl on my hands and knees towards the kettle, praying there is water inside, given I'm not sure I can make it to the bathroom and back. *There is a God!* I try to stand but my legs shake and the room is spinning. *Hurry up, I need coffee!* Gripping the bed, I pull myself up and perch delicately on the end, staring into the mirror opposite. I've aged a decade over night. My face looks like it's been painted with a permanent worried fix, deeply rooted and cemented in to give it longevity, red eyes sit between swollen lids and dark circles and my face is dry and tight and salty.

My hands tremble as I empty the coffee sachet into the plain white cup, spilling most of it onto the saucer below. I try to pull back the foil of the tiny milk carton but my motor skills are on go-slow and I can't quite manage the required level of coordination.

I'll drink it black.

Time to face the music.

Dressed and almost ready to leave, there is one more thing I need to do: ring my mother and tell her I need her advice. Because I do.

Unplugging the charger, I switch the phone on. *What the . . . ? Twenty-seven messages and thirty-eight missed calls!* Someone is taking the piss and I'm not in the mood for it. I listen to the first couple of messages left by Chantelle getting her knickers in a twist over something or other. I'll soon be there to put it all right. *Oops, they found the title deeds on my desk!* That one will take some explaining.

I delete the messages one by one until I hear my mother's frantic tone. She knows! She knows I'm not away on holiday. *Shit!* They all do. *Where am I?* I listen on as the messages become more hysterical – from her, Sam, and Chantelle, each one of them begging for me to contact them. But it's my dad's voice that gets to me and crushes me to the point of no return.

The messages grow more bizarre. What are they talking about? Press coverage? Radio and TV appeals for my safe return? *What?*

The contents of my stomach explodes through my mouth and splatters across the room. The nausea cripples me and I continue vomiting until there is nothing left but bile. The back of my throat feels like sandpaper and as I swallow a burning liquid acid trickles down into an empty stomach with eroded lining.

I don't understand it. I'm on holiday. I'm not a missing person. How has it come to this? Chantelle knows I'm not missing, I only spoke to her the other day. I spoke to Kate at midnight and she didn't mention it . . . I've only been gone a week.

What have I done?

Perhaps it might be better for everyone if I was missing.

27

Down on all fours, I scrub the carpet with the complimentary facecloth, removing the bulk of the mess which unfortunately does very little to alleviate the hellish stench. Every now and then I have to run to the window and hang out to avoid a repeat performance, and even the dirty Manchester air is better than the putrid smell of this hotel room.

With the facecloth in the bin, I scrub my hands and splash ice-cold water on my face, not even caring that it's gone in my hair and will frizz up by the time I've counted to ten. On a scale of what's happening in my life right now, I don't think I'll ever care about my personal appearance again. Besides, nobody will see me in Siberia which is where I belong, on my own where I can't fuck things up. I can't understand how they think I'm missing. I'm in Crete.

Desperate to know what's happened but not quite ready to speak to my family yet even though I know their agony is prolonged with each extended moment, I stare at the phone wondering who the hell to call first. The police? My sister? Kate? My mum? *Definitely not*

Kate! I wonder why Kate never said anything to me? Perhaps she doesn't know, or perhaps she's too preoccupied with correcting her own life right now? Maybe she is happy for me to stay missing?

Bang bang bang bang! A continued knocking on the hotel door lifts me from my soporific state and I grab the holdall, weak with exertion.

"I'm leaving now!" I call out, conscious that my checkout is an hour overdue. My voice is hoarse and strained. The banging continues and I shuffle to the door wearily, pulling it open, my body shaking with the strain.

I rub my eyes with utter disbelief. I must be seeing things.

"Hello, Tina," he says calmly.

Okay, it speaks. I'm definitely not dreaming.

"Can I come in?"

I nod, speechless, stepping back to let him past me as he takes the holdall from my quivering hand. My lips purse and hard as I try, I can't stop the tears from falling.

"Simon."

I fall into his open arms, oblivious to the smell of my breath and pale grey face, so thankful to see someone I know. "What are you doing here?" I hiccup. "How did you know where to find me?"

Simon holds me tightly. His arm is wrapped around my shoulder and he pulls me towards him where I rest my head on him. The fatigue of it all is starting to kick in and I've only enough energy left to breathe. My body is burnt out and my head is awash with disturbing images of an unpleasant future, one that I should have seen coming. *They* should have seen this coming.

He shakes his head solemnly. "You're in a bit of a

mess, I see," he says with grave concern and I nod pathetically. "As soon as I heard you were missing I had a fair idea of what you were up to."

"But how?"

"I could hardly forget a title like *Stiffs*, could I ?" The corners of his mouth turn up a fraction. "I kept trying to remember the conversation you had on the hands-free the other week even though I wasn't listening," He grins half-heartedly. "I remembered the guy who rang was called Gerry so I contacted every casting agent in the North West until I found him and he told me where you were staying." He releases his hold but continues to talk. "When the hotel told me you'd checked out of there I guessed you'd still be local so I made a list of all Manchester hotels and called them until I found you."

"Does my mother know?" I keep my fingers crossed behind my back and sigh with relief when he gestures not.

"No-one knows I'm here, Tina, but I think we need to make contact with your family immediately." He takes the phone. "Have you any idea how worried they've been?"

I turn away in embarrassment. I'm too much of a idiot to even look him in the eye. "Please don't shout at me," I whisper. "It was never my intention for this to happen. I thought I could get away with being on holiday and keep the whole thing secret until I was ready to tell them." I pause with sad reflection. "Obviously not."

"I'm not here to shout at you." He touches my face softly. "I'm here to help you."

I can't believe Simon has come to my aid. Again. 'Touched' isn't the word, I'm suddenly in complete awe of him and his ability to fix things, like me. I hang my head in shame.

"I don't deserve rescuing," I sob. "But there's something else, Simon, something that's going to ruin me."

"Worse than your family thinking you're dead?"

"I might be better off dead."

"Tina, don't be so dramatic!" he scolds me, harsh in tone. "Your acting days are over now."

"Actually." I pause flatly. "That's where you're wrong."

I grimace at the costly sight of it all. Every last item has been put into a black bin-liner and will be removed from my life forever. I had no idea I was surrounded by so much stuff but, if I'm honest, most of it was kept hidden apart from the odd swing of the dowsing here and a scattering of crystals there. I tear up pages of handwritten notes, desperate to read them again to see if they make sense.

"Just throw them away, Tina, it's all nonsense."

Most of the writing is mine. I made regular notes concerning the content of my dreams and then tried to pick out key messages from them, I scoured my dream dictionary until I found the interpretation which best suited my mood that day, and each time I congratulated myself for my developing psychic skills.

Simon stands in front of me, a dominating sight I thought I'd never see. "All of it," he orders, pointing to some ridiculous pieces of art work I drew after a bottle of wine. The more I drank the more convinced I was that I could draw after all – I am creative, I told myself.

Not any more you're not!

"Go through your phone and delete the numbers, Tina." He hands me the phone, with a facial expression not be messed with. I obey a man who isn't my father for once in my life. I've always had a problem with guys telling me what to do but in this instance I both need it and deserve it and Simon has been a breath of fresh air from the moment he arrived at my hotel room.

He lifts the bag and throws it into the back of his car. *BMW 5 series. Nice!*

"What happened to your old Porsche?"

He slams the boot closed. "It died on me – it was old and clapped out."

Sounds a bit like how I feel.

"Come on, Tina. It's time."

The drive to my parents' house feels like forever. The events of the past few months create so much noise in my head that I shut my eyes and try to focus on something else but it's impossible. I am consumed with emotional bedlam and still in a state of stupor from the clear-out. The stuff I threw away was really quite remarkable – horoscope and destiny magazines, stones, gems, crystals, tarot cards, a mini crystal ball. The list goes on and on. So determined was I to bring my psychic powers to the surface, I purchased the crystal ball from a web site and spent hours staring into it trying to capture images and turn them into predictions. The only vision I ever had was of the wine bottle reflecting back at me, or on a good day I would see, well, just what it was I wanted to see. Nothing that my mind's eye couldn't have shown me and nothing that couldn't have been planned if I really wanted to achieve it. Alone and through sheer grit and determination.

I plan what I'm going to say to them, having talked it over with Simon first. We decided that no-one needs to know about the psychic stuff – the less they have to worry about the better.

Simon tells me about the press coverage and my parents' appeal for my safe return but after a while I tell him to stop, I can't bear to listen any more.

I really thought I had it in the bag and for something as drastic as this to come out of what started off being a little white lie could only happen to me. The only person I've been lying to is myself. But I really did put closure on my failed acting career all those years back and it was only when I kept hearing *'you gave in too soon'* and all the other crap I swallowed naively that I chose to put one and one together to make three. I took out of each reading just what I wanted it to mean, I put together real-life scenarios off the back of bogus predictions and a bunch of spoofs supposedly reading my future. I can't believe I fell for it all, hook, line and sinker but by God has it cost me. I may well have lost everything: my business, my family, my best friend, but come what may I'm going to fight to regain my life and get back in the driving seat.

I sit dutifully at the long table in between my mum and dad. The room is packed full of ravenous journalists and camera crew. There's no escaping them. The press officer talked me through some of the questions I was likely to be asked. We pre-rehearsed the answers and she even told me who was going to ask them and explained their background, which allowed me to feel a little more prepared.

My mum and dad have a tight grip of each of my hands, rested on the table for all to see, as advised. Happy families.

I'll never forget the look on my mother's face as I walked through the door and into her living room. She went to stand but couldn't. I'm not sure she quite believed it was really me and she hasn't let go of me since. I had really done it for her. I wanted to make her proud. I wanted her to be able to affirm to her friends that I merely had been taking time out. I wanted to relive the dream for her more than me.

"Tina, how does it feel to be home?"

I pause calmly to consider my reply. "Amazing." My eyes well and I squeeze my mother's hand. "But I didn't actually know I'd been reported as missing."

"Where were you?" the same journalist asks inquisitively.

"I'm not at liberty to say," I tell him solemnly. "My lawyer has forbidden me to discuss it for the moment." This is true.

I told Simon about the other two series, making it abundantly clear that I didn't want to star in them and needed a get-out clause. As soon as he was confident I wouldn't change my mind, again, he told me to leave it with him but to keep my lips firmly sealed in order to buy him time for our defence. I always knew Simon was a lawyer but I never realised he was a corporate lawyer. I suppose I never asked him or showed any interest. I paid more attention to his creased wardrobe and general slovenliness and never sought to ascertain facts beyond his external appearance. Kate told me I was shallow but I never believed it. I do now.

"Were you in any danger?"

I suppress a giggle at the ambiguity of this question. "No, I wasn't, but I can say no more about what I was doing until I meet with my lawyer."

"What's next for you then, Tina?" a heftily built woman calls to me.

That's an easy one.

"Firstly I have some things to put right with my family and explain why I did what I did. Secondly I want to continue to build my business, Harding Homes, my estate agent's."

The PR guru clears her throat to capture my attention but I ignore her. Any publicity is good publicity and when else am I likely to get the chance to plug this? I need all the help I can get for it to succeed while I play on with the role of fiancé to the most evil man in Britain.

"It's on High Street but I'm opening a second shop in Camberwell Road shortly," I say quickly, seeing the PR woman move closer.

She steps up to the raised platform, holding her hand up to the room.

"No more questions, thank you."

She throws me a look of annoyance.

Sorry but it was there for the taking! I'm not going out without a fight. Welcome back, Tina Harding!

Simon waits patiently in the reception area equipped with pinstriped suit and obligatory briefcase. His defence is a little risky but it's a risk he is prepared to take, he told me off the record, and it's quite contrary to his usual pertinent approach of drowning in stacks of corroborative paperwork.

He grips the burgundy leather briefcase, a tool for

intimidation. I giggled earlier as he showed me its content of empty sweet wrappers and chewed pens. Simon explained that he has a proposition to put to Nick, one which sits outside of the law he has practised for so long and one which requires no text-book analysis, just a pair of steel balls.

"He's free to see you now." The receptionist points in the direction of the room. "Second door on the left."

"Thank you."

Simon glides through the building with convincing arrogance, me trooping behind trying to put up an equal show of confidence. He throws open the door and we enter.

Simon seizes the hand of the gentleman and shakes. I do likewise.

"Nick Hand."

Nick sits down, gesturing for Simon to do the same. "Good handshake," he says to Simon, wincing.

"Simon Heath-Jones, lawyer for Christina Harding." Simon talks sternly and purposefully. He goes straight for the jugular. "We need to talk, Mr Hand."

Simon places the paper in front of Nick. "It's all clearly documented. We will fulfil our side of the deal once you've signed, giving permission for the release of Miss Harding. Naturally, there is a clause banning you from discussing this private arrangement with anyone." He stares him out with elfish green eyes. "Anyone at all."

We stands to leave.

"I'm sure you'll make the right decision, Mr Hand," says Simon.

We exit via the stairway, taking the steps two by two. Simon literally jumps through the door, loosening his tie and mopping sweat from his forehead. His hands shake as he runs them through his damp sandy hair and his mouth is dry and tight.

Then he looks at me and smiles. "A strange case for an even stranger girl," he says.

"Surprise!"

I jerk backwards in total shock as a room full of familiar faces yells at me excitedly. *A party. For me?* I stand there completely mute and unable to move. I expected reactions of hostility crossed with relief. I anticipated playing the role of dutiful daughter, sister and employer but I certainly didn't expect to be greeted with such warmth and openness. I don't deserve it.

I'm grabbed, hugged, playfully strangled and generally mobbed by all the people I know and love and I can't recall a single other moment in my life where I've felt so wanted and so utterly forgiven. Don't get me wrong – I've never been the type to have a chip on my shoulder, in fact far from it – it's just that taking in the view of these people, all here for me, tells me that life is about something other than my own personal satisfaction and my own thoughtless agenda. It's about others and what they want and need in equal measures and how I can be a part of that.

The humility was squeezed dry from me for a while and my head has been up my own arse, giving me blinkered vision and a bleak lack of direction, but suddenly it all makes sense. Watching my family, Chantelle and Heather, Kate, Tim, and aunts, uncles and cousins not seen for far too long, the penny drops. *This is what it's all about. Family. Happiness. Security. Openness.* It's not about bagging the richest guy or having celebrity status, nor is it about regression, it's about the simple things in life that come absolutely free.

I swing from Kate's tiny frame and she embraces me with a full-on friendly snog before giving me a firm dig in the arm. "Knobhead!" she whispers in my ear. "I'll tell you what though, Tina, you must have done bloody well in that audition to get the part." She mouths '*bitch*' at me. "What spurred you on then, you big looney?"

It's the million-dollar question really. Do I tell her the truth that I took a whole host of cranks at face value and came up with my own rather creative agenda? Perhaps not.

"I had nothing to lose, Kate," I tell her frankly. "I was in the right place at the right time and I guess in this instance there just was no pressure. Not like the old days."

This is partly right. I don't bother explaining those voices in my head driving me to do it. Neither do I tell her of the ridiculous other events that occurred that weekend. *I saw you but I actually hid! My man walked out on me . . . although it was after I ran out on him right in the throes of passion . . . did I tell you I nearly had a threesome with an old school friend? What do you mean you don't remember a Hazel Topping?*

If it wasn't so outstandingly bizarre it might actually be quite comical. The art classes, the kids from hell, a wedding boycott, a frightened lover – not that we ever got that far. What was I thinking?

You weren't, Tina. That's just it.

The words of those ridiculous readings clung to me with fierce talons and much as I tried to shake them off, I couldn't. They were stronger than me and so often I felt like I was in a trance, under a powerful spell that needed something other than a bit of willpower to break. It never occurred to me that I could fight it, dismiss it, even laugh at it and at them. I lost my sense of humour. Subconsciously, their words became my words and then my actions until I reached a point where I felt unable to make a simple decision without consulting one of them. I imagined the next reading would be the right one, that I'd discover the truth and my future pathway would be revealed plain and simple. But it never happened like that. Every reading was filled with a vague ambiguity and every indicative crossroads carried a blank sign and an arrow pointing to nowhere.

Kate's posture straightens out as does her face. "I'm so sorry, Tina." Her eyes are watery. "I spent too much time telling you to appreciate what you had that I made it impossible for you to confide in me." She shrugs her shoulders in admittance. "You should have been able to talk to me and tell me how you were feeling but instead I made myself unapproachable." She pauses. "I'm sorry."

"What are you on about, Kate?" I'm taken aback by her uncharacteristic admission. "I'm the one who should be apologising to you! For not listening to your advice, for lying to you, for hiding . . ."

"Hiding?"

"Erm, never mind about that – but your warnings, Kate, about the people, the hours, the phoneys were right and I'd forgotten it. Plus I could have wrecked your career with my stupid actions."

"True but if I'd been approachable enough for you to tell me about it, I could have warned you about that prick Raymond. I knew he'd got that role and I was quite relieved I didn't get my part so I wouldn't have to be in the same room as him, to say nothing of simulating sex with him."

I grimace at the mention of his name.

"The funny thing is," Kate snorts, "I've never had so many offers coming in."

"What?" My voice lifts an octave.

"I know, I can't believe it." She leans forward, whispering in my ear. "I've got a photo shoot lined up with *Just for Him* magazine next week and I can't believe what they're paying me."

She laughs her signature laugh, coarse and suggestive, and I'm consoled that she's back in true Kate style.

"So you'll be thanking me then for all that free publicity?" I tease.

"I think you've got your own publicity issues to worry about," she replies gravely. "What was it, Tina, what was that thing that made you do it one more time?"

"I suppose I see you looking so glam and always on the telly, then you're buying a docklands apartment and generally making it all look so simple that I . . ."

Kate stands as tall as she can get at five-feet nothing. "Simple? Are you crazy. I go for ten castings and am lucky if I get one job. I work fourteen-hour days and have to practically starve myself to keep this body the way it is." She takes my shoulders, gripping them hard. "Tell me you're through with it now, Tina."

I look down at her in my four-inch heels, biting my lip. *It's time to open up to her.* "I wish I could, Kate." *I wish I could.*

But thank God I've got a saving grace. A clear-sighted lawyer helping me and doing something by the book for once. Something black and white and legitimate.

28

I can't believe I'm back at work, sitting in the same leather chair I bought when I started out. I've missed it. I've also missed the nine-to-five lifestyle – in fact, I've missed everything so much that I want to go around kissing it all.

My desk is clear and a huge bouquet of flowers is sitting pretty and smelling of a fresh, new day, thanks to my staff.

Much as I grabbed the odd conversation with Chantelle at the party, I didn't feel it was the time or place to start grovelling, plus everything's been so full-on that I needed the weekend to consider a tactical but sincere approach. The truth is that I can't survive without her. Yes, there are a dozen other managers I could employ who could perform the role suitably, but to find someone with her integrity, her positive outlook on life and her amazing ability to instantaneously disarm people is not something you come across every day. I spent a lot of time thinking about how invaluable she is to me and, depending on the outcome of future circumstances, I have a proposition to put to her.

My phone shrills with high-pitched urgency and I

glance down to see that it's Simon calling. I snatch it nervously, anxious to hear his progress on getting me out of this current mess which once upon a time would have been referred to as a triumph.

"Hi, Simon."

"Tina, meet me at the Hastings Hotel at three p.m. sharp and dress to impress," Simon orders.

"Simon, you're my lawyer," I snap at him. "This is no time for a date."

He exhales with exasperation. "Tina, just do it!"

The line is dead. The cheeky sod has cut me off. He'd better not make a pass at me or think I owe him one for rescuing me.

I look at the chrome wall clock. It's past eleven now and by the time I go home to change and then drive into town for three . . . I reckon I'll have to leave just after lunchtime. *The timing is abysmal.*

I take each stair one by one, still a little apprehensive of Chantelle and conscious that we haven't had a chance to discuss her employer-employee relationship. It was on our agenda for this afternoon but that's obviously been knocked on the head.

Chantelle puts the phone down and smiles at me warmly. She's been pretty quiet today and in fact she was too at the party and, if I know her well enough, I'd say she's biding her time and waiting for the right moment to resign. She wouldn't kick a girl when she's down, this much I do know.

"I have to go out shortly, Chantelle. I'll get back as quickly as I can though."

Her position shifts and her body language becomes clearly defensive.

"Where are you going to?" Her voice is clipped but calm. "I thought we were going to talk this afternoon?" She looks tired.

What on earth do I tell her? Only Kate knows of the additional-episode balls-up and until Simon pulls out his lawyer finger I don't see the point of communicating it to anyone else.

"I'm meeting Simon at the Hastings Hotel." The truth feels good. It's a weight off my heavy shoulders.

"For what?"

"I don't know," I tell her honestly (well, technically so). "He told me to meet him there at three."

She turns away from me so I can't see her facial expression but I swear I can see her bottom lip quivering. "You told me you were over all that stuff, Tina."

Her voice wobbles and I rush over to her, putting my arm around her shoulders but she shrugs me off.

"I am, I swear to God!" I'm upset that she doesn't believe me but is it any bloody wonder?

"Well, then, tell me why it's so important to that you have to cancel our chat about my possible resignation, Tina?" Her voice cracks and she bites her nails in an attempt to distract herself from crying. "I thought you said I was indispensable?"

I decide to tell Chantelle of my whereabouts of the past few months. She of all people needed an explanation for my frequent Paul Daniels disappearing acts and lengthy phone calls and I know the secret will go with her to the grave. *"I'll always be there for you," she told me. "Just be honest with me, that's all I ask . . ."*

As usual, she listens a lot and says very little.

"Chantelle, I didn't mean to get into this tangle and

now I only want to get out of it," I finish up, practically begging her to believe me. "I swear on my life."

She throws me a look of utter disgust and jumps out of her seat, grabbing her coat from the back of the kitchen door.

"I'm sorry, Tina, but enough is enough," she hiccups. "I've held the fort while you've done your invisible tricks and all the time I thought you were out on appointments. I held it again while you were supposedly on holiday." Mascara runs down her wet cheeks and a single drop spills onto her starched white shirt collar. "You got off the hook while I stood there and took all the shit and now you have the audacity to tell me more lies." With her coat thrown on, Chantelle grabs her bag. "I don't care about picking up the pieces, nor the mistakes," she sniffs. "But I can't work where there is no trust, Tina. And right now I can't trust you so there is no solid ground for a continuing relationship."

She turns to leave but looks back at me with a wistful expression.

"Only a fool lies to themselves, Tina, and I never had you down as one of those. But I really don't know who you are any more."

My knees knock together as I watch her empty chair spinning with loneliness and the door chimes loudly, bidding her farewell. *Maybe it's time to shut up shop, Tina.*

I wobble up the steps of the Hastings Hotel, thankful for the automatic doors. I have a continuing problem with the revolving type. It does feel rather strange to be prancing around in a fitted black dress and killer heels mid-afternoon, but I'm only following orders. The dress is not so fitted actually, what with a gruelling film schedule lasting a week and a half and the projectile evacuation of my entire stomach contents, including its lining. I haven't been this thin in years but I don't feel good and for once that's because I don't feel good on the inside. Everything is beginning to make perfect sense to me now and it's like I'm a proper adult. For some reason I've matured more in the last week than in my entire thirty-two years, but my heart is still heavy and burdened for what I put my family through and the sheer disdain on Chantelle's beautiful face is haunting my conscience.

Simon is waiting for me in the reception area and standing right next to him is Nick Hand.

I tremble with anticipation as I walk towards them, greeting the two of them shakily but trying hard to suppress it. Their facial expressions bear no indication of the outcome, assuming they've reached one of course, nor do they even look in opposition to each other which they should have done because after all, what one wants, the other doesn't.

Nick steps forward, kissing me on both cheeks in true Thespian style while Simon remains aloof and simply nods to me. I obediently follow them into a side conference room where a boardroom table has been laid out with a dozen or so chairs surrounding it.

Simon pulls out a chair and I sit between him and Nick, feeling wildly intimidated and not knowing what to say or do.

"So, Tina, you're unwilling to continue with the production?" Nick cuts to the chase.

"Well, erm . . ." He's caught me by surprise. "It's just that . . ."

Simon interrupts abruptly. "Nick is offering you a get-out clause, Tina."

The hairs on my arms stand on end. *Oh God, please, please.*

Nick thrusts a sheet of paper under my nose and clicks on the pen before handing it to me in poised position.

"Sign here, Tina, and you're free to go."

I grab the pen from him without any hesitation and scribble my name with absolute delight. Nick signs below me and Simon deftly retrieves the paper.

"I'll send you a copy by post, Mr Hand." He puts it in his empty briefcase. "Thank you." Simon looks at his watch and points to the open room. "Tina, you've got thirty minutes to prepare with Nick. You owe him one!"

He stands, shaking Nick's hand, smiling for the first time since they met but showing me no sign of emotion whatsoever. Then he leaves.

"Okay, Tina, here's the deal."

Nick paces around the room pensively, his long legs creating easy access to the four corners. He suddenly changes direction and strides back up to the table to lean across it, facing me head on.

"I'm going to kill you," he tells me solemnly.

Help!

"Kill me?"

"Kill you." He pulls his face back from mine, giving me much-needed space. "I don't want to but you've left me with little choice."

I can't move a muscle. He's turned into some kind of deranged psycho. I force myself to speak, to bargain with him.

"You can't kill me," I implore. "Oh God, Nick, I didn't mean to make you this cross – I'm sorry!"

Nick's face creases with stifled humour, then his mouth opens wide, letting out a belt of laughter. He smirks at me with his elongated face, in keeping with his lengthy build.

"Classic!" he teases. "Kill you off as Balmy, you idiot!"

My heart rate slows dramatically and I immediately feel the blood-supply flowing around my body once again with understated relief. Once upon a time I would have been with it enough to have realised the joke for what it was, but these days finding clarity in my mind is like searching for a diamond in a mud bath. I used to be intelligent.

"God, Nick, I thought I was a goner for a moment." The corners of my mouth turn up and the stupidity of my reaction sets in and I too reciprocate but with embarrassed laughter.

Nick comes to sit next to me and I relax on seeing his easy posture. "Seriously though, Tina, I will have to have you written out. Obviously we'll still need you for a day or two to film those scenes but then you're free to go." He leans back against the blue fabric. "I think you're making a mistake though."

I sit upright, feeling strong and assertive and sure. "You know what, Nick," I tell him unequivocally. "I'm not. This feels totally right for me and I've a business empire to build up. That's where I belong and it's taken this experience to make me realise it."

"This thing is going to be big, Tina." He cocks his head to one side. "But it will be even bigger once you've fulfilled your side of the deal. And that also involves a television interview which I've taken the liberty of setting up for an hour's time."

Dress to impress, indeed.

Crammed into my mum's lounge we sit like sardines on the sofas with barely enough room to move. My lips struggle to reach the glass of wine as my elbows are pinned down by the person on each side, which is possibly a good thing actually, given I have pledged to drink less these days. Never turn to alcohol when you're down – it's the worst thing you can do. *Plus it makes you fat!*

Everyone has turned up to watch it and I'm actually quite excited to see the interview. The show was recorded yesterday afternoon but is being aired this evening and it really is the strangest thing to almost be turned into an overnight celebrity as a result of an AWOL disappearance.

Simon, extremely cleverly, devised a plan where my missing-person status could be turned into something positive and he put it to Nick that his advertising budget need not be touched. Why pay for air time when I was all they needed? I could save them a fortune. Nick jumped at the chance to take advantage of my unfortunate circumstances to get low-cost publicity and keep his production pot ready for the show's potential expansion. A well-laid plan. Contrary to his hollow words, there is no way he's sad to see me go. Not after he made comments like "I couldn't have planned this better myself" and "You've been all over the press, Tina – what better exposure can a show get!"

Similarly, I'm not sad to go and it's not because of the

saga with Raymond, which seems so trivial now on a scale of things although at the time I don't ever recall Kate being so removed from her usual self. Any wonder she forgot to tell me I was missing. It's a whole host of reasons and, as for fourteen-hour days, one would surely have to ask themselves *"Why?"* Why the instability? Why the uncertainty of not knowing when your next cheque was coming in? Why drive six hours to a casting just to turn up and know full well you just weren't quite what they were looking for? You could see it in their eyes, sense their visible hesitation.

"Mum," Sam screeches, "it's starting!" She rubs my hand lovingly. Her other hand is firmly wrapped around Tim's. A match made in heaven.

Simon managed to bag the only available armchair and is sitting back, looking rather chilled and extremely comfortable in his sloppy jeans and T-shirt, a look I'd almost go so far as to say that I've missed. Every now and then we exchange knowing glances but nothing that anyone else would pick up on, and I know he is secretly gloating. I can tell. And why wouldn't he? He deserves it and I have to hand it to him – it took some balls to steer away from his usual text-book approach and put a more streetwise proposition to Nick. I'm still coming to terms with how changeable he was as my learned lawyer. He was cold, aggressive, arrogant and pompous, all the things I usually love in a guy for some reason, but I know it was all an act. Thank God. And he did it for me. Again.

Major Heath-Jones is too wrapped up in his own self-importance to even notice his own wife, let alone the surreptitious glances between his son and the weird youngest daughter from the Harding family.

Mum and Dad are busying themselves, hosting perfectly, and I note how happy they look, how content. Watching them gives me the most amazing feeling of satisfaction that right now I would be willing to trade my own happiness for all eternity just to see their contentment prevail. My self-absorbed days are over and right now I am fuelled with everyone else's joy, a welcome epidemic.

The titles stop rolling, the music fades and the host skips into view. He is greeted by a rhapsodic applause from the live audience as he takes centre stage in front of the auto-cue.

"Welcome to *The Today Show.*" He welcomes the audience with a responsive gesture and an open invitation to be deafened with planned popularity. The audience cheer again and again just as rehearsed. "You may recall hearing of the missing girl, Christina Harding. Well, she joins us today to give us her side of the story." The camera closes in on him. "Don't miss it." More staged cheers.

I squirm uncomfortably. It's been a long time since I've see myself on TV and I'm a little apprehensive, although watching myself as bland, boring Balmy will be far worse, I imagine, but thankfully short-lived.

The camera pulls back to a wide shot revealing every inch of me and then closes in focusing on my upper half. *I don't look too bad actually.*

Simon is glued to the television and this time doesn't return my furtive glance.

"Ladies and gentlemen, just to refresh your memory, here is the first interview after Christina handed herself in."

Cheeky sod, I'm not a bloody convict. They show a clip of the press conference and my mum dabs her eyes with a tissue. *Ever the drama queen.* Dad squeezes her hand fondly and they both glance across at me, mesmerised and consumed with love. My stomach flips.

The show's host, John Kennedy, joins me on the sofa, shaking my hand and welcoming me to the show. As the camera freezes on me the entire living room breaks into a frenzied acclamation. *Oh stop!*

"So, Christina, to cut to the chase," he casts a grave look directly at the camera, "you told everyone you were going on holiday with a friend, but you didn't." He pauses. "Your friend then rang you at work looking for you . . . but of course you weren't there . . . and that's when it came out that you were missing." He shakes his head at the audience, inviting a hum of antagonism. "You didn't answer your phone or even try to contact home and nobody knew where you were."

I simply nod, although inside I'm squirming.

"I imagine they thought you were dead?"

A loud tut echoes from the audience.

Get over it.

"So talk us through your version of what actually happened and explain to us where you where?"

"Well, John, I was working on a TV production called *Stiffs.*" *There you go Nick – the very first sentence.* I turn to the audience. "I told my family and my work colleagues that I was going on holiday so that I could surprise them when the show was aired." I shrug with fabricated humour, only this time I'm not convincing myself that I am telling the truth. "They knew how long I'd wanted to be an actress so I chose to keep the filming a secret from them until the very last moment, only . . ." I chuckle affably, "only it didn't quite work out that way." I pose sheepishly, looking deliberately pitiful. "Hence the small lie I concocted to cover my disappearance. It was all very innocent and supposed to be a huge surprise . . . especially for my mother of all people."

Mum mouths to me '*I love you*' and I swear my heart is near bursting point.

The black dress is so flattering. It is a little dark for the spring season but it never fails to impress and the loss of a few pounds allows it to sit perfectly around my hips and not crease up like it usually does. My face is caked in make-up but beneath the heavy lights it looks faded and natural. I grin with wonderment at how a man like Simon can have known me so well that he ordered me to dress with glamour, knowing this would have been top of my agenda, certainly for a television appearance. We had only met on a handful of occasions and on each one of those I had behaved like a total freak.

"Why didn't you tell them the truth about what you were doing?"

I decide to answer him honestly. "Because I'd already tried my hand at acting and, while I had some successes, it wasn't enough to carve a career out of it." I clear my throat. "Plus I didn't really know why I was doing it, especially with a business to run, so all things considered it wouldn't have gone down well with anyone." *Apart from my mum.* "I got the part by sheer default and, to be honest, it never ever felt right seeing it through so I lied about it." I don't mention Kate who warned me to steer clear of her.

John raises his eyebrows towards the live crowd who

are *oohing* and *aahing* their way through the show. I tell all how it was when I auditioned for the role, right through to being found out, planting the odd white lie here and there to glamorize it, but mostly I plug the show at every given opportunity. It was so tempting to talk about Harding Homes but that wasn't the deal and I'm a woman of my word. And I want out.

The crowd gasp with excitement as I tell of my trip to the funeral parlour and I leak authorised snippets of the storyline to wet their appetite.

"What's next for you then, Christina?" John asks.

"Watch the show and see for yourself. I can say no more than that." I smile at him and he stands up, leaning forward to kiss me on the cheek.

"Thank you for telling us your story, Christina."

He takes centre stage, once again reading from the auto-cue.

"That's it from *The Today Show,* ladies and gentlemen." The camera zooms in. "Just remember that honesty really is the best policy."

The camera takes one last shot of me sitting there serenely without a care in the world. *If only they knew.*

I activate the alarm and yank the door closed as I leave.

Today was a long, lonely day without Chantelle and it felt like I had lost my right arm. I miss her, I need her, and all the more to keep me grounded after last night's show was aired. I have barely been able to walk down the street without being mobbed. Okay, slight exaggeration, but I have lost count of how many autographs I've signed today and the most irritating part of it all is that I'm desperate to sell houses and get on with business as usual. But everyone else wants to focus on the celebrity gossip and the apparent glamour of this rather peculiar industry. Momentarily I imagine how life would look with a permanent role in a long-running, successful series or more importantly, in my temporary vision, how much money I would earn. And then I laugh. I don't care.

Glad to see the long day drawing to a close, I lock the door, thrusting against it with my hip to check it's firmly secured. Stepping back I feel my heel penetrate something soft and a loud yelp belts down my right ear.

I swing around. "I'm so sorry!" I apologise to the owner of the foot and then look up at him. "Brian!"

He hops around like a fool, rubbing the front of his expensive suede shoe. "Why do women never wear flat shoes?"

"Some do."

"Like who?"

I stop dead, pensively. "Traffic Wardens!"

Brian pulls me towards him, planting his lips on mine. How I've missed them! Missed him. And by the looks of things he's missed me.

"Uniforms – now we're talking," he replies indecently. He behaves like we have never been apart. His blue eyes are alight and incandescent as he checks me out sinfully. "You were great last night by the way." He surveys me, making no attempt to hide his lustful scrutiny.

You're not so bad yourself, Mr Steen. I look towards the sky, praying silently. *Thank you, God! Oh, by the way, there's just one other thing I need some help with . . .*

The small row of town houses are immaculately groomed and the street is free from debris. A neighbour waves across at me, continuing to scrub the small doorstep on her hands and knees. The scent of bleach stings the warm air, cleaning it abrasively.

I press down on the metal latch of the rusty gate, pushing it back as it creaks with aged fatigue. The narrow concrete path is lined with an array of potted plants bursting with colour and oozing a summer scent slightly premature for this time of year, and the small square of grass is immaculately mown with newly turned borders.

At a snail's pace my feet travel up the short path until I can walk no further and I stop and simply stare at the replica front door. The shiny brass greets me with my own reflection and it echoes my apprehension. I'm nervous. More nervous than I've been for a long long time and I desperately need the outcome of this to be positive, otherwise I'm finished. Okay, maybe '*finished*' is a little dramatic, given I started off on my own, but Chantelle has been instrumental in helping me grow the business and I realise that I need her more than she needs me.

I flip the matching brass letterbox a few times, letting it fall back with a tinny clang. My fingerprints leave their trace on its highly polished surface and I quickly rub them away with my sleeve.

An elegant lady, perfectly preened, surveys me. Her eyes squint with scrutiny and for a moment I feel exposed, revealed. She clasps her hands together. "Tina, how wonderful to see you!" She takes hold of my arm, leading me into the box-sized hallway. "My eyesight isn't what it used to be." She laughs. "And how are things with you, dear?"

I follow her into the kitchen and plonk myself down

on a chair while she lifts a teapot, clad in its knitted garment and shakily pours it into three matching mugs. I watch her hand tremble and my emotions almost capsize at the thought of anything happening to her.

"Arthritis," she explains. "It's crippling me but still I shouldn't complain. There's always someone worse off than me, isn't that right, dear?"

From the moment I met Grace I fell in love with her and her amazing outlook on life and I can clearly see where Chantelle's humility derives from. Her name encapsulates the very essence of her soul and her magic continues to live on through her beautiful and gracious granddaughter.

"Where's Chantelle?" I cringe, wondering just how much Grace knows.

"She's upstairs." She sips her drink unsteadily. "Be a dear and tell her there is some tea for her, please. Or take it up to her perhaps?"

I prise myself reluctantly from the chair.

"It's not like her to be unwell, is it, Tina?"

I'm not sure whether that's a rhetorical question or if there was any hidden agenda behind such a statement, but I pick up the mug and make my way up the freshly hoovered stairs, leaving a trail of flattened prints behind me.

Tapping anxiously on her bedroom door, I will her not to answer so I can leave the tea outside and run away fast.

"Come in, Tina."

Still in her pyjamas, Chantelle is propped against the pillows, staring at the portable television on her antique dressing table. She pulls her legs up to her chest, giving me room to sit down on the end of the bed. I glance around, wondering how she survives there – I feel claustrophobic already.

"How did you know it was me?"

"I heard you downstairs." She lifts the mug of tea. "Thanks."

I face her head on, keeping my fingers crossed behind my back.

"Chantelle, I know I'm probably the last person you want to see right now but please hear me out," I beg her. "I've got a proposition for you."

29

The party spills out onto the street and passersby stop to watch the commotion. One by one they're yanked in for complimentary drinks, their pockets stuffed with business cards.

The room has been tastefully decorated with earthy corporate colours of stone, clay and vanilla. It feels bright and airy but still exudes a homely ambience.

Matching pearlised balloons float gracefully on the newly plastered ceiling with tightly curled satin ribbons falling elegantly beneath. Large banners of the company's logo sit proudly on the three available walls and freshly printed marketing material is prominently displayed at eye level for easy reading and housed in easy-to-clean transparent boxes. The room reeks of success.

The groomed waitresses squeeze through the crowds, holding high trays of canapés with scallops, crayfish and fois gras and chilled champagne flows plentifully, served from borrowed flutes, its giddy effects taking their toll on some of the guests. The atmosphere is rich with enthusiasm as all enjoy the free-for-all. Today is an open house and a perfect opportunity for me to play the hostess role that I so love and all with the support of my family close by me.

Camberwell Road is a perfect party venue. Not only does it hold double the capacity of the High Street office, it also offers more competition from the other estate agents who have set up shop on the main strip of this double-sided street. At one stage I might have felt threatened by that, but in the past it's actually worked in my favour. People shop around usually, hopping from agent to agent, but once Chantelle and I have them in our grasp, we won't lose them. But in my opinion, there's only one estate agency I can see penetrating the marketplace around here. And that's mine. I've never felt such a fierce determination to make this work. Not even when I first started out. And the prospect of losing all of this has made me want it all the more.

The local press have arrived as requested and are snapping away at poor unassuming folk. *No press is bad press,* as they say. I did try to get the national press involved with me being a familiar name and that but it's so true, what is one day's news is the next day's chip-wrappers and no-one really cares now that I've turned up alive and well. How dull is that? I imagine next week when *Stiffs* is aired their response might be somewhat different but I dare not cross that line with Nick. My word is my honour and if it weren't for him, and Simon of course, this party wouldn't exist. I'd be chained to the camera with heavy bags under my eyes, working with a bunch of shallow knobs.

This launch not only represents achievement and success, it represents a new chapter in my life, a new dawning and a way of living which encompasses everything that's important to me: trust, self-belief and grounding. It took me a while to learn these simple ethics.

I caved in and told my family about my roller-coaster journey of readings and the rationale, or lack of it, behind the strange series of events. My parents as always were empathetic, but Sam, she just threw her head back and laughed until she cried and just when I thought she was calming down, she'd start all over again at which point I started to see the funny side of it. The pair of us chortled away like we did when we used to sneak into each other's bedrooms, pretending to be asleep whenever we heard Mum or Dad coming up to check on us. I've missed her so much. I feel like I've been leading a double life and wearing a mask which restricted seeing who I really was, but I'm back now and while it's been a difficult ride I can honestly say that I wouldn't change a thing. What's the point? It's the crap life throws at you that makes you who and what you are – it develops you and if you've any sense you'll learn from it and embrace it.

"Tina, the car's pulling up!" Lucy squeals.

Lucy is the new sales advisor for Camberwell Road and has natural ability in shed-loads. She's young and can learn at an accelerated pace and my gut tells me she's going to need to be a fast learner the way the housing market is moving.

"Move the cones, please, Lucy, thanks." My voice quakes with excitement.

We pile outside to see the Mercedes pulling up and Lucy removes the cones to make available their reserved parking space. I glance at my mum who already has tears in her eyes. *No more champagne for her!* My dad has his video camera rolling away to capture the moment although he's promised not to come anywhere near me with it, or else!

The car rolls to a smooth halt and the driver jumps out, opening the rear door. His hands are clothed with pristine white gloves and he lends one of them to the lady who exits with graceful poise. Her consort follows and they stand together waiting to be announced.

"Ladies and gentlemen," the driver announces. "Lady Mayoress and her consort."

The gathering breaks into an uproar, clapping loudly and stamping their feet.

I step forward with my hand extended and curtsey simultaneously, a move I've been practising at great length.

"Thank you for coming." My voice is a little shaky and I'm more scared than I thought I'd be. "Are you ready?" I ask her, bowing ever so slightly to show total respect.

Lady Mayoress smiles at me with a warm assurance and takes the scissors from my hand.

"Stand back, please!" I yell to the crowd as she makes her way towards the open door which is dressed with a thick band of silk purple ribbon.

She attaches the scissors to the centre of it, holding them there, and pausing for effect she turns to the crowd.

"Ladies, gentlemen, boys and girls," her voice is audible and confident, "it is with great pleasure that I witness the opening of this new enterprise in our town." She looks directly at me before snipping the ribbon which falls down weightlessly. "I wish you every success. Let us celebrate by raising our glasses to the Harding and Hungerford Partnership."

Ouch! Chantelle's nails dig into my hand and I whisper in her ear for her to let go. *Now!*

"That's my name up there and it's taking up more space than yours!" she gloats, takes a massive gulp of champagne, then clinks her glass against mine. "I've got more letters! I've got more letters!"

"Well, at least I know I've hired someone who can count."

Chantelle coughs with an air of importance. "Actually, Ms Harding, you haven't hired me," she scolds. "We are equal business partners for this shop, might I remind you."

As if I could forget.

I grin with pride at her sudden air of confidence and self-belief. She'll never let it go to her head, she's not like that, but she will give it everything she's got, that much I know. Why else would I have created such a proposition? Apart from the fact that she deserves it of course.

"How do you get on with Lucy?"

"She's brilliant, Tina." Chantelle beckons Lucy over. "Nothing is too much trouble and it's mainly down to her that we'll be ready for business on Monday morning."

Lucy stands in between us and we raise our glasses to girl power and an all-female business.

"Wait for me!" Heather excuses herself through the foot traffic but, substantially overweight, she's pretty slow in getting here. She bounces off the poor folk standing in her way, sending them flying with her hefty frame.

"Hurry up, Heather!" Chantelle shouts authoritatively. "I'm gasping to KB this!"

Heather arrives, panting from the mere six-foot journey. "KB?" she frowns and Lucy laughs loudly.

"Knock Back, Heather," she tells her. "It's slang."

Heather salutes us all with her full glass and drinks its entire content in a single gulp. She surveys our faces smugly. "Slang, don't make me laugh. Actions speak louder than words, you lightweights!"

I make a point of finding out who is who. It's always good to have allies and like-minded people you can turn to when the need arises. Quite a few faces are already familiar, although perhaps I recognise them from the plethora of visits here, one visit in particular which I can't forget. Talking of the man himself, Brian and his team are all here. They've turned up to support us and, regardless of the minor issues we've had personally, I can honestly say I couldn't have done it without him. He gave me the contract and provided all the building work and, most importantly, he gave me the biggest confidence booster I've ever had. *Him.* There are times when I ask myself whether I've just used him for suitability, but I think not. Maybe he used me? But regardless of how I won the contract, only we at Harding Homes sold those apartments, perhaps with a slightly unusual sales strategy but still we did it and no-one can take the credit for that away from us. *And my bitch of a best friend for buying one!*

I watch Brian chatting to Lucy. She knows of him but hasn't been formerly introduced. I make my way over, waving behind them to my dad who gives me the thumbs-up. He's still trying to capture a '*You've been framed*' clip. He's a typical accountant in that he'll do anything for money.

"Have you two been properly introduced?" I take in Brian's delight at talking to the young Lucy.

"Miss Harding." He bows slightly. "We're not worthy, it appears."

I see Lucy grimace from the corner of my eye but choose to ignore her. She really doesn't know him from Adam and, besides, she's young and probably not a good judge of character at her tender age.

"Nonsense." I shake his hand formally as part of the act. "I couldn't have done it without you, Brian, and I mean that with all sincerity." He looks shocked at my formality but now is not the time to flirt with him. There is only one firm agenda behind today and that involves myself and my new business partner.

Surveying the room, taking in its hustle and the hum of contented guests, I spot Simon arriving late as usual and in desperate need of a shave. I observe his confidence as he walks through the gathering, smiling sincerely and excusing himself profusely, a gentleman through and through.

"Will you excuse me, please, Brian?" I disappear before he can answer, conscious that I have another person to whom I owe much gratitude.

I tap Simon on the shoulder, ducking down to hide as he turns around. "Boo!" I jump up, almost head-butting him, and he pretends to be taken aback.

"Blimey, you're scary!" He acts pretty well but then again just look at his vocation. I don't know a lawyer that isn't a born performer. "No, I really mean it, Tina, you are scary!" he teases solemnly.

"Cheeky sod, have you looked in the mirror lately?" I wink at him fondly, pausing to collect myself for a moment of paramount importance. "You know I never really got the chance to thank you for what you did." I feel like the entire room has gone silent but I can only focus on what's going on in front of me. "You've saved me so many times, Simon, and all I've done is treat you like crap." My heart aches as I reflect on my condescending attitude towards him. "From the bottom of my heart, thank you so very very much."

I reach forward, kissing him on his pale cheek, capturing his boyish scent. The hairs on his face are soft and a few days old, tinged with a citrus fragrance. He pulls on his sleeve, pretending to be repulsed, and scrubs away at his face with a montage of hilarious gestures.

"Tina." He escorts me speedily to a less crowded corner of the room.

"What are you doing?"

"Don't ever change, will you?" he whispers urgently.

"What?"

"Don't ever change." He delicately pushes a strand of hair from my face. "Always be yourself."

Hang on, isn't that the wrong way round?

"Don't change for anyone, Tina," he repeats. "Always be yourself and you won't go wrong."

His words and the compassion of his delivery have stunned me. I thought he would have called me all the idiots under the sun. It's nothing I wouldn't have deserved.

"Earth calling Tina!" Simon digs me in the arm, sensing my shock at his statement, clearly trying to make light of it. I think he's a little embarrassed. "What's going on in that head of yours . . . or shouldn't I ask?"

I'm growing up, that's what's going on and I'm prioritising my life. On my own! Yippee!

"Okay, then I won't change," I reply matter of factly, taking a huge swig of champagne. I know he meant it with great earnestness but I'm taking nothing seriously from now on and I'm so in the mood for a bit of playful banter.

With childish retaliation, Simon pokes me just below the ribs and the champagne sprays from my mouth, soaking his faded rugby shirt. He glances down at it, unperturbed. "There's no need to wash this shirt for another week now." He grins.

"Sorry, Simon, but I'm so ticklish there."

He penetrates my skin with his stare. "I know you are."

My faces flushes and I look around the room for the nearest emergency exit while my body chemically reacts to his imaginary touch. Sensing my embarrassment, he grabs my hand, drags me roughly towards one of the waiting staff and snatches two drinks from the silver tray.

"To your success!" he congratulates, holding the glass high.

"And to your success," I reciprocate fondly. "Although I imagine you are already quite successful, Simon. You know, I never ever asked you what you did." I ignore the chilled flute just inches from my lips. "How rude was that?"

He grins impishly. "That was very rude, you bad girl. But I wouldn't have you any other way!"

"Yes but –"

"Tina, stop analysing what's in the past and drink up," he orders firmly. "If I don't have to carry you out of here, there's something terribly wrong!"

I join my family, at the back of the room keeping

themselves to themselves. It amazing to have them back on board and I keep asking myself why I lied to them about so many things. Perhaps the same reason I lied to myself?

Sam calls me over.

"Where's your drink, Sam?" I wave across to one of the waitresses.

"It's here." She points to her drink set down on the floor.

"It's our opening bash, Sam! Get some champers down your neck!"

Sam breaks into a fixed grin. She looks at me and pats her stomach.

"No!" *I can't speak in case I'm right.*

"Yes!" she squeals. "You're going to be an aunt."

I can't move.

"What if you have a boy, Sam? Does that mean she'll be an uncle?" Simon peals with laughter while I just stand there staring at my sister, basking in her pregnancy glow.

How could I have even missed it? She's never been so radiant.

I fling myself on her while she ruffles my hair fondly. She'll make a great mother. Better than me, I'm sure. It's a good job there's one stable daughter in our family.

"Oh guys, I am so delighted for you both." I hug Tim affably. If I wasn't all cried-out I'd probably have tears of joy to shed but I've done enough whinging to last me a lifetime. "Hey, I have some experience with children if you ever want –"

"Them to be abandoned!" Simon pipes up. "Or left in some designer shop!"

I curse him for his avid memory and wish he'd have kept his mouth shut. I'll be the best aunt there is.

Sam sees the hurt expression. "Don't be cruel, Simon," she chides him. "Tina will make a wonderful aunt."

I smirk at Simon as my big sister defends me.

"As long as she doesn't have to change nappies, clean sick –"

My faces warps. *I forgot about all that stuff!*

With the wondrous news of an impending birth and a massively successful party, I think today has got to be one of the best days of my life. Just a few weeks ago I truly believed it was all over. On a positive day I had a glimmer of hope that I might be able to keep High Street open, but that would be the limit of my success. It would barely break even by the time I had paid a decent salary for a full-time manager to replace me. But now I know where I stand. I know where feels comfortable and I know where feels like home and somewhere in the not too distant future there will be one of our shops on every major high street.

"I was just kidding, Tina," Simon concedes. "About the aunt comment. I think you'll be wonderful."

I eye him cautiously.

"All you can do is try, Simon," I preach. "And by God I'll try to be the best aunt I possibly can be." My voice breaks at the prospect of a miniature new arrival. A baby Sam. I can't wait.

"And what makes you think you'll be a great uncle? You can't even look after yourself, never mind get a baby ready!"

"Do you mind!" He tuts. "It takes me ages to get this slept-in look!"

Hilary strolls over to join us, looking extremely regal in her wide-brimmed hat and matching lilac suit. She looks more like she's attending a royal wedding than a shop opening but I'm flattered at the effort.

"I couldn't help overhearing, Tina," she says softly. "You know, when Simon was at secondary school I went in one morning to wake him up . . ."

Simon's face reddens.

"And as I pulled the covers from him I saw his shirt collar sticking out from beneath his pyjama top!" She titters shyly. "He'd worn his pyjamas over his school uniform so he wouldn't have the bother of getting dressed in the morning!"

"Yuck! How gross are you?" I prod his ribs, enjoying my revenge.

Simon raises his eyebrows at Hilary. "Any other embarrassing stories you'd like to share, Mother?"

"Actually, lots." Hilary links her arm through mine, a sign of much physical affection from a woman so timid, but changing slowly under my mother's influence. "But I don't want to put her off you, Simon." She hesitates. "A girl like Tina would be good for you."

I throw him a snide look, sticking my tongue out like a schoolgirl. "Yeah, *too* bloody good for you!"

"Suits you!" he sniggers.

"Dream on, loser!" I snort.

Simon clears his throat cockily. "Young lady, if my memory serves me correctly, I didn't lose . . . I won."

Hilary looks from him back to me with a confused expression.

"Okay, I'll give you that one," I concede.

Chantelle and I pose for the *Mersey Times*. We've been in stitches doing it, mainly at the expense of the poor photographer who looks petrified,. We pout like pin-ups while our bodies are moulded into the most flattering positions chosen by ourselves, chin up, chest out. We decided to make our pictures sexy and sassy so they'd stand out – no-one wants to see a formal picture of a suited businesswoman, they want something easy on the eye, something that jumps out at them, and between the two of us I'd say we've pulled it off.

I escort the photographer from the premises, thanking him profusely for his attendance and patience with us. We were rather trying, but that's what champagne does for you and it is our day after all.

Outside, I take a moment to inhale the early summer air, marvelling as its warmth hits my lungs, feeling the light breeze caress my face with tenderness. I'd forgotten what a wonderful day it was with our new state-of-the-art glass and its anti-reflective glare.

I gaze up at the sign, shiny and new. *We did it!* I tell myself silently. *We're on our way!* It's an absolute privilege to have Chantelle on board as a business partner. It was the only way I could tie her down without a ball and chain shackled to her ankle. I put a proposition to her that I knew she couldn't refuse. Ordinarily an exchange of funds would take place when someone buys in, but I knew Chantelle didn't have them to give so I proposed to her that she settled for the lowest salary possible, using the remainder to buy her shares in the partnership, that way she wouldn't start off in any debt. Plus we agreed a fifty-fifty split of the commission. Any wonder she nearly bit my hand off!

"Miss Harding." His dulcet tones demand my immediate attention and I look up to see Brian standing in the doorway clad in dark denim jeans which flatter his perfect build. He never ceases to be anything other than sex on legs.

"Mr Steen."

Brian joins me outside and we stand together looking up at the pristine new lettering.

"I did mean it, Brian – you've been an integral part of my success and I really couldn't have done it without you." I watch him intently.

"Then you can make it up to me if you like?" He inches forward slightly and my stomach churns with lust.

A loud squeal distracts me and I peer through glass to see Chantelle prancing around waving her arm in the air. I watch Tim fetch a chair, forcing Sam to put her feet on it, and I take in Simon and my dad looking incredibly at ease with one another, laughing and joking. And why wouldn't they get on? They're both wonderful people.

What?

I'm stunned at my reaction. *Wonderful?* An admission that I didn't even know existed. *Where the hell did that come from? My dad, yes. But Simon . . .*

Brian edges forward a little more. "So how about it then, Miss Harding?"

I think about the times when Simon rescued me. When he held the drunken me up for the wedding dance and practically carried me to bed. When he got me out of a legal contract that could have crippled me. Where he told me to be me. Just me.

"You know what, Brian . . . I think I need some space."

The past few months have been so full-on that I think I need to be on my own for a while. The prospect of two men to consider is far too overwhelming and maybe I'll regret it but my instinct tells me to go with it. To just be me for a little while, wise words from a very special person. Whatever will be shall manifest itself suitably as and when the timing is right, but I'm no longer prepared to interfere with my life. I'm happy to simply let it be and work away doing the things I love to do, being around the people I adore.

"Brian," I give him a peck on his cheek, determined not to linger any longer than necessary even if it is killing me, "my mother once told me never to mix business with pleasure."

I head towards the front door, eager to join in the boisterous merriment. I brush past the loosely hanging purple ribbon symmetrically cut by our special guest and spin around to see Brian standing there, affronted.

"And it kills me to say it," I add, "but I think she was right!"